PE

# THE
# DA VINCI
# CODE

# DAN BROWN

# THE DA VINCI CODE

## ABRIDGED EDITION

PENGUIN BOOKS

PENGUIN BOOKS

UK | USA | Canada | Ireland | Australia
India | New Zealand | South Africa

Penguin Books is part of the Penguin Random House group of companies
whose addresses can be found at global.penguinrandomhouse.com.

www.penguin.co.uk
www.puffin.co.uk
www.ladybird.co.uk

Penguin
Random House
UK

*The Da Vinci Code* first published in the UK by Bantam Press,
an imprint of Transworld Publishers, 2003
Abridged edition published 2016
003

Typeset in 11/17 pt Dante MT Std by Jouve (UK), Milton Keynes
Printed in Great Britain by Clays Ltd, St Ives plc

A CIP catalogue record for this book is available from the British Library

ISBN: 978–0–141–37256–3

www.greenpenguin.co.uk

MIX
Paper from
responsible sources
FSC® C018179

Penguin Random House is committed to a
sustainable future for our business, our readers
and our planet. This book is made from Forest
Stewardship Council® certified paper.

*For Blythe . . . again. More than ever.*

# Acknowledgements

Special thanks for this young adult edition to Bill Scott-Kerr, Barbara Marcus, Beverly Horowitz, Shannon Cullen and Sue Cook, and all the talented people at the Penguin Random House Children's Group in both the US and UK.

To my friend and editor, Jason Kaufman, for working so hard on this project and for truly understanding what this book is all about. And to the incomparable Heidi Lange – tireless champion of *The Da Vinci Code*, agent extraordinaire and trusted friend.

I cannot fully express my gratitude to the exceptional team at Doubleday, for their generosity, faith and superb guidance. Thank you especially to Bill Thomas and Steve Rubin, who believed in this book from the start. My thanks also to the initial core of early in-house supporters, headed by Michael Palgon, Suzanne Herz, Janelle Moburg, Jackie Everly and Adrienne Sparks, and to the talented people of Doubleday's sales force.

For their generous assistance in the research of the book, I would like to acknowledge the Louvre Museum, the French Ministry of Culture, Project Gutenberg, Bibliothèque Nationale, the Gnostic Society Library, the Department of Paintings Study and Documentation Service at the Louvre, Catholic World News, Royal Observatory Greenwich, London Record Society, the

Muniment Collection at Westminster Abbey, John Pike and the Federation of American Scientists, and the five members of the Opus Dei (three active, two former) who recounted their stories, both positive and negative, regarding their experiences inside Opus Dei.

My gratitude also to Water Street Bookstore for tracking down so many of my research books; my father, Richard Brown – mathematics teacher and author – for his assistance with the Divine Proportion and the Fibonacci sequence; Stan Planton; Sylvie Baudeloque; Peter McGuigan; Francis McInerney; Margie Wachtel; Andre Vernet; Ken Kelleher at Anchorball Web Media; Cara Sottak; Karyn Popham; Esther Sung; Miriam Abramowitz; William Tunstall-Pedoe; and Griffin Wooden Brown.

And finally, in a novel drawing so heavily on the sacred feminine, I would be remiss if I did not mention the two extraordinary women who have touched my life. First, my mother, Connie Brown – fellow scribe, nurturer, musician and role model. And my wife, Blythe – art historian, painter, front-line editor and without a doubt the most astonishingly talented woman I have ever known.

Dear Reader,

**I have always loved secrets and codes.**

There is something magical that happens when you suddenly see what lies hidden . . . right before your eyes.

When I was ten years old, I encountered my first code – a series of strange symbols scrawled on a slip of paper hanging from our Christmas tree. When I finally deciphered those symbols, I discovered that the message was from my parents, announcing that we would all be leaving in a few hours on a surprise family vacation.

Ever since that morning, I've been fascinated by codes – those secret messages that must be untangled before they can be understood. I've spent my life exploring that cryptic world, and a few years ago my journey brought me face to face with the most mysterious code I had ever encountered.

The code was ancient . . . and puzzling. And best of all, it was hidden in plain sight, right there for the entire world to see.

According to legend, this code protected an astonishing secret. Some claimed the secret was so shocking that if you learned it, you would never see the world in the same light again. Others claimed the secret was just a myth . . . nothing but empty whispers in the mist.

Either way, the book in your hands tells the tale of a man and a woman on a quest to decipher that code and unveil its hidden mysteries. Whether or not you choose to believe the secrets you are about to discover, I hope the journey inspires you to keep searching for your own truth, whatever that may be.

Without wax,

Dan Brown

# Fact:

The Priory of Sion – a European secret society founded in 1099 – is a real organization. In 1975, Paris's Bibliothèque Nationale discovered parchments known as *Les Dossiers Secrets,* identifying numerous members of the Priory of Sion, including scientist Sir Isaac Newton, artist and sculptor Sandro Botticelli, writer Victor Hugo, and artist and inventor Leonardo da Vinci.

Opus Dei is a deeply devout Catholic sect that has been the topic of recent controversy due to reports of extreme practices. Opus Dei has built a $47-million national headquarters in New York City.

All descriptions of artwork, architecture, documents and secret rituals in this novel are accurate.

# Prologue

*Louvre Museum, Paris*
*10:46 p.m.*

Renowned curator Jacques Saunière staggered through the vaulted archway of the museum's Grand Gallery. He lunged for the nearest painting he could see, a Caravaggio. Grabbing the gilded frame, the seventy-six-year-old man heaved the seventeenth-century masterpiece from the wall and collapsed backwards in a heap beneath the canvas.

As he had anticipated, a thundering iron gate fell nearby, barricading the entrance to the suite. The parquet floor shook. Far off, an alarm began to ring.

The curator lay a moment, gasping for breath, taking stock. *I am still alive.* He crawled out from under the canvas and scanned the cavernous space for somewhere to hide.

A voice spoke, chillingly close. 'Do not move.'

On his hands and knees, the curator froze, turning his head slowly.

Only fifteen feet away, outside the sealed gate, the mountainous silhouette of his attacker stared through the iron bars. He was broad and tall, with ghost-pale skin and thinning white hair. His irises were pink with dark red pupils. The albino drew a pistol from his coat and aimed the barrel through the bars, directly at the curator. 'You should not have run.' His accent was not easy to place. 'Now tell me where it is.'

'I – I told you already,' the curator stammered. 'I have no idea what you are talking about!'

'You are lying.' The man stared at him, perfectly immobile except for the glint in his ghostly eyes. 'You and your brethren possess something that is not yours. Tell me where it is hidden, and you will live.' The man levelled his gun at the curator's head. 'Is it a secret you will die for?'

Saunière could not breathe.

The man tilted his head, peering down the barrel of his gun.

Saunière held up his hands in defence. 'Wait,' he said slowly. 'I will tell you what you need to know.' The curator spoke his next words carefully – a lie he had rehearsed many times.

When the curator had finished speaking, his assailant smiled smugly. 'Yes. This is exactly what the others told me.'

Saunière recoiled. *The others?*

'I found them too,' the huge man taunted. 'All three of them. They confirmed what you have just said.'

*It cannot be!* The curator's true identity, along with the identities of his three *sénéchaux*, was almost as sacred as the ancient secret they protected. Saunière now realized his *sénéchaux*, following strict procedure, had told the same lie before their own deaths.

The attacker aimed his gun again. 'When you are gone, I will be the only one who knows the truth.'

*The truth.* In an instant, the curator grasped the true horror of the situation. *If I die, the truth will be lost forever.* He tried to scramble for cover.

The gun roared, and the curator felt a searing heat as the bullet lodged in his stomach. He fell forward . . . struggling against the pain. Slowly, Saunière rolled over and stared back through the bars at his attacker.

The man was now taking dead aim at his head.

Saunière closed his eyes, his thoughts a swirling tempest of fear and regret.

The click of an empty chamber echoed through the corridor.

The curator's eyes flew open.

The man glanced down at his weapon, looking almost amused. He reached for a second clip, but then seemed to reconsider, smirking calmly at Saunière's gut.

The curator looked down and saw the bullet hole in his white linen shirt. There was a small circle of blood a few inches below his breastbone. *My stomach.* From his war experiences he knew he had fifteen minutes to live.

'My work here is done,' the man said. Then he was gone.

Alone, Jacques Saunière turned his gaze again to the iron gate. The doors could not be reopened for at least twenty minutes. By the time anyone got to him, he would be dead. Even so, the fear that now gripped him was a fear far greater than that of his own death.

*I must pass on the secret.* He found the strength to try to get up.

Staggering to his feet, he pictured his three murdered brethren.

He thought of the generations who had come before them . . . of the mission with which they had all been entrusted.

*An unbroken chain of knowledge.*

Now, despite all the precautions . . . despite all the fail-safes . . . Jacques Saunière was the only remaining link, the sole guardian of one of the most powerful secrets ever kept.

Shivering, he pulled himself to his feet.

*I must find some way . . .*

He was trapped inside the Grand Gallery, and there existed only one person on earth to whom he could pass the torch. Saunière gazed up at the walls of his opulent prison. A collection of the world's most famous paintings seemed to smile down on him like old friends.

Wincing in pain, he summoned all of his faculties and strength. The desperate task before him, he knew, would require every remaining second of his life.

# Chapter 1

Robert Langdon awoke slowly.

A telephone was ringing in the darkness – a tinny, unfamiliar ring. He fumbled for the bedside lamp and turned it on. Squinting at his surroundings, he saw a plush bedroom with antique eighteenth-century furniture, hand-frescoed walls and a colossal mahogany four-poster bed.

*Where am I?*

The jacquard bathrobe hanging on his bedpost bore the monogram *Hôtel Ritz Paris*.

Slowly, the fog began to lift. Sitting up, he gazed tiredly into the full-length mirror across the room. The man staring back at him was a stranger – tousled and weary, his usually sharp blue eyes hazy and drawn. A dark stubble was shrouding his strong jaw, and around his temples the grey highlights were advancing, making their way deeper into his thicket of coarse black hair.

He picked up the receiver. 'Hello?'

'Monsieur Langdon?' a man's voice said. 'I hope I have not awoken you?'

Dazed, Langdon looked at the bedside clock. It was 12:32 a.m. He had been asleep only an hour, but he felt like the dead.

'This is the concierge, monsieur. I apologize for this intrusion, but you have a visitor. He insists it is urgent.'

Langdon still felt fuzzy. *A visitor?* His eyes focused on a crumpled flyer on his bedside table.

### THE AMERICAN UNIVERSITY OF PARIS
*proudly presents*
#### AN EVENING WITH ROBERT LANGDON
#### PROFESSOR OF RELIGIOUS SYMBOLOGY,
#### HARVARD UNIVERSITY, USA

Langdon groaned. His books on religious paintings and symbols had made him a reluctant celebrity in the art world, and tonight's lecture – a slide show about pagan symbolism hidden in the stones of Chartres Cathedral – had probably ruffled some conservative feathers in the audience. Most likely, some religious scholar had trailed him home to pick a fight.

'I'm sorry,' Langdon said, 'but I'm very tired and –'

'*Mais, monsieur,*' the concierge pressed, lowering his voice to an urgent whisper. 'Your guest is an important man. He is even now en route to your room.'

Langdon was wide awake now. 'You sent someone to my *room?*'

'I apologize, monsieur, but a man like this . . . I cannot presume the authority to stop him.'

'Who exactly *is* he?'

But the concierge was gone.

Almost immediately, a heavy fist pounded on Langdon's door.

Uncertain, Langdon slid off the bed, feeling his toes sink deep into the carpet. He donned the hotel bathrobe and moved towards the door. 'Who is it?'

'Mr Langdon? I need to speak with you.' The man's English was accented – a sharp, authoritative bark. 'My name is Lieutenant Jérôme Collet. Direction Centrale Police Judiciaire.'

Langdon paused. *The Judicial Police?* Why would the DCPJ, roughly equivalent to the FBI, be coming to see him?

Leaving the security chain in place, he opened the door a few inches. The face staring back at him was thin and washed out. The man was lean, dressed in an official-looking blue uniform.

'May I come in?' the agent asked.

Langdon hesitated, feeling uncertain. 'What is this all about?'

'My *capitaine* requires your expertise in a private matter.'

'Now?' Langdon managed. 'It's after midnight.'

'Am I correct that you were scheduled to meet with the curator of the Louvre this evening?'

Langdon felt a sudden surge of uneasiness. He and the revered curator Jacques Saunière had made an appointment to meet for drinks after the lecture – but Saunière had never shown up. 'Yes. How did you know that?'

'We found your name in his daily planner.'

'I trust nothing is wrong?'

The agent gave a dire sigh and slid a Polaroid snapshot through the narrow opening in the door.

When Langdon saw the photo, his entire body went rigid.

'This photo was taken less than an hour ago. Inside the Louvre.'

As Langdon stared at the bizarre image, his initial revulsion and shock gave way to an upwelling of anger.

'We had hoped that you might help us answer that very question, considering your knowledge of symbology and your plans to meet Saunière.'

Langdon's horror was now laced with fear. 'This symbol here,' he began, 'and the way his body is so oddly . . .'

'Positioned?' the agent offered.

Langdon nodded, feeling a chill as he looked up. 'I can't imagine who could do this to someone.'

The agent looked grim. 'You don't understand, Mr Langdon. What you see in this photograph . . .' He paused. 'Monsieur Saunière did that to himself.'

# Chapter 2

One mile away, the hulking albino named Silas limped through the front gate of a luxurious residence on Rue La Bruyère. He wore a spiked chain around his thigh – a *cilice*. All true followers of *The Way* wore this device – a leather strap, studded with sharp metal barbs that caused pain as a perpetual reminder of Christ's suffering on the cross. His soul sang with satisfaction of service to the Lord.

Silas went through the lobby and climbed the stairs quietly, not wanting to awaken anyone. His bedroom door was open; locks were forbidden here. He entered, closing the door behind him.

The room was spartan – hardwood floors, a pine dresser, a canvas mat in the corner that served as his bed. He was a visitor here in Paris this week, and yet for many years he had been blessed with a similar sanctuary in New York City.

*The Lord has provided me shelter and purpose in my life.*

Tonight, at last, Silas felt he had begun to repay his debt. Hurrying to the dresser, he found the cellphone hidden in his bottom drawer and placed a call.

'Yes?' a male voice answered.

'Teacher, I have returned.'

'Speak,' the voice commanded, sounding pleased to hear from him.

'All four are gone. The three *sénéchaux* . . . and the *Grand Master* himself.'

There was a momentary pause, as if for prayer. 'Then I assume you have the information?'

'All four said the same thing. Independently.' Silas paused, knowing that the information he had gleaned from his victims would come as a shock. 'Teacher, all four confirmed the existence of the *clef de voûte* . . . the legendary *keystone*.'

He heard a quick intake of breath over the phone and could feel the Teacher's excitement. 'The *keystone* . . .'

According to lore, the brotherhood had created a map of stone – a *clef de voûte*, or *keystone* – an engraved tablet that revealed the final resting place of the brotherhood's greatest secret: a secret so powerful that its protection was the reason for the brotherhood's very existence.

'When we possess the keystone,' the Teacher whispered, 'we will be only one step away.'

'We are closer than you think. The keystone is here in Paris.'

'Paris? Incredible. It is almost too easy.'

Silas relayed the earlier events of the evening . . . how all four of his victims, moments before death, had told Silas the exact same thing: that the keystone was ingeniously hidden at a precise location inside one of Paris's ancient churches – the Church of Saint-Sulpice.

'Inside a house of the Lord!' the Teacher exclaimed. 'How they mock us!'

'As they have for centuries.'

The Teacher fell silent, as if letting the triumph of this moment settle over him. Finally, he spoke. 'You have done a great service to God. Now, Silas, you must retrieve the stone for me. Immediately. Tonight.'

And the Teacher explained what was to be done.

When Silas hung up the phone, his skin tingled with anticipation. *One hour*, he told himself, grateful that the Teacher had given him time to carry out the necessary penance before entering a house of God. *I must purge my soul of today's sins.*

'*Pain is good*,' he whispered.

# Chapter 3

The crisp April air whipped through the open window of the DCPJ car as it skimmed across Paris. In the passenger seat, Robert Langdon tried to clear his thoughts. His quick shower and shave had left him looking reasonably presentable but had done little to ease his anxiety. The frightening image of the curator's body remained locked in his mind.

*Jacques Saunière is dead.*

He could not help but feel a deep sense of loss at the curator's death. Despite Saunière's reputation for being reclusive, his dedication to the arts made him an easy man to revere, and Langdon had been very much looking forward to meeting him.

Outside, the city was just now winding down – street vendors wheeling carts of candied *amandes*, waiters carrying bags of garbage to the kerb, a late-night couple cuddling to stay warm in a breeze scented with jasmine blossom. The Citroën navigated the chaos with authority, its dissonant two-tone siren parting the traffic like a knife.

'*Le capitaine* was pleased to discover you were still in Paris tonight,' the agent said as he gunned the sedan through the northern entrance of the famed Tuileries Gardens – a place Langdon had always considered to be almost sacred ground. These were the gardens in which the artist Claude Monet had experimented with form and colour, and literally inspired the birth of the Impressionist movement.

The agent turned off the blaring siren and Langdon exhaled, savouring the sudden quiet. The Citroën swerved left now, angling west down the park's central boulevard, curling around a circular pond, and then cutting across a desolate avenue and into a wide quadrangle. Now they could see the end of the Tuileries Gardens – a spot marked by a giant stone archway.

Arc du Carrousel.

Those who loved the arts revered this place. From here, four of the finest art museums in the world could be seen . . . one at each point of the compass. Out of the right-hand window, south, Langdon could see the dramatically lit facade of the old train station – now the esteemed Musée d'Orsay. Glancing left, he could make out the top of the ultramodern Pompidou Centre, which housed the Museum of Modern Art. Behind him to the west, he knew the ancient obelisk of Ramses rose above the trees, marking the Musée du Jeu de Paume.

But it was straight ahead, to the east, through the archway, that Langdon could now see the Renaissance palace that had become the most famous art museum in the world.

Musée du Louvre.

Shaped like an enormous horseshoe, the Louvre was the longest building in Europe, stretching further than three Eiffel Towers laid end to end. The building rose like a citadel against the Paris sky – a magnificent structure with a million square feet of open plaza between the museum's wings. He remembered the first time he had walked the Louvre's entire perimeter, an astonishing three-mile journey.

It had been estimated that it would take a visitor five weeks to properly appreciate the 65,300 pieces of art in this building, but most tourists chose an abbreviated experience Langdon referred to as 'Louvre Lite' – a fast sprint through the museum to see the three most famous objects: the oil painting *Mona Lisa*, and the marble sculptures *Venus de Milo* and *Winged Victory*.

The driver pulled out a hand-held walkie-talkie and spoke in rapid-fire French. *'Monsieur Langdon est arrivé. Deux minutes.'* He turned to Langdon. 'You will meet the *capitaine* at the main entrance.' Then he revved the engine and gunned the Citroën up over the kerb. The Louvre's main entrance was visible now, rising boldly in the distance.

*La Pyramide.*

This entrance – a seventy-one-foot-tall neo-modern glass pyramid designed by Chinese-born American architect I. M. Pei – had become almost as famous as the museum itself, though it was surrounded with controversy.

'Do you like our pyramid?' the agent asked.

Langdon frowned. He knew it was a loaded question. Admitting you liked the pyramid made you appear tasteless, and expressing dislike was an insult to the French.

'Mitterrand was a bold man,' he replied, splitting the difference. The late French president, who had commissioned the pyramid, was said to have suffered from a 'Pharaoh complex', filling Paris with Egyptian obelisks, art and artefacts.

'What is the captain's name?' Langdon asked, changing the subject.

'Bezu Fache,' the driver said. 'We call him *le Taureau*.'

Langdon glanced over at him. *'The Bull?'*

The man arched his eyebrows. 'Your French is better than you admit, Monsieur Langdon.'

*My French stinks,* Langdon thought, *but my knowledge of the zodiac is pretty good.* Astrology was much the same all over the world, and Taurus was always the bull.

The agent pulled the car to a stop and pointed between two fountains to a large revolving door in the side of the pyramid. 'My orders are to leave you here. I have other business to attend to. Good luck, monsieur.'

Langdon heaved a sigh and climbed out, then strode to the main entrance as the car sped away. He raised his hand to bang on the glass, but out of the darkness below, a figure appeared, striding up the curving staircase. The man was stocky and dark, with wide shoulders and squat, powerful legs. He motioned for Langdon to enter.

'I am Bezu Fache,' he announced as Langdon pushed through the door. 'Captain of the Direction Centrale Police

Judiciaire – the DCPJ.' His tone was fitting – a guttural rumble . . . like a gathering storm.

Langdon held out his hand to shake. 'Robert Langdon.'

Fache's enormous palm wrapped around Langdon's with crushing force. 'Mr Langdon.' The captain's ebony eyes locked on. 'Come.'

# Chapter 4

Captain Bezu Fache carried himself like an angry ox, his wide shoulders thrown back and his chin tucked hard into his chest.

Langdon followed him down the famous marble staircase into the sunken atrium beneath the glass pyramid. As they descended, they passed between two armed Judicial Police guards with machine guns. The message was clear: nobody goes in or out tonight without the blessing of Captain Fache.

Langdon fought a rising sense of unease. Fache's presence was anything but welcoming, and the Louvre itself had an almost sepulchral aura at this hour. The staircase, like the aisle of a dark cinema, was illuminated by subtle tread lighting embedded in each step, and he could hear his own footsteps reverberating off the glass overhead. As Langdon glanced up, he could see the faint illuminated wisps of mist from the fountains fading away outside the transparent roof.

'Do you approve?' Fache asked, nodding upwards with his broad chin.

Langdon sighed, too tired to play games. 'Yes, your pyramid is magnificent.'

Fache grunted. 'A scar on the face of Paris.'

*Strike one.* Langdon sensed his host was a hard man to please. He wondered if Fache had any idea that this pyramid, at President Mitterrand's explicit demand, had been constructed of exactly 666 panes of glass – a bizarre request that had always been a hot topic among conspiracy buffs who claimed 666 was a number representing Satan.

Langdon decided not to bring it up.

As they dropped further into the subterranean foyer, the yawning space slowly emerged from the shadows. Built fifty-seven feet beneath ground level, the Louvre's newly constructed 70,000-square-foot lobby spread out like an endless grotto. Constructed in warm ochre marble to be compatible with the honey-coloured stone of the Louvre facade above, the hall was usually vibrant with sunlight and tourists. Tonight, however, the lobby was barren and dark, giving the entire space a cold, crypt-like atmosphere.

'Where are the museum's regular security staff?' Langdon asked.

'*En quarantaine,*' Fache replied, as if Langdon were questioning his decisions. 'Obviously, someone gained entry tonight who should not have. All Louvre night wardens are being questioned. My own agents have taken over museum security for the evening.'

Langdon nodded, moving quickly to keep pace with Fache.

'How well did you know Jacques Saunière?' the captain asked.

'Actually, not at all. We'd never met.'

Fache looked surprised. 'Your first meeting was to be tonight?'

'Yes. We'd planned to meet at the American University reception following my lecture, but he never showed up.'

As Fache scribbled some notes in a little book, Langdon caught a glimpse above of the Louvre's lesser-known pyramid – *La Pyramide Inversée,* a huge inverted skylight that hung from the ceiling like a stalactite.

'Who requested tonight's meeting?' Fache asked suddenly, guiding Langdon up a short set of stairs. 'You or he?'

The question seemed odd. 'Mr Saunière did,' Langdon replied as they entered the tunnel to the Denon Wing, the most famous of the Louvre's three sections. 'His secretary contacted me a few weeks ago via email. She said the curator had heard I would be lecturing in Paris this month and wanted to discuss something with me while I was here.'

'Discuss what?'

'I don't know. Art, I imagine. We share similar interests.'

Fache looked sceptical. 'You have *no* idea what your meeting was about?'

Langdon did not. He'd been curious at the time but had not felt comfortable demanding specifics. The venerated Jacques Saunière liked his privacy and granted very few appointments; Langdon was grateful simply for the opportunity to meet him.

'Mr Langdon, can you at least *guess* what our murder victim might have wanted to discuss with you on the night he was killed? It might be helpful.'

The pointedness of the question made Langdon uncomfortable. 'I really can't imagine. I didn't ask. I felt honoured to have been contacted at all. I'm an admirer of Mr Saunière's work. I use his texts often in my classes.'

Fache made note of that fact in his book.

The two men were now halfway up the Denon Wing's entry tunnel, and Langdon could see the twin ascending escalators at the far end, both motionless. 'We'll take the elevator,' Fache said. 'As I'm sure you're aware, the gallery is quite a distance on foot.' He ran a meaty hand across his hair. 'So you shared interests with Saunière?' he continued as the lift doors opened.

'Yes. In fact, I've spent much of the last year writing the draft for a book that deals with Mr Saunière's primary area of expertise. I was looking forward to learning his thoughts on the topic.'

'I see. And what topic is that?'

Langdon hesitated, uncertain exactly how to put it. 'Essentially, the manuscript is about goddess worship – the concept of female sanctity and the art and symbols associated with it.'

'And Saunière was knowledgeable about this?'

'Nobody more so.'

'I see.'

'Perhaps Jacques Saunière knew of your manuscript?' Fache suggested. 'And he called the meeting to offer his help on your book.'

Langdon shook his head. 'Actually, nobody knows about my manuscript yet. It's still in draft form, and I haven't shown it to anyone except my editor.'

'You and Mr Saunière,' the captain said as the elevator began to move, 'you never spoke at all? Never corresponded? Never sent each other anything in the mail?'

Another odd question. Langdon shook his head. 'No. Never.'

Fache cocked his head, as if making a mental note of that fact. Saying nothing, he stared dead ahead at the chrome doors. In the reflection of the shiny elevator door, Langdon noticed the captain's tie clip – a silver crucifix with thirteen embedded pieces of black onyx. The symbol was known as a *crux gemmata* – a cross bearing thirteen gems – a graphic symbol for Christians of Christ and His twelve apostles. Somehow Langdon had not expected the captain of the French police to broadcast his religion so openly. Then again, this was France; Christianity was not a religion here so much as a birthright.

The elevator jolted to a stop. Langdon glanced up to find Fache's eyes on him in the reflection.

He stepped quickly out into the hallway, then stopped short, surprised.

Fache glanced over. 'I gather, Mr Langdon, you have never seen the Louvre after hours?'

*I guess not,* Langdon thought, trying to get his bearings.

The Louvre galleries had famously high ceilings and were usually brightly lit. Tonight, however, it was startlingly dark. A muted red glow seemed to emanate upwards from the baseboards – intermittent patches of red light spilling out on to the tile floors.

As Langdon gazed down the murky corridor, he realized he

should have expected this. Virtually all major galleries employed red service lighting at night – low-level, non-invasive lights that allowed staff and security to find their way around yet kept the paintings in relative darkness to help slow the fading effects of overexposure to light. 'This way,' Fache said, turning sharply right and setting out through a series of interconnected galleries.

Langdon followed, his vision slowly adjusting to the dark. All around, large-format oils began to materialize like photos developing before him in an enormous darkroom . . . their eyes following as he moved through the rooms. Mounted high on the walls, the visible security cameras sent a clear message to visitors: *We see you. Do not touch anything.*

'Any of them real?' Langdon asked, motioning to the cameras.

Fache shook his head. 'Of course not.'

Langdon was not surprised. With acres of galleries to watch over, the Louvre would need several hundred staff members simply to watch the video feeds. Most large museums now used containment security. *Forget keeping thieves out. Keep them in.* Containment was activated after hours, and if an intruder removed a piece of artwork, exits would snap shut around that particular gallery, and the thief would find himself behind bars even before the police arrived.

The sound of voices echoed down the marble corridor up ahead. The noise seemed to be coming from a large recessed alcove that lay ahead on the right. A bright light spilled out into the hallway.

'Office of the curator,' the captain said.

As he and Fache drew nearer the alcove, Langdon peered down a short hallway, into Saunière's luxurious study – with its warm wood and Old Master paintings. A handful of police agents bustled about the room, talking on phones and taking notes. One of them was seated at Saunière's enormous antique desk, typing into a laptop. Apparently, the curator's private office had become the police's command post for the evening.

'*Messieurs,*' Fache called out, and the men turned. '*Ne nous dérangez pas sous aucun prétexte. Entendu?*'

Langdon had hung enough NE PAS DERANGER signs on hotel room doors to catch the gist of the captain's orders. Fache and Langdon were not to be disturbed under any circumstances.

Everyone inside the office nodded their understanding.

Leaving the small congregation of agents behind, Fache led Langdon further down the darkened hallway. Thirty yards ahead loomed the gateway to the Louvre's most popular section – *la Grande Galerie* – a seemingly endless corridor that housed the Louvre's most valuable Italian masterpieces. Langdon knew that *this* was where Saunière's body lay; the Grand Gallery's famous parquet floor had been unmistakable in the photo.

As they approached, he saw the entrance was blocked by an enormous steel grate that looked like something used by medieval castles to keep out marauding armies.

'Containment security,' Fache said as they neared the grate.

Langdon peered through the bars into the dimly lit caverns of the Grand Gallery.

'After you, Mr Langdon,' Fache said. He motioned towards the floor at the base of the grate where the barricade was raised about two feet. 'Please slide under.'

Langdon stared at the narrow crawl space at his feet and then up at the massive iron grate. *He's kidding, right?* The barricade looked like a guillotine waiting to crush intruders.

Fache grumbled something in French and checked his watch. Then he dropped to his knees and slithered his bulky frame underneath the grate. On the other side, he stood up and looked back at Langdon through the bars.

Langdon sighed. Placing his palms flat on the polished parquet, he lay on his stomach and pulled himself forward. As he slid underneath, the nape of his tweed jacket snagged on the bottom of the grate, and he cracked the back of his head on the iron.

*Very smooth, Robert,* he thought, fumbling and then finally pulling himself through. As he stood up, Langdon was beginning to suspect it was going to be a very long night.

# Chapter 5

The Opus Dei world headquarters and conference centre is located at 243 Lexington Avenue in New York City. The 133,000-square-foot tower contains over one hundred bedrooms, six dining rooms, libraries, living rooms, meeting rooms and offices. Its seventeenth floor is entirely residential. Men enter the building through the main doors on Lexington Avenue, while women – kept separate from the men at all times – enter through a side street.

Earlier that evening, within the sanctuary of his penthouse apartment, Bishop Manuel Aringarosa had packed a small travel bag and dressed in a traditional black cassock. On his finger was his fourteen-carat gold bishop's ring with a purple amethyst, large diamonds, and its design of a hand-tooled mitre-crozier.

As president-general of Opus Dei, Bishop Aringarosa had spent the last decade of his life spreading the message of 'God's Work' – literally, *Opus Dei*. Founded in 1928 by the Spanish priest Josemaría Escrivá, the congregation promoted a return to strict Catholic values as spelled out in Escrivá's book *The Way*. Now, with over four million copies of the book in circulation in forty-two languages, Opus Dei was a global force with residence halls, teaching centres, and even universities in almost every major city on earth. The head of the Catholic Church, the pope – together with his cardinals in the Vatican – had given the group his full approval and blessing.

The wealth and power of Opus Dei, however, meant that they were a magnet for suspicion.

'Many call Opus Dei a brainwashing cult,' reporters often challenged. 'Others call you an ultra-conservative Christian secret society. Which are you?'

'Opus Dei is neither,' the bishop would patiently reply. 'We are a Catholic Church – a congregation of Catholics who have chosen as our priority to follow Catholic doctrine as rigorously as we can in our own daily lives. Thousands of Opus Dei members have families and do God's Work in their own communities. Others choose to live a religious life within our residences. These choices are personal, but everyone in Opus Dei shares the goal of bettering the world by doing the Work of God. Surely this is an admirable quest.'

Reason seldom worked, though. The media loved scandal, and Opus Dei, like most large organizations, had within its membership a few misguided souls who cast a shadow over the entire group. The media was now referring to Opus Dei as 'God's Mafia' and 'the Cult of Christ'.

*We fear what we do not understand,* Bishop Aringarosa thought.

Five months ago, however, the kaleidoscope of power had been shaken badly. Aringarosa was still reeling from the blow.

Now, sitting aboard a commercial airliner bound for Rome, he gazed out of the window at the dark Atlantic. The sun had already set, but the bishop knew his own star was on the rise again. *Tonight the battle will be won,* he thought, amazed that only months ago he had felt so powerless. *They know not the war they have begun.* For an instant, his eyes refocused, lingering on the reflection of his awkward face – dark and oblong, dominated by a flat, crooked nose that had been shattered by a fist in Spain when he was a young missionary. The physical flaw barely registered now. Aringarosa's was a world of the soul, not of the flesh.

As the jet passed over the coast of Portugal, the cellphone in his cassock began vibrating. The bishop knew this was a call he could not miss. Only one man possessed this number, the man who had mailed Aringarosa the phone.

Excited, he answered quietly. 'Yes?'

'Silas has located the keystone,' the caller said. 'It is in Paris. Within the Church of Saint-Sulpice.'

Bishop Aringarosa smiled. 'Then we are close.'

'We can obtain it immediately. But we need your influence.'

'Of course. Tell me what to do.'


Five hundred miles away, the albino named Silas stood over a small basin of water cleaning his back, another of his personal rituals. *Purge me with hyssop, and I shall be clean,* he prayed, quoting Psalms. *Wash me, and I shall be whiter than snow.*

For the last decade, Silas had been following *The Way,* cleansing himself of sins, rebuilding his life, erasing the violence in his past. *Jesus's message is one of peace . . . of love.* This was the message he had been taught from the beginning, and the message he held in his heart.

The message the enemies of Christ now threatened to destroy.

*Those who threaten God with force will be met with force,* he murmured.

Tonight, Silas had been called to battle.

# Chapter 6

Having squeezed beneath the security gate, Robert Langdon now stood just inside the entrance to the Grand Gallery, home to the Louvre's most famous Italian art. On either side of the gallery, stark walls rose thirty feet, evaporating into the darkness above. The reddish glow of the service lighting sifted upward, casting an unnatural smoulder across a staggering collection of still lifes, and religious scenes made by Da Vinci and other great masters.

As Langdon's gaze shifted to the diagonal slats of the parquet floor, thought by some to be the wing's most stunning offering, his eyes stopped short on an unexpected object lying on the floor a few yards to his left, surrounded by police tape. He spun towards Fache. 'Is that . . . a *Caravaggio*?'

Fache nodded without even looking.

The painting, Langdon guessed, was worth more than two million dollars, and yet it was lying on the floor like a discarded poster. 'What on earth is it doing there?'

Fache glowered. 'This is a crime scene, Mr Langdon. We have touched nothing. That canvas was pulled from the wall by the curator. It was how he activated the security system. We believe he was attacked in his office, fled into the Grand Gallery, and then pulled that painting from the wall. The gate fell immediately, sealing off all access.'

Langdon felt confused. 'So the curator actually captured his attacker inside the Grand Gallery?'

Fache shook his head. 'The security gate *separated* Saunière from his attacker. The killer was locked out there in the hallway and shot Saunière through this gate.' Fache pointed towards an orange tag hanging from one of the bars on the gate under which they had just passed. 'Saunière died in here alone.'

Langdon looked out at the enormous corridor before them. 'So where is his body?'

Fache straightened his cruciform tie clip and began to walk. 'As you probably know, the Grand Gallery is quite long.'

The exact length, if Langdon recalled correctly, was around fifteen hundred feet. As he followed Fache up the corridor, he felt almost disrespectful to be racing past so many masterpieces without pausing for so much as a glance. Yet still he saw no corpse. 'Jacques Saunière went this *far*?'

'Mr Saunière suffered a bullet wound to his stomach. He died very slowly. Perhaps over fifteen or twenty minutes. He was obviously a man of great personal strength.'

Langdon turned, appalled. 'Security took *fifteen* minutes to get here?'

'Of course not. Louvre security responded immediately to the alarm and found the Grand Gallery sealed. Through the gate, they could hear someone moving around at the far end of the corridor, but they could not see who it was. They followed protocol and called us in. We were here within fifteen minutes, and when we arrived, we raised the barricade enough to slip underneath, and I sent a dozen armed agents inside. They swept the length of the gallery to corner the intruder.'

'And?'

'They found no one inside. Except . . .' He pointed further down the hall. 'Him.'

Langdon lifted his gaze and followed Fache's outstretched finger. Thirty yards down the hall, a single spotlight on a portable stand shone down on the floor, creating a stark island of white light in the dark gallery. In the centre of the light, like an insect under a microscope, lay the corpse of the curator.

Langdon felt a deep chill as they approached the body. Before him was one of the strangest images he had ever seen. The naked corpse of Jacques Saunière lay on the parquet floor exactly as it appeared in the photograph. The curator's body was perfectly aligned with the long axis of the room, his arms and legs were sprawled outwards in a wide spreadeagle and his clothes were arranged neatly nearby. Just below his breastbone, a bloody smear marked the spot where the bullet had entered. The wound had bled surprisingly little, leaving only a small pool of blackened blood.

Saunière's left index finger was also bloody. He had apparently dipped it into the wound and, using his own blood as ink and his naked abdomen as a canvas, drawn a simple symbol on his flesh – five straight lines that intersected to form a five-pointed star.

*A pentacle.*

Langdon felt a deepening uneasiness.

*He did this to himself.*

'Mr Langdon?' Fache's dark eyes settled on him again.

'It's a pentacle,' Langdon offered, his voice feeling hollow in the huge space. 'One of the oldest symbols on earth. Used over four thousand years before Christ.'

'And what does it mean?'

Langdon always hesitated when he got this question. Telling someone what a symbol 'meant' was like telling them how a song should make them feel. 'Symbols carry different meanings in different settings,' he said. 'Primarily, the pentacle is a pagan religious symbol.'

Fache nodded. 'Devil worship.'

'No,' Langdon corrected, immediately realizing he hadn't chosen his words well. Nowadays, the term *pagan* had become almost another way of saying devil worship – which was very wrong. The word's roots actually reached back to the Latin *paganus*, meaning country-dwellers. 'Pagans' were literally simple country folk who clung to the old, rural religions. 'The pentacle,' he clarified, 'is a pre-Christian symbol that relates to Nature worship. The ancients thought of their world as having two halves – masculine and feminine. Yin and yang, as many in the East describe it. When male and female were balanced, there was harmony in the world. When they were unbalanced, there was chaos.' He motioned to Saunière's stomach. 'This pentacle is representative of the *female* half of all things – what religious historians call the "sacred feminine" or the "divine goddess". Saunière, of all people, would know this.'

'Saunière drew a *goddess* symbol on his stomach?'

Langdon had to admit, it seemed odd. 'The pentacle symbolizes Venus – the goddess of female sexual love and beauty.'

Fache eyed the naked man and grunted.

'Early religion was based on the divine order of Nature. The goddess Venus and the planet Venus were one and the same,' Langdon added, 'no matter what name Venus was known by.'

Fache looked more troubled now, as if he somehow preferred the idea of devil worship. 'Mr Langdon,' he said abruptly. 'Obviously, the pentacle must *also* relate to the devil. Your American horror films make that point clearly.'

Langdon frowned. *Thank you, Hollywood.* The five-pointed star was now a virtual cliché in horror films about Satanists – he was always frustrated when he saw the symbol in this context.

'I assure you,' he said, 'that despite what you see in the movies, it is historically wrong to link the pentacle with the devil. The symbolism of the pentacle has been distorted over the millennium. In this case, through bloodshed.'

'I'm not sure I follow.'

Langdon glanced at Fache's crucifix, uncertain how to phrase his next point. 'The Church, sir. Symbols are very resilient, but the pentacle was altered by the early Roman Catholic Church. As part of the Vatican's campaign to wipe out pagan religions and convert the masses to Christianity, the Church launched a campaign against the pagan gods and goddesses, making sure their symbols were seen as evil.'

'Go on.'

'This is very common in times of turmoil,' Langdon continued. 'A newly emerging power takes over the existing symbols and, over time, changes their meaning. In the battle between pagan symbols and Christian symbols, the pagans lost; Poseidon's trident became the devil's pitchfork, the wise crone's pointed hat became the symbol of a witch, and Venus's pentacle became a sign of the devil.'

'Interesting.' Fache nodded towards the spreadeagled corpse. 'And the positioning of the body? What do you make of that?'

Langdon shrugged. 'Repeating a symbol is the simplest way to strengthen its meaning. Jacques Saunière positioned himself in the shape of a five-pointed star.'

Fache's eyes followed the five points of Saunière's arms, legs and head as he again ran a hand across his slick hair. 'And the *nudity*?' He grumbled as he spoke the word, sounding repulsed by the sight of an ageing male body. 'Why did he remove his clothing?'

*Good question*, Langdon thought. He'd been wondering the same thing ever since he first saw the photo. 'Mr Fache, I obviously can't tell you why Mr Saunière drew that symbol on himself or placed himself in this way,' he said, 'but I *can* tell you that a man like Jacques Saunière would certainly consider the pentacle a sign of the sacred female.'

'And the use of his own blood as ink?'

'Obviously he had nothing else to write with.'

Fache was silent a moment. 'Actually, I believe he used blood so that the police would follow certain forensic procedures.' He gestured. 'Look at his left hand.'

Uncertain, Langdon circled the corpse and crouched down, noting with surprise that the curator was clutching a large felt-tipped marker.

'Saunière was holding it when we found him,' Fache said, leaving Langdon and moving several yards to a portable table covered with investigation tools, cables and assorted electronic gear. 'As I told you,' he said, rummaging around the table, 'we have touched nothing. Are you familiar with this kind of pen?'

Langdon knelt down further to see the pen's label.

STYLO DE LUMIERE NOIRE.

He glanced up in surprise. The black-light pen or watermark stylus was a specialized felt-tipped marker originally designed by museums, restorers and forgery police to place invisible marks on items. The stylus wrote in a noncorrosive, alcohol-based fluorescent ink that was visible only under black light. Nowadays, museum maintenance staffs carried these markers on their daily rounds to place invisible 'tick marks' on the frames of paintings that needed restoration.

As Langdon stood up, Fache walked over to the spotlight and turned it off, plunging the gallery into sudden darkness. He reappeared a moment or so later, carrying a portable light source.

'As you may know,' the captain said, his eyes luminescing in the violet glow, 'police use black-light illumination to search crime scenes for blood and other forensic evidence. So you can imagine our surprise . . .' Abruptly he pointed the light down at the corpse.

Langdon looked down and jumped back in shock.

Scrawled in luminescent handwriting, the curator's final words glowed purple beside his corpse. As Langdon stared at the shimmering text, he felt the fog that had surrounded this entire night growing thicker.

He read the message again and looked up at Fache. 'What the devil does this mean?'

Fache's eyes shone white. '*That*, monsieur, is precisely the question you are here to answer.'

# Chapter 7

The Church of Saint-Sulpice had a modest dwelling on the first floor of the church itself, to the left of the choir balcony. It had been home to Sister Sandrine Bieil for over a decade – the sixty-year-old nun had made herself quite comfortable there.

She was responsible for overseeing all the non-religious aspects of the church – general maintenance, hiring support staff and guides, securing the building after hours, ordering supplies like communion wine and wafers.

Tonight, asleep in her small bed, she awoke to the shrill of her telephone. Tiredly, she lifted the receiver.

'*Soeur Sandrine. Eglise Saint-Sulpice.*'

'Hello, Sister,' the man said in French.

Sister Sandrine sat up. *What time is it?* Although she recognized her boss's voice, in fifteen years she had never been awoken by him. The abbé was a deeply pious man who went home to bed immediately after mass.

'I apologize if I have awoken you, Sister,' the abbé said, his own voice sounding groggy and on edge. 'I have a favour to ask of you. I just received a call from an influential American bishop. Perhaps you know him? Manuel Aringarosa?'

'The head of Opus Dei?' *Of course I know of him. Who in the Church doesn't?*

Opus Dei made her feel uneasy – and their views on women were medieval at best. Sister Sandrine had been shocked to learn that female numeraries were forced to clean the men's residence halls for no pay while the men were at mass; women slept on hardwood floors, while the men had straw mats . . . all as added penance for Original Sin. She knew too that Opus Dei had become suddenly more powerful in recent years, just after the wealthy sect had allegedly transferred almost one billion dollars into the Vatican's Institute for Religious Works – commonly known as the Vatican Bank.

'Bishop Aringarosa called to ask me a favour,' the abbé told her, his voice nervous. 'One of his numeraries is in Paris tonight . . . and he has always dreamed of seeing Saint-Sulpice.'

'By night? But the church is far more interesting by day.'

'Sister, I agree, and yet I would consider it a personal favour if you could let him in tonight. He can be there at . . . say, one o'clock? That's in twenty minutes.'

Sister Sandrine frowned. 'Of course. It would be my pleasure.'

The abbé thanked her and hung up.

Swinging her legs off the bed, Sister Sandrine stood slowly, chilled by the cold stone on the soles of her bare feet.

As the chill rose through her flesh, she felt an unexpected apprehension.

*Women's intuition?*

A follower of God, Sister Sandrine had learned to find peace in the calming voices of her own soul. Tonight, however, those voices were as silent as the empty church around her.

# Chapter 8

Langdon couldn't tear his eyes off the glowing purple text scrawled across the parquet floor. Jacques Saunière's final communication seemed as unlikely a departing message as any Langdon could imagine.

The message read:

*13-3-2-21-1-1-8-5*
*O, Draconian devil!*
*Oh, lame saint!*

Although Langdon had not the slightest idea what it meant, he did understand Fache's instinct that the pentacle had something to do with devil worship.

*O, Draconian devil!*

Saunière had left a literal reference to the devil. Equally bizarre was the series of numbers. 'Part of it looks like a numeric cipher.'

'Yes,' Fache said. 'Our cryptographers are already working on it. We believe these numbers may be the key to who killed him. Maybe a telephone exchange or some kind of personal identification? Do the numbers have any symbolic meaning to you?'

Langdon looked again at the digits. The numbers appeared to be totally random. When numbers were used as part of a system of symbols, they usually made some sort of sense – a progression or pattern, for instance. But nothing here – the pentacle, the text, the numbers – seemed to have a link to each other.

'You said earlier,' Fache said, 'that Saunière's actions here were all in an effort to send some sort of message . . . goddess worship or something in that vein? How does this message fit in?' He paused. 'This text appears to be an accusation of some sort. Wouldn't you agree?'

Langdon tried to imagine the curator's final minutes trapped alone in the Grand Gallery, knowing he was about to die. It seemed logical. 'An accusation against his murderer makes sense, I suppose.'

'My job, of course, is to put a name to that person. Let me ask you this, Mr Langdon. To your eye, beyond the numbers, what about this message is most strange?'

*Most strange?* A dying man had barricaded himself in the gallery, drawn a pentacle on himself and scrawled a mysterious accusation on the floor. What about all that *wasn't* strange?

'Saunière was a Frenchman,' Fache said flatly. 'He lived in Paris. And yet he chose to write this message . . .'

'In English,' Langdon said, now realizing the captain's meaning.

Fache nodded. '*Précisément.* Any idea why?'

Langdon knew Saunière spoke impeccable English – but why he would choose English as the language in which to write his final words escaped him. He shrugged.

Fache motioned back to the pentacle on Saunière's abdomen. 'Nothing to do with devil worship? Are you still certain?'

Langdon was certain of nothing any more. 'The symbology and text don't seem to go together. I'm sorry I can't be of more help.'

'Perhaps this will make it clearer.' Fache backed away from the body and raised the black light again, letting the beam spread out in a wider angle. 'And now?'

To Langdon's amazement, a rudimentary circle glowed around the curator's body. Saunière had apparently lain down and swung the pen around himself in several long arcs, essentially inscribing himself inside a circle.

In a flash, the meaning became clear.

'The Vitruvian Man,' Langdon gasped.

Da Vinci's The Vitruvian Man had become a modern-day icon of culture, appearing on posters, mouse pads and T-shirts around the world. The celebrated drawing consisted of a perfect circle in which was inscribed a nude male, his arms and legs outstretched in a naked spreadeagle.

Da Vinci. Langdon felt a shiver of amazement. The clarity of Saunière's intentions could not be denied. In his final moments of life, the curator had stripped off his clothing and arranged his body in a life-sized replica of Leonardo da Vinci's most famous sketch.

The circle had been the missing critical element. A feminine symbol of protection, the circle around the naked man's body completed Da Vinci's male and female harmony. The question now, though, was *why* Saunière would imitate a famous drawing.

'Mr Langdon,' Fache said, 'certainly a man like yourself is aware that Leonardo da Vinci had a tendency towards the darker arts.'

Langdon was surprised by Fache's knowledge of Da Vinci, and it certainly went a long way towards explaining the captain's suspicions about devil worship. Da Vinci had always been an awkward subject for historians, especially in the Christian tradition. The genius artist had been a homosexual; he cut up corpses to study human anatomy; he kept mysterious journals in illegible reverse handwriting; he believed he could use alchemy to turn lead into gold, and possibly even cheat God by creating an elixir to postpone death.

*Misunderstanding breeds distrust,* Langdon thought.

'I understand your concerns,' he said, 'but Da Vinci never really practised any dark arts. He was an exceptionally spiritual man, though his beliefs put him in conflict with the Church.' He weighed his words carefully. 'Saunière's views actually had a lot in common with Da Vinci . . . including a shared frustration with how the Church demonized the idea of the goddess.'

Fache's eyes hardened. 'You think Saunière is calling the Church a lame saint and a Draconian devil?'

Langdon had to admit it seemed far-fetched. 'All I am saying is that Mr Saunière dedicated his life to studying the history of the goddess – and nothing has done more to erase that history than the Catholic Church. It seems reasonable that Saunière might have chosen to express his disappointment in his final goodbye.'

'Disappointment?' Fache demanded, sounding hostile now. 'This message sounds more *enraged* than disappointed, wouldn't you say?' His jaw tightened as he spoke. 'Mr Langdon, I have seen a lot of death in my work, and let me tell you something. When a man is murdered by another man, I do not believe his final thoughts are to write an obscure spiritual statement that no one will understand. I believe he is thinking of one thing only.' Fache's whispery voice sliced the air. '*La vengeance*. I believe Saunière wrote this note to tell us who killed him.'

Langdon stared. 'But that makes no sense whatsoever.'

'No?'

'No,' he fired back, tired and frustrated. 'You told me Saunière was attacked in his office by someone he had apparently invited in.'

'Yes.'

'So it seems reasonable to conclude that the curator *knew* his attacker.'

Fache nodded. 'Go on.'

'So if Saunière *knew* the person who killed him, why do all this?' He pointed at the floor. 'Numeric codes? Lame saints? Draconian devils? Pentacles on his stomach? It's all too cryptic. No, I would assume that if Saunière wanted to tell you who killed him, he would have written down somebody's *name*.'

As Langdon spoke those words, a smug smile crossed Fache's lips for the first time all night. *'Précisément,'* he said.

Not far away, inside Saunière's office, was Lieutenant Collet, huddled over the curator's enormous desk. With the exception of the eerie, robot-like doll of a medieval knight that seemed to be staring at him from the corner of Saunière's desk, Collet was comfortable. He adjusted his headphones and checked the input levels on the hard-disk recording system. All systems were go. The audio feed of the conversation inside the Grand Gallery was crystal clear.

Turning now to his laptop computer, the lieutenant checked the GPS tracking system. The onscreen image revealed a detailed floor plan of the gallery where the curator's body lay.

Deep in the heart of the Grand Gallery blinked a tiny red dot.

*La marque.*

Fache was keeping his prey on a very tight leash tonight. Wisely so. For Robert Langdon seemed to be one cool customer.

# Chapter 9

To make sure his conversation with Mr Langdon would not be interrupted, Bezu Fache had turned off his phone. Unfortunately, it was an expensive model equipped with a two-way radio feature, which, contrary to his orders, was now being used by one of his agents to page him.

'*Capitaine?*' The phone crackled like a walkie-talkie.

Fache felt his teeth clench in rage. He gave Langdon a calm look of apology. 'One moment, please.' He pulled the phone from his belt and pressed the radio transmission button. '*Oui?*'

'*Capitaine, un agent du Département de Cryptographie est arrivé.*'

Fache's anger stalled momentarily. *A cryptographer had arrived?* This was probably good news. Fache, after finding Saunière's cryptic text on the floor, had uploaded photographs of the entire crime scene to the Cryptography Department, hoping someone there could tell him what Saunière was trying to say. If a codebreaker had now arrived, it most likely meant someone had decrypted the message.

'I'm busy at the moment,' he radioed back, leaving no doubt in his tone that a line had been crossed. 'Ask the cryptographer to wait at the command post. I'll speak to him when I'm done.'

'*Her,*' the voice corrected. 'It's Agent Neveu.'

Fache was becoming less amused with this call with every passing moment. Thirty-two-year-old Sophie Neveu had been foisted on Fache two years ago as part of the ministry's attempt to include more women in the police force.

The man on the radio said, 'Agent Neveu insisted on speaking to you immediately, Captain. I tried to stop her, but she's on her way into the gallery.'

Fache recoiled in disbelief. 'Unacceptable! I made it very clear –'

'*Excusez-moi, messieurs.*'

A woman's voice chimed out behind Langdon, and he turned to see a young woman approaching. Her thick burgundy hair fell unstyled to her shoulders, and she was dressed casually in a knee-length, cream-coloured Irish sweater over black leggings.

To Langdon's surprise, the woman walked directly up to him and extended a polite hand. 'Monsieur Langdon, I am Agent Sophie Neveu from the Cryptology Department.' She had a muted Anglo-French accent. 'It is a pleasure to meet you.'

Langdon took her palm in his and felt himself momentarily fixed in her strong gaze. Her eyes were olive-green – incisive and clear.

'Captain,' she said, turning quickly to face Bezu Fache, 'please excuse the interruption, but –'

'*Ce n'est pas le moment!*' Fache sputtered.

'I tried to phone you,' Sophie continued in English, as if out of courtesy to Langdon. 'I've deciphered the numeric code.'

Langdon felt a pulse of excitement. *She broke the code?*

'Before I explain,' Sophie said, 'I have an urgent message for Mr Langdon.'

Fache's expression turned to one of deepening concern. 'For Mr Langdon?'

She nodded, turning back to Langdon. 'You need to contact the US Embassy, Mr Langdon. They have a message for you from the States.'

Langdon reacted with surprise, his excitement over the code giving way to a sudden ripple of concern. *A message from the States?* He tried to imagine who could be trying to reach him. Only a few of his colleagues even knew he was in Paris.

Fache's broad jaw had tightened with the news. 'The US Embassy?' he demanded, sounding suspicious. 'How would they know to find Mr Langdon *here*?'

Sophie shrugged. 'Apparently they called Mr Langdon's hotel, and the concierge told them Mr Langdon had been collected by the Judicial Police. The police then told me they had a message waiting for Mr Langdon and asked me to pass it along.'

Fache's brow furrowed in confusion. He opened his mouth to speak, but Sophie had already turned back to Langdon.

'Mr Langdon,' she said, pulling a small slip of paper from her pocket, 'this is the number for your embassy's messaging service. They asked that you phone in as soon as possible.' She handed him the paper with an intent gaze. 'While I discuss the code with

Captain Fache, you need to make this call.' She began to pull a cellphone from her sweater pocket.

Fache waved her away. He now looked like a volcano about to erupt. Without taking his eyes off Sophie, he produced his own cellphone and handed it to Langdon. 'This line is secure, Mr Langdon. You may use it.' He marched Sophie several steps away and began telling her off in hushed tones.

Disliking the captain more and more, Langdon switched on the cellphone and dialled the number Sophie Neveu had given him – a Paris number with an extension.

The line began to ring.

One ring . . . two rings . . . three rings . . .

Finally, the call connected.

Langdon expected to hear an embassy operator, but he found himself instead listening to an answering machine. Oddly, the voice on the tape was familiar – it was that of Sophie Neveu herself! Confused, he turned back towards Sophie. 'I'm sorry, Ms Neveu? I think you may have given me –'

'No, that's the right number,' Sophie interjected quickly, as if anticipating Langdon's confusion. 'The embassy has an automated message system. You have to dial an access code to pick up your messages.'

Langdon stared. 'But –'

'It's the three-digit code on the paper I gave you.' Sophie flashed Langdon a silencing glare. Her eyes sent a crystal-clear message. *Don't ask questions. Just do it.*

Bewildered, Langdon punched in the extension on the slip of

paper: 454. The outgoing message immediately cut off, and he heard an electronic voice announce in French: 'You have *one* new message.' Apparently, 454 was Sophie's remote access code for picking up her messages while away from home.

*I'm picking up this woman's messages?*

The message began to play – and the voice on the line was Sophie's.

'Mr Langdon,' the message began in a fearful whisper. 'Do *not* react to this message. Just listen calmly. You are in danger right now. Follow my directions very closely.'

# Chapter 10

Silas sat behind the wheel of the black Audi the Teacher had arranged for him and gazed out at the great Church of Saint-Sulpice. Lit from beneath by banks of floodlights, the church's two bell towers rose like stalwart sentinels. On either flank, a shadowy row of sleek buttresses jutted out like the ribs of a beautiful beast.

*The heathens used a house of God to conceal their keystone.* He was looking forward to finding it and giving it to the Teacher so they could recover what the brotherhood had long ago stolen from the faithful.

*How powerful that will make Opus Dei.*

Parking the Audi, Silas exhaled, telling himself to clear his mind for the task at hand. The memories of his life before Opus Dei had saved him still haunted his soul . . .

His birth name had not been Silas – he couldn't now even recall the name his parents had given him. He had left home when he was seven. His drunken father, a burly dockworker in the city of

Marseilles, blamed his mother for the boy's embarrassing condition.

One night, there had been a horrific fight, and Silas's mother never got up again. The boy stood over his lifeless mother and felt unbearable guilt.

*This is my fault!*

As if some kind of demon were controlling his body, he had walked to the kitchen and grabbed what he needed, then moved to the bedroom where his father lay on the bed in a drunken stupor. Without a word, the boy made his father pay for what he had done.

He fled once the deed was done, but his strange appearance made him an outcast among the other young runaways on the city streets, and he was forced to live alone in the basement of a dilapidated factory, eating stolen fruit and raw fish from the docks. *A ghost,* people would whisper to each other, their eyes wide with fright as they stared at his white skin. *A ghost with the eyes of a devil!*

And Silas had felt like a ghost . . . transparent . . . floating from seaport to seaport until, at eighteen, his crimes led him to a prison in Andorra.

Twelve years there, and his flesh and soul had withered until he knew he had become transparent.

*I am a ghost.*

*Yo soy un espectro . . .*

One night a mighty hand shook the mortar of his stone cell and the ghost awoke to the screams of other inmates. As he jumped to his feet, a large boulder toppled on to the very spot where he had been sleeping, leaving a hole in the trembling wall. Beyond it was a sight he had not seen in over ten years. The moon.

Even while the earth still shook, the ghost found himself scrambling through a narrow tunnel, staggering out, and tumbling down a barren mountainside into the woods. He ran all night, delirious with hunger, following the tracks of a railway, and eventually stumbling across an empty freight car into which he crawled to rest.

When he awoke, the train was moving; someone was yelling at him, and throwing him out of the freight car. He wandered away from the tracks and came upon a road. Exhausted, he lay down beside it and slipped into unconsciousness . . .

The light came slowly, and the ghost wondered how long he had been dead. *A day? Three days?* It didn't matter. His bed was soft, the air around him smelled sweet with candles, and Jesus was there, staring down at him.

*I am here,* Jesus whispered to him. *The stone has been rolled aside, and you are born again. You are saved, my son. Blessed are those who follow my path.*

Again he slept.

A scream of anguish startled the ghost from his slumber. He staggered down a hallway towards the sounds of shouting. Entering a kitchen, he saw a large man beating up a smaller man. The ghost grabbed the large man and hurled him backwards against a wall, and the man ran, leaving the ghost standing over the body of a young man in priest's robes. Lifting the priest, who had a badly shattered nose, the ghost carried him to a couch.

'Thank you, my friend,' the priest said in awkward French. 'The offertory money is tempting for thieves . . .' He smiled. 'My name is Manuel Aringarosa, and I am a missionary from Madrid, sent here – to the north of Spain – to build a church. What is your name, my friend?'

The ghost could not remember. 'Where am I?' His voice sounded hollow. 'How did I get here?'

'You were on my doorstep. You were ill, so I fed you, cared for you. You've been here many days,' Aringarosa said softly.

The ghost studied his young caretaker. Years had passed since anyone had shown him any kindness. 'Thank you, Father.'

The priest touched his bloody lip. 'It is I who am thankful, my friend.'

When the ghost awoke in the morning, he was surprised to find a newspaper clipping on his bedside table. The article was in French and was a week old. When he read the story, he was filled with fear, for it told of an earthquake in the mountains that had destroyed a prison and freed many dangerous criminals.

*The priest knows who I am!* He sprang from the bed, ready to run.

'The Book of Acts,' a voice said from the door, and the young priest entered, smiling. His nose was awkwardly bandaged, and he was holding out an old Bible. 'The chapter is marked.'

Uncertain, the ghost took the Bible.

*Acts 16.*

The verses told of a prisoner named Silas who lay naked and beaten in his cell, singing hymns to God. When the ghost reached Verse 26, he gasped in shock.

'Suddenly there was a great earthquake, so that the foundations of the prison were shaken, and all the doors fell open.'

The priest smiled warmly. 'From now on, my friend, if you have no other name, I shall call you Silas.'

The ghost nodded blankly. *Silas*. He had been given flesh. *My name is Silas.*

'It's time for breakfast,' the priest said. 'You will need your strength if you are to help me build this church.'


Twenty thousand feet above the Mediterranean, Bishop Aringarosa barely noticed as the flight bounced in turbulence. His thoughts were with the future of Opus Dei. He wished he could phone Silas in Paris. But he could not.

'It is for your own safety,' the Teacher had explained, speaking in English with a French accent. 'Communications can be intercepted. The results could be disastrous for you.'

Aringarosa knew he was right. The Teacher seemed an exceptionally careful man – he had not even revealed his real identity to Aringarosa. But he was a man well worth obeying. After all, he had somehow obtained very secret information: *the names of the brotherhood's four top members!*

'Bishop,' the Teacher had told him, 'I have made all the arrangements. For my plan to succeed, you must allow Silas to answer *only* to me for several days. The two of you will not speak.

I do this to protect your identity, Silas's identity . . . and my investment.'

*Twenty million euros,* the bishop thought. *A pittance for something so powerful.* He allowed himself a rare smile. Only five months ago, he had feared for the future of the Faith. Now, as if by the will of God, the solution had presented itself. If all went as planned tonight, Aringarosa would soon be in possession of something that would make him the most powerful man in Christendom.

The Teacher and Silas would not fail.

The Teacher was acting for money, Silas for faith.

Both money and faith were strong motives to succeed.

# Chapter 11

'A joke!' Bezu Fache was livid, glaring at Sophie Neveu in disbelief. A *numeric joke?* 'Your professional assessment of Saunière's code is that it is some kind of mathematical prank?'

'This code,' Sophie explained, 'is so simple that Jacques Saunière must have known we would see through it immediately.' She pulled a scrap of paper from her sweater pocket and handed it to Fache. 'Here is the decryption.'

Fache looked at the card.

$$1-1-2-3-5-8-13-21$$

'This is it?' he snapped. 'All you did was put the numbers in increasing order!'

Sophie actually had the nerve to give a satisfied smile. 'Exactly.'

Fache's tone lowered to a guttural rumble. 'Agent Neveu, I have no idea where you're going with this, but I suggest you get there fast.' He shot an anxious glance at Langdon, who stood nearby with the phone pressed to his ear, apparently still listening to his phone message from the US Embassy. From Langdon's ashen expression, Fache sensed the news was bad.

'Captain,' Sophie said, her tone dangerously defiant, 'the sequence of numbers you have in your hand happens to be one of the most famous mathematical progressions in history. This is the Fibonacci sequence,' she declared, nodding towards the piece of paper in Fache's hand. 'A progression in which each number is equal to the sum of the two preceding numbers.'

Fache studied the numbers. Each was indeed the sum of the two previous numbers, and yet Fache could not imagine what the relevance of all this was to Saunière's death.

'Mathematician Leonardo Fibonacci created this succession of numbers in the thirteenth century. Obviously there can be no coincidence that *all* the numbers Saunière wrote on the floor belong to Fibonacci's famous sequence.'

Fache stared at the young woman for several moments. 'Fine, but would you tell me *why* Jacques Saunière chose to do this? What is he saying? What does this *mean*?'

She shrugged. 'Absolutely nothing. That's the point. It's a simple joke. Like taking the words of a famous poem and shuffling them at random to see if anyone recognizes what all the words have in common.'

Fache took a menacing step forward, placing his face only inches from Sophie's. 'I certainly hope you have a much more satisfying explanation than *that*.'

Sophie's soft features grew surprisingly stern as she leaned in. 'Captain, considering what you have at stake here tonight, I thought you might appreciate knowing that Jacques Saunière might be playing games with you. Apparently not. I'll inform the director of Cryptography you no longer need our services.'

With that, she turned on her heel and marched off the way she had come.

Stunned, Fache watched her disappear into the darkness. *Is she out of her mind?* He faced Langdon, who was still on the phone and seemed even more concerned than before. By the time he hung up, he looked ill.

'Is everything all right?' Fache asked.

Weakly, Langdon shook his head.

*Bad news from home,* Fache sensed, noticing his suspect was sweating slightly as Fache took back his cellphone.

'An accident,' Langdon stammered, looking at Fache with a strange expression. 'A friend . . .' He hesitated. 'I'll need to fly home first thing in the morning.'

Fache had no doubt the shock on Langdon's face was genuine, and yet he sensed another emotion there too, as if a distant fear were suddenly simmering in the American's eyes. 'I'm sorry to hear that,' he said, watching Langdon closely. 'Would you like to sit down?' He motioned to one of the viewing benches in the gallery.

Langdon nodded absently and took a few steps towards the bench, then he paused. 'Actually, I think I'd like to use the toilet.'

Fache frowned inwardly at the delay. 'The toilet. Of course. Let's take a break for a few minutes.' He motioned back down the long hallway in the direction they had come from. 'The toilets are back towards the curator's office.'

Langdon hesitated, pointing in the other direction towards the far end of the Grand Gallery corridor. 'I believe there's a much closer one at the end.'

Fache realized Langdon was right. They were two-thirds of the way down, and the Grand Gallery dead-ended at a pair of toilets. 'Shall I accompany you?'

Langdon shook his head, already moving deeper into the gallery. 'Not necessary. And . . . I think I'd like a few minutes to myself.'

Fache was not wild about the idea of Langdon wandering down the corridor alone, but he knew the Grand Gallery had just the one doorway – the gate under which they had entered – and he had guards on every ground-floor exit. Langdon could not possibly leave without Fache knowing about it.

'I need to return to Mr Saunière's office for a moment,' he said. 'Please come and find me there when you are ready. There is more we need to discuss.' Turning, he marched angrily back as Langdon disappeared into the darkness in the opposite direction. Arriving at the gate, Fache slid under and stormed over to his agents in Saunière's office.

'Who let Sophie Neveu into this building?' he bellowed.

Collet was the first to answer. 'She told the guards outside she'd broken the code.'

Fache looked around. 'Has she gone?'

'She's not with you?'

'She left.' Fache glanced out at the darkened hallway.

For a moment, he considered contacting the guards below and telling them to drag her back up here before she could leave the premises. He thought better of it.

Pushing her from his mind, he stared for a moment at the miniature knight standing on Saunière's desk. Then he turned back to Collet. 'Do you have him?'

Collet gave a curt nod and spun the laptop towards Fache. The red dot was clearly visible on the floor plan overlay, blinking methodically in a room marked TOILETTES PUBLIQUES.

'Good,' Fache said, stalking into the hall. 'I've got a phone call to make. Be sure our suspect doesn't leave the premises.'

# Chapter 12

Robert Langdon felt light-headed as he trudged towards the end of the Grand Gallery. Sophie's phone message played over and over in his mind.

Finding the men's room door, Langdon entered and turned on the lights.

The room was empty.

Walking to the sink, he splashed cold water on his face and tried to wake up. Harsh fluorescent lights glared off the stark tiles, and the room smelled of disinfectant. As he towelled off, the door creaked open behind him. He spun round.

Sophie Neveu entered, her green eyes flashing fear. 'Thank God you came. We don't have much time.'

Langdon stood beside the sinks, staring in bewilderment at the police cryptographer. Only minutes ago, he had listened to her phone message, and the more he listened, the more he sensed Sophie Neveu was speaking in earnest. *Do not react to this message. Just listen calmly. You are in danger right now. Follow my directions very closely* . . . Langdon had decided to do exactly as Sophie advised.

'I wanted to warn you, Mr Langdon,' she began, still catching her breath, 'that you are *sous surveillance cachée*. Under a guarded observation.' As she spoke, her accented English resonated off the tiled walls, giving her voice a hollow quality.

'But . . . why?' Langdon demanded.

'Because,' she said, stepping towards him, 'Fache's primary suspect in this murder is *you*. Look in the left pocket of your jacket. You'll find proof that they are watching you.'

Langdon felt his apprehension rising. *Look in my pocket?* It sounded like some kind of cheap magic trick.

'Just look.'

Bewildered, Langdon reached his hand into his tweed jacket's left pocket – one he never used. Feeling around inside, he found nothing at first, but then his fingers brushed against something unexpected. Small and hard. Pinching the tiny object between his fingers, Langdon pulled it out and stared in astonishment. It was a metallic button-shaped disc, about the size of a watch battery. He had never seen it before. 'What the . . . ?'

'GPS tracking dot,' Sophie said. 'Continuously transmits its location to a Global Positioning System satellite. It's accurate within two feet anywhere on the globe. They have you on an electronic leash. The agent who picked you up at the hotel would have slipped it inside your pocket before you left your room.'

Langdon's mind flashed back to the hotel room . . . his quick shower, getting dressed, the police lieutenant politely holding out Langdon's tweed coat as they left.

Sophie's gaze was keen. 'Fache can't know you've found it.'

She paused. 'They tagged you because they thought you might run. In fact, they *hoped* you would run; it would make their case stronger.'

'Why would I run?' Langdon demanded. 'I'm innocent!' Angrily, he stalked towards the trash receptacle to dispose of the tracker.

'No!' Sophie grabbed his arm and stopped him. 'Leave it in your pocket. If you throw it out, the signal will stop moving and they'll know you found it. If Fache thinks you've discovered what he's doing . . .' She did not finish the thought. Instead, she prised the metallic disc from Langdon's hand and slid it back into his coat. 'The dot stays with you. At least for the moment.'

Langdon felt lost. 'How could Fache possibly believe I killed Jacques Saunière?'

'There is a piece of evidence here that you have not yet seen.' Sophie's expression was grim. 'Do you recall the three lines of text that Saunière wrote on the floor?'

Langdon nodded. The numbers and words were imprinted on his mind.

Sophie's voice dropped to a whisper. 'There was a *fourth* line that Fache photographed and then wiped clean before you arrived.'

Langdon knew the soluble ink of a watermark stylus could easily be wiped away – but why would Fache remove evidence?

'The last line of the message,' Sophie said, 'was something Fache did not want you to know about.' She paused. 'At least not until he was done with you.' She produced a computer printout of a photo from her sweater pocket and began unfolding it. 'This is the *complete* message.' She handed the page to Langdon.

He looked at the image. The final line hit him like a kick in the gut.

13-3-2-21-1-1-8-5
*O, Draconian devil!*
*Oh, lame saint!*
*P.S. Find Robert Langdon*

For several seconds, he stared in wonder at the photograph. *P.S. Find Robert Langdon*. He felt as if the floor were tilting beneath his feet. *Saunière left a postscript with my name on it?* In his wildest dreams, he could not fathom why.

'Now do you understand,' Sophie said, her eyes urgent, 'why Fache ordered you here tonight, and why you are his primary suspect?'

The only thing Langdon understood at the moment was why Fache had looked so smug when Langdon suggested Saunière would have accused his killer by name.

*Find Robert Langdon.*

'Why would Saunière write this?' Langdon demanded, his confusion now giving way to anger. 'Why would I want to kill him?'

'Fache has yet to uncover a motive, but he has been recording his entire conversation with you tonight in hopes you might reveal one.'

Langdon opened his mouth, but still no words came.

'He's fitted with a miniature microphone,' Sophie explained. 'It's connected to a transmitter in his pocket that radios the signal back to the command post.'

'This is impossible,' Langdon stammered. 'I have an alibi. I went directly back to my hotel after my lecture. You can ask the hotel desk.'

'Fache already did. His report shows you retrieving your room key from the concierge at about ten thirty. Unfortunately, the time of the murder was closer to eleven. You easily could have left your hotel room unseen.'

'This is madness! Fache has no evidence!'

Sophie's eyes widened as if to say: *No evidence?* 'Mr Langdon, your name is written on the floor beside the body, and Saunière's diary says you were due with him at approximately the time of the murder. Fache has more than enough reason to take you into custody for questioning.' She sighed. 'Jacques Saunière was a very prominent and well-loved figure in Paris, and his murder will be news in the morning. Fache will be under a lot of pressure to find his murderer, and he will look a lot better if he has a suspect in custody. Whether or not you are guilty, you most certainly will be held by the police until they can figure out what really happened.'

Langdon felt like a caged animal. 'Why are you telling me all this?'

'Because, Mr Langdon, I believe you are innocent.' Sophie looked away for a moment and then back into his eyes. 'And also because it is partially *my* fault that you're in trouble.'

'I'm sorry? It's *your* fault Saunière is trying to frame me?'

'Saunière wasn't trying to frame you. It was a mistake. That message on the floor was meant for me.'

Langdon needed a minute to process that one. 'I beg your pardon?'

'That message wasn't for the police. He wrote it for *me*. I think he was forced to do everything in such a hurry that he just didn't realize how it would look to the police.' Sophie paused. 'The numbered code is meaningless – Saunière wrote it to make sure the police investigation would include calling in cryptographers, meaning that *I* would know as soon as possible what had happened to him.'

Langdon felt himself losing touch fast. 'But why do you think his message was for you?'

'*The Vitruvian Man*,' she said flatly. 'That particular sketch has always been my favourite Da Vinci work. Tonight he used it to catch my attention.'

'Hold on. You're saying the curator *knew* your favourite piece of art?'

She nodded. 'I'm sorry. This is all coming out of order. Jacques Saunière and I . . .' Sophie's voice caught. 'We had a falling-out ten years ago,' she said, her voice a whisper now. 'We've barely spoken since. Tonight, when Crypto got the call that he had been murdered, and I saw the images of his body and text on the floor, I realized he was trying to send me a message.'

'Because of *The Vitruvian Man*?'

'Yes. And the letters P.S.'

'Post Script?'

She shook her head. 'P.S. are my initials.'

'But your name is Sophie Neveu.'

She looked away. 'P.S. is the nickname he called me when I lived with him.' She blushed. 'It stood for *Princess Sophie*. Silly, I know. But it was years ago. When I was a little girl.'

'You knew him when you were a little *girl*?'

'Quite well,' she said, her eyes welling with emotion. 'Jacques Saunière was my grandfather.'

# Chapter 13

It was time.

Silas felt strong as he stepped from the black Audi, the night-time breeze rustling his loose-fitting robe. *The winds of change are in the air.*

'Hago la obra de Dios,' he whispered, moving towards the church entrance. *I do the work of God . . .*

He raised his ghost-white fist and banged three times on the door. Moments later, the bolts of the enormous wooden portal began to move and Sister Sandrine greeted him.

She was a small woman with quiet eyes, and Silas knew he could overpower her easily, but he had vowed not to use force unless absolutely necessary. *She is a woman of the cloth, and it is not her fault the brotherhood chose her church as a hiding place for their keystone. She should not be punished for the sins of others.*

'You're an American,' she said as she led him into the sanctuary. The cavernous nave was as silent as a tomb, the only hint of life the faint smell of incense from mass earlier that evening.

'French by birth,' Silas responded. 'I had my calling in Spain, and I now study in the United States.'

The nun nodded. 'And you have *never* seen Saint-Sulpice?'

'I realize this is almost a sin in itself.'

'She is more beautiful by day.'

'I am certain. Nonetheless, I am grateful that you would provide me this opportunity tonight.'

'The abbé requested it. You obviously have powerful friends.'

*You have no idea,* Silas thought.

As he followed Sister Sandrine down the main aisle, he was surprised by the austerity of Saint-Sulpice. It was stark and cold inside, with an almost barren quality that reminded him of the ascetic cathedrals of Spain. As he gazed up into the soaring ribbed vault of the ceiling, he imagined he was standing beneath the hull of an enormous overturned ship.

*A fitting image,* he thought. The brotherhood's ship was about to be capsized forever. Feeling eager to get to work, he wished Sister Sandrine would leave him.

'I am embarrassed, Sister, that you were awoken on my behalf.'

'Not at all. You are in Paris a short time. Where would you like to begin your tour?'

Silas felt his eyes focus on the altar. 'A tour is unnecessary. I can show myself around.'

'It is no trouble,' she said.

Silas stopped walking. They had reached the front pew now, and the altar was only fifteen yards away. He turned his massive body fully towards the small woman, and he could sense her recoil as she gazed up into his red eyes. 'If it does not seem too rude, Sister, I am not accustomed to walking into a house of God and simply taking *a tour*. I wish to take some time alone to pray before I look around.' He put a soft but heavy hand on her shoulder and peered down. 'Sister, please, you should return to bed. Prayer is a solitary joy.'

'As you wish.' But she looked uneasy.

Silas took his hand from her shoulder. 'Sleep well, Sister. May the peace of the Lord be with you.'

'And also with you.'

As Sister Sandrine headed for the stairs, Silas turned and knelt in the front pew, feeling the *cilice* cut into his leg.

*Dear God, I offer up to you this work I do today . . .*

# Chapter 14

Sophie wondered how long it would take Fache to figure out she had not left the building. Seeing that Langdon was clearly overwhelmed, she wasn't sure either whether she had done the right thing by cornering him.

*But what else was I supposed to do?*

There was a time when her grandfather had meant the world to her, yet tonight, Sophie was surprised to feel almost no sadness for the man. Jacques Saunière was a stranger to her now. Their relationship had evaporated in a single instant one March night when she was twenty-two.

*Ten years ago.*

Sophie had witnessed her grandfather doing something she was obviously not supposed to see.

*If I hadn't seen it with my own eyes . . .*

Too stunned to listen to her grandfather's pained attempts to explain, Sophie immediately moved out on her own, taking money she had saved and getting a small apartment with some roommates. She told her grandfather never to call her again.

Over the years, he had sent her numerous cards and letters, begging her to meet him so he could explain – she possessed a decade's worth of unopened letters – but to his credit, he had never once disobeyed her request and phoned her.

*Until this afternoon.*

'Sophie?' His voice had sounded startlingly old on her answering machine. 'I have abided by your wishes for so long . . . and it pains me to call now, but I must speak to you. Something terrible has happened.'

Standing in the kitchen of her Paris apartment, Sophie felt a chill to hear her grandfather's voice again after all these years. It brought back a flood of memories.

'Sophie, please listen.' He was speaking English to her, as he always did when she was a little girl. *Practise French at school. Practise English at home.* 'You cannot be mad forever. Do you not yet understand?' He paused. 'We must speak at once. Please grant your grandfather this one wish. Call me at the Louvre. Right away. I believe you and I are in grave danger.'

Sophie stared at the answering machine. *Danger?* What was he talking about?

'Princess . . .' Her grandfather's voice cracked with an emotion Sophie could not place. 'I know I've kept things from you, and I know it has cost me your love. But it was for your own safety. Now you must know the truth. Please . . . I must tell you the truth about your family.'

Suddenly, Sophie could hear her own heart. *My family?* Her parents had died when she was only four. Their car had gone off a bridge into fast-moving water, killing not only them but her grandmother and younger brother, too, who had also been in the car. Her entire family had been wiped out in an instant. She had the newspaper clippings to confirm it.

'Sophie . . .' her grandfather said on the machine. 'I have been waiting for years to tell you. Call me at the Louvre. As soon as you get this. I'll wait here all night. There's so much you need to know.'

The message ended.

*My family.* His words had sent an unexpected surge of longing through Sophie's bones.

Now, standing in the darkness of the men's toilets, she heard the echoes of the message. *Sophie, you and I are in grave danger . . . Call me.*

She had not called him. Now her grandfather lay murdered inside his own museum. And he had written a code on the floor.

A code for *her.*

Despite not understanding the meaning of his message, Sophie was sure the words were intended for her. Her passion and aptitude for cryptography were a product of growing up with Jacques Saunière – a fanatic himself for codes, word games and puzzles. *How many Sundays did we spend doing the puzzles and crosswords in the newspaper?*

At the age of twelve, Sophie could finish the daily crossword without any help, so her grandfather introduced her to crosswords in English, mathematical puzzles and substitution ciphers. Sophie devoured them all. Eventually, she turned her passion into her career by becoming a code-breaker for the police.

Tonight, her grandfather had used a simple code to unite two total strangers – Sophie Neveu and Robert Langdon.

The question was *why?*

Unfortunately, from the bewildered look in Langdon's eyes, Sophie sensed the American had no more idea than she did why her grandfather had thrown them together.

She pressed again. 'You and my grandfather had planned to meet tonight. What about?'

Langdon looked truly perplexed. 'His secretary arranged the meeting and I didn't ask why – I just thought it would be fun to meet for drinks after my talk.'

Sophie took a deep breath and probed further. 'My grandfather called me this afternoon and told me he and I were in grave danger. Does *that* mean anything to you?'

Langdon's blue eyes now clouded with concern. 'No, but considering what just happened . . .'

Sophie nodded. After tonight's events, she would be a fool not to be frightened. Feeling drained, she walked to the small plate-glass window at the far end of the washroom and gazed out in silence through the mesh of alarm tape embedded in the glass. They were high up – forty feet at least. Below them, the road – the Place du Carrousel – ran almost flush with the building. She could see the usual traffic jam of the city's night-time delivery trucks as they sat idling, waiting for the traffic lights to change.

'I don't know what to say,' Langdon said, coming up behind her. 'I'm sorry I'm so little help.'

Sophie turned from the window, sensing sincere regret in Langdon's deep voice. Even with all the trouble around him, he obviously wanted to help. As a code-breaker, she made her living finding meanings in seemingly senseless data, and tonight, her best guess was that Robert Langdon – whether he knew it or not – somehow possessed information that she desperately needed. *Princess Sophie, Find Robert Langdon.* How much clearer could her grandfather's message be? She needed more time with Langdon. Time to think. Time to sort out this mystery together.

Gazing up at Langdon, she said, 'Bezu Fache will take you into custody at any minute. I can get you out of this museum. But we need to act now.'

Langdon's eyes went wide. 'You want me to *run*?'

'It's the smartest thing you could do. You could spend weeks in jail while the French police and the US Embassy fight over which courts should try the case. But if we could get you out of here and make it to your embassy, your government can protect you while you and I prove you had nothing to do with this murder.'

Langdon looked not even vaguely convinced. 'Forget it! Fache has armed guards on every single exit! Even if we escape without being shot, running away only makes me look guilty. You need to tell Fache that the message on the floor was for *you*, and that my name is not there as an accusation.'

'I *will* do that,' Sophie said, speaking hurriedly, 'but I'll do it *after* you're safely inside the US Embassy. It's only about a mile away, and my car is parked just outside the museum. Dealing with Fache from here is too much of a gamble. Don't you see? Fache has made it his mission tonight to prove you are guilty. The only reason he didn't arrest you right away was so he could watch you in the hope you said or did something that would make his case stronger.'

'Exactly. Like *running*!'

Sophie sighed. Turning back towards the window, she gazed down to the pavement below. A leap from this height would leave Langdon with a couple of broken legs. At best.

Nonetheless, she made her decision.

Robert Langdon was about to escape the Louvre, whether he wanted to or not.

# Chapter 15

'Where's Langdon?' Fache demanded.

'Still in the men's room, sir,' Lieutenant Collet replied.

Fache grumbled, 'Taking his time, I see.' He eyed the GPS dot over Collet's shoulder. Ideally, the subject of an observation was allowed as much time and freedom as possible, lulling him into a false sense of security. Langdon needed to return of his own volition. Still, it had been almost ten minutes now.

*Too long.*

'Captain?' one of the DCPJ agents now called from across the office. 'I think you had better take this call.'

'Who is it?' Fache said.

The agent frowned. 'It's the director of our Cryptography Department.'

'And?'

'It's about Sophie Neveu, sir. Something is not quite right . . .'

A few minutes later, Fache terminated the call and marched over to Collet, demanding that he get Agent Neveu on the line. When Collet failed to reach her, Fache began to pace. 'What do you mean she's not answering? You're calling her cellphone, right? I know she's carrying it.'

'Maybe her battery is dead. Or her ringer's off.' The lieutenant ventured a question. 'Why did Crypto call?'

Fache turned. 'To tell us they found no references to Draconian devils and lame saints . . . and also to tell us that they had just identified the numerics as Fibonacci numbers, but they suspected the series was meaningless.'

Collet stammered. 'But they already sent Agent Neveu to tell us that.'

Fache shook his head. 'They didn't send Neveu.'

'What?'

'According to the director, he asked his entire team to come in and look at the images I'd shared with him, and when Agent Neveu arrived, she took one look at the photos of Saunière and the code and left the office without a word. The director said he didn't question her behaviour because it was understandable that the photos would make her upset.'

'Upset? Why?'

Fache was silent a moment. 'I was not aware of this, and it seems neither was the director until a co-worker informed him – but apparently Sophie Neveu is Jacques Saunière's granddaughter.'

Before this revelation could be pondered further, an alarm shattered the silence of the deserted museum. *Grande Galerie!* an agent called. *Toilettes Messieurs!*

A broken window in the men's toilets?

Fache wheeled to Collet. 'Where's Langdon?'

'Still in the toilets.' Collet pointed to the blinking red dot on his laptop schematic. 'But . . . my God,' he exclaimed, eyeing the screen, 'a broken window in the men's toilet? Langdon's moving to the window ledge!'

Fache was already in motion. Yanking his revolver from his shoulder holster, the captain dashed out of the office.

Collet watched the screen as the blinking dot arrived at the window ledge and then did something utterly unexpected. The dot moved *outside* the perimeter of the building.

*Jesus!* He jumped to his feet. Fumbling with the controls, Collet recalibrated the GPS. Zooming in, he could see the exact location of the signal.

It lay at a dead stop in the middle of Place du Carrousel. No longer moving.

Langdon had jumped!

His radio call to Fache blared over the distant sound of the alarm. 'He jumped!' Collet was yelling. 'The signal shows he's out on Place du Carrousel!'

Fache heard the words, but they made no sense. He kept running. The hallway seemed never-ending. As he sprinted past Saunière's body, he set his sights on the partitions at the far end of the Denon Wing.

'Wait!' Collet's voice came again over the radio. 'He's moving! My God, he's alive. Langdon's moving! . . . He's heading down Carrousel. Wait . . . he's picking up speed. He's moving too fast!'

Arriving at the partitions, Fache snaked his way through them and ran for the door of the toilets.

The walkie-talkie was barely audible now over the alarm. 'He must be in a car! I think he's in a car! I can't –'

Collet's words were swallowed by the alarm as Fache burst into the men's room with his gun drawn. Wincing against the piercing shrill, he scanned the area.

It was deserted. Fache's eyes moved immediately to the shattered window. He ran to the opening and looked over the edge. Langdon was nowhere to be seen.

Collet's voice came again as the alarm finally shut off. '. . . moving south . . . faster . . . he's crossing the Seine on Pont du Carrousel!'

Fache looked to his left. The only vehicle on Pont du Carrousel was an enormous twin-bed delivery truck moving southwards away from the Louvre. The truck's open-air bed was covered with a vinyl tarp, roughly resembling a giant hammock. Fache felt a shiver of apprehension. That truck, only moments ago, had probably been stopped at a red light directly beneath the bathroom window.

*An insane risk,* Fache told himself. Langdon could have had no way of knowing what the truck was carrying beneath that tarp. A forty-foot leap? It was madness.

'He's turning right on Pont des Saints-Pères!' Collet called.

Sure enough, the truck that had crossed the bridge was slowing down and making a right turn on to Pont des Saints-Pères. Amazed, Fache watched the truck disappear round the corner.

*It's over,* Fache knew. The truck would be surrounded within minutes. He radioed Collet. 'Bring my car round. I want to be there when we make the arrest.'

As he jogged back down the length of the Grand Gallery, he wondered if Langdon had even survived the fall.

Not that it mattered.

*Langdon ran. Guilty as charged.*

Only fifteen yards from the toilets, Langdon and Sophie stood in the darkness of the Grand Gallery, their backs pressed to one of the large partitions that hid the toilets from the gallery. They had barely managed to hide themselves before Fache darted past them, gun drawn, and disappeared into the bathroom.

The last sixty seconds had been a blur.

Langdon had been standing inside the men's room refusing to run from a crime he didn't commit, when Sophie began eyeing the alarm mesh running through the plate-glass window.

'With a little aim, you can get out of here,' she said, ignoring the sudden ringing of her cellphone.

*Aim?* Uneasy, Langdon peered out of the window.

Up the street, an enormous twin-bed eighteen-wheeler was headed for the stop light beneath the window. Langdon hoped Sophie was not thinking what she seemed to be thinking.

'Sophie, there's no way I'm jump–'

'Take out the tracker.'

Bewildered, Langdon fumbled in his pocket until he found the tiny metallic disc. Sophie took it from him and strode immediately to the sink. She grabbed a thick bar of soap and used her thumb to push the tracker down into it. As the disc sank into the soft surface, she pinched the hole closed, firmly embedding the device in the bar.

Handing the bar to Langdon, she retrieved a heavy, cylindrical rubbish bin from under the sinks. Before Langdon could protest, Sophie ran at the window, holding the bin before her like a battering ram. Driving the bottom of the bin into the centre of the window, she shattered the glass.

Alarms erupted overhead at ear-splitting decibel levels.

'Give me the soap!' Sophie yelled, barely audible over the alarm.

Langdon thrust the bar into her hand.

Palming the soap, she peered out of the shattered window at the eighteen-wheeler idling below. As the traffic lights prepared to change, Sophie took a deep breath and lobbed the bar of soap out into the night.

The soap plummeted down towards the truck, landing on the edge of the blue vinyl tarp that covered its load, and slid into the cargo bay just as the traffic light turned green.

'Congratulations,' Sophie said, dragging him towards the door. 'You just escaped from the Louvre.'

Fleeing the men's toilets, they moved into the shadows . . . just as Fache rushed past.

# Chapter 16

'There's an emergency stairwell about fifty metres back into the Grand Gallery,' Sophie said. 'Now that the guards are away from the perimeter, we can get out of here.'

Emerging from the shadows, they moved stealthily up the deserted Grand Gallery corridor. As he moved, Langdon felt like he was trying to assemble a jigsaw puzzle in the dark. 'Do you think,' he whispered, 'that maybe *Fache* wrote that message on the floor?'

Sophie didn't even turn. 'Impossible.'

Langdon wasn't so sure. 'He seems pretty intent on making *me* look guilty. Maybe he thought writing my name on the floor would help his case?'

'The Fibonacci sequence? The P.S.? All the Da Vinci and goddess symbolism? That *had* to be my grandfather.'

Langdon knew Sophie was right. The symbols of the clues meshed too perfectly – a pentacle, *The Vitruvian Man*, Da Vinci, the goddess, even the Fibonacci sequence. *A clear symbolic set.*

'And his phone call to me this afternoon,' Sophie added. 'My grandfather said he had to tell me something. I'm certain his message at the Louvre was his final effort to reveal something important, something he thought you could help me understand.'

Langdon frowned. *O, Draconian devil! Oh, lame saint!* He wished he could work out the message, both for Sophie's well-being and for his own. Things had definitely got worse since he had first laid eyes on the cryptic words. His staged leap out of the bathroom window was not going to help Langdon's popularity with Fache one bit. Somehow he doubted the captain of the French police would see the humour in chasing down and arresting a bar of soap.

'The doorway isn't much further,' Sophie said.

'Do you think there's a possibility that the *numbers* in your grandfather's message hold the key to understanding the other lines?' Langdon had once worked on a series of seventeenth-century manuscripts that contained ciphers in which certain lines of code were clues as to how to decipher the other lines.

'I've been thinking about the numbers all night, but I don't see anything. Mathematically, they're arranged at random. To a code-breaker, they are just gibberish.'

'And yet they're all part of the Fibonacci sequence. That can't be coincidence.'

'It's not. Using Fibonacci numbers was my grandfather's way of waving another flag at me – like writing the message in English, or arranging himself like my favourite piece of art, or drawing a pentacle on himself. All of it was to catch my attention.'

'The pentacle has meaning to you?'

'Yes. I didn't get a chance to tell you, but the pentacle was a special symbol between my grandfather and me when I was growing up. We used to play tarot cards for fun, and my indicator card *always* turned out to be from the suit of pentacles. I'm sure he stacked the deck, but pentacles got to be our little joke.'

Langdon felt a chill. *They played tarot?* The medieval Italian card game – originally devised as a secret means to pass along belief systems banned by the Church – was full of hidden symbols. The game's twenty-two cards bore names like *The Female Pope, The Empress* and *The Star.*

*The tarot suit for feminine divinity is pentacles,* he thought.

They arrived at the emergency stairwell, and Sophie carefully pulled open the door and led Langdon down a tight set of switchback stairs towards ground level, picking up speed as they went.

'Your grandfather,' Langdon said, hurrying behind her, 'when he told you about the pentacle, did he mention goddess worship or any resentment of the Catholic Church?'

Sophie shook her head. 'I was more interested in the mathematics of it – the Divine Proportion, Phi, Fibonacci sequences, that sort of thing.'

Langdon was surprised. 'Your grandfather taught you about the number Phi?'

'Of course. The Divine Proportion.' Her expression turned sheepish. 'In fact, he used to joke that I was half divine . . . you know, because of the letters in my name.'

Langdon considered it a moment and then groaned.

*s-o-PHI-e.*

Still descending, Langdon refocused on Phi. He was starting to realize that Saunière's clues were even more consistent than he had first imagined.

*Da Vinci . . . Fibonacci numbers . . . the pentacle.*

Incredibly, all of these things were connected by a single concept so fundamental to art history that Langdon often gave a series of lectures on the topic.

*Phi. 1.618.*

Langdon thought back to his Symbolism in Art course at Harvard. 'Who can tell me what this number on the board is?' he had asked his class.

A math student at the back raised his hand. 'That's the number Phi.' He pronounced it *fee*.

'Nice job, Stettner,' Langdon said. 'Everyone, meet Phi.'

'Not to be confused with pi,' Stettner added.

'This number Phi,' Langdon continued, 'one-point-six-one-eight, is a very important number in art. It is generally considered the most beautiful number in the universe.'

As Langdon loaded his presentation, he explained that the number Phi was derived from the Fibonacci sequence, and that the dimensions of plants, animals and even human beings all had properties that adhered with eerie exactitude to the ratio of Phi to 1.

'Phi's presence is everywhere in nature,' Langdon said, killing the lights. 'So the ancients assumed the number must have been preordained by the Creator of the universe – *the Divine Proportion.*'

'Hold on,' said a female student in the front row. 'I've never seen this Divine Proportion in biology.'

'No?' Langdon grinned. 'Ever study the relationship between females and males in a honeybee community?'

'Sure. The female bees always outnumber the male bees.'

'Correct. And did you know that if you divide the number of female bees by the number of male bees in any beehive in the world, you always get the same number? Phi.' Langdon projected an image of a spiral seashell. 'Recognize this?'

'It's a type of mollusc,' said a student on the right.

'Correct. And can you guess what the ratio is of each spiral's diameter to the next? That's right. Phi. The Divine Proportion. One-point-six-one-eight to one.'

Langdon began racing through photos now – the head of a sunflower, pine-cone petals, leaf arrangements on plant stalks, insect anatomy – all displaying astonishing obedience to the Divine Proportion.

'This is amazing!' someone cried out.

'Yeah,' someone else said, 'but what does it have to do with *art*?'

'Aha!' Langdon said. 'Glad you asked.' He pulled up a picture of Leonardo da Vinci's famous male nude – *The Vitruvian Man*, named for Marcus Vitruvius, a brilliant Roman architect who had written about the Divine Proportion in relation to architecture.

'In his day, nobody understood better than Da Vinci the structure of the human body. Da Vinci actually *exhumed* and cut up corpses to measure the exact proportions of human bone structure. He was the first to show that the human body is literally made of building blocks whose proportional ratios *always* equal Phi.' He smiled. 'We'll be seeing a lot more of Da Vinci in this course . . . there are symbols hidden in places you would never imagine.'

'Come on,' Sophie whispered. 'What's wrong? We're almost there. Hurry!'

Langdon glanced up, paralysed by a revelation.

*O, Draconian devil! Oh, lame saint!*

Sophie was looking back at him.

*It can't be that simple,* he thought.

But he knew of course that it was.

There in the bowels of the Louvre . . . with images of Phi and Da Vinci swirling through his mind, Robert Langdon suddenly and unexpectedly deciphered Saunière's code.

'O, Draconian devil!' he said. 'Oh, lame saint! It's the simplest kind of code!'

Sophie had stopped on the stairs below him, staring up in confusion.

'You said it yourself.' Langdon's voice reverberated with excitement. 'Fibonacci numbers only have meaning in their proper order. Otherwise they're mathematical gibberish.'

Sophie had no idea what he was talking about.

'The scrambled Fibonacci sequence is a clue,' Langdon said, taking the printout. 'The numbers are a hint as to how to decipher the rest of the message. Your grandfather wrote the sequence out of order to tell us to apply the *same* concept to the text. *O, Draconian devil? Oh, lame saint?* Those lines mean *nothing*. They are simply *letters* written out of order.'

'You think this message is . . . *an anagram?*' She stared at him.

Without another word, Langdon pulled a pen from his jacket pocket and rearranged the letters in each line.

O, Draconian devil!
Oh, lame saint!

was a perfect anagram of . . .

Leonardo da Vinci!
The Mona Lisa!

# Chapter 17

*The Mona Lisa.*

For an instant, standing in the exit stairwell, Sophie forgot all about trying to leave the Louvre.

Her shock over the anagram was matched only by her embarrassment at not having deciphered the message herself. 'I can't imagine,' Langdon said, staring at the printout, 'how your grandfather created such an intricate anagram in the minutes before he died.'

Sophie knew the explanation, and the realization made her feel even worse. *I should have seen this!* She now recalled that her grandfather had entertained himself as a young man by creating anagrams of famous works of art. In fact, one of his anagrams had got him in trouble when Sophie was a little girl. While being interviewed by an American art magazine, Saunière had expressed his distaste for the early twentieth-century Cubist movement by noting that Picasso's masterpiece *Les Demoiselles d'Avignon* was a perfect anagram of *vile meaningless doodles*. Picasso fans were not amused.

'My grandfather probably created this *Mona Lisa* anagram long ago,' Sophie said, glancing up at Langdon. *And tonight he was forced to use it as a makeshift code.* Her grandfather's voice had called out from beyond with chilling precision.

*Leonardo da Vinci!*

*The Mona Lisa!*

Why his final words to her would reference the famous painting, Sophie had no idea, but she could think of only one possibility. A disturbing one.

*Those were not his final words . . .*

Was she supposed to visit the *Mona Lisa*? Had her grandfather left her a second message there? The idea seemed perfectly plausible. After all, the famous painting hung in a private viewing chamber accessible only from the Grand Gallery. In fact, Sophie now realized, the doors to that chamber were only twenty metres away from where her grandfather had been found dead.

She gazed back up the emergency stairwell and felt torn. She knew she should get Langdon out of the museum immediately, and yet her instinct urged her to seek out the *Mona Lisa*. If her grandfather had a secret to tell her, few places on earth would make a more apt rendezvous.

'She's just a little bit further,' her grandfather had whispered on her first childhood visit to the Denon Wing, clutching Sophie's tiny hand as he led her through the deserted museum after hours.

Sophie was six years old. She felt small and insignificant as she gazed up at the enormous ceilings and down at the dizzying pattern on the floor. The empty museum frightened her, although she was not about to let her grandfather know that. She set her jaw firmly and let go of his hand.

Sophie had seen pictures of the *Mona Lisa* in books and didn't like it at all. She couldn't understand why everyone made such a fuss.

As they entered the Salle des Etats, the room where the *Mona Lisa* was kept, her eyes scanned the narrow room and settled on the obvious spot of honour – the centre of the right-hand wall, where the lone portrait hung behind protective Plexiglas. Her grandfather motioned towards the painting. 'Go ahead, Sophie. Not many people get a chance to visit her alone.'

Swallowing her apprehension, Sophie moved slowly across the room. After everything she'd heard about the *Mona Lisa,* she felt as if she were approaching royalty. She held her breath and looked up, taking it in all at once.

She was not sure what she had expected to feel, but it most certainly was not this. No jolt of amazement. No instant of wonder. The famous face looked as it did in books. Sophie stood in silence for what felt like forever, waiting for something to happen.

'So what do you think?' her grandfather whispered, arriving behind her. 'Beautiful, yes?'

'She's too little.'

Saunière smiled. 'You're little and you're beautiful.'

*I am not beautiful,* she thought. Sophie hated her red hair and freckles, and she was bigger than all the boys in her class. She looked back at the *Mona Lisa* and shook her head. 'She looks like she knows something . . . like when kids at school have a secret.'

Her grandfather laughed. 'That's part of why she is so famous. People like to guess why she is smiling.'

'Do *you* know why she's smiling?'

'Maybe.' Her grandfather winked. 'Someday I'll tell you all about it.'

Sophie stamped her foot. 'I told you I don't like secrets!'

'Princess.' He smiled. 'Life is filled with secrets. You can't learn them all at once.'

'I'm going back up,' Sophie declared, her voice hollow in the stairwell.

'To the *Mona Lisa?*' Langdon recoiled. *'Now?'*

Sophie considered the risk. 'I'm not a murder suspect. I'll take my chances. I need to understand what my grandfather was trying to tell me.'

'What about going to the US Embassy?'

Sophie felt guilty, turning Langdon into a fugitive only to abandon him, but she saw no other option. She pointed down the stairs to a metal door. 'Go through that door and follow the illuminated exit signs – they lead to a security turnstile where you can get out.' She handed Langdon her car keys. 'Mine is the red SmartCar parked in the employee lot. Do you know how to get from here to your embassy?'

Langdon nodded, eyeing the keys in his hand.

'Listen,' Sophie said, her voice softening. 'I think my

grandfather may have left me a message at the *Mona Lisa* – some kind of clue as to who killed him. Or why I'm in danger.' *Or what happened to my family.* 'I have to go and see.'

'But if he wanted to warn you that you were in danger, why wouldn't he simply write it on the floor where he died? Why this complicated word game?'

'Whatever my grandfather was trying to tell me, I don't think he wanted anyone else to learn it. Not even the police. As strange as it may sound, I think he wants me to get to the *Mona Lisa* before anyone else does.'

'I'll come.'

'No! We don't know how long the Grand Gallery will stay empty. You have to go.' She gave him a grateful smile. 'I'll see you at the embassy, Mr Langdon.'

Langdon looked displeased. 'I'll meet you there on *one* condition,' he replied, his voice stern.

She paused, startled. 'What's that?'

'That you stop calling me *Mr* Langdon.'

Sophie detected the faint hint of a lopsided grin growing across Langdon's face, and she felt herself smile back. 'Good luck, Robert.'

When Langdon reached the landing at the bottom of the stairs, the unmistakable smell of linseed oil and plaster dust assaulted his nostrils. Ahead, an illuminated SORTIE/EXIT displayed an arrow pointing down a long corridor.

Saunière's clever anagrams were still on Langdon's mind, and he wondered what Sophie would find at the *Mona Lisa* . . . if anything. She had seemed certain her grandfather meant for her to go and see the famous painting one more time. It seemed plausible – but Langdon felt haunted now by a troubling question.

*P.S. Find Robert Langdon.*

Saunière had written *his* name on the floor, instructing Sophie to find him. Why? Merely so he could help her break an anagram? It seemed unlikely. After all, Saunière had no reason to think Langdon was especially skilled at anagrams.

*Sophie was supposed to break that anagram on her own.* Langdon was suddenly feeling more certain about this, and yet the conclusion left an obvious gap in the logic of Saunière's actions.

*Why me?* he wondered, heading down the hall. *What is it that Saunière thinks I know?*

With an unexpected jolt, he stopped short. Eyes wide, he dug in his pocket and yanked out the computer printout. He stared at the last line of Saunière's message.

*P.S. Find Robert Langdon.*

He fixated on two letters.

*P.S.*

In that instant, he felt Saunière's puzzling mix of symbolism fall into stark focus. Like a peal of thunder, a career's worth of knowledge of symbols and history came crashing down around him. Everything Jacques Saunière had done tonight suddenly made perfect sense.

Langdon's thoughts raced as he tried to assemble the

implications of what this all meant. Reeling, he stared back in the direction from which he had come.

*Is there time?*

He knew it didn't matter.

Without hesitation, he sprinted back towards the stairs.

# Chapter 18

Sophie arrived breathless outside the large wooden doors of the room that housed the *Mona Lisa*. Before entering, she gazed further down the hall, twenty yards or so, to the spot where her grandfather's body still lay under the spotlight.

The remorse that gripped her was powerful, a deep sadness laced with guilt. Her grandfather had reached out to her so many times over the past ten years, and yet Sophie left his letters and packages unopened, denying his efforts to see her. *He lied to me! Kept appalling secrets! What was I supposed to do?*

Now her grandfather was dead, and he was talking to her from the grave.

*The Mona Lisa.*

She reached for the huge wooden doors and pushed. The entryway yawned open. Sophie stood on the threshold a moment, scanning the large rectangular chamber beyond. It too was bathed in a soft red light.

Even before Sophie entered, though, she knew she was missing something. *A black light*. If her grandfather had written anything in here, he almost certainly would have written it with the watermark stylus.

Taking a deep breath, she hurried down to the well-lit crime scene. Unable to look at her grandfather's body, she focused solely on the scene-of-crime tools. Finding a small ultraviolet penlight, she slipped it in the pocket of her sweater and hurried back up the hallway. A ghostly figure emerged suddenly from out of the reddish haze. Sophie jumped back.

'There you are!' Langdon's hoarse whisper cut the air as his silhouette slid to a stop in front of her.

Her relief was only momentary. 'Robert, I told you to get out of here! If Fache –'

'Where were you?'

'I had to get the black light,' she whispered, holding it up. 'If my grandfather left me a message –'

'Sophie, listen.' Langdon caught his breath as his blue eyes held hers firmly. 'The letters P.S. . . . do they mean anything else to you? *Anything at all?*'

Afraid their voices might echo down the hall, Sophie pulled him closer to the *Mona Lisa* and closed the enormous twin doors silently, sealing them inside. 'I told you, the initials mean Princess Sophie.'

'I know, but did you ever see them anywhere *else*? Did your grandfather ever use P.S. in any other way? Maybe on stationery or on some personal item?'

The question startled her. *How would Robert know that?* Sophie had indeed seen the initials P.S. once before, on the day before her ninth birthday. She was secretly combing the house, searching for hidden birthday presents. Even then, she could not bear secrets being kept from her. *What did Grand-père get for me this year?* She dug through cupboards and drawers.

Eventually, she mustered the courage to sneak into her grandfather's bedroom. The room was off-limits to her, but her grandfather was downstairs, asleep on the couch.

*I'll just take a fast peek!*

Tiptoeing across the creaky wood floor to his wardrobe, Sophie peered on the shelves behind his clothing. Nothing. Next she searched under the bed. Still nothing. Moving to his bureau, she opened the drawers and one by one began pawing carefully through them. *There must be something for me here!* Dejected, she opened the final drawer and pulled aside some black clothes she had never seen him wear. She was about to close the drawer when her eyes caught a glint of gold in the back of the drawer.

*A necklace?*

Sophie carefully pulled a chain from the drawer. To her surprise, on the end was a brilliant gold key. Heavy and shimmering. Spellbound, she held it up. It looked like no key she had ever seen. Most keys were flat with jagged teeth, but this one had a triangular column with little pockmarks all over it. Its large golden head was in the shape of a cross, or really more like a plus sign. Embossed in the middle of the cross was a strange symbol – two letters intertwined with some kind of flowery design.

'P.S.,' she whispered, scowling as she read the letters. *Whatever could this be?*

'Sophie?' her grandfather said from the doorway.

Startled, she spun, dropping the key on the floor with a loud clang. 'I . . . was looking for my birthday present,' she said, hanging her head, knowing she had betrayed his trust.

For what seemed like an eternity, her grandfather stood silently in the doorway. Finally, he let out a long troubled breath. 'Pick up the key, Sophie.'

Sophie did as he asked.

'Sophie, you need to respect other people's privacy.' Gently, he knelt down and took the key. 'This key is very special. If you had lost it . . .'

Her grandfather's quiet voice made Sophie feel even worse. 'I'm sorry, *Grand-père*. I really am.' She paused. 'I thought it was a necklace for my birthday.'

He gazed at her for several seconds. 'I'll say this once more, Sophie, because it's important. You need to learn to respect other people's privacy.'

'Yes, *Grand-père*.'

'We'll talk about this some other time. Right now, the garden needs to be weeded.'

Sophie hurried outside to do her chores.

The next morning, she received no birthday present from her grandfather. She hadn't expected one, not after what she had done. But he didn't even wish her happy birthday all day. Sadly, she trudged up to bed that night. As she climbed in, though, she found a card with a simple riddle lying on her pillow. *I know what this is! A treasure hunt!*

Eagerly, she pored over the riddle until she solved it. The solution pointed her to another part of the house, where she found another card and another riddle. She solved this one too, racing on to the next card. Running wildly, she darted back and forth across the house, from clue to clue, until at last she found one that directed her back to her own bedroom. Sophie dashed up the stairs, rushed into her room and stopped in her tracks. There in the middle of the room sat a shining red bicycle with a ribbon tied to the handlebars. Sophie shrieked with delight.

'I know you asked for a doll,' her grandfather said, smiling in the corner. 'I thought you might like this even better.'

'*Grand-père,*' Sophie said, hugging him. 'Thank you . . . and I'm really sorry about the key.'

'I know, sweetie. You're forgiven. I can't possibly stay mad at you. Grandfathers and granddaughters always forgive each other.'

Sophie knew she shouldn't ask, but she couldn't help it. 'What does it open? I never saw a key like that. It was very pretty.'

Her grandfather was silent a long moment, and Sophie could see he wasn't sure how to answer. *Grand-père never lies.* 'It opens a box,' he finally said. 'Where I keep many secrets.'

Sophie pouted. 'I hate secrets!'

'I know, but these are important secrets. And someday you'll learn to appreciate them as much as I do.'

'I saw letters on the key, and a flower.'

'Yes, that's my favourite flower. It's called a fleur-de-lis. We have them in the garden. The white ones. In English we call that kind of flower a lily.'

'I know those! They're *my* favourite too!'

'Then I'll make a deal with you.' Her grandfather's eyebrows rose. 'If you can keep my key a secret, and *never* talk about it ever again, to me or anybody, then someday I will give it to you.'

Sophie couldn't believe her ears. 'You *will?*'

'I promise. When the time comes, the key will be yours. It has your name on it.'

Sophie scowled. 'No, it doesn't. It said P.S. My name isn't P.S.!'

Her grandfather lowered his voice and looked around as if to make sure no one was listening. 'OK, Sophie, if you *must* know, P.S. is a code. It's your secret initials.'

Her eyes went wide. 'I have secret initials?'

'Of course. Granddaughters *always* have secret initials that only their grandfathers know.' He tickled her. *'Princess Sophie.'*

She giggled. 'I'm not a princess!'

He winked. 'You are to me.'

From that day on, they never again spoke of the key. And she became his Princess Sophie.

'The initials,' Langdon repeated. 'Have you seen them?'

Sophie sensed her grandfather's voice whispering in the corridors of the museum. *Never speak of this key, Sophie. To me or to anyone.* Could she break his trust again?

*P.S. Find Robert Langdon.* Her grandfather wanted Langdon to help . . .

Sophie nodded. 'Yes, I saw the letters P.S. once. When I was very young. On something very important to him.'

Langdon locked eyes with her. 'Sophie, this is crucial. Can you tell me if they appeared with a symbol? A fleur-de-lis?'

Sophie felt herself staggering backwards in amazement. 'But . . . how could you possibly know that?'

Langdon exhaled and lowered his voice. 'I'm fairly certain your grandfather was a member of a secret society. A very old covert brotherhood.'

Sophie felt a knot tighten in her stomach. She was certain of it too. For ten years she had tried to forget the incident that had confirmed that for her. When she had witnessed something unthinkable. *Unforgivable.*

'The fleur-de-lis,' Langdon said, 'combined with the initials P.S., is the brotherhood's official device. Their coat of arms. Their logo.'

'How do you know this?' Sophie was praying Langdon was not going to tell her that he *himself* was a member.

'I've written about this group,' he said, his voice tremulous with excitement. 'The *Prieuré de Sion* – the Priory of Sion. They are one of the oldest surviving secret societies on earth.'

Sophie had never heard of them.

Langdon was talking in rapid bursts now. 'The Priory's membership has included some of history's most cultured individuals: men like Botticelli, Sir Isaac Newton, Victor Hugo.' His voice was brimming with academic zeal. 'And Leonardo da Vinci.'

Sophie stared. 'Da Vinci was in a secret society?'

'Da Vinci presided over the Priory between 1510 and 1519 as the brotherhood's Grand Master, which might help explain your grandfather's passion for Leonardo's work. The two men would share a historical bond. And it all fits perfectly with both men's fascination for goddess icons, feminine deities and contempt for the Church. The Priory has a history of reverence for the sacred feminine.'

'You're telling me this group is a pagan goddess-worship cult?'

'More like *the* pagan goddess-worship cult. But more important, they are known as the guardians of an ancient secret. One that made them immeasurably powerful.'

Despite the total conviction in Langdon's eyes, Sophie's gut reaction was one of stark disbelief. *A secret pagan cult? Once headed by Leonardo da Vinci?* It all sounded utterly absurd. And yet, even as she dismissed it, she felt her mind flashing back ten years – to the night she had mistakenly surprised her grandfather and witnessed what she still could not accept. *Could that explain – ?*

'The identities of living Priory members are kept extremely secret,' Langdon said. 'But the P.S. and fleur-de-lis that you saw as a child are proof. It could *only* have been related to the Priory.'

Sophie realized now that she needed Langdon to help her understand her grandfather's actions. 'I can't afford to let them catch you now, Robert. There's a lot we must discuss. You need to *go*!'

Langdon heard only the faint murmur of her voice. He wasn't going anywhere. He was lost in another place. Slowly, as if moving underwater, he turned his head and gazed through the reddish haze towards the *Mona Lisa*.

*The fleur-de-lis . . . the flower of Lisa . . . the Mona Lisa.*

It was all intertwined – a silent symphony echoing the deepest secrets of the Priory of Sion and Leonardo da Vinci.

# Chapter 19

Saint-Sulpice, like most churches, had been built in the shape of a giant Roman cross. Its long central section – the nave – led directly to the main altar, where a shorter section known as the transept cut across.

Kneeling in the first pew, Silas pretended to pray as he scanned the layout. Turning his head to the right, he gazed into the south transept, towards the open area of floor beyond the end of the pews.

*There it is.*

Embedded in the grey granite floor, a thin polished strip of brass glistened in the stone . . . a golden line slanting across the church's floor.

*The Rose Line.*

Slowly, Silas let his eyes trace the path of the brass strip as it made its way across the floor from his right to left, slanting in front of him at an awkward angle, not in tune at all with the symmetry of the church, finally reaching the base of a most unexpected structure.

A colossal Egyptian obelisk.

Here, the glistening Rose Line took a ninety-degree *vertical* turn and continued directly up the face of the obelisk itself, ascending thirty-three feet to the very tip of the pyramid.

*The Rose Line,* Silas thought. *The brotherhood hid the keystone at the Rose Line.*

Earlier that night, when Silas told the Teacher that the Priory keystone was hidden inside Saint-Sulpice, the Teacher had sounded doubtful. But when Silas added that his victims had all told him of a brass line running through the church, the Teacher had gasped with understanding. 'You speak of the Rose Line!'

The Teacher quickly told Silas of Saint-Sulpice's famed architectural oddity – a strip of brass that ran across the sanctuary on a perfect north–south axis. The line bore graduated markings, like a ruler. It was an ancient sundial of sorts, he explained, known as the Rose Line, and it was famous. For centuries, the symbol of a rose had been associated with maps – a compass rose, drawn on almost every map, indicated north, east, south and west. To this day, the primary navigational instrument was still known as a compass rose, its northernmost direction marked by an arrowhead . . . or, more commonly, an image of a fleur-de-lis.

On a globe, a Rose Line – also called a meridian or longitude line – was any imaginary line drawn from the North Pole to the South Pole. There were, of course, an infinite number of Rose Lines because every point on the globe could have a line drawn through it connecting the North and South Poles. The question for early navigators was *which* of these lines would be called *the* Rose Line – the zero longitude, or prime meridian – the line from which all other longitudes on earth would be measured.

Today that line was in Greenwich, England. As it had been since 1888.

But before then, the zero longitude of the entire world had passed directly through Paris, through the Church of Saint-Sulpice. The brass line in Saint-Sulpice, the original Rose Line, was therefore the world's first prime meridian.

'And so the legend is true,' the Teacher had told Silas. 'The Priory keystone has been said to lie "beneath the Sign of the Rose".'

Standing now, Silas faced the altar and genuflected three times. Then he turned left and followed the brass line towards the obelisk. He felt taut with exhilaration as he knelt at the base of the structure, not out of reverence, but out of necessity.

*The keystone is hidden beneath the Rose Line.*

*At the base of the Sulpice obelisk.*

All the brothers had told him the same thing.

On his knees now, Silas ran his hands across the stone floor. He began rapping softly with his knuckles on the floor, knocking on each tile adjacent to the brass line. Finally, one of them echoed strangely.

*There's a hollow area beneath the floor!*

Silas smiled. His victims had spoken the truth.

Crouching in the shadows of the choir balcony high above the altar, Sister Sandrine peered silently through the balustrade at the cloaked monk below. Her darkest fears had just been confirmed. This visitor was not who he seemed. The mysterious Opus Dei monk had come to Saint-Sulpice for another purpose.

A secret purpose.

But Sister Sandrine Bieil was more than the keeper of this church. She was a sentry. And tonight, the arrival of this stranger at the base of the obelisk was a signal to her to act.

# Chapter 20

The *Mona Lisa* was still twenty yards ahead when Sophie turned on the black light, and the bluish crescent of penlight fanned out on the floor in front of them. She swung the beam back and forth across the floor like a minesweeper, searching for any hint of luminescent ink.

It was all intertwined – the Priory of Sion and Leonardo de Vinci, the fleur-de-lis . . . and the *Mona Lisa*. Now they just had to figure out how deep the connection was.

The painting's status as the most famous piece of art in the world, Langdon knew, had nothing to do with her enigmatic smile. Quite simply, the *Mona Lisa* was famous because Leonardo da Vinci claimed she was his finest accomplishment. He carried the painting with him whenever he travelled and, if asked why, would reply that he found it hard to part with his most sublime expression of female beauty.

Even so, many art historians suspected Da Vinci's reverence for the *Mona Lisa* had nothing to do with the quality of the painting but rather something far deeper: a hidden message in the layers of paint.

The *Mona Lisa* was, in fact, one of the world's most documented inside jokes. Its collage of double entendres and playful references had been revealed in most art history books, and yet, incredibly, the public at large still considered her smile a great mystery.

*No mystery at all*, Langdon thought, moving forward and watching as the faint outline of the painting began to take shape. *No mystery at all.*

He remembered how he had shared the *Mona Lisa*'s secret with a rather unlikely group – a dozen inmates in a prison. His seminar there was part of a university programme to bring education into the prison system.

'You may notice,' Langdon told them, walking up to a projected image of the *Mona Lisa* on the library wall, 'that the background behind her face is uneven.' He motioned to the glaring discrepancy. 'Da Vinci painted the horizon line on the left significantly lower than the right.'

'He messed it up?' one of the inmates asked.

Langdon chuckled. 'No. Da Vinci didn't do that too often. Actually, this is a little trick Da Vinci played. By lowering the countryside on the left, he made Mona Lisa look much larger from the left side than from the right side. A little Da Vinci joke. Historically, left sides are female, and right sides male. Da Vinci was a big fan of the feminine, so he made Mona Lisa look more majestic from the *left* than the right.'

'Hey, Mr Langford,' a muscle-bound man said. 'I've heard that the *Mona Lisa* is actually a picture of Da Vinci in drag.'

'It's quite possible,' Langdon said, once the laughter had died down. 'Da Vinci was a prankster. But more than that, he was in tune with the *balance* between male and female. He believed that a human soul could not be enlightened unless it had both male and female elements, and his Mona Lisa is neither male nor female, but a fusion of both.' He paused. 'Has anyone here ever heard of the Egyptian gods Amon and Isis?'

The question met with silence.

Langdon grabbed a marker and headed for the whiteboard. 'They are the Egyptian gods of fertility. So we have the male god, Amon.' He wrote it down. 'And the female goddess, Isis, whose ancient pictogram was once called L'Isa.'

He stepped back to let the group see.

## AMON L'ISA

'Ring any bells?'

'Mona Lisa . . .' somebody gasped.

Langdon nodded. 'Gentlemen, not only does the face of Mona Lisa look both male and female, but her name is based on the divine union of male and female. And *that,* my friends, is the reason for Mona Lisa's knowing smile.'

'My grandfather *was* here,' Sophie said, dropping suddenly to her knees, now only ten feet from the *Mona Lisa*. She pointed the black light tentatively to a spot on the parquet floor.

At first Langdon saw nothing. Then, as he knelt beside her, he saw a tiny droplet of dried liquid that was luminescing. *Ink?*

Suddenly, he recalled what black lights were actually used for. *Blood.* His senses tingled. Sophie was right. Jacques Saunière had indeed paid a visit to the *Mona Lisa* before he died.

'He wouldn't have come here without a reason,' Sophie whispered, standing up. 'I know he left a message for me here.' Quickly striding the final few steps to the *Mona Lisa,* she illuminated the floor directly in front of the painting. She waved the light back and forth across the bare parquet.

'There's nothing here!'

At that moment, Langdon saw a faint purple glimmer on the protective glass before the *Mona Lisa.* Reaching down, he took Sophie's wrist and slowly moved the light up to the painting itself.

They both froze.

On the glass, six words glowed in purple, scrawled directly across the *Mona Lisa*'s face.

# Chapter 21

A few miles away, on the Paris river bank, the bewildered driver of a twin-bed truck watched as the captain of the Judicial Police let out a guttural roar of rage and heaved a bar of soap out into the turgid waters of the Seine.

Frowning, Fache pulled out his phone.

The night operator of the US Embassy was reading a magazine when the phone rang.

'US Embassy,' she answered.

'Good evening.' The caller spoke English accented with French. 'I need some assistance.' His tone was gruff and official. 'I was told you had a phone message for me on your automated system. The name is Langdon. Unfortunately, I have forgotten my three-digit access code. If you could help me, I would be most grateful.'

The operator paused, confused. 'I'm sorry, sir. Your message must be quite old. That system was removed two years ago.'

'You have *no* automated phone system?'

'No, sir. Any message for you would be handwritten in our services department. What was your name again?'

But there was no reply. The man had hung up.


Bezu Fache paced the banks of the river Seine. He had *seen* Langdon dial a local number, enter a code and then listen to a recording. *But if Langdon hadn't phoned the embassy, then who did he call?*

Suddenly, he realized the answers were in the palm of his hand. *Langdon had used his phone.*

He pulled up the list of recently dialled numbers, dialled the last one and waited.

Finally, a woman's voice answered. *'Bonjour, vous êtes bien chez Sophie Neveu,'* the recording announced. *'Je suis absente pour le moment, mais . . .'*

Minutes later, seated at Saunière's desk, Lieutenant Collet pressed the phone to his ear in disbelief as his captain called in.

'A bar of soap? But how could Langdon have known about the GPS tracker?'

'Sophie Neveu.'

'But, Captain . . . if she told Langdon, then where is he *now*?'

'Have any fire alarms gone off there?'

'No, sir.'

'And no one has come out under the Grand Gallery gate?'

'No. We've got a Louvre security officer there. Just as you requested. And nobody has seen them leave.'

'OK, then Langdon must still be inside the Grand Gallery.'

# Chapter 22

Langdon stared in astonishment at the six words glowing on the Plexiglas. The text seemed to hover in space, casting a jagged shadow across Mona Lisa's mysterious smile.

'The Priory,' Langdon whispered. 'This proves your grandfather was a member!'

Sophie looked at him in confusion. 'You *understand* this?'

Langdon nodded, his thoughts churning. 'It's a statement of one of the Priory's most fundamental philosophies.'

Sophie looked baffled in the glow of the message scrawled across the *Mona Lisa*'s face.

## SO DARK THE CON OF MAN

'Sophie,' Langdon said, 'the Priory's tradition of goddess worship is based on a belief that powerful men in the early Christian Church "conned" the world by spreading lies that successfully converted it from pagan beliefs that had reverence for goddesses and the female to a Christianity that values the masculine and pretty much demonized the sacred feminine, obliterating the goddess from modern religion forever.'

Sophie's expression remained uncertain. 'My grandfather sent me to this spot to find this. He must be trying to tell me more than *that*.'

Langdon understood her meaning. *She thinks this is another code.* Whether a hidden meaning existed here or not, Langdon could not immediately say. His mind was still grappling with the bold clarity of Saunière's outward message.

*So dark the con of man*, he thought. *So dark indeed.*

Nobody could deny the enormous good the modern Church did in today's troubled world, and yet it had a history of violence and deceit. Their brutal crusade to 're-educate' the pagan and feminine-worshipping religions spanned three centuries, and was often horrific. The clergy was instructed to locate, torture and destroy those deemed 'witches', a term that included female scholars, priestesses, gypsies, mystics, nature lovers, herb gatherers and any women 'suspiciously attuned to the natural world'. Midwives were killed for using medicines to ease the pain of childbirth – this pain was a suffering, the Church claimed, that was God's rightful punishment for Eve's eating of the Apple of Knowledge in the Garden of Eden, the Original Sin. Ultimately, an astounding five *million* women were burned at the stake.

The propaganda and bloodshed worked. Today's world was living proof.

'Robert!' Sophie said, her whisper yanking him back. 'Someone's coming!'

He heard the approaching footsteps out in the hallway.

'Over here!' Sophie extinguished the black light and seemed to evaporate before Langdon's eyes.

For an instant, he felt totally blind. *Over where?* As his vision cleared he saw Sophie's silhouette racing towards the centre of the room and ducking out of sight behind the octagonal viewing bench. He was about to dash after her when a booming voice stopped him cold.

'*Arrêtez!*' a man commanded from the doorway. *Stop!*

Langdon was face down on the floor in a matter of seconds. The security guard hurried over and kicked his legs apart.

Langdon found little humour in the irony of his position. *The Vitruvian Man*, he thought. *Face down.*

# Chapter 23

Inside Saint-Sulpice, Silas carried the heavy iron votive candleholder from the altar back towards the obelisk. The shaft would do nicely as a battering ram, though he realized he could not possibly shatter the tiles without making a considerable noise.

Iron on marble. It would echo off the vaulted ceilings.

Would the nun hear him? She should be asleep again by now. Even so, it was a chance Silas preferred not to take. Looking around for a cloth to wrap over the tip of the iron pole, he saw nothing except the altar's linen mantle, which he refused to defile. *My cloak*, he thought. He untied it and slipped it off his body. As he removed it, he felt a sting as the wool fibres pulled at the fresh wounds on his back.

Naked now except for a small loincloth, Silas wrapped his cloak over the end of the iron rod. Then, aiming at the centre of the floor tile, he drove the tip into it. A muffled thud. The stone did not break. He drove the pole into it once more. Again a dull thud, but this time accompanied by a crack. On the third swing, the covering finally shattered, and stone shards fell into a hollow area beneath the floor.

*A compartment!*

Quickly pulling the remaining pieces from the opening, Silas gazed into the void. His blood pounded as he knelt down before it and reached inside.

At first he felt nothing. The floor of the compartment was bare, smooth stone. Then, feeling deeper, reaching his arm in under the Rose Line, he touched something! A thick stone tablet. He gripped it firmly and gently lifted it out. As he stood and examined his find, he realized he was holding a rough-hewn stone slab with engraved words and he felt for an instant like a modern-day Moses.

As Silas read the words on the tablet, he felt surprise. He had expected the keystone to be a map, or a complex series of directions, perhaps even encoded. The keystone, however, bore the simplest of inscriptions.

*A verse from the Book of Job. Chapter thirty-eight. Verse eleven.*

Although Silas did not recall the exact contents of verse eleven by heart, he knew the Book of Job told the story of a man whose faith in God survived repeated tests. *Appropriate*, he thought, barely able to contain his excitement.

In breathless silence, Sister Sandrine left the balcony and raced down the hall to her quarters. Getting down on her hands and knees, the nun reached beneath her wooden bed frame and retrieved the sealed envelope she had hidden there years ago.

Tearing it open, she found four Paris phone numbers.

Trembling, she began to dial.

Downstairs, Silas laid the stone tablet on the altar and turned his eager hands to the leather Bible. His long white fingers were sweating now as he thumbed the pages. Flipping through the Old Testament, he found the Book of Job, chapter thirty-eight. As he ran his finger down the column of text, he anticipated the words he was about to read.

*They will lead The Way!*

Locating verse number eleven, Silas read the text. It was only seven words. Confused, he read it again, sensing something had gone terribly wrong. The verse simply read:

*Hitherto shalt thou come, but no further.*

# Chapter 24

Security guard Claude Grouard simmered with rage as he stood over his prostrate captive in front of the *Mona Lisa*. He yanked his walkie-talkie off his belt and attempted to radio for backup – but all he heard was static.

Grouard began backing slowly to the entrance, stopping short when he saw a woman moving through the darkness towards him. In front of her, a purplish beam of light swung back and forth across the floor, as if she were searching for something with a coloured flashlight.

'Scene of crime,' the woman announced calmly, still scanning the floor with her light.

'*Votre nom!*' Grouard yelled.

'*C'est moi,*' the voice responded in calm French. '*Sophie Neveu.*'

The security guard hesitated, still only getting static.

'You know me. *I am Jacques Saunière's granddaughter,*' the woman called. 'And Robert Langdon did not kill my grandfather. Believe me.'

As he continued to inch backwards he could see the woman

raising her UV light and pointing it up at a large painting that hung directly opposite the *Mona Lisa*.

Sophie Neveu knew that the guard would not actually kill her or Langdon, but she felt a cold sweat breaking across her forehead as she scanned the entire area around the masterpiece – another Da Vinci. She was sure she had deciphered her grandfather's message correctly. *What else could he possibly have meant?*

The masterpiece she was examining was a five-foot-tall canvas: *Madonna of the Rocks*. The scene Da Vinci had painted included an awkwardly posed Virgin Mary sitting with Baby Jesus, John the Baptist and the Angel Uriel on a perilous outcropping of rocks. When Sophie was a little girl, no trip to the *Mona Lisa* had been complete without her grandfather dragging her across the room to see this second painting.

*Think!* The painting before her had no protective glass on which to write a message, and Sophie knew her grandfather would never have defaced it by writing on the painting itself. She paused. *At least not on the front.* Her eyes shot upward. Long cables dangled from the ceiling to support the canvas.

*Could that be it?*

Grabbing the left side of the carved wood frame, she pulled it towards her. The painting was large and the backing flexed as she swung it away from the wall. Sophie slipped her head and shoulders in behind the painting and raised the black light to inspect the back.

It took only seconds to realize her instinct had been wrong.

The back of the painting was pale and blank. There was no purple text here, only the mottled brown backing of ageing canvas and –

*Wait.*

Her eyes locked on an incongruous glint of lustrous metal lodged near the bottom edge of the frame. A shimmering gold chain. To Sophie's utter amazement, the chain was affixed to a familiar gold key. *The* key. The broad, sculpted head was in the shape of a cross and on it was the engraved seal. A fleur-de-lis with the initials P.S. She had not seen it since she was nine years old.

In that instant, Sophie felt the ghost of her grandfather whispering in her ear. *When the time comes, the key will be yours.*

A tightness gripped her throat as she realized that, even in death, he had kept his promise. *This key opens a box,* his voice was saying, *where I keep many secrets.*

Sophie now realized that the entire purpose of tonight's word game had been this key. Her grandfather must have had it with him when he was killed and had hidden it behind this painting, devising an ingenious treasure hunt to ensure only she would find it.

She snatched the key from behind the painting and slipped it deep in her pocket, along with the UV penlight. Peering out from behind the canvas, she could see that the guard was still trying desperately to raise someone on his walkie-talkie.

*He can't reach anyone yet,* Sophie realized, remembering how the extra security wiring in the walls made it virtually impossible to get a signal unless you stepped out into the hall. But he was nearly at the exit now, so she knew she had to act immediately.

Leonardo da Vinci, for the second time tonight, would have to help her.

'*Arrêtez! Ou je la détruis!*' the woman's voice echoed across the room. *Stop! Or I will destroy it!*

Grouard glanced over and stopped in his tracks. '*Mon dieu, non!*' Through the reddish haze, he could see that the woman had actually lifted the large painting off its cables and propped it on the floor in front of her. And then the canvas started to bulge in the middle, the fragile outlines of the Virgin Mary, Baby Jesus, and John the Baptist beginning to distort.

'*Non!*' Grouard screamed, watching the priceless Da Vinci stretch as the woman pushed her knee into the centre of the canvas from behind! '*NON!*'

'Set down your gun and radio,' the woman said in calm French, 'or I'll put my knee through this painting. I think you know how my grandfather would feel about that.'

Raising his hands over his head, the guard did as she asked.

'Thank you,' the woman said. 'Now continue to do exactly as I tell you, and everything will work out fine.'

Moments later, Langdon's pulse was still thundering as he ran beside Sophie down the stairs towards the ground level. Neither of them had said a word since leaving the trembling Louvre guard. Langdon was awkwardly clutching the man's pistol in his hand.

Taking the stairs two at a time, he said as they ran, 'You chose a valuable hostage.'

'*Madonna of the Rocks*,' she replied. 'But I didn't choose it – my grandfather did. He left me a little something behind the painting.'

Langdon shot her a startled look. 'What? But how did you know which painting? Why *Madonna of the Rocks*?'

'So dark the con of man.' She flashed a triumphant smile. 'I missed the first two anagrams, Robert. I wasn't about to miss the third.'

# Chapter 25

'They're dead!' Sister Sandrine stammered into the telephone in her Saint-Sulpice residence. She was leaving a message on an answering machine. 'Please pick up! Everyone else is dead!'

The first three phone numbers on the list had produced terrifying results – a hysterical widow, a detective working late at a murder scene, and a sombre priest consoling a bereaved family. And now, as she called the fourth and final number – the number she was not supposed to call unless the first three could not be reached – she only got an answering machine that simply asked the caller to leave a message.

'The floor panel has been broken!' she pleaded as she left the message. 'The other three are dead!'

Sister Sandrine did not know the identities of the four people she protected, but the phone numbers hidden beneath her bed were for use on only one condition. *If that floor panel is ever broken,* the faceless messenger had told her, *it means there has been a serious breach. One of us will have been mortally threatened and been forced to tell a desperate lie. Call the numbers. Warn the others. Do not fail us.*

It was a silent alarm. Foolproof in its simplicity. If one brother was in trouble, he could tell a lie that would set in motion a process to warn the others. Tonight, however, it seemed that more than one of them had been compromised.

'Please answer,' she whispered in fear. 'Where are you?'

'Hang up the phone,' a deep voice said from the doorway.

Turning in terror, Sister Sandrine saw the massive albino monk from Opus Dei. He was clutching the heavy iron candle stand. Shaking, she set the phone back in the cradle.

'They are dead,' the monk said. 'All four of them. And they have played me for a fool. Tell me where the keystone is.'

'I don't know!' Sister Sandrine said truthfully.

The man advanced, his white fists gripping the iron stand. 'You are a sister of the Church, and yet you serve *them*?'

'Jesus had but one true message,' Sister Sandrine said defiantly. 'I cannot see that message in Opus Dei.'

A sudden explosion of rage erupted behind the monk's eyes. He lunged, lashing out with the candle stand like a club. As Sister Sandrine fell, her last feeling was an overwhelming sense of foreboding.

*All four are dead.*

*The precious truth is lost forever.*

# Chapter 26

The security alarm on the west end of the Denon Wing sent the pigeons in the nearby Tuileries Gardens scattering as Langdon and Sophie dashed out into the Paris night. As they ran across the plaza to Sophie's car, Langdon could hear police sirens wailing in the distance.

'That's it there,' Sophie called, pointing to a red snub-nosed two-seater parked on the plaza.

*She's kidding, right?* The vehicle was easily the smallest car Langdon had ever seen.

'SmartCar,' she said. 'A hundred kilometres to the litre.'

Langdon had barely thrown himself into the passenger seat before Sophie gunned the SmartCar up and over a kerb and the car shot out across the sidewalk and bounced back down on to the roundabout at Carrousel du Louvre.

For an instant, Sophie seemed to consider ploughing straight ahead, through the perimeter hedge and across the large circle of grass in the centre.

'No!' Langdon shouted, knowing the hedges around Carrousel

du Louvre were there to hide the perilous chasm in the centre – *La Pyramide Inversée* – the upside-down pyramid skylight he had seen earlier from inside the museum. It was large enough to swallow their SmartCar in a single gulp. Fortunately, Sophie decided on the more conventional route, jamming the wheel hard to the right, circling properly until she exited, then cutting left and accelerating away.

The two-tone police sirens blared louder behind them, and Langdon turned in his seat, craning his neck to look out of the rear window towards the Louvre. The police did not seem to be chasing them. The sea of blue lights was assembling at the museum.

He turned back round. 'That was interesting.'

Sophie didn't seem to hear. Her eyes remained fixed ahead. Langdon settled into his seat.

*So dark the con of man.*

Sophie's quick thinking had been impressive.

*Madonna of the Rocks.*

Sophie had said her grandfather left her something behind the painting. *A final message?* Langdon could not help but marvel over Saunière's brilliant hiding place. Saunière, it seemed was reinforcing his fondness for Leonardo da Vinci at every turn.

As Sophie gunned the car up the Champs-Elysées, he said, 'The painting. What was behind it?'

Her eyes remained on the road. 'I'll show you once we're safely inside the embassy.'

'You'll *show* it to me?' Langdon was surprised. 'He left you a *physical* object?'

Sophie gave a curt nod. 'Embossed with a fleur-de-lis and the initials P.S.'

Langdon couldn't believe his ears.

*We're going to make it*, Sophie thought. The embassy was less than a mile away now. She was finally feeling like she could breathe normally again.

Even as she drove, her mind remained locked on the key in her pocket, her memories of seeing it many years ago, the gold head shaped as an equal-armed cross, the triangular shaft, the indentations, the embossed flowery seal and the letters P.S.

Although the key had barely entered Sophie's thoughts through the years, its peculiar tooling no longer looked so mystifying. *Laser-tooled. Impossible to duplicate.* This key had a complex series of laser-burned pockmarks that were examined by an electric eye. If the eye determined that the hexagonal pockmarks were correctly spaced, arranged and rotated, then the lock would open.

The cross on top implied the key belonged to some kind of Christian organization, and yet Sophie had never heard of any churches that used this sort of key.

*Besides, my grandfather was no Christian.*

Sophie had witnessed proof of that ten years ago. Ironically, it had been another *key* – a far more normal one – that had revealed his true nature to her . . .

The afternoon had been warm when she landed at Charles de Gaulle Airport and hailed a taxi home. *Grand-père will be so surprised to see me,* she thought. Returning from university in Britain for spring break a few days early, Sophie couldn't wait to see him and tell him all about her studies.

When she arrived at their Paris home, however, her grandfather was not there. Disappointed, she knew he had not been expecting her and was probably working at the Louvre. *But it's Saturday afternoon,* she realized. He seldom worked on weekends. On weekends, he usually –

Grinning, Sophie ran out to the garage. Sure enough, his car was gone. It was the weekend. Jacques Saunière despised city driving and owned a car for one destination only – his holiday château in Normandy, west of Paris. Sophie, after months in the congestion of London, was eager for the smells of nature. It was still early evening, so she decided to leave immediately and surprise him. Borrowing a friend's car, she drove west, winding into the deserted moon-swept hills. She arrived just after ten o'clock, turning down the long private driveway towards her grandfather's retreat. The access road was over a mile long, and she was halfway down it before she could start to see the house through the trees – a mammoth old stone château nestled in the woods on the side of a hill.

Sophie had half expected to find her grandfather asleep at this hour, so she was excited to see instead the house twinkling with lights. Her delight turned to surprise, however, when she arrived to find the driveway filled with parked cars – Mercedes, BMWs, Audis and a Rolls-Royce.

Sophie stared a moment and then burst out laughing. *My*

*grand-père, the famous recluse!* Jacques Saunière, it seemed, was far less solitary than he liked to pretend. Clearly he was throwing a party while Sophie was away at school, and from the looks of the cars, some of Paris's most influential people were among the guests.

She hurried to the front door. When she got there, though, she found it locked. She knocked. Nobody answered. Puzzled, she walked round and tried the back door. It too was locked. No answer.

Confused, she stood a moment and listened. The only sound she heard was the cool Normandy air letting out a low moan as it swirled through the valley.

No music.

No voices.

Nothing.

In the silence of the woods, Sophie hurried to the side of the house and clambered up on a woodpile, pressing her face to the living-room window. What she saw inside made no sense at all.

'Nobody's here!'

The entire floor looked deserted.

*Where are all the people?*

Heart racing, Sophie dashed to the woodshed and got the spare key her grandfather kept hidden under the kindling box. She ran to the front door and let herself in. As she stepped into the deserted hall, the control panel for the security system started blinking red – a warning that the entrant had ten seconds to type in the proper code before the burglar alarms went off.

*He has the alarm on during a party?*

Sophie quickly typed in the code and deactivated the system.

Entering, she found the entire house uninhabited. Upstairs too. As she descended again to the deserted living room, she stood a moment in the silence, wondering what could possibly be happening.

It was then that she heard it.

Muffled voices. And they seemed to be coming from underneath her . . . Crouching, she put her ear to the floor and listened. Yes, the sound was definitely coming from below. The voices seemed to be singing, or . . . *chanting?* She was frightened. Almost more eerie than the sound itself was her realization that this house did not even have a basement.

*At least none I've ever seen.*

Turning now and scanning the living room, Sophie's eyes fell on the only object in the entire house that seemed out of place – her grandfather's favourite antique, a sprawling Aubusson tapestry. It usually hung on the east wall beside the fireplace, but tonight it had been pulled aside on its brass rod, exposing a bare wooden wall behind it.

Walking towards it, Sophie sensed the chanting getting louder. Hesitant, she leaned her ear against the wood. The voices were clearer now. People were definitely chanting . . . intoning words Sophie could not discern.

*The space behind this wall is hollow!*

Feeling around the edge of the panels, Sophie found a recessed fingerhold. It was discreetly crafted. *A sliding door.* Heart pounding, she placed her finger in the slot and pulled it. With noiseless precision, the heavy wall slid sideways. From out of the darkness beyond, the voices echoed up.

Sophie slipped through the door and found herself on a rough-hewn stone staircase that spiralled downwards. She'd been coming to this house since she was a child and yet had no idea this staircase even existed!

As she descended, the air grew cooler. The voices grew clearer. She heard men and women now. Her line of sight was limited by the spiral of the staircase, but the last step was now coming into view. Beyond it, she could see a small patch of the basement floor – stone, illuminated by the flickering orange blaze of firelight.

Holding her breath, Sophie inched down another few steps and crouched to look.

It took her several seconds to understand what she was seeing. The room was a grotto – a coarse chamber that appeared to have been hollowed from the granite of the hillside. The only light came from torches on the walls. In the glow of the flames, thirty or so people stood in a circle in the centre of the room.

*I'm dreaming,* Sophie told herself. *A dream. What else could this be?*

Everyone in the room was wearing a mask. They looked like pieces in a giant chess set. The women were dressed in white gossamer gowns and golden shoes. Their masks were white, and in their hands they carried golden orbs. The men wore long black tunics, and their masks were black. Everyone in the circle rocked back and forth as they chanted in reverence. And there was something on the floor before them – something Sophie could not see.

The chanting grew steady again. Then accelerating. Thundering. Faster. The participants all took a step inwards now and knelt – and in that instant, Sophie could finally see what they all were watching . . .

She staggered back in horror, but the image felt as if it had seared itself into her memory forever. Overtaken by nausea, Sophie spun, clutching at the stone walls as she clambered back up the stairs. Pulling the door closed, she fled the deserted house and drove in a tearful stupor back to Paris.

That night, believing her life shattered by disillusionment and betrayal, she packed her belongings and left her home. On the dining-room table, she left a note.

I was there. Don't try to find me.

Beside the note, she laid the old spare key from the château's woodshed.

'Sophie!' Langdon's voice intruded. 'Stop! *Stop!*'

Emerging from the memory, Sophie slammed on the brakes, skidding to a halt. As Langdon pointed down the long street before them, her blood went cold. A hundred yards ahead, the intersection was blocked by a couple of Judicial Police cars, parked askew, their purpose obvious. *They've sealed off the road!*

Langdon gave a grim sigh. 'I take it the US Embassy is now off-limits this evening?'

*OK, Sophie, turn round very slowly.*

Putting the SmartCar in reverse, she performed a composed three-point turn and reversed her direction. As she drove away, she heard the sound of squealing tyres behind them, and sirens blared to life.

Cursing, she slammed down the accelerator.

# Chapter 27

As Sophie's SmartCar tore through the streets, Langdon sat white-knuckled in the passenger seat. He suddenly wished he had not decided to run. Although Sophie seemed to have lost the police, at least for the moment, he doubted their luck would hold for long.

Behind the wheel Sophie was fishing in her sweater pocket. She removed a small metal object and held it out for him. 'Robert, you'd better have a look at this. This is what my grandfather left me behind *Madonna of the Rocks*. It's a laser-cut key.'

Feeling a shiver of anticipation, Langdon took the object and examined it. *A key?* He had never seen anything like it before.

'Look at the other side,' Sophie said, changing lanes and sailing through an intersection.

When Langdon turned the key, he felt his jaw drop. There, intricately embossed on the centre of the cross, was a stylized fleur-de-lis with the initials P.S. 'Sophie,' he said, 'this is the seal I told you about! The official device of the Priory of Sion.'

She nodded. 'This is the object I saw a long time ago. My grandfather told me never to speak of it again.'

Langdon's eyes were still riveted on the embossed key. Its high-tech tooling and age-old symbolism gave out an eerie fusion of ancient and modern worlds.

'He said only that the key opened a box where he kept many secrets,' she said.

Langdon felt a chill. The Priory existed for the sole purpose of protecting a secret. A secret of incredible power.

'Do you know what it opens?' he asked.

Sophie looked disappointed. 'I was hoping *you* knew.'

Langdon remained silent as he turned the key in his hand.

'It looks Christian,' Sophie pressed.

Langdon was not so sure about that. The head of this key was a *square* cross – with four arms of equal length – which predated Christianity by fifteen hundred years. This kind of cross was not the same as the longer-stemmed Latin cross, designed by the Romans for torture and *crucifixion* . . .

'Sophie,' he said, 'all I can tell you is that equal-armed crosses like this one are considered *peaceful* crosses. The balance between the vertical and horizontal elements conveys a natural union of male and female – as a symbol, the square cross is very consistent with what the Priory of Sion believes.'

'OK, we have to get off the road.' Sophie checked her rear-view mirror. 'We need a safe place where we can figure out what that key opens.'

Langdon thought longingly of his comfortable room at the

Ritz. Obviously, that was not an option. 'You must know people. You live here.'

'Fache will check my phone and email records, talk to my colleagues at work. So, no. Finding a hotel is no good either because they all ask for ID.'

'Perhaps we should call the US Embassy,' Langdon suggested. 'I can explain the situation and have them send someone out to meet us somewhere.'

'Meet us?' Sophie turned and stared at him as if he were crazy. 'Robert, you're dreaming.' She shook her head. 'If you call your embassy right now, they will tell you to turn yourself in to Fache. Then they'll promise to use diplomatic channels to get you a fair trial.' She gazed up the line of elegant storefronts on the Champs-Elysées. 'How much cash do you have?'

Langdon checked his wallet. 'A hundred dollars. A few euros. Why?'

'Credit cards?'

'Of course.'

Sophie's eyes were on the rear-view mirror again. 'We lost them for the time being,' she said, 'but we won't last another five minutes if we stay in this car.' She paused, then nodded grimly and gunned the SmartCar forward and on to a roundabout. 'Trust me.'

Langdon made no response. Trust had not got him very far this evening. Pulling back the sleeve of his jacket, he checked his watch – a vintage, collector's-edition Mickey Mouse wristwatch that had been a gift from his parents on his tenth birthday.

Although its juvenile dial often drew odd looks, Langdon had never owned any other watch. Disney cartoons had been his first introduction to the magic of form and colour, and the image of Mickey now served as his daily reminder to stay young at heart. At the moment, however, Mickey's arms were skewed at an awkward angle, indicating an equally awkward hour.

2:51 a.m.

'Interesting watch,' Sophie said.

'Long story,' he said, pulling his sleeve back down.

'I imagine it would have to be.' She gave him a quick smile and exited a roundabout, heading away from the city centre. They'd left the rich, tree-lined streets of the diplomatic neighbourhood and soon plunged into a gloomier industrial area. A moment later, Langdon realized where they were.

Gare Saint-Lazare. *The railway station.*

European train stations never slept. Even at this hour, a half-dozen taxis idled near the main entrance. Vendors manned stalls selling sandwiches and mineral water, and grungy kids in backpacks emerged from the station rubbing their eyes, looking around as if trying to remember what city they were in now. Sophie pulled in behind the line of taxis and parked. Before Langdon could ask what was going on, she was out of the car. She hurried to the window of the cab in front of them and began speaking to the driver.

As Langdon got out, he saw Sophie hand the taxi driver a big wad of cash. The taxi driver nodded and then, to Langdon's bewilderment, sped off without them.

'What happened?' he demanded, joining Sophie on the kerb as the taxi disappeared.

Sophie was already heading for the station entrance. 'Come on. We're buying two tickets on the next train out of Paris.'

# Chapter 28

A small unimpressive black Fiat collected Bishop Aringarosa from the airport in Rome. Bundling his black cassock around himself, Aringarosa climbed into the back seat and settled in for the drive to Castel Gandolfo. It would be the same ride he had taken five months ago.

*Last year's trip to Rome,* he sighed. *The longest night of my life.*

Five months ago, the Vatican had phoned to request Aringarosa's immediate presence in Rome – with no explanation. He had no choice but to accept the invitation, albeit reluctantly – Aringarosa, like many of the conservative clergy, was not a fan of the new pope, an unprecedented liberal who had settled into his first year in office declaring that his papal mission was to be a 'rejuvenation of Vatican doctrine and updating Catholicism into the third millennium'.

Aringarosa feared this meant that the man was actually arrogant enough to think he could rewrite God's laws to win back the hearts of those who felt the demands of true Catholicism had become too inconvenient in a modern world. Aringarosa did not agree. *People need structure and direction from the Church,* he insisted. And he had been using all of his influence – substantial, considering the size and wealth of Opus Dei – to persuade the pope and his advisers to take a different course.

On that night, months ago, Aringarosa had been surprised to find himself being driven not towards Vatican City but rather eastwards up a sinuous mountain road. 'Where are we going?' he had demanded of his driver.

'Alban Hills,' the man replied. 'Your meeting is at Castel Gandolfo.'

*The pope's summer residence?* Aringarosa had never been, nor had he ever desired to see it. The sixteenth-century citadel was not only the pope's summer holiday home, but it also housed the Specola Vaticana – the Vatican Observatory, which was one of the most advanced astronomical observatories in Europe. Aringarosa himself had never been comfortable with the Vatican's desire to dabble in science. Why try to fuse science and faith?

Perched at the very edge of a cliff, the castle was a sight to behold – an impressive example of tiered, defensive architecture, echoing the potency of its dramatic cliffside setting. Sadly, in Aringarosa's opinion, the Vatican had ruined the building by constructing two huge aluminium telescope domes atop the roof, leaving the once dignified structure looking like a proud warrior wearing a couple of party hats.

When he got out of the car, a young Jesuit priest hurried out and greeted him. 'Bishop, welcome. I am Father Mangano. An astronomer here.'

Aringarosa grumbled his hello and followed him into the castle's foyer – a wide-open space whose decor included both Renaissance art and images of astronomy. Following his escort up the wide marble staircase, Aringarosa saw signs for conference centres, science lecture halls and tourist information services. *The Vatican has gone mad,* he thought. The Church just kept softening at every turn.

The top-floor corridor led in only one direction – towards a huge set of oak doors with a brass sign.

## BIBLIOTECA ASTRONOMICA

Aringarosa had heard of this place – the Vatican's Astronomy Library – rumoured to contain more than twenty-five thousand volumes, including rare works from philosophers and scientists from the fifteenth to eighteenth centuries, like Copernicus, Galileo, Kepler, Newton and Secchi. Allegedly, it was also where the pope's highest officers held private meetings . . . those meetings they chose not to hold within the walls of Vatican City.

Approaching the door, Bishop Aringarosa would never have imagined the shocking news he was about to receive inside, or the deadly chain of events it would put into motion. An hour later, as he staggered from the meeting, the devastating implications settled in.

*Six months from now!* he had thought. *God help us!*

Now, with just one month to go to that deadline, heading back to Castel Gandolfo again, Bishop Aringarosa clenched his fists as he thought about that first meeting. He wished his cellphone would ring with the news he needed to hear.

*Why hasn't the Teacher called me? Silas should have the keystone by now.*

Silas, crouched on the floor in his spartan room in the Opus Dei house in Paris, was gripped with anguish.

*Everything is lost.*

The brothers had lied, choosing death instead of revealing the truth of their secret. Not only had Silas now killed the only four people in the world who knew where the keystone was hidden, he had also killed a nun. He did not have the strength to call the Teacher and confess his failure.

The death of Sister Sandrine complicated matters greatly. Bishop Aringarosa had made the phone call that gave Silas entrance into Saint-Sulpice; what would the abbé think when he discovered the nun was dead? And the damage to the tiled floor in the church?

*I have endangered the bishop.*

Silas gazed blankly at the floor and pondered taking his own life. After all, it had been Aringarosa who gave Silas life in the first place . . . in that small rectory in Spain, educating him, giving him purpose.

'My friend,' Aringarosa had told him, 'you were born an albino. Do not let others shame you for this. Do you not understand how special this makes you? Were you not aware that Noah himself was an albino?'

'Noah of the Ark?' Silas had never heard this.

Aringarosa was smiling. 'Indeed, Noah of the Ark. An albino. Like you, he had skin white like an angel. Consider this. Noah saved all life on the planet. You are destined for great things, Silas. The Lord has freed you for a reason. He needs your help to do His work.'

Kneeling on the wooden floor, Silas prayed now for forgiveness. Then, stripping off his robe, he reached for his whip . . .

# Chapter 29

The inside of the station looked like every other railway station in Europe. Sophie raised her eyes to the enormous departure board overhead. The topmost listing read:

## LILLE – RAPIDE – 3:06

'I wish it left sooner,' she said, 'but Lille will have to do.'

*Sooner?* Langdon checked his watch: 2:59 a.m. The train left in seven minutes and they didn't even have tickets yet.

Sophie guided Langdon towards the ticket window and said, 'Buy us two tickets with your credit card.'

'I thought credit card usage could be traced by –'

'Exactly.'

Langdon decided to stop trying to keep ahead of Sophie Neveu. Using his Visa card, he purchased two tickets to Lille and handed them to Sophie.

But instead of heading for the platform, Sophie put her arm through Langdon's and led him in the exact *opposite* direction – through a side lobby, past an all-night café, and finally out through a side door on to a quiet street on the west side of the station.

Where a lone taxi sat idling by the doorway.

The driver saw Sophie and flicked his lights.

As the taxi pulled away from the station, Langdon and Sophie in the back seat, Sophie took out their newly purchased train tickets and tore them up.

Langdon sighed. *Seventy dollars well spent.*

As the taxi left Paris, Langdon began to feel they'd actually got away.

'It doesn't make sense,' he said slowly, 'that your grandfather would go to so much trouble to give you a key without letting you know what it opened. Are you sure he didn't write anything else on the back of the painting?'

'I searched the whole area. This is all there was. This key, wedged behind the painting. I saw the Priory seal, stuck the key in my pocket, and then we left.'

Langdon frowned, peering at the blunt end of the triangular shaft. Nothing. Squinting, he brought the key close to his eyes and examined the rim of the head. Nothing there either. He held the key to his nose and sniffed. 'I think this key was cleaned recently . . . it smells like somebody polished it with a cleaner.' He flipped it over. 'Yes, it's alcohol-based, like –' He stopped.

'What?'

He angled the key to the light and looked at the smooth surface on the broad arm of the cross. It seemed to shimmer in places . . . like it was wet. 'How well did you look at the back of this key before you put it in your pocket?'

'What? Not well. I was in a hurry.'

Langdon turned to her. 'Do you still have the black light?'

Sophie reached into her pocket and produced the UV penlight. Langdon took it and switched it on, shining the beam on the back of the key.

The back luminesced instantly. There was writing there. In penmanship that was hurried but legible.

'Well,' Langdon said, smiling, 'I guess we know what the alcohol smell was.'

Sophie stared in amazement at the purple writing on the back of the key.

## 24 RUE HAXO

*An address! My grandfather wrote down an address!*

'Where is this?' Langdon asked.

Sophie had no idea. She leaned forward and excitedly asked the driver the very same question.

The driver thought a moment and then nodded. He told Sophie it was out near the tennis stadium on the western outskirts of Paris. She asked him to take them there immediately, then sat back and looked again at the key, wondering what they could possibly find at 24 Rue Haxo.

*A church? Some kind of Priory headquarters?*

Her mind filled again with images of the secret ritual she had witnessed ten years ago, and she heaved a long sigh. 'Robert, I have a lot of things to tell you.' She paused, locking eyes with him as the taxi raced westwards. 'But first I want you to tell me everything you know about this Priory of Sion.'

# Chapter 30

'Tell me about the Priory of Sion,' Sophie repeated.

As Langdon gathered his thoughts, their taxi entered a heavily forested park – the Bois de Boulogne – and began heading west on the cobblestone thoroughfare. He wondered where to begin. The brotherhood's history spanned more than a millennium, an astonishing chronicle of secrets, blackmail, betrayal and even brutal torture at the hands of one particular pope.

'The Priory of Sion,' he began, 'was founded in Jerusalem in 1099 by a French king named Godefroi de Bouillon, immediately after he had conquered the city.'

Sophie nodded, her eyes riveted on him.

'King Godefroi allegedly possessed a powerful secret – a secret that had been in his family since the time of Christ. Fearing his secret might be lost when he died, he founded a secret brotherhood – the Priory of Sion – and charged them with protecting this secret by quietly passing it on from generation to generation. The Priory then learned of documents buried beneath the ruins of Herod's temple in Jerusalem – a temple that had been built on top of the earlier ruins of Solomon's temple. These hidden documents, they believed, proved the truth of the secret they were sworn to protect – and were also so explosive in nature that the Church would stop at nothing to get them.'

Sophie looked uncertain.

'The Priory vowed that these documents must be recovered from the rubble beneath the temple and protected forever, so the truth would never die. To do so, they created a military arm – a group of nine knights called the Order of the Poor Knights of Christ and the Temple of Solomon.' Langdon paused. 'They are more often known as the Knights Templar.'

Sophie glanced up with a surprised look of recognition. 'I thought the Templars were created to protect the Holy Land.'

'A common misunderstanding. The protection of pilgrims was just a guise under which the Templars ran their real mission in the Holy Land – a mission with the true goal of retrieving the documents from beneath the ruins of the temple.'

'So did they find them?'

Langdon grinned. 'Nobody knows for sure, but the one thing on which all academics agree is this: the Knights discovered *something* down there in the ruins . . . something that made them wealthy and powerful beyond anyone's wildest imagination.'

He gave Sophie a quick summary of the accepted Knights Templar history, explaining how the Knights were in the Holy Land during the Second Crusade – in the middle of the twelfth century. They told King Baldwin II of Jerusalem – who led the Crusader army – that they were there to protect Christian pilgrims, and that they needed basic shelter. He gave them permission to take up residence in the stables under the ruins of the temple – an odd choice of lodging, but one that had been anything but random. The Knights believed the documents the Priory sought were buried deep under the devastated shrine – beneath the Holy of Holies, a sacred chamber where God Himself was believed to reside. Literally, the very centre of the Jewish faith. For almost a decade, the nine Knights lived in the ruins, excavating in total secrecy through solid rock.

Sophie looked over. 'And you said they discovered something?'

'They certainly did,' Langdon said, explaining how it had taken them nine years, but the Knights finally found what they had been searching for. They took the treasure from the temple and travelled to Europe, where the pope of that time – Innocent II – immediately issued an unprecedented papal bull that afforded them limitless power and declared them 'a law unto themselves'. With this freedom, the Knights Templar expanded at a staggering rate, both in numbers and political power, amassing vast estates in over a dozen countries – they even had enough money to lend funds to bankrupt royals and charge interest in return, thereby establishing modern banking.

By the 1300s, the Knights had built up so much power that the pope of the time, Clement V, decided that something had to be done. Working with the French king, the pope set up an operation to quash the Templars and seize their treasure. He issued secret sealed orders to be opened simultaneously by his soldiers all across Europe on Friday, 13 October 1307.

At dawn on this day, his orders were unsealed and their appalling contents revealed. Clement's letter claimed that God had visited him in a vision and warned him that the Knights Templar were heretics guilty of devil worship, homosexuality, defiling the cross and other blasphemous behaviour. He stated that he had been asked by God to cleanse the earth by rounding up all the Knights and torturing them until they confessed their crimes against God.

It worked with clockwork precision. On that one day, countless Knights were captured, tortured mercilessly and finally burned at the stake as heretics. Echoes of the tragedy still remained in modern culture; to this day, Friday the thirteenth is considered unlucky.

Sophie looked confused. 'The Knights Templar were obliterated? I thought they still existed today.'

'They do, under a variety of names. Despite Clement's false charges and best efforts to eradicate them, the Knights had powerful allies, and some did manage to escape. Their treasure trove of documents – most likely their source of power over the Church – was Clement's true objective, but that slipped through his fingers. For the documents from beneath the temple had long since been entrusted to the Priory of Sion – an organization so secret that the Vatican had not attacked them in their onslaught on the Knights – and the Priory smuggled the documents away by ship.'

'Where did the documents go?'

Langdon shrugged. 'The answer to that is known only to the

Priory of Sion, but they are believed to have been moved and rehidden several times. Current speculation places the documents somewhere in the United Kingdom.'

Sophie looked uneasy.

'For a thousand years,' Langdon continued, 'legends of this secret have been passed on. The entire collection of documents, its power and the secret it reveals have become known by a single name – *Sangreal*. Hundreds of books have been written about it.'

'The Sangreal? Does the word have anything to do with the French word *sang* or the Spanish *sangre* – meaning "blood"?'

Langdon nodded. Blood was the backbone of the Sangreal, and yet not in the way Sophie probably imagined. 'The legend is complicated, but the important thing to remember is that the Priory guards the proof of the secret, and is supposedly waiting for the right moment in history to reveal the truth.'

'What truth? What secret could possibly be that powerful?'

Langdon took a deep breath and gazed out at the shadowy woods. 'Sophie, the word *Sangreal* is an ancient word. It has evolved over the years into another term . . . a more modern name.' He paused. 'When I tell you its modern name, you'll realize you already know a lot about it. In fact, almost everyone on earth has heard the story of the Sangreal.'

Sophie looked sceptical. 'I've never heard of it before.'

'Sure you have.' Langdon smiled. 'You're just used to hearing it called by a different name – the Holy Grail.'

# Chapter 31

Sophie stared at Langdon. *You're joking.* 'The Holy Grail?'

Langdon nodded, his expression serious. His claim still made no sense to Sophie.

'I thought the Holy Grail was a *cup.* Not a collection of documents.'

'Yes, but the Sangreal documents are only *half* of the Holy Grail treasure. They are buried with the Grail itself . . . and reveal its true meaning. The documents gave the Knights Templar so much power because the pages revealed the true nature of the Grail.'

*The true nature of the Grail?* Sophie felt even more lost now. The Holy Grail, she had thought, was the cup that Jesus drank from at the Last Supper, before he was taken by the Romans and charged with crimes that would lead to his crucifixion. 'The Holy Grail is the Cup of Christ,' she said. 'How much simpler could it be?'

'Sophie,' Langdon whispered, leaning towards her now, 'according to the Priory of Sion, the Holy Grail is not a cup at all. They claim the Grail legend – that of a *chalice* – is actually a clever allegory. That the Grail story uses the *chalice* as a metaphor for something else, something far more powerful.' He paused. 'Something that fits perfectly with everything your grandfather has been trying to tell us tonight, including all his references to the sacred feminine.'

'Non!' Sophie's shouts cut into his thoughts and Langdon jumped as she leaned forward and yelled at the taxi driver. Langdon could see the driver was speaking into his radio mouthpiece.

Sophie turned and plunged her hand into the pocket of Langdon's tweed jacket. Before he knew what had happened, she had yanked out the pistol he had taken from the security guard at the Louvre, swung it round and pressed it to the back of the driver's head. The driver instantly dropped his radio, raising his one free hand overhead.

'Sophie!' Langdon choked. 'What the hell –'

'Arrêtez!' Sophie commanded the driver. *Stop!*

Trembling, the driver obeyed.

It was then that Langdon heard the metallic voice of the taxi company's dispatcher coming from the dashboard – a voice that was suddenly reading out their *names*. His muscles turned rigid. *They found us already?*

Sophie waved the trembling taxi driver out of the car; he kept his arms over his head as he took several steps backwards. Sophie had rolled down her window and continued to aim the gun at the cabbie. 'Robert,' she said quietly, 'take the wheel. You're driving.'

Langdon was not about to argue. He climbed out of the car and jumped back in behind the wheel.

'Come on,' Sophie said from the back seat, 'drive us out of here.'

Langdon looked down at the car's controls and hesitated. *Oh no!* He groped for the gearstick and tentatively put a foot on the clutch pedal. 'Sophie? Maybe you –'

'Go!' she yelled.

Langdon depressed the clutch and jostled the stick into what he hoped was first gear. He touched the accelerator, testing the gas – then let in the clutch. The tyres howled as the taxi leaped forward, fishtailing.

'*Doucement!*' Sophie said as the car lurched down the road. '*Gently!* What are you doing?'

'I tried to warn you!' he shouted over the sound of gnashing gears. 'I can only drive an automatic!'

# Chapter 32

Struggling with the gears, Langdon managed to manoeuvre the hijacked taxi to the exit of the park, where he jammed on the brakes. 'You'd better drive.'

Sophie looked relieved as she jumped behind the wheel, handing him the gun as she did so. Within seconds she had the car humming smoothly westwards along the road.

'Which way is Rue Haxo?' Langdon asked.

Sophie's eyes remained focused on the road. 'The cab driver said it's adjacent to the tennis stadium. I know that area.'

Langdon pulled the heavy key from his pocket again, feeling the weight in his palm. He sensed it was an object of enormous consequence. Earlier, while telling Sophie about the Knights Templar, he had realized the equal-armed cruciform was also the symbol of the Knights – their white tunics were emblazoned with an equal-armed red cross. *A square cross. Just like the one on this key.*

He felt his imagination starting to run wild as he fantasized about what they might find. *The Holy Grail.* He almost laughed out loud at the absurdity of it. Most historians believed that the

Grail was somewhere in England, buried in a chamber beneath one of the many Templar churches, where it had been hidden since at least 1500.

*The era of Grand Master Da Vinci.*

Wherever it was, two important facts remained:

*Leonardo da Vinci knew where the Grail was during his lifetime.*

*That hiding place had probably not changed to this day.*

For this reason, Grail enthusiasts still pored over Da Vinci's art and diaries in hopes of unearthing a hidden clue as to the Grail's current location.

*Everyone loves a conspiracy.*

'Is it possible,' Sophie asked, putting into words what he barely dared to imagine, 'that the key you're holding actually unlocks the hiding place of the Holy Grail?'

Langdon's laugh sounded forced, even to him. 'I really can't imagine. Besides, the Grail is most likely in the United Kingdom somewhere, not France.' He gave her the quick history.

'But the Grail seems the only rational conclusion,' she insisted. 'We have an extremely secure key, stamped with the Priory of Sion seal, delivered to us by a member of the Priory of Sion – a brotherhood which, you just told me, is the guardian of the Holy Grail.'

Langdon knew her train of thought was logical, and yet intuitively he could not accept it. 'I really don't see how this could have anything to do with the Grail.'

'Because the Grail is supposed to be in England?'

'Not only that. The location of the Holy Grail is one of the best-kept secrets in history. Although the Priory brotherhood is very large, only *four* members at any given time know where the Grail is hidden – the Grand Master and his three *sénéchaux*. The probability of your grandfather being one of those four top people is very slim.'

'My grandfather *was* one of them,' Sophie said, pressing down on the accelerator. She had an image stamped in her memory that confirmed her grandfather's status within the brotherhood beyond any doubt.

'And even if your grandfather *were* in the upper echelon, he would never be allowed to reveal anything to anyone outside the brotherhood. It is inconceivable that he would bring you into the inner circle. There!' Langdon said suddenly, pointing to the huge tennis complex looming ahead.

Sophie snaked her way towards the stadium. After several passes, they found Rue Haxo and turned on to it.

*We need number twenty-four,* Langdon told himself, realizing he was secretly scanning the horizon for the spires of a church. *Don't be ridiculous. A forgotten Templar church in this neighbourhood?*

'There it is!' Sophie exclaimed, pointing.

*What in the world?*

Langdon's eyes followed hers to the structure ahead. The building was modern. A squat citadel with a giant, neon, equal-armed cross emblazoned atop its facade. Beneath the cross were the words:

## DEPOSITORY BANK OF ZURICH

Langdon had entirely forgotten that the peaceful, equal-armed cross had been adopted as the perfect symbol for a country – for the flag of neutral Switzerland.

At least the mystery was solved.

Sophie and Langdon were holding the key to a Swiss bank deposit box.

# Chapter 33

Outside Castel Gandolfo, an updraught of mountain air gushed over the top of the cliff and across the high bluff, sending a chill through Bishop Aringarosa as he stepped from the Fiat. *I should have worn more than this cassock,* he thought, fighting the reflex to shiver. The last thing he needed to appear tonight was weak or fearful.

The castle was dark save the windows at the very top of the building, which glowed ominously. *The library,* Aringarosa thought. *They are awake and waiting.* He ducked his head against the wind and continued on without so much as a glance towards the observatory domes.

The priest who greeted him at the door looked sleepy. He was the same priest who had welcomed Aringarosa five months ago. 'We were worried about you, Bishop,' he said, checking his watch and looking more perturbed than worried. 'They are waiting upstairs. I will escort you up.'

The library was a vast square room with dark wood from floor to ceiling. On all sides, towering bookcases groaned with volumes. The floor was amber marble with black basalt trim, a handsome reminder that this building had once been a palace.

'Welcome, Bishop,' a man's voice said from across the room.

Aringarosa tried to see who had spoken, but the lights were ridiculously low – much lower than they had been on his first visit, when everything was ablaze. *The night of stark awakening.* Tonight, these men sat in the shadows, as if they were somehow ashamed of what was about to transpire.

Aringarosa entered slowly, regally even. He could see the shapes of three men at a long table on the far side of the room. The silhouette of the man in the middle was immediately recognizable – the obese Secretarius Vaticana, the man in charge of all legal matters within Vatican City, the heart of the Catholic Church. The other two were high-ranking cardinals.

Aringarosa crossed the library towards them. 'My humble apologies for the hour. We're on different time zones. You must be tired.'

'Not at all,' the secretarius said, his hands folded on his enormous belly. 'We are grateful you have come so far. The least we can do is be awake to meet you. Can we offer you some coffee or refreshments?'

'I'd prefer we don't pretend this is a social visit. I have another plane to catch. Shall we get down to business?'

'Of course,' the secretarius said. 'You have acted more quickly than we imagined.'

'Have I?'

'You still have a month.'

'You made your concerns known five months ago,' Aringarosa said. 'Why should I wait?'

'Indeed.'

Aringarosa's eyes travelled the length of the long table to a large black briefcase. 'Is that what I requested?'

'It is.' The secretarius sounded uneasy. 'Although, I must admit, we are concerned with the request. It seems quite . . .'

'Dangerous,' one of the cardinals finished. 'Are you certain we cannot wire it to you somewhere? The sum is exorbitant.'

*Freedom is expensive.* 'I have no concerns for my own safety. God is with me.'

The men actually looked doubtful.

'The funds are exactly as I requested?'

The secretarius nodded. 'Large-denomination bearer bonds from the Vatican Bank. Negotiable as cash anywhere in the world.'

Aringarosa walked to the end of the table and opened the briefcase. Inside were two thick stacks of bonds.

The secretarius looked tense. 'I must say, Bishop, all of us would feel less apprehensive if these funds were in *cash*.'

*Twenty million euros? I could not lift that much cash,* Aringarosa thought, closing the case. 'Bonds are negotiable as cash. You said so yourself.' *We are all in this together now.* 'This is a perfectly legal transaction,' he defended. 'His Holiness can disperse monies however he sees fit. No law has been broken here.'

'True, and yet . . .' The secretarius leaned forward and his chair creaked under the burden. 'We have no knowledge of what you intend to do with these funds, and if it is in any way illegal . . .'

'Considering what you are asking of me,' Aringarosa countered, 'what I do with this money is not your concern . . . Now, I imagine you have something for me to sign?'

They all jumped, eagerly pushing the paper towards him, as if they wished he would simply leave.

Aringarosa eyed the sheet before him. It bore the papal seal. He was surprised how little emotion he felt as he signed it. The three men present, however, seemed to sigh in relief.

'Thank you, Bishop,' the secretarius said. 'Your service to the Church will never be forgotten.'

Aringarosa picked up the briefcase, turned and headed for the door.

'Bishop?' one of the cardinals called out as Aringarosa reached the threshold.

'Yes?'

'Where will you go from here?'

'Paris,' Aringarosa said, and walked out of the door.

# Chapter 34

The Depository Bank of Zurich was a twenty-four-hour *Geldschrank* bank offering totally anonymous services in the tradition of the Swiss numbered account.

As Sophie pulled the taxi to a stop in front of their destination, Langdon gazed out at the building's uncompromising architecture – a windowless rectangle that seemed to be forged entirely of dull steel.

An imposing gate blocked the bank's driveway – a cement-lined ramp that descended beneath the building – with a video camera mounted directly overhead and an electronic podium on the driver's side. An LCD screen, with a triangular hole beneath, provided directions in seven languages. Topping the list was English.

**INSERT KEY**

'Here we go.' Sophie stuck the key in the hole, and the door swung inwards with a low hum. She drove in, and the gate shut with a thud behind them. She repeated the procedure at the next gate, and then headed down into the underground car park. She and Langdon got out of the car and made their way up to ground level again.

The foyer of the Depository Bank of Zurich was very intimidating. Where most banks used polished marble and granite, this one had opted for wall-to-wall metal and rivets. The grey metal was everywhere – the floor, walls, counters, doors, even the lobby chairs appeared to be fashioned of moulded iron.

A large man behind the counter glanced up as they entered. He turned off the small television he was watching and greeted them with a pleasant smile. Despite his enormous muscles and visible sidearm, his voice chimed with polished courtesy.

'*Bonsoir,*' he said. 'How may I help you?'

Sophie simply laid the gold key on the counter in front of the man.

The man glanced down and immediately stood straighter. 'Of course. Your elevator is at the end of the hall. I will alert someone that you are on your way.'

Sophie nodded and took her key back. 'Which floor?'

The man gave her an odd look. 'Your key instructs the elevator which floor.'

She smiled. 'Ah, yes.'

Langdon had no idea how many floors they descended before the lift doors finally opened. A host was already there to greet them, an elderly and pleasant man in a neatly pressed flannel suit that made him look oddly out of place – an old-world banker in a high-tech world.

'Good evening,' the man said. 'Would you be so kind as to follow me, *s'il vous plaît*?' Without waiting for a response, he spun on his heel and strode briskly down a narrow metal corridor.

They followed him past several large rooms filled with computers, until finally arriving at a steel door. '*Voici,*' their host said, opening it for them. 'Here you are.'

Langdon and Sophie stepped into another world. Gone were the metal and rivets, replaced with oriental carpets, dark oak furniture, and cushioned chairs. On the broad desk in the middle of the small room, two crystal glasses sat beside an opened bottle of Perrier, its bubbles still fizzing. A pewter pot of coffee steamed beside it.

The man gave a perceptive smile. 'I sense this is your first visit to us?'

Sophie hesitated and then nodded.

'Understood. Keys are often passed on as part of an inheritance, and our first-time users are almost always uncertain of the protocol.' He motioned to the table of drinks. 'This room is yours as long as you care to use it. Shall I run through the process of accessing your box?'

Sophie nodded again. 'Please.'

Their host swept an arm across the luxurious salon. 'This is your private viewing room. Once I leave, you may spend all the time you need in here to review and modify the contents of your safe-deposit box, which arrives . . . over here.' He walked them to the far wall, where a wide conveyor belt entered the room in a graceful curve, vaguely resembling a baggage-claim carousel. 'You insert your key in that slot there.' The man pointed to a large electronic podium facing the conveyor belt. The podium had a familiar triangular hole. 'Then you enter your account number, and your safe-deposit box will be retrieved robotically from the vault below. When you are finished, you place the box back on the conveyor belt, insert your key again, and the process is reversed. Your total privacy is guaranteed. If you need anything at all, simply press the call button on the table in the centre of the room.'

Sophie was about to ask a question when a telephone rang. The man looked puzzled and embarrassed. 'Excuse me, please.' He walked over to the phone, which was sitting on the table beside the coffee and Perrier. '*Oui?*' he answered. His brow furrowed as he listened to the caller. '*Oui . . . oui . . .*' He hung up and gave them an uneasy smile. 'I'm sorry, I must leave you now.' He moved quickly towards the door.

'Excuse me,' Sophie called. 'Could you clarify something before you go? You mentioned that we enter an *account* number?'

The man paused at the door, looking pale. 'But of course. Like most Swiss banks, our safe-deposit boxes are attached to a *number,* not a name. You have a key and a personal account number known only to you. Your key is only half of your identification. Your personal account number is the other half. Otherwise, anyone could use your key if you lost it.'

Sophie hesitated. 'But if my benefactor gave me no account number?'

The banker gave them a calm smile. 'I will ask someone to help you. He will be in shortly.'

He left the room, closing the door behind him and twisting a heavy lock, sealing the two of them inside.

Across town, Lieutenant Collet was coordinating the police investigation at the railway station when his phone rang.

It was Fache. 'Interpol got a tip,' he said. 'Forget the train. Langdon and Neveu just walked into the Paris branch of the Depository Bank of Zurich. Twenty-four Rue Haxo. I want your men over there right away.'

Collet understood. 'Right away, Captain.'

# Chapter 35

'Good evening,' said André Vernet, president of the Paris branch of the Depository Bank of Zurich, his eyes finding his clients. 'I am André Vernet. How can I be of serv—' The rest of the sentence lodged somewhere beneath his Adam's apple.

'I'm sorry, do we know each other?' Sophie asked. She did not recognize the banker, but he looked for a moment as if he'd seen a ghost.

'No . . .' the bank president fumbled. 'I don't . . . believe so. Our services are anonymous.' He exhaled and forced a calm smile. 'My assistant tells me you have a gold key but no account number? Might I ask how you came by this key?'

'My grandfather gave it to me,' Sophie replied, watching the man closely. His uneasiness seemed more evident now.

'Really? Your grandfather gave you the key but failed to give you the account number?'

'I don't think he had time,' Sophie said. 'He was murdered tonight.'

Her words sent the man staggering backwards. 'Jacques

Saunière is dead?' he demanded, his eyes filling with horror. 'But . . . how?'

Now it was Sophie who reeled, numb with shock. 'You *knew* my grandfather?'

Banker André Vernet looked equally astounded, steadying himself by leaning on an end table. 'Jacques and I were dear friends. When did this happen?'

'Earlier this evening. Inside the Louvre.'

Vernet sank into a deep leather chair and glanced up at Langdon, then back to Sophie. 'Did either of you have anything to do with his death?'

'No!' Sophie declared. 'Absolutely not.'

Vernet's face was grim, and he paused, pondering. 'Your pictures are being circulated by Interpol. You're wanted for murder.'

Sophie slumped. *Fache had run an Interpol broadcast already?* It seemed the captain was more motivated than Sophie had anticipated. She quickly told Vernet who Langdon was and what had happened inside the Louvre tonight.

Vernet looked amazed. 'And as your grandfather was dying, he left you a message telling you to find Mr Langdon?'

'Yes. And this key.' Sophie laid the gold key on the coffee table in front of Vernet, placing the Priory seal face down.

Vernet glanced at the key but made no move to touch it. 'He left you only this key? Nothing else? No slip of paper?'

Sophie knew she had been in a hurry inside the Louvre, but she was certain she had seen nothing else behind *Madonna of the Rocks*. 'No. Just the key.'

Vernet gave a helpless sigh. 'I'm afraid every key is electronically paired with a ten-digit account number that functions as a password. Without that number, your key is worthless . . . and I truly can do nothing. Clients select their own account numbers via a secure terminal, meaning account numbers are known only to the client and the computer. This is one way we ensure anonymity. And the safety of our employees.'

Sophie understood. Twenty-four-hour stores did the same thing.

She sat down beside Langdon, glanced down at the key and then up at Vernet. 'Monsieur Vernet,' she pressed, 'my grandfather called me tonight and told me he and I were in grave danger. He said he had to give me something, and it turned out to be a key to your bank. Now he is dead. Anything you can tell us would be helpful.'

Vernet broke into a sweat. 'I just know that we need to get you out of the building. I'm afraid the police will arrive shortly. My security guard felt obliged to call Interpol.' Just then, his cell-phone rang, and he snatched it off his belt. *'Oui?'* He listened a moment, his expression one of surprise and growing concern. *'La police? Si rapidement?'* He gave some quick directions in French, then hung up the phone and turned back to Sophie. 'The police have responded far more quickly than usual. They are arriving as we speak.'

Sophie had no intention of leaving empty-handed. 'Tell them we came and went already. If they want to search the bank, you can demand a search warrant – that will take them time to get.'

'Listen,' Vernet said, 'Jacques was a friend, and my bank does not need this kind of press. So for those two reasons, I have no intention of allowing this arrest to be made on my premises. Give me a minute and I will see what I can do to help you leave the bank undetected. Beyond that, I cannot get involved.' He stood up and hurried for the door. 'Stay here. I'll be right back.'

'But the safe-deposit box,' Sophie declared. 'We can't just leave.'

'There's nothing I can do,' Vernet said, hurrying out of the door. 'I'm sorry.'

Sophie stared after him a moment, wondering if maybe the account number was buried in one of the countless unopened letters and packages her grandfather had sent her over the years.

Langdon stood suddenly, and Sophie sensed an unexpected glimmer of excitement in his eyes.

'Robert? You're smiling.'

'Your grandfather was a genius.'

'I'm sorry?'

'Ten digits?'

Sophie had no idea what he was talking about.

'The account number,' he said, a familiar lopsided grin now crossing his face. 'I'm pretty sure he left it for us after all.'

'Where?'

Langdon produced the printout of the crime scene photo and

spread it out on the coffee table. Sophie needed only to read the first line to know that he was correct.

13-3-2-21-1-1-8-5
O, Draconian devil!
Oh, lame saint!
P.S. Find Robert Langdon

# Chapter 36

Langdon was already moving towards the electronic podium near the conveyor belt. Sophie grabbed the computer printout and followed.

The podium had a keypad similar to that of an ATM. Beside it was a triangular hole. Sophie wasted no time inserting the shaft of her key into the hole.

The screen refreshed instantly.

ACCOUNT NUMBER:

– – – – – – – – – –

The cursor blinked. Waiting.

*Ten digits.* Sophie read the numbers off the printout, and Langdon typed them in.

ACCOUNT NUMBER:

1 3 3 2 2 1 1 1 8 5

When he had typed the last digit, a message in several languages appeared on the screen. English was on top.

> CAUTION:
> Before you strike the enter key, please check
> the accuracy of your account number. For your
> own security, if the computer does not recognize
> your account number, this system will automatically
> shut down.

'Looks like we only get one try,' Sophie said, frowning.

'The number looks right,' Langdon confirmed, carefully checking what they had typed and comparing it to the printout. He motioned to the ENTER key. 'Fire away.'

Sophie extended her index finger towards the keypad but hesitated, an odd thought now hitting her.

'Go ahead,' Langdon urged. 'Vernet will be back soon.'

'No.' She pulled her hand away. 'This isn't the right account number.'

'Of course it is! Ten digits. What else would it be?'

'It's too random.' Sophie deleted everything they had just typed in and looked up at Langdon, her gaze self-assured. 'It's far too coincidental that this supposedly *random* account number could be rearranged to form the Fibonacci sequence.' She began entering a different number, as if from memory. 'Moreover, I believe my grandfather would have chosen an account number that had meaning to him, something he could easily remember.'

She finished typing the entry and gave a sly smile. 'Something that appeared random . . . but was *not.*'

Langdon looked at the screen.

ACCOUNT NUMBER:

1 1 2 3 5 8 1 3 2 1

It took him an instant, but when Langdon spotted it, he knew she was right.

*The Fibonacci sequence.*

1-1-2-3-5-8-13-21

When the Fibonacci sequence was melded into a single ten-digit number, it became virtually unrecognizable. *Easy to remember, and yet seemingly random.* A brilliant ten-digit code that Saunière would never forget.

Sophie reached down and pressed the ENTER key.

Nothing happened.

At least nothing they could detect.

At that moment, beneath them, in the bank's cavernous subterranean vault, a robotic claw sprang to life. Sliding on a double-axis transport system attached to the ceiling, the claw headed off in search of the proper coordinates. On the cement floor below, hundreds of identical plastic crates lay aligned on an enormous grid . . . like rows of small coffins in an underground crypt.

Whirring to a stop over the correct spot on the floor, the claw dropped down, an electric eye confirming the barcode on the box. Then, with computer precision, the claw grasped the heavy handle and hoisted the crate vertically. New gears engaged, and the claw transported the box to the far side of the vault, coming to a stop over a stationary conveyor belt.

Gently now, the retrieval arm set down the crate and retracted.

Once the arm was clear, the conveyor belt whirred to life . . .

Upstairs, Sophie and Langdon exhaled in relief to see the conveyor belt move. It entered the room on their right through a narrow slit beneath a retractable door. The metal door slid up, and a huge plastic box appeared, emerging from the depths on the inclined conveyor belt. The box was black, made of heavy moulded plastic. It coasted to a stop directly in front of them.

Langdon and Sophie stood there, silent, staring at the mysterious container. Sophie thought it looked like a giant toolbox. Wasting no time, she unhooked the two buckles facing her. Then she glanced over at Langdon. Together, they raised the heavy lid and let it fall back; then they leaned forward and peered down into the crate.

Sitting at the bottom was a lone item – a polished wooden box about the size of a shoe box with ornate hinges. The wood was a lustrous deep purple with a strong grain. *Rosewood,* Sophie realized. Her grandfather's favourite. The lid bore a beautiful inlaid design of a rose.

'The five-petal rose,' Langdon whispered, 'is a Priory symbol for the Holy Grail.'

Sophie leaned in and grabbed the box, lifting it out. *My God, it's heavy!* she thought as she carried it gingerly to a large receiving table and set it down.

'It's a perfect size,' Langdon whispered, 'to hold . . . a chalice.' *But it can't be a chalice.*

Sophie pulled the box towards her across the table, preparing to open the lid. As she moved it, though, something unexpected happened. The box let out an odd gurgling sound.

Sophie did a double take. 'Did you just hear . . . ?'

Langdon nodded. 'Liquid, do you think?'

Reaching forward, Sophie slowly unhooked the clasp and raised the lid.

The object inside was unlike anything Langdon had ever seen. One thing was immediately clear to both of them, however. This was definitely *not* the Cup of Christ.

# Chapter 37

'Mademoiselle Neveu, the police are blocking the street,' André Vernet said, walking into the waiting room. 'Getting you out will be difficult.'

Sophie immediately closed the lid of the box and looked up. 'We had the account number after all,' she said.

'Will you be taking the item with you or returning it to the vault before you leave?' he asked.

Sophie glanced at Langdon and then back to Vernet. 'We need to take it.'

He nodded. 'Very well. Then I suggest you wrap it in your jacket. I would prefer nobody else see it.'

As Langdon shed his jacket, Vernet hurried over to the conveyor belt, closed the now empty crate and typed in a series of simple commands. The conveyor began moving again, carrying the plastic container back down to the vault. Pulling the gold key from the podium, he handed it back to Sophie.

'This way, please. Hurry.'

When they finally reached the rear loading dock, Sophie could see the flash of police lights filtering through the underground garage. They were probably blocking the ramp. Vernet motioned to one of the bank's small armoured trucks. 'In the back,' he said, heaving open the massive rear door to reveal a glistening steel compartment.

Vernet hurried across to the office, collected the keys for the truck and put on a driver's cap and jacket, stuffing a pistol inside. Back at the truck, he swung the heavy back doors closed on Langdon and Sophie, locking them inside, then got in behind the wheel and revved the engine.

As the truck powered up the ramp, the gate swung inwards to let them pass, the exit beckoning.

Four patrol cars were parked out front, and a few yards from the roadblock, a lanky officer stepped out and waved Vernet to a stop.

'Je suis Jérôme Collet,' the agent said, identifying himself. He motioned to the truck's cargo hold. 'Qu'est-ce qu'il y a là dedans?' What's inside the truck?

'Hell if I know,' Vernet replied in crude French. 'I'm only a driver.'

Collet looked unimpressed. 'We're looking for two criminals.' He held up a passport picture of Robert Langdon. 'Was this man in your bank tonight?'

Vernet shrugged. 'No clue. They don't let us anywhere near the clients. You need to go in and ask the front desk.'

'Your bank is demanding a search warrant before we can enter.'

Vernet put on a disgusted look. 'Administrators. Don't get me started.'

'Open your truck, please.' Collet motioned towards the cargo hold.

Vernet stared at the agent and forced an obnoxious laugh. 'Open the truck? You think I have keys? You think they trust us? You should see the rubbish wages I get paid.'

Collet's head tilted to one side. 'You're telling me you don't have keys to your own truck?'

Vernet shook his head. 'Not the back of it. Ignition only. These security trucks get sealed by overseers on the loading dock. The truck just sits here while someone drives the cargo keys to the drop-off point. Once we get the call that they are at their destination, I get the OK to drive there. Not a second before. I never know what the hell I'm lugging.'

'When was *this* truck sealed?'

'Must have been hours ago. I'm driving all the way up to St Thurial tonight. Cargo keys are already up there.' A drop of sweat was preparing to slide down Vernet's nose. 'You mind?' he said, wiping his nose with his sleeve and motioning to the police car blocking his way. 'I'm on a tight schedule.'

'Do all the drivers wear Rolexes?' the agent asked, pointing to Vernet's wrist.

Vernet glanced down and saw the glistening band of his absurdly expensive watch peeking out from beneath the sleeve of his jacket. 'This piece of rubbish? Bought it for twenty euros from a Taiwanese street vendor in the market. I'll sell it to you for forty.'

Collet paused and finally stepped aside. 'No thanks. Have a safe trip.'

# Chapter 38

*Twenty million euros.*

The sum would buy him power far more valuable than that.

As his car sped back towards Rome, Aringarosa again found himself wondering why the Teacher had not yet contacted him. Pulling his cellphone from his cassock pocket, he checked the carrier signal. Extremely faint.

'Mobile service is poor up here,' the driver said, glancing at him in the rearview mirror. 'In about five minutes, we'll be out of the mountains, and service improves.'

'Thank you.' Aringarosa felt a sudden surge of concern. *No service in the mountains?* Maybe the Teacher had been trying to reach him all this time. What might he think if he had been repeatedly calling with no answer?

In Paris, Silas lay prone on the canvas mat in his room. Tonight's second session had left him dizzy and weak. Still, he felt he deserved it.

*I have failed the Church.*

*Far worse, I have failed the bishop.*

Tonight was supposed to be Bishop Aringarosa's salvation. Five months ago, the bishop had returned from a meeting at the Vatican Observatory, where he had learned something that left him deeply changed. He had finally shared the news with Silas.

'But this is impossible!' Silas had cried out in shock. 'I cannot accept it!'

'It is true,' Aringarosa said. 'Unthinkable, but true. In only six months.'

Silas had prayed for deliverance, and even in those dark days, his trust in God and *The Way* never wavered. It was only a month later that the clouds parted miraculously and the light of possibility shone through.

*Divine intervention,* Aringarosa had called it. 'Silas,' he whispered, 'God has bestowed upon us an opportunity to protect *The Way.* Our battle, like all battles, will take sacrifice. Will you be a soldier of God?'

Silas fell to his knees before Bishop Aringarosa – the man who had given him a new life – and said, 'I am a lamb of God. Shepherd me as your heart commands.'

Aringarosa put Silas in contact with the man who had proposed the plan – a man who called himself the Teacher. Although the Teacher and Silas never met face to face, each time they spoke by phone, Silas was awed, both by the depth of the Teacher's faith and by the scope of his power. 'Do as the Teacher commands you,' the bishop told Silas, 'and we will be victorious.'

*Victorious.* Silas now gazed at the bare floor and feared victory had eluded them. The Teacher had been tricked. The keystone was a devious dead end. And with the deception, all hope had vanished.

He wished he could call Bishop Aringarosa and warn him, but the Teacher had cut off their lines of direct communication tonight. *For our safety.*

Finally, overcoming enormous trepidation, Silas knew he must report on the night's events. He crawled to his feet and found his robe, which lay on the floor. He dug his cellphone from the pocket. Hanging his head in shame, he dialled.

'Teacher,' he whispered, 'all is lost.' He told the man how he had been tricked.

'You lose your faith too quickly,' the Teacher replied. 'I have just received news. The secret lives still. Jacques Saunière passed on information to someone else before he died. I will call you soon – our work tonight is not yet done.'

# Chapter 39

Riding inside the dimly lit cargo hold of the armoured truck was like being transported inside a cell for solitary confinement. Langdon's legs were stiff from sitting cross-legged on the metal floor, and he winced to feel the blood pouring back into his lower body as he moved. In his arms, he still clutched the bizarre treasure they had extricated from the bank.

He laid the precious bundle on the floor, unwrapped his jacket and extracted the box, pulling it towards him. Sophie shifted her position so they were sitting side by side. Langdon felt like they were two kids huddled over a Christmas present.

In contrast to the warm colours of the rosewood box, the inlaid rose had been crafted of a pale wood, probably ash, which shone clearly in the dim light. *The Rose*. Entire armies and religions had been built on this symbol, as had secret societies. *The Rosicrucians. The Knights of the Rosy Cross.*

'Go ahead,' Sophie said. 'Open it.'

Langdon took a deep breath. He stole one more admiring

glance at the intricate woodwork, and then, unhooking the clasp, he opened the lid.

Nestled snugly inside lay an object Langdon could not even begin to comprehend. Crafted of polished white marble, it was a cylinder approximately the size of a tennis-ball can. More complicated than a simple column of stone, however, the cylinder appeared to have been assembled from many pieces. Five doughnut-sized discs of marble had been stacked and affixed to one another within a delicate brass framework. It looked like some kind of tubular, multiwheeled kaleidoscope. Each end of the cylinder was closed off with an end cap, also marble, making it impossible to see inside. Having heard liquid within, Langdon assumed the cylinder was hollow.

As mystifying as the construction of the cylinder was, however, it was the engravings around the tube's circumference that drew Langdon's primary focus. Each of the five discs had been carefully carved with the same unlikely series of letters – the entire alphabet.

'Amazing, isn't it?' Sophie whispered.

Langdon glanced up. 'I don't know. What the hell is it?'

Now there was a glint in Sophie's eye. 'My grandfather used to craft these as a hobby. They were invented by Leonardo da Vinci.'

Even in the diffuse light, she could see Langdon's surprise. 'Da Vinci?' he muttered, looking again at the canister.

'Yes. It's called a cryptex. According to my grandfather, the blueprints come from one of Da Vinci's secret diaries.'

'What is it for?'

'It's like a safe,' she said. 'For storing secret information.'

Langdon's eyes widened further.

Sophie explained that creating models of Da Vinci's inventions was one of her grandfather's best-loved hobbies.

'He made me one of these when I was little,' she said. 'But I've never seen one so ornate and large.'

Langdon's eyes hadn't left the box. 'I've never heard of a cryptex.'

Sophie was not surprised. 'Most of Leonardo's unbuilt inventions had never been studied or even named. The term *cryptex* could even have been my grandfather's creation. It's an apt title for this device that used the science of *cryptology* to protect information written on the contained scroll, or *codex*.' As their armoured truck roared down the highway, Sophie told Langdon that the cryptex had been Da Vinci's solution to the dilemma of sending secure messages over long distances.

'We require a password,' Sophie said, pointing out the lettered dials. 'A cryptex works much like a bicycle's combination lock. If you align the five dials in the proper position, the lock will open and the entire cylinder slides apart. Inside there's a hollow central compartment, which can hold a scroll of paper. That's where the information you want to keep private is written.'

Langdon looked incredulous. 'And you say your grandfather built these for you when you were younger?'

'Some smaller ones, yes. A couple of times for my birthday, he gave me a cryptex and told me a riddle. The answer to the riddle was the password, so once I figured it out I could open the cryptex and find my birthday card.'

'A lot of work for a card.'

'No, the cards always contained another riddle or clue. My grandfather loved creating treasure hunts around our house, a string of clues that eventually led to my real present. Each treasure hunt was a test, to make sure I earned my rewards. And the tests were never simple.'

Langdon eyed the device again, still looking sceptical. 'But why not just prise it apart? Or smash it? The metal looks delicate, and marble is a soft rock.'

Sophie smiled. 'Because Da Vinci was too smart for that. He designed the cryptex so that if you try to force it open in any way, the information self-destructs.' She reached into the box and carefully lifted out the cylinder. 'Any information to be inserted is first written on a papyrus scroll.'

She tipped the cryptex, and the liquid inside gurgled. 'A vial of liquid.'

'Liquid *what*?'

Sophie smiled. 'Vinegar.'

Langdon hesitated a moment and then began nodding. 'Brilliant.' *Vinegar and papyrus.* If someone attempted to force open the cryptex, the glass vial would break, and the vinegar would quickly dissolve the papyrus. By the time anyone extracted the secret message, it would be just a glob of meaningless pulp.

'So,' Sophie told him, 'the only way to access the information inside is to know the proper five-letter password. And with five dials, each with twenty-six letters, that's a lot of possible combinations. Approximately twelve million possibilities.' She paused, closing the box lid and eyeing the five-petal rose inlaid on it. 'Did you say earlier that the Rose is a symbol for the Grail?'

'Exactly. In Priory symbolism, the Rose and the Grail mean the same thing.'

Sophie furrowed her brow. 'That's strange, because my grandfather always told me the Rose meant *secrecy*. He used to hang a rose on his office door at home when he was having a confidential phone call and didn't want me to disturb him. He encouraged me to do the same.'

'*Sub rosa*,' Langdon said. 'The Romans hung a rose over meetings to indicate the meeting was confidential. Whatever was said *under the rose* – or *sub rosa* – had to remain a secret.' His expression seemed to tighten suddenly. '*Sub . . . rosa*,' he choked. 'It can't be.'

'What?'

Langdon slowly raised his eyes. 'Under the sign of the Rose,' he whispered. 'This cryptex . . . I think I know what it actually is.'

He could scarcely believe his own supposition, and yet, considering *who* had given this stone cylinder to them, *how* he had given it to them, and now the inlaid rose on the container, Langdon could formulate only one conclusion.

*I am holding the Priory keystone.*

The legend was specific.

*The keystone is an encoded stone that lies beneath the sign of the Rose.*

'Robert?' Sophie was watching him. 'What's going on?'

Langdon needed a moment to gather his thoughts. 'Did your grandfather ever speak to you of something called *la clef de voûte*?'

'The key to the vault?' Sophie translated.

'No, that's the literal translation. *Clef de voûte* is a common architectural term – *voûte* means a vault in an archway. Like a *vaulted* ceiling.'

'But vaulted ceilings don't have keys.'

'Actually, they do. Every stone archway requires a central, wedge-shaped stone at the top, which locks the pieces together and carries all the weight. This stone is, in an architectural sense, the key to the vault. In English we call it a keystone.' Langdon watched her eyes for any spark of recognition.

Sophie shrugged, glancing down at the cryptex. 'But this obviously is not a keystone.'

Langdon didn't know where to begin. The use of wedged keystones to build vaulted archways had been one of the best-kept secrets of the early Masonic brotherhood – part of the wisdom that had made the Masons such wealthy craftsmen. And yet the stone cylinder in the rosewood box was obviously something quite different. The Priory keystone – if this was indeed what they were holding – was not at all what Langdon had imagined.

'The Priory keystone is not my speciality,' he admitted. 'My interest in the Holy Grail is mostly to do with the symbols, so I tend to ignore all the discussions about how to actually find it.'

Sophie's eyebrows arched. '*Find* the Holy Grail?'

Langdon gave an uneasy nod, speaking his next words carefully. 'Sophie, according to Priory lore, the keystone is an encoded map . . . a map that reveals the hiding place of the Holy Grail.'

Sophie's face went blank. 'And you think this is it?'

Langdon didn't know what to say. Even to him it sounded unbelievable, and yet the keystone was the only logical conclusion he could muster. *An encrypted stone, hidden beneath the sign of the Rose.*

The idea that the cryptex had been designed by Leonardo da Vinci – former Grand Master of the Priory of Sion – shone as another tantalizing indicator that this was indeed the Priory keystone. *A former Grand Master's blueprint . . . brought to life centuries later by another Priory member.*

For the last decade, historians had been searching for the keystone in French churches. Grail seekers believed that *la clef de voûte* was a literal keystone – an architectural wedge, an engraved, encrypted stone, inserted into a vaulted archway in a church. *Beneath the sign of the Rose.*

'This cryptex *can't* be the keystone,' Sophie argued. 'It's not old enough. I'm certain my grandfather made this. It can't be part of any ancient Grail legend.'

'Actually,' Langdon replied, feeling a tingle of excitement ripple through him, 'the keystone is believed to have been created by the Priory sometime in the past couple of decades.'

Sophie's eyes flashed disbelief. 'But if this cryptex reveals the hiding place of the Holy Grail, why would my grandfather give it to *me*? I have no idea how to open it or what to do with it. I don't even know what the Holy Grail *is*!'

Langdon realized to his surprise that she was right. He had not yet had a chance to explain to Sophie the true nature of the Holy

Grail. That story would have to wait. At the moment, they were focused on the keystone.

*If that is indeed what this is . . .*

Against the hum of the bulletproof wheels beneath them, Langdon quickly explained to Sophie everything he had heard about the keystone. Allegedly, for centuries, the Priory's biggest secret – the location of the Holy Grail – was never written down. For security's sake, it was passed on verbally to each new rising *sénéchal* at a secret ceremony. Then, at some point during the last century, it was believed that the policy had changed – they vowed never again even to *speak* the location of the sacred hiding place.

'But then how could they pass on the secret?' Sophie asked.

'That's where the keystone comes in,' Langdon explained. 'When one of the top four members died, the remaining three would choose the next candidate to ascend as *sénéchal*. Rather than *telling* the new *sénéchal* where the Grail was hidden, they gave him a test through which he could prove he was worthy.'

'So the keystone is a proof of merit,' Sophie said.

Langdon nodded. 'Sophie, if this is indeed the keystone, it means that your grandfather was one of the highest four members within the Priory of Sion.'

Sophie sighed. 'He was powerful in a secret society. I'm certain of it. I can only assume now it was the Priory.'

Langdon did a double take. 'You *knew* he was in a secret society?'

'I saw some things I wasn't supposed to see ten years ago. We haven't spoken since.' She paused. 'My grandfather was not only a ranking top member of the group . . . I believe he was *the* top member.'

Langdon could not believe what she had just said. 'Grand Master? But . . . there's no way you could know that!'

'I'd rather not talk about it.' Sophie looked away, her expression as determined as it was pained.

Langdon sat in stunned silence. *Jacques Saunière? Grand Master?* And he had been scheduled to *meet* Saunière earlier. *The Priory Grand Master called a meeting with me. Why? Just to chat about art?* It suddenly seemed unlikely. And why would Saunière do something as risky as giving his granddaughter the keystone, when there were three *sénéchaux* who also possessed the secret and therefore guaranteed the Priory's security, especially when he and Sophie weren't even in touch? *Why involve me . . . a total stranger?*

The answers were apparently going to have to wait. The sound of the slowing engine caused them both to look up. Gravel crunched beneath the tyres and the truck slowed down to a crawl, lurching over unexpectedly rough terrain. Sophie shot Langdon an uneasy look, hastily closing the cryptex box and latching it. Langdon slipped his jacket back on.

When the truck came to a stop, the engine remained idling as the locks on the rear doors began to turn. When the doors swung open, Langdon was surprised to see they were parked in a wooded area, well off the road. Vernet stepped into view, a strained look in his eye.

In his hand, he held a pistol.

# Chapter 40

André Vernet looked awkward with a gun in his hand, but his eyes shone with a determination that Langdon sensed would be unwise to test.

'I'm afraid I must insist,' Vernet said, training the weapon on the two of them in the back of the idling truck. 'Set the box down.'

Sophie clutched it to her chest. 'You said you and my grandfather were friends.'

'I have a duty to protect your grandfather's assets,' Vernet replied. 'And that is exactly what I am doing. Now set the box on the floor.' He turned, and Langdon watched the gun barrel swing in his direction. 'Mr Langdon,' Vernet said, 'you will now bring the box over to me. And be aware that I'm asking you because *you* I would not hesitate to shoot.'

Langdon stared at the banker in disbelief. 'Why are you doing this?'

'Why do you imagine?' Vernet snapped, his accented English terse now. 'To protect my client's assets.'

'*We* are your clients now,' Sophie said.

Vernet's visage turned ice-cold. 'Mademoiselle Neveu, I don't know *how* you got that key and account number tonight, but had I known the extent of your crimes, I would never have helped you leave the bank.'

'I told you,' Sophie said, 'we had nothing to do with my grandfather's death!'

Vernet looked at Langdon. 'The radio claims you are wanted not only for the murder of Jacques Saunière but for the murders of three *other* men as well.'

'What?' Langdon was thunderstruck. *Three more murders? The three sénéchaux?* His eyes dropped to the rosewood box. *If the sénéchaux were murdered, Saunière had no choice – he had to transfer the keystone to someone . . .*

'The police can sort it all out when I turn you in,' Vernet said. 'I have got my bank involved too far already. Whatever this box contains, I have no intention of letting it become a piece of catalogued evidence in a police investigation. Mr Langdon, bring me the box.'

Sophie shook her head. 'Don't do it.'

A gunshot roared, and a bullet tore into the wall above Langdon. The reverberation shook the back of the truck as a spent shell clinked on to the floor.

Langdon froze.

Box in hand, he moved across the hold towards the open door. *I've got to do something!* he thought. *I'm about to hand over the Priory keystone!*

Vernet took several steps back, repositioning himself six feet away. 'Place the box beside the door,' he commanded.

Seeing no option, Langdon knelt down and set the rosewood box at the edge of the cargo hold, directly in front of the open door.

'Now stand up.'

Langdon began to stand up but paused, spotting the small spent pistol shell on the floor beside the truck's precision-crafted doorsill. He eyed the metal threshold, then as he stood, he discreetly brushed the shell over the edge on to the narrow ledge that was the door's lower sill. Fully upright now, he stepped backwards.

'Return to the back wall and turn round.'

Langdon obeyed.

Vernet could feel his own heart pounding as he laid the gun down on the bumper, lifted the wooden box with two hands and set it on the ground, immediately grabbing the gun again and aiming it back into the hold. Neither of his prisoners had moved.

*Perfect.* Now all that remained was to lock them in again. He began to heave the heavy metal door closed. It shut with a thud, and Vernet quickly grabbed the bolt, pulling it to the left – but the bolt crunched to an unexpected halt, not lining up with its sleeve. *The door isn't fully closed!* Feeling a surge of panic, Vernet turned to throw his full shoulder into the door, but the door exploded outwards, striking him in the face and sending him reeling back on to the ground, his nose shattering in pain and the gun flying out of his hand.

Moments later, the banker felt a cloud of dirt and exhaust billowing over him and heard the crunch of tyres on gravel. He sat up just in time to see the truck's wide wheelbase fail to navigate a turn. There was a crash as the front bumper clipped a tree. The armoured car lurched away, bumper dragging on the ground. When it reached the paved access road, a shower of sparks lit up the night, trailing behind as it sped away.

Vernet turned his eyes back to the ground where the truck had been parked. Even in the faint moonlight he could see there was nothing there.

The wooden box was gone.

# Chapter 41

Even at a modest sixty kilometres an hour, the dangling front bumper of the armoured truck grated against the deserted suburban road with a grinding roar, spraying sparks up on to the hood.

*We've got to get off the road,* Langdon thought. He could barely even see where they were headed since the truck's lone working headlight had been knocked off-centre and was casting a skewed sidelong beam into the woods beside the country road.

Sophie sat in the passenger seat, staring blankly at the rosewood box on her lap.

'Are you OK?' Langdon asked.

Sophie looked shaken. 'Do you believe him?'

'About the three additional murders? Absolutely. It answers a lot of questions – your grandfather's desperation to pass on the keystone, and the intensity with which Fache is hunting me.'

'No, I meant about Vernet trying to protect his bank.'

Langdon glanced over. 'As opposed to?'

'Taking the keystone for himself. He knew my grandfather. He might have decided he wanted the Grail for himself.'

Langdon shook his head. 'In my experience, there are only two reasons people seek the Grail. Either they believe they are searching for the long-lost Cup of Christ . . .'

'Or?'

'Or they know the truth and are threatened by it. Many groups throughout history have sought to destroy the Grail.'

The silence between them accentuated the sound of the scraping bumper. They had driven a few miles now, and as Langdon watched the cascade of sparks coming off the front of the truck, he made up his mind.

'I'm going to see if I can bend this bumper back.'

Pulling on to the hard shoulder, he brought the truck to a stop.

Silence at last.

As he walked towards the front, Langdon felt surprisingly alert. News of the three additional murders had dire implications. *The Priory has been infiltrated. They are compromised.* It seemed to explain why Saunière might have transferred the keystone to Sophie and Langdon – people *outside* the brotherhood. He examined the truck. Its front end looked worse than he had imagined, the left headlight gone and the right one looking like an eyeball dangling from its socket. He straightened it, and it dislodged again. The only good news was that the front bumper had been torn almost clean off. Langdon gave it a hard kick and it broke off with a crash.

*We need help,* he decided. *Professional help.*

In the world of the Holy Grail and the Priory of Sion, he knew of only one man . . .

Inside the armoured car, Sophie opened the rosewood box and eyed the cryptex's dials. *Think, Sophie! Use your head. Grand-père is trying to tell you something!*

*A proof of merit.* She could feel her grandfather's hand at work. Lifting the cryptex out, she ran her fingers over the dials. *Five letters.* She rotated the dials one by one. The mechanism moved smoothly as she aligned the discs so that her chosen letters lined up between the cryptex's two brass alignment arrows at either end of the cylinder. The dials now spelled a five-letter word that Sophie knew was absurdly obvious.

G-R-A-I-L

Gently, she held the two ends of the cylinder and pulled. The cryptex didn't budge. She heard the vinegar inside gurgle and stopped pulling. Then she tried again.

V-I-N-C-I

Again, no movement.

V-O-U-T-E

Nothing. The cryptex remained locked solid.

As the armoured truck accelerated again, Langdon was pleased how much more smoothly it drove. 'Do you know how to get to Versailles?'

Sophie eyed him. 'Sightseeing?'

'No, I have a plan. There's a religious historian I know who lives near Versailles. I can't remember exactly where, but we can look it up. I've been to his estate a few times. His name is Leigh Teabing. He's a former British Royal Historian.'

'And he lives in Paris?'

'Teabing's lifelong passion is the Grail – about fifteen years ago, he moved to France to search churches here in hopes of finding it. He may be able to help us figure out how to open the cryptex and what to do with the contents.'

Sophie's eyes were wary. 'Can you trust him?'

'Trust him to what? Not steal the information?'

'And not to turn us in.'

'I don't intend to tell him we're wanted by the police. I'm hoping he'll take us in until we can sort all this out.'

'Robert, has it occurred to you that every television in France is probably broadcasting our pictures?' Sophie asked. 'Is this man a good enough friend? Fache will definitely be offering a reward for information.'

Langdon laughed. 'Believe me, money is the last thing this guy needs.' Leigh Teabing was wealthy in the way small countries were wealthy. A descendant of Britain's first Duke of Lancaster, Teabing had got his money the old-fashioned way – he'd inherited it. His estate outside Paris was a seventeenth-century palace with two private lakes.

Langdon had first met Teabing several years ago through the BBC, when he had been chosen as one of three historians to back up Teabing's approach for a documentary about the Holy Grail. The BBC had flown him to Teabing's Paris estate for the filming.

'Robert,' Sophie asked, 'you're *certain* we can trust this man?'

'Absolutely. We're colleagues, he doesn't need money, and I happen to know he dislikes the French authorities – the government taxes him at absurd rates because he bought a historic landmark. He'll be in no hurry to cooperate with Fache.'

Sophie stared out at the dark roadway. 'If we go to him, how much do you want to tell him?'

'Believe me, Leigh Teabing knows more about the Priory of Sion and the Holy Grail than anyone on earth.'

Sophie eyed him. 'More than my grandfather?'

'I meant more than anyone *outside* the brotherhood.'

'How do you know Teabing isn't a member of the brotherhood?'

'Teabing has spent his life trying to broadcast the truth about the Holy Grail. The Priory's oath is to keep its true nature hidden.'

'Sounds to me like a conflict.'

Langdon understood her concerns. 'We don't need to tell Teabing about the keystone immediately. Or at all, even. His house will give us a place to hide and think, and maybe when we talk to him about the Grail, you'll start to have an idea why your grandfather gave this to you.'

'*Us,*' Sophie reminded him.

Langdon felt a humble pride and wondered yet again why Saunière had included him.

'Do you know more or less where Mr Teabing lives?' Sophie asked.

'His estate is called Château Villette.'

Sophie turned with an incredulous expression. '*The* Château Villette?'

'That's the one. You know the estate?'

'I've passed it. It's about twenty minutes from here – which will give you enough time to tell me what the Holy Grail *really* is. Please explain this to me.'

Langdon paused. 'I'll tell you at Teabing's. He and I specialize in different areas of the legend, so between the two of us, you'll get the full story.' He smiled. 'Besides, the Grail has been Teabing's life, so hearing the story of the Holy Grail from Leigh Teabing will be like hearing the Theory of Relativity from Einstein himself.'

'Let's hope Leigh doesn't mind middle-of-the-night visitors.'

'For the record, it's *Sir* Leigh.' Langdon had made that mistake only once.

Sophie looked over. 'You're kidding, right?'

Langdon gave an awkward smile. 'We're on a Grail quest, Sophie. Who better to help us than a knight?'

# Chapter 42

The sprawling 185-acre estate of Château Villette was one of Paris's most significant historical châteaus. Built in 1668, it was more of a modest castle than a mansion, fondly known as *la Petite Versailles*.

Langdon brought the armoured truck to a shuddering stop at the foot of the mile-long driveway. Beyond the imposing security gate, Sir Leigh Teabing's residence rose on a meadow in the distance. The sign on the gate was in English: PRIVATE PROPERTY. NO TRESPASSING. Langdon leaned across Sophie to press the intercom button. A telephone began ringing over the small speaker, and finally an irritated French accent spoke. 'Château Villette. Who is calling?'

'This is Robert Langdon,' Langdon called out. 'I'm a friend of Sir Leigh Teabing. I need his help.'

'My master is sleeping. What is your business with him?'

'It is a private matter. One of great interest to him. It's quite important.'

'As is Sir Leigh's sleep. If you are a friend, then you are aware he is in poor health.'

Sir Leigh Teabing had suffered from polio as a child and now wore leg braces and walked with crutches, but Langdon had found him such a lively and colourful man on his last visit that it hardly seemed a disability. 'If you would, please tell him I have uncovered new information about the Grail. Information that cannot wait until morning.'

Langdon and Sophie waited, the truck idling loudly.

A full minute passed.

Finally, someone spoke. 'My good man, I dare say you are still on Harvard Standard Time.' The voice was crisp and light.

Langdon grinned, recognizing the thick English accent. 'Leigh, my apologies for waking you at this obscene hour.'

'My manservant tells me that not only are you in Paris, but you speak of the Grail.'

'I thought that might get you out of bed.'

'And so it has.'

'Any chance you'd open the gate for an old friend?'

'Those who seek the truth are more than friends. They are brothers. Indeed I will open the gate,' Teabing proclaimed. 'But first I must confirm your heart is true. A test of your honour. You will answer three questions.'

Langdon groaned, whispering to Sophie, 'Bear with me here. Sir Leigh is something of a character.'

'Your first question,' Teabing declared, his tone Herculean. 'Shall I serve you coffee or tea?'

Langdon knew Teabing's feelings about the American love of coffee. 'Tea,' he replied. 'Earl Grey.'

'Excellent. Your second question. Milk or sugar?'

Langdon hesitated.

'*Milk,*' Sophie whispered in his ear. 'I think the English always put milk in their tea.'

'*Milk,*' Langdon said.

Silence.

*Wait!* Langdon now recalled the drink he had been served on his last visit and realized this question was a trick. '*Lemon!*' he declared. 'Earl Grey with *lemon.*'

'Indeed.' Teabing sounded deeply amused now. 'And finally, I must make the most grave of enquiries.' He paused and then spoke in a solemn tone. 'In which year did a Harvard oarsman last outrow an Oxford man at Henley?'

Langdon had no idea, but he could imagine only one reason the question had been asked. 'Surely such a travesty has never occurred.'

The gate clicked open. 'Your heart is true, my friend. You may pass.'

# Chapter 43

As Langdon and Sophie drove up the winding, poplar-lined driveway towards the house, Sophie could feel her muscles relaxing.

They turned into the sweeping circular driveway, and Château Villette came into view on their right. Three storeys tall and at least sixty yards long, the building had grey stone facing illuminated by outside spotlights. It was surrounded by immaculately landscaped gardens. The inside lights were just now coming on.

Langdon pulled into a parking area nestled in the evergreens. 'No reason to risk being spotted from the road,' he said. 'Or having Leigh wonder why we arrived in a wrecked armoured truck.'

Sophie nodded. 'What do we do with the cryptex? If Leigh sees it, he'll certainly want to know what it is.'

'Not to worry,' Langdon said, removing his jacket as he stepped out of the truck. He wrapped the tweed coat around the box and held the bundle in his arms like a baby.

Sophie looked dubious. 'Subtle.'

La Pyramide Inversée at the Louvre, from above

Arago Medallions

LEFT:
*Mona Lisa*
by Leonardo da Vinci

BELOW LEFT:
*The Madonna of the Rocks*
by Leonardo da Vinci

BELOW RIGHT:
*The Virgin of the Rocks*
by Leonardo da Vinci

*The Garden of Earthly Delights* by Hieronymus Bosch

*Les Dossiers Secrets*

Caesar Box Codes

**Code:**
TIARHSEBIASOSCAX

Broken into four equal lines:

```
T  I  A  R
H  S  E  B
I  A  S  O
S  C  A  X
```

Each column read vertically:

```
T │ I │ A │ R
H │ S │ E │ B
I │ S │ A │ S
S │ C │ A │ X
```

**Deciphered code:**
THIS IS A CAESAR BOX

Château Villette

*The Last Supper* by Leonardo da Vinci

Knights' Effigies, Temple Church

### Hebrew Alphabet

| | |
|---|---|
| א | ALEPH |
| ב | BEYT |
| ג | GIMEL |
| ד | DALET |
| ה | HEY |
| ו | VAV |
| ז | ZAYIN |
| ח | HHET |
| ט | TET |
| י | YUD |
| כ | KAPH |
| ל | LAMED |
| מ | MEM |
| נ | NUN |
| ס | SAMECH |
| ע | AYIN |
| פ | PEY |
| צ | TSADEY |
| ק | QUPH |
| ר | RESH |
| ש,שׂ | SHIN,SIN |
| ת | TAV |

Altar, Saint-Sulpice

Rose Line, Saint-Sulpice

Obelisk, Saint-Sulpice

Westminster Abbey

Sir Isaac Newton Monument

Rosslyn Chapel

Encoded Ceiling, Rosslyn Chapel

Pillars of Rosslyn Chapel (Boaz and Jachin)

'Teabing never answers his own door – so I'll find somewhere inside to stash this before he joins us.'

The pathway to the main entrance was hand-laid cobblestone. It curved to a door of carved oak and cherry with a brass knocker the size of a grapefruit. Before Sophie could knock, however, the door swung open and a prim and elegant butler stood before them, making final adjustments to the white tie and tuxedo he had apparently just donned. He looked to be about fifty, with an austere expression that left little doubt he was unamused by their presence here.

'Sir Leigh will be down presently,' he declared, his accent thick French. 'He is dressing. He prefers not to greet visitors while wearing only a nightshirt. May I take your coat?' He scowled at the bunched-up tweed in Langdon's arms.

'Thank you, I'm fine.'

'Of course you are. Right this way, please.'

The butler guided them through a lush marble foyer into an exquisitely adorned drawing room, softly lit by tassel-draped Victorian lamps. Against the far wall, flanked between two glistening suits of armour, was a rough-hewn fireplace large enough to roast an ox. Walking to the hearth, the butler knelt and touched a match to a pre-laid arrangement of oak logs and kindling. A fire quickly crackled to life. The butler stood, straightening his jacket. 'His master requests that you make yourselves at home.' With that, he departed, leaving Langdon and Sophie alone.

Langdon unwrapped the cryptex from his coat, walked over to

a velvet divan and slid the wooden box deep underneath it, well out of sight. Then, shaking out his jacket, he put it back on and smiled at Sophie as he sat down directly over the stashed treasure.

Sophie took a seat beside him. As she stared into the growing fire, enjoying the warmth, she had the sensation that her grandfather would have loved this room.

She pictured the cryptex under the divan and wondered if Leigh Teabing would have any idea how to open it. *Or if we even should ask him.*

'Sir Robert!' a voice bellowed somewhere behind them. 'I see you travel with a maiden.'

Langdon stood up, and Sophie jumped to her feet as well. The voice had come from the top of a curled staircase that snaked up to the shadows of the first floor. 'Good evening,' Langdon called up. 'Sir Leigh, may I present Sophie Neveu.'

'An honour.' Teabing moved into the light.

'Thank you for having us,' Sophie said, now seeing the man wore metal leg braces and used crutches. He was coming down one stair at a time. 'I realize it's quite late.'

Portly and ruby-faced, Sir Leigh had bushy red hair and jovial hazel eyes that seemed to twinkle as he spoke. He wore pleated trousers and a roomy silk shirt under a paisley waistcoat. He walked over to them and extended a hand to Langdon. 'Robert, you've lost weight.'

Langdon grinned. 'And you've found some.'

Teabing laughed heartily, patting his rotund belly. Turning

now to Sophie, he gently took her hand, bowing his head slightly, breathing lightly on her fingers and diverting his eyes. 'M'lady.'

Sophie glanced at Langdon, feeling she'd somehow stepped back in time.

The butler now entered carrying a tea service, which he arranged on a table in front of the fireplace.

'This is Rémy Legaludec,' Teabing said, 'my manservant.'

The slender butler gave a stiff nod and disappeared yet again.

'Rémy is from Lyon,' Teabing whispered. 'But he does sauces quite nicely.'

Langdon looked amused. 'I would have thought you'd import an English staff.'

'Good heavens, no! I would not wish an English chef on anyone except the French tax collectors.' Teabing looked at Langdon. 'Something has happened. You both look shaken.'

Langdon nodded. 'We've had an interesting night, Leigh.'

'No doubt. You tell me, is this indeed about the Grail, or did you simply say that because you know it is the one topic for which I would rouse myself in the middle of the night?'

*A little of both,* Sophie thought, picturing the cryptex hidden beneath the couch.

'Leigh,' Langdon said, 'we'd like to talk to you about the Priory of Sion.'

Teabing's bushy eyebrows arched with intrigue. 'The keepers? So this is indeed about the Grail. You say you come with information? Something new, Robert?'

'Perhaps. We're not quite sure. We might have a better idea if we could get some information from you first.'

Teabing wagged his finger. 'Ever the wily American. Very well. I am at your service. What is it I can tell you?'

Langdon sighed. 'I was hoping you would be kind enough to explain to Ms Neveu the true nature of the Holy Grail.'

Teabing looked stunned. 'She doesn't *know*?' He turned eagerly to Sophie. 'How much *do* you know, my dear?'

Sophie quickly outlined what Langdon had explained earlier – the Priory of Sion, the Knights Templar, the Sangreal documents, and how the Holy Grail was not a cup . . . but rather something far more powerful.

'That's *all*?' Teabing fired Langdon a scandalized look, then locked Sophie in his twinkling gaze. 'Trust me, you will never forget what I am about to tell you . . .'

Meanwhile, outside the Château Villette, hidden in the undercarriage of the armoured truck, a tiny transponder blinked into life.

# Chapter 44

Sir Leigh Teabing was beaming as he awkwardly paced before the open fire, his leg braces clicking on the stone hearth.

'The Holy Grail,' he said, his voice sermonic. 'Most people ask me only *where* it is. I fear that is a question I may never answer.' He turned and looked directly at Sophie. 'However . . . the far more relevant question is this: *What* is the Holy Grail? To fully appreciate that, we must first understand the Bible. How well do you know the New Testament?'

Sophie shrugged. 'Not at all, really. I was brought up by a man who worshipped Leonardo da Vinci.'

Teabing looked both startled and pleased. 'An enlightened soul. Superb! Then you must be aware that Leonardo was one of the keepers of the secret of the Holy Grail. And he hid clues in his art.'

'Robert told me as much, yes.'

'And Da Vinci's views on the New Testament?'

'I have no idea.'

Teabing's eyes turned mirthful as he motioned to the

bookshelf across the room. 'Robert, would you mind? On the bottom shelf.'

Langdon went over to the bookcase and found a large art book, brought it back and set it down on the table between them. Teabing flipped open the heavy tome and pointed inside the end cover to a series of quotations. 'From one of Da Vinci's notebooks,' he said, indicating one quote in particular. 'I think you'll find this relevant to our discussion.'

Sophie read the words.

> *Many have made a trade of delusions and false miracles,*
> *deceiving the stupid multitude.*
> – Leonardo da Vinci

'Here's another,' Teabing said, pointing to a different quote.

> *Blinding ignorance does mislead us. O! Wretched*
> *mortals, open your eyes!*
> – Leonardo da Vinci

Sophie felt a little chill. 'Da Vinci is talking about the Bible?'

Teabing nodded. 'Leonardo's feelings about the Bible relate directly to the Holy Grail. In fact, Da Vinci painted the true Grail – which I will show you in a moment. But first we must speak of the Bible.' He smiled. 'And everything you need to know about the Bible can be summed up by this: the Bible is a product of *man*, my dear. Not of God. The Bible did not fall magically from the clouds. *Man* created it, and it has evolved through countless translations, additions and revisions. History has never had a definitive version.'

'OK.'

Teabing paused to sip his tea and then placed the cup back on the mantel. 'More than *eighty* gospels were considered for the New Testament, and yet only a relative few were chosen for inclusion – Matthew, Mark, Luke and John among them.'

'Who chose which gospels to include?' Sophie asked.

'Aha!' Teabing burst in with enthusiasm. 'The true irony of Christianity! The Bible, as we know it today, was collated by the pagan Roman emperor Constantine the Great.'

'I thought Constantine was a Christian,' Sophie said.

'Hardly,' Teabing scoffed. 'He was a lifelong pagan who was baptized on his deathbed, too weak to protest. In Constantine's day, Rome's official religion was sun worship, and Constantine was its head priest. Unfortunately for him, a growing religious turmoil was gripping Rome as, three centuries after the crucifixion of Jesus Christ, the number of those who followed Christ's teachings was increasing rapidly. The conflict between the Christians and the pagans was so great that it threatened to split Rome in two. Constantine decided something had to be done, so in AD 325, he decided to unify Rome under a single religion. Christianity.'

Sophie was surprised. 'Why would a pagan emperor choose *Christianity* as the official religion?'

Teabing chuckled. 'Constantine was a very good businessman.

He could see that Christianity was on the rise, and he simply backed the winning horse. Historians still marvel at the brilliance with which Constantine converted the sun-worshipping pagans to Christianity. By fusing pagan symbols, dates and rituals into the growing Christian tradition, he created a kind of combined religion that everyone was happy with.'

'It's called transmogrification,' Langdon said. 'The remnants of pagan religion in Christian symbols are undeniable. Egyptian sun discs became the haloes of Catholic saints. Pictograms of Isis nursing her son Horus – a miraculous conception – became the blueprint for our modern images of the Virgin Mary nursing Baby Jesus. And virtually all the elements of the Catholic ritual: the mitre, the altar, Holy Communion – bread and wine as the body and blood of Christ – were taken directly from earlier pagan rituals.'

Teabing groaned. 'Don't get an expert on symbols started. Nothing in Christianity is original. Even Christianity's weekly holy day was stolen from the pagans.'

'What do you mean?'

'Originally,' Langdon said, 'Christianity honoured the Jewish Sabbath of Saturday, but Constantine shifted it to coincide with the pagan's veneration day of the sun.' He paused, grinning. 'To this day, most churchgoers attend services on Sunday morning with no idea that they are there on account of the pagan sun god's weekly tribute – Sunday.'

Sophie's head was spinning. 'And all of this relates to the Grail?'

'Indeed,' Teabing said. 'During this fusion of the two

religions – Christianity and paganism – Constantine decided that he needed to strengthen the new Christian tradition, so he held a famous meeting known as the Council of Nicaea. Here, they debated and voted upon lots of different aspects of Christianity, including the date of Easter, the role of the bishops, the rituals – like baptism – and, of course, the *divinity* of Jesus.'

'I don't follow. His divinity?'

'My dear,' Teabing declared, 'until that moment in history, Jesus was viewed by His followers as a mortal prophet . . . a great and powerful man, but a *man* nonetheless. A mortal.'

'Not the Son of God?'

'Right,' Teabing said. 'Jesus's establishment as the Son of God was officially proposed and voted on by the Council of Nicaea.'

'Hold on. You're saying Jesus's divinity was the result of a *vote*?'

'Quite a close vote at that,' Teabing added. 'Nonetheless, by officially endorsing Jesus as the Son of God, Constantine turned Jesus into a deity. This not only put a stop to further pagan challenges to Christianity, but now the followers of Christ were able to redeem themselves *only* if they became members of the established sacred channel – the Roman Catholic Church.'

Sophie glanced at Langdon, and he gave her a soft nod of agreement.

'It was all about power,' Teabing continued. 'Christ as Messiah meant that Church and state worked together. Many scholars claim that the early Church literally *stole* Jesus from His original followers, hijacking His human message to expand their own power. I've written several books on the topic.'

'And I assume devout Christians send you hate mail on a daily basis?'

'Why would they?' Teabing countered. 'The vast majority of educated Christians know the history of their faith. Jesus was indeed a great and powerful man, and nobody is saying he was a fraud, or denying that He walked the earth and inspired millions to better lives. All we are saying is that Constantine took advantage of Christ's influence and importance. And in doing so, he shaped the way we see Christianity today.'

Sophie glanced at the art book before her, eager to move on and see the Da Vinci painting of the Holy Grail.

'The twist is this,' Teabing said, talking faster now. 'Constantine's upgrade of Jesus's status from man to Son of God took place almost four centuries *after* His death, so there were thousands of documents – *gospels* – already in existence that told the story of His life as a *mortal* man. To rewrite the history books, Constantine knew he would need a bold stroke. From this sprang a very important moment in Christian history.' Teabing paused, eyeing Sophie. 'Constantine paid for a new Bible, which left out any gospels that spoke of Christ's *human* traits and embellished those that made Him godlike. The rejected gospels were outlawed, gathered up and burned.'

'An interesting note,' Langdon added. 'The word *heretic* derives from that moment in history. The Latin word *haereticus* means "choice". Those who "chose" the original history of Christ were the world's first *heretics*.'

'Fortunately for historians,' Teabing said, 'some of the gospels that Constantine attempted to destroy managed to survive. The Dead Sea Scrolls were found in the 1950s hidden in a cave in the Judaean desert. And, of course, the Coptic Scrolls in 1945 at Nag Hammadi in Egypt. These documents speak of Christ's ministry in very human terms – *and* tell the true Grail story. The Vatican, of course, tried very hard to suppress the release of these scrolls. And why wouldn't they? The scrolls tell us that the modern Bible was put together by men who wanted power.'

'And yet,' Langdon went on, 'it's important to remember that the Church's attempt to suppress these documents comes from a sincere belief in their view of Christ. The Vatican is made up of deeply pious men who truly believe these other documents could only be false testimony.'

Teabing chuckled as he eased himself into a chair opposite Sophie. 'Robert is right when he says that the modern clergy believe these other gospels are contrived. That's understandable. Constantine's Bible has been their truth for centuries.'

'What he means,' Langdon said, 'is that we worship the gods of our fathers.'

'What I mean,' Teabing countered, 'is that almost everything our fathers taught us about Christ is *false*. As are the stories about the Holy Grail.' He reached for the art book and flipped the pages towards the centre. 'And finally, before I show you Da Vinci's paintings of the Holy Grail, I'd like you to take a quick look at this.' He opened the book to a colourful graphic that spanned both full pages. 'I assume you recognize this fresco?'

*He's kidding, right?* Sophie was staring at *The Last Supper*, Da

Vinci's legendary painting in which Jesus and His disciples were portrayed at the moment when Jesus announced one of them would betray Him. 'I recognize this, yes.'

'Then perhaps you would indulge me in a little game? Close your eyes if you would.'

Uncertain, Sophie closed her eyes.

'Where is Jesus sitting?' Teabing asked.

'In the centre.'

'Good. And what food are He and His disciples breaking and eating?'

'Bread.' *Obviously.*

'Superb. And what drink?'

'Wine. They drank wine.'

'Great. And one final question. How many wineglasses are on the table?'

Sophie paused, realizing it was a trick question. 'One cup,' she said slowly. 'The chalice.' *The Cup of Christ. The Holy Grail.* 'Jesus passed a single chalice of wine, just as modern Christians do at Communion.'

Teabing sighed. 'Open your eyes.'

She did. Teabing was grinning smugly as Sophie looked down at the painting, seeing to her astonishment that *everyone* at the table had a glass of wine, including Christ. Thirteen cups. Moreover, the cups were tiny, stemless and made of glass. There was no chalice in the painting. No Holy Grail.

Teabing's eyes twinkled. 'Oddly, Da Vinci appears to have

forgotten to paint the Cup of Christ.' He paused. 'This fresco, in fact, is the entire key to the Holy Grail mystery.'

Sophie scanned the work eagerly. 'Are you saying that *The Last Supper* tells us what the Grail really is?'

'Not *what* it is,' Teabing whispered. 'But rather *who* it is. The Holy Grail is not a thing. It is, in fact . . . a *person*.'

# Chapter 45

Sophie stared at Teabing a long moment and then turned to Langdon. 'The Holy Grail is a person?'

Langdon nodded. 'A woman, in fact.'

'Robert, perhaps this is the moment for you to clarify?' Teabing went to a nearby end table, found a piece of paper and laid it in front of Langdon.

Langdon pulled a pen from his pocket. 'Sophie, I assume you are familiar with the modern icons for male and female.' He drew the common male symbol and female symbol.

'These,' he said quietly, 'are not the original symbols for male and female. These were ancient symbols for the planet-god Mars and planet-goddess Venus. The original symbols are far simpler.' Langdon drew another icon on the paper.

'This symbol is the original icon for *male*,' he told her. 'The female symbol, as you might imagine, is the exact opposite.' He drew another symbol on the page. 'This is called the chalice.'

Sophie glanced up, looking surprised.

Langdon could see she had made the connection. 'The chalice,' he said, 'resembles a cup or vessel and, more important, it resembles the shape of a woman's womb.' He looked directly at her now. 'Sophie, legend tells us the Holy Grail is a chalice – a cup. But the Grail's description as a *chalice* is actually an allegory to protect the true nature of the Holy Grail. That is to say, the legend uses the chalice as a *metaphor* for something far more important.'

'A woman,' Sophie said.

'Exactly.' Langdon smiled. 'The Grail is literally the ancient symbol for womanhood, and the *Holy* Grail represents the sacred feminine and the goddess, which of course has now been lost, erased by the Church. The power of the female and her ability to produce life was once very sacred, but it posed a threat to the rise of a Church headed by men. It was *man*, not God, who created the concept of Original Sin, whereby Eve tasted of the apple in the Garden of Eden and caused the downfall of the human race. Woman, once the sacred giver of life, became the enemy.'

'I should add,' Teabing chimed in, 'that this concept of woman as life-bringer was the foundation of ancient religion. Childbirth was mystical and powerful. Sadly, Christian philosophy decided to ignore this and make *man* the Creator. The Book of Genesis in the Old Testament of the Bible tells us that Eve was created from Adam's rib – woman as an offshoot of man. And a sinful one at that. Genesis was the beginning of the end for the goddess.'

'The Grail,' Langdon said, 'is a symbol of the lost goddess. When Christianity came along, the old pagan religions did not die easily. Knights who claimed to be on a quest for the Holy Grail, "searching for the chalice", were speaking in code as a way to protect themselves from a Church that burned non-believers.'

Sophie shook her head. 'I'm sorry, when you said the Holy Grail was a person, I thought you meant it was an actual person.'

'It is,' Langdon said.

'And not just *any* person,' Teabing blurted, clambering excitedly to his feet. 'But a woman who carried with her a secret so powerful that, if revealed, it threatened to destroy the very foundation of Christianity!'

Sophie looked overwhelmed. 'Is this woman well known in history?'

Teabing collected his crutches and motioned down the hall. 'If we adjourn to the study, my friends, it would be my honour to show you Da Vinci's painting of her.'

Two rooms away, in the kitchen, Rémy Legaludec stood in silence before a television. The TV was showing photos of a man and woman . . . the same two individuals to whom he had just served tea.

# Chapter 46

Collet's cellular phone rang. It was the command post at the Louvre.

'We just got a tip. We have the exact location where Langdon and Neveu are hiding. I have an address in the suburbs. Somewhere near Versailles.'

'Does Captain Fache know?' Collet asked.

'Not yet. He's busy on an important call.'

'I'm on my way. Have him call me as soon as he's free.' Collet took down the address and jumped into his car. He radioed the five cars accompanying him. 'No sirens, men. Langdon can't know we're coming.'

Thirty miles away, a black Audi pulled off a rural road and parked in the shadows on the edge of a field. Silas got out and peered through the rungs of the wrought-iron fence that encircled the vast compound before him. He gazed up the long moonlit slope to the château in the distance.

The downstairs lights were all ablaze. *Odd for this hour,* Silas thought, smiling. The information the Teacher had given him was obviously accurate. *I will not leave this house without the keystone,* he vowed. *I will not fail the bishop and the Teacher.*

Checking the ammunition in his pistol, Silas heaved himself up and over the fence, dropping to the ground on the other side, and began the long trek up the grassy slope.

# Chapter 47

Teabing's 'study' was like no study Sophie had ever seen. The boundless tile floor was dotted with clustered islands of worktables buried beneath books, artwork, artefacts and a surprising amount of electronic gear – computers, projectors, microscopes, photocopiers and flatbed scanners.

'I converted the ballroom,' Teabing said, looking sheepish as he shuffled into the room. 'I have little occasion to dance.'

Sophie felt as if the entire night had become some kind of twilight zone where nothing was as she expected. 'This is all for your work?'

'Learning the truth has become my life's love,' Teabing said. 'And the Sangreal is my favourite mistress.'

*The Holy Grail is a woman,* Sophie thought, her mind full of ideas that seemed to make no sense. 'You said you had a *picture* of this woman who you claim is the Holy Grail.'

'Yes, but it is not I who *claims* she is the Grail. Christ Himself made that claim.'

'Which one is the painting?' Sophie asked, scanning the walls.

'Hmmm . . .' Teabing made a show of seeming to have forgotten. 'The Holy Grail. The Sangreal. The chalice.' He wheeled suddenly and pointed to the far wall. On it hung an eight-foot-long print of *The Last Supper*, the same exact image Sophie had just been looking at. 'There she is!'

Sophie was certain she had missed something. 'That's the same painting you just showed me.'

He winked. 'I know, but the enlargement is so much more exciting.'

Sophie turned to Langdon for help. 'I'm lost.'

Langdon smiled. 'As it turns out, the Holy Grail *does* indeed make an appearance in *The Last Supper*. Leonardo included her prominently.'

'Hold on,' Sophie said. 'You told me the Holy Grail is a *woman*. *The Last Supper* is a painting of thirteen men.'

'Is it?' Teabing arched his eyebrows. 'Take a closer look.'

Uncertain, Sophie made her way closer to the painting, scanning the thirteen figures – Jesus Christ in the middle, six disciples on His left, and six on His right. 'They're all men,' she confirmed.

'Oh?' Teabing said. 'How about the one seated in the place of honour, at the right hand of the Lord?'

Sophie examined the figure to Jesus's immediate right, focusing in. As she studied the person's face and body, a wave of astonishment rose within her. The individual had flowing red hair, delicate folded hands and the hint of a bosom. It was, without a doubt . . . female.

'That's a woman!' Sophie exclaimed.

Teabing was laughing. 'Surprise, surprise. Believe me, it's no mistake. Leonardo was skilled at painting the difference between the sexes.'

Sophie could not take her eyes off the woman beside Christ. *The Last Supper is supposed to be thirteen men. Who is this woman?* She was young and pious-looking, with a demure face, beautiful red hair and hands folded quietly. *This is the woman who single-handedly could crumble the Church?*

'Everyone misses it,' Teabing said. 'We see what we expect to see.'

Sophie moved closer to the image. 'Who is she?' she asked.

'That, my dear,' Teabing replied, 'is Mary Magdalene.'

Sophie turned. 'The prostitute?'

Teabing drew a short breath, as if the word had injured him personally. 'Magdalene was no such thing. That opinion is the legacy of a smear campaign launched by the early Church. The Church needed to defame Mary Magdalene in order to cover up her dangerous secret – her role as the Holy Grail.'

'Her *role*?'

'As I mentioned,' Teabing clarified, 'the early Church needed to convince the world that the mortal prophet Jesus was a *divine* being. Therefore any gospels that described *earthly* aspects of Jesus's life had to be omitted from the Bible. Unfortunately, one particularly troubling earthly theme kept turning up in the gospels. Mary Magdalene.' He paused. 'More specifically, her marriage to Jesus Christ.'

'I beg your pardon?' Sophie's eyes moved to Langdon and then back to Teabing.

'It's a matter of historical record,' Teabing said, 'and Da Vinci was certainly aware of that fact. *The Last Supper* practically shouts at the viewer that Jesus and Magdalene were a couple.'

Sophie glanced back to the fresco.

'Notice that Jesus and Magdalene are clothed as mirror images of one another.' Teabing pointed to the two individuals in the centre.

Sophie was mesmerized. Even the colour of their clothes showed this. Jesus wore a red robe and blue cloak; Mary Magdalene wore a blue robe and red cloak. *Yin and yang. The female and the male.*

'Venturing into the more bizarre,' Teabing said, 'note that Jesus and His bride appear to be joined at the hip and are leaning away from one another as if to create a particular shape to the space between them.'

Even before Teabing traced the contour for her, Sophie saw it. It was the same symbol Langdon had drawn earlier for the Grail, the chalice and the female womb.

'Finally,' Teabing said, 'if you view Jesus and Magdalene not as people but as elements of Da Vinci's composition of the painting, you will see another obvious shape leap out at you.' He paused. 'A *letter* of the alphabet.'

Sophie saw it at once. In fact, it was suddenly all she could see: the unquestionable outline of an enormous, flawlessly formed letter M.

She weighed the information. 'I'll admit, the hidden M is

intriguing – although I assume nobody is claiming it is proof of Jesus's marriage to Magdalene.'

'No, no,' Teabing said, going to a nearby table of books. 'As I said earlier, the marriage of Jesus and Mary Magdalene is part of the historical record.' He began pawing through his book collection. 'Moreover, Jesus as a married man makes much more sense than our standard biblical view of Jesus as single.'

'Why?' Sophie asked.

'Because Jesus was a Jew,' Langdon said, 'and at that time it was virtually forbidden for a Jewish man to be unmarried. Every Jewish father was obliged to find a suitable wife for his son. If Jesus were not married, at least one of the Bible's gospels should have mentioned it and given some reason for His unnatural state of bachelorhood.'

Teabing located a huge book and pulled it towards him across the table. The leather-bound edition was poster-sized, like a huge atlas. The cover read *The Gnostic Gospels*. He heaved it open, and Langdon and Sophie joined him. Sophie could see it contained photographs of what appeared to be magnified passages of ancient documents – tattered papyrus with handwritten text. She did not recognize the ancient language, but there were typed translations on the facing pages.

'These are photocopies of the scrolls, which I mentioned earlier,' Teabing said. 'The earliest Christian records – which do not match up with the gospels in the Bible.' Flipping towards the middle of the book, he pointed to a passage. 'The Gospel of Philip is always a good place to start.'

Sophie read the passage:

> *And the companion of the Saviour is Mary Magdalene.*
> *Christ loved her more than all the disciples and used to*
> *kiss her often on her mouth. The rest of the disciples were*
> *offended by it and expressed disapproval. They said to*
> *him, 'Why do you love her more than all of us?'*

The words surprised Sophie, and yet they hardly seemed conclusive. 'It says nothing of marriage.'

Teabing smiled, pointing to the first line. 'The word *companion*, in those days, literally meant spouse.' He flicked through the book and motioned to another passage. 'This is from the Gospel of Mary Magdalene.'

Sophie had not known a gospel existed in Magdalene's words. She read the text:

> *And Peter said, 'Did the Saviour really speak with a*
> *woman without our knowledge? Are we to turn about*
> *and all listen to her? Did he prefer her to us?'*
>
>     *And Levi answered, 'Peter, you have always been hot-*
> *tempered. Now I see you contending against the woman*
> *like an adversary. If the Saviour made her worthy, who*
> *are you indeed to reject her? Surely the Saviour knows her*
> *very well. That is why he loved her more than us.'*

'The woman they are speaking of,' Teabing explained, 'is Mary Magdalene. Peter – Jesus's disciple – is jealous of her.'

'Because Jesus preferred Mary?'

'Not only that. The stakes were far higher. At this point in the gospels, Jesus suspects He will soon be captured and crucified. So He gives Mary Magdalene instructions on how to carry on His Church after He is gone. Peter doesn't want to play second fiddle to a woman.'

Sophie was trying to keep up. 'This is *Saint Peter*, right? The "rock" on which Jesus built His Church.'

'The same, except for one catch. According to these unaltered gospels, it was not *Peter* who Christ told to establish the Christian Church. It was *Mary Magdalene*.'

Sophie looked at Teabing. 'You're saying the Christian Church was to be carried on by a *woman*?'

'That was the plan. Jesus was the original feminist. And Peter had a problem with that,' Langdon said, pointing to *The Last Supper*. 'That's Peter there. You can see that Da Vinci was well aware of how Peter felt about Mary Magdalene.'

Again, Sophie was speechless. In the painting, Peter was leaning menacingly towards Mary Magdalene and slicing his blade-like hand across her neck.

'And here too,' Langdon said, pointing now to the crowd of disciples near Peter. 'A bit ominous, no?'

Sophie squinted and saw a hand emerging from the crowd of disciples. 'Is that hand wielding a *dagger*?'

'Yes. Now count the arms – and you'll see that this hand belongs to . . . no one at all. It's disembodied. Anonymous.'

Sophie was starting to feel overwhelmed. 'I'm sorry, I still don't understand how all of this makes Mary Magdalene the Holy Grail.'

'Aha!' Teabing exclaimed again. 'Therein lies the rub! Few people realize that Mary Magdalene, in addition to being Christ's right hand, was a powerful woman, already part of a royal family.'

'But I was under the impression she was poor.'

Teabing shook his head. 'Magdalene was recast as a prostitute in order to get rid of any evidence of her powerful family ties.'

Sophie found herself again glancing at Langdon, who again nodded. She turned back to Teabing. 'But why would the early Church *care* if Magdalene had royal blood?'

The historian smiled. 'My dear child, it was not Mary Magdalene's royal blood that concerned the Church so much as it was the idea of her with Christ – who *also* had royal blood. He was of the house of David, a descendant of King Solomon – King of the Jews. By marrying Mary, Jesus joined together two royal bloodlines. It was a union with the potential of making a legitimate claim to the throne. Together Jesus and Mary could have restored the line of kings as it was under Solomon.'

Sophie sensed that Teabing was at last getting to the point.

He looked excited now. 'The legend of the Holy Grail is about royal blood. When Grail legend speaks of "the chalice that held the blood of Christ", it speaks, in fact, of Mary Magdalene – the female womb that carried Jesus's royal bloodline.'

The words seemed to echo across the ballroom and back before they fully registered in Sophie's mind. *Mary Magdalene carried the royal bloodline of Jesus Christ?* 'But how could Christ have a bloodline unless . . . ?' She paused and looked at Langdon.

He smiled. 'Unless they had a child.'

Sophie stood transfixed.

'Behold,' Teabing proclaimed, 'the greatest cover-up in human history. Not only was Jesus Christ married, but He was a father. My dear, *Mary Magdalene was the Holy Vessel*. She was the chalice that bore the royal bloodline of Jesus Christ!'

Sophie felt the hairs stand up on her arms. 'And the Sangreal documents held by the Priory?' she asked. 'Do they contain proof that Jesus had a royal bloodline?'

'They do.'

'So the entire Holy Grail legend is all about royal blood?'

'Quite literally,' Teabing said. 'The word *Sangreal* derives from *San Greal* – or Holy Grail. But in its most ancient form, the word *Sangreal* was divided in a different spot.' He wrote on a piece of scrap paper and handed it to her.

She read what he had written.

*Sang Real*

Instantly, Sophie translated it into English.
*Sang Real* literally meant *Royal Blood*.

# Chapter 48

The male receptionist in the lobby of the Opus Dei headquarters in New York City was surprised to hear Bishop Aringarosa's voice on the line. 'Good evening, sir.'

'Have I had any messages?' the bishop demanded, sounding unusually anxious.

'Yes, sir. I'm very glad you called in. You had an urgent phone message about half an hour ago.'

'Yes?' The bishop sounded relieved by the news. 'Did the caller leave a name?'

'No, sir, just a number.' The operator relayed it.

'That's a French number, am I right?'

'Yes, sir. Paris. The caller said it was critical you contact him immediately.'

'Thank you. I have been waiting for that call.' Aringarosa quickly severed the connection. *The Teacher* was *trying to reach me,* he thought as the Fiat approached the exit for Rome's airport. *Things must have gone well in Paris tonight.* He felt excited to know he would soon be there. He had a chartered plane waiting for the short flight to France.

He dialled the number and the line began to ring.

A female voice answered. *'Direction Centrale Police Judiciaire.'*

Aringarosa felt himself hesitate. The French police? This was unexpected. 'Ah, yes . . . I was asked to call this number?'

*'Qui êtes-vous?'* the woman said. 'Your *name*, monsieur?'

'Bishop Manuel Aringarosa.'

*'Un moment.'* There was a click on the line.

After a long wait, another man came on, his tone gruff and concerned. 'Bishop, I am glad I finally reached you. You and I have much to discuss.'

# Chapter 49

Sangreal . . . *Sang Real* . . . *San Greal* . . . *Royal Blood* . . . *Holy Grail*.
It was all intertwined.

*The Holy Grail is Mary Magdalene . . . the mother of the royal bloodline of Jesus Christ*. Sophie stood in the silence of the ballroom and stared at Robert Langdon. The more pieces Langdon and Teabing laid on the table tonight, the more unpredictable this puzzle became.

'As you can see, my dear,' Teabing said, hobbling towards a bookshelf, 'Leonardo is not the only one who has been trying to tell the world the truth about the Holy Grail. The royal bloodline of Jesus Christ has been chronicled in exhaustive detail by scores of historians.' He ran a finger down a row of several dozen books.

Sophie tilted her head and scanned the list of titles:

*THE TEMPLAR REVELATION:*
*Secret Guardians of the True Identity of Christ*

### THE WOMAN WITH THE ALABASTER JAR:
*Mary Magdalene and the Holy Grail*

### THE GODDESS IN THE GOSPELS:
*Reclaiming the Sacred Feminine*

'Here is perhaps the best-known tome,' Teabing said, pulling a tattered hardcover from the stack and handing it to her.

The cover read:

### HOLY BLOOD, HOLY GRAIL:
*The Acclaimed International Bestseller*

Sophie glanced up. 'An international bestseller? I've never heard of it.'

'You were too young then. This caused quite a stir back in the 1980s. The authors brought the idea of Christ's bloodline into the mainstream.'

'What was the Church's reaction?'

'Outrage, of course. But that was to be expected. After all, this was a secret the Vatican had tried to bury in the fourth century. That's part of what the Crusades were about. Gathering and destroying information.'

Sophie glanced at Langdon, who nodded. 'Sophie, the historical evidence supporting this is substantial.'

'You must understand,' Teabing said, 'that the Church had

powerful motivations for such a cover-up. A child of Jesus would undermine all they taught about Christ's divinity – and how the Christian Church was the only way in which people could access the divine and gain entrance to the kingdom of heaven.'

'The five-petal rose,' Sophie said, pointing suddenly to the spine of one of Teabing's books. *The same exact design inlaid on the rosewood box.*

Teabing glanced at Langdon and grinned. 'She has a good eye.' He turned back to Sophie. 'That is the Priory symbol for the Grail, Mary Magdalene. Because her name was forbidden by the Church, Mary Magdalene became secretly known by many pseudonyms – the Chalice, the Holy Grail . . . and the Rose.'

'The point here,' Langdon said, 'is that all of these books support the same historical claim.'

'That Jesus was a father?' Sophie was still uncertain.

'Yes,' Teabing said. 'And that Mary Magdalene was the womb that carried His royal lineage. The Priory of Sion, to this day, still worships Mary Magdalene as the Goddess, the Holy Grail, the Rose and the Divine Mother.'

Sophie again flashed on the ritual she had seen in the basement of her grandfather's house.

'According to the Priory,' Teabing continued, 'Mary Magdalene was pregnant at the time of the crucifixion. For the safety of Christ's unborn child, she had no choice but to flee the Holy Land. With the help of Jesus's trusted uncle, Joseph of Arimathea, Mary Magdalene secretly travelled to France, then known as Gaul. There she found safe refuge in the Jewish community. It was here in France that she gave birth to a daughter. Her name was Sarah.'

Sophie glanced up. 'They actually know the child's *name*?'

'Far more than that. Magdalene and Sarah's lives were scrupulously chronicled. The Jews in France considered Magdalene sacred royalty. Countless scholars of that era chronicled Mary Magdalene's days in France, including the birth of Sarah and the subsequent family tree.'

Sophie was startled. 'There exists a *family tree* of Jesus Christ?'

'Indeed. And it is purportedly one of the cornerstones of the Sangreal documents. A complete genealogy of the early descendants of Christ.'

'But what good is a document showing a family tree?' Sophie asked. 'It's not *proof*. Historians could not possibly confirm whether or not it was true.'

Teabing chuckled. 'The same applies to the Bible.'

'Meaning?'

'Meaning that history is always written by the winners. When two cultures clash, the loser is wiped out, and the winner writes the history books – books that glorify their own cause. The Sangreal documents simply tell the *other* side of the Christ story. In the end, which side of the story you believe becomes a matter of faith and personal exploration, but at least the information has survived. The Sangreal documents include tens of thousands of pages of information – eyewitness accounts describe the treasure as being carried in four enormous trunks. In those trunks are reputed to be the Purist Documents – thousands of pages of unaltered, pre-Constantine documents, written by the early followers of Jesus, revering Him as a wholly human teacher and prophet. Also rumoured to be part of the treasure is the legendary "Q" Document – a manuscript that even the Vatican admits they believe exists. Allegedly, it is a book of Jesus's teachings, possibly written in His own hand.'

'Writings by Christ Himself?'

'Of course,' Teabing said. 'Why wouldn't Jesus have kept a record of His ministry? Most people did in those days. Another explosive document believed to be in the treasure is a manuscript called the Magdalene Diaries – Mary Magdalene's personal account of her relationship with Christ, His crucifixion and her time in France.'

Sophie was silent for a long moment. 'And these four chests of documents were the treasure that the Knights Templar found under Solomon's temple?'

'Exactly. The documents that made the Knights so powerful. Documents that have been the object of countless Grail quests throughout history.'

'But you said the Holy Grail was *Mary Magdalene*. If people are searching for documents, why would you call it a search for the Holy Grail?'

Teabing eyed her, his expression softening. 'Because the hiding place of the Holy Grail includes . . . a sarcophagus.' He spoke more quietly now. 'The quest for the Holy Grail is literally the quest to kneel before the bones of Mary Magdalene. A journey to pray at the feet of the outcast one, the lost sacred feminine.'

Sophie felt an unexpected wonder. 'The hiding place of the Holy Grail is actually . . . a *tomb*?'

Teabing's hazel eyes grew misty. 'It is. A tomb containing the body of Mary Magdalene and the documents that tell the true story of her life. At its heart, the quest for the Holy Grail has always been a quest for the Magdalene – the wronged Queen, entombed with proof of her family's rightful claim to power.'

'Over all these years then, members of the Priory,' Sophie said thoughtfully, 'have protected the Sangreal documents and the tomb of Mary Magdalene?'

'Yes, but the brotherhood also had another, more important duty – to protect the *bloodline* itself.'

The words hung in the huge space, and Sophie felt an odd vibration, as if her bones were reverberating with some new kind of truth. *Descendants of Jesus who survived into modern times.* Her grandfather's voice again was whispering in her ear. *Princess, I must tell you the truth about your family.*

A chill raked her flesh.

*Royal blood.*

She could not imagine.

*Princess Sophie.*

'Sir Leigh?' The manservant's words crackled through the intercom on the wall, and Sophie jumped. 'If you could join me in the kitchen a moment?'

Teabing scowled at the ill-timed intrusion. He went over to the intercom and pressed the button. 'Rémy, as you know, I am busy with my guests. Thank you and goodnight.'

'A word with you before I retire, sir. If you would.'

Teabing looked incredulous. 'It cannot wait until morning?'

'No, sir. My question won't take a minute.'

Teabing rolled his eyes and looked at Langdon and Sophie. 'Sometimes I wonder who is serving whom.' He pressed the button again. 'I'll be right there, Rémy.'

# Chapter 50

*Princess Sophie.*

Sophie felt hollow as she listened to the clicking of Teabing's crutches fade down the hallway. Numb, she turned and faced Langdon in the deserted ballroom. He was already shaking his head as if reading her mind.

'No, Sophie,' he whispered, his eyes reassuring. 'The same thought crossed my mind as soon as you told me your grandfather was in the Priory, and when I realized you said he wanted to tell you a secret about your family. But it's impossible.' Langdon paused. 'Saunière is not a Merovingian name.'

Sophie wasn't sure whether to feel relieved or disappointed. 'And Chauvel?' she asked. *Chauvel* was her mother's maiden name.

Again he shook his head. 'I'm sorry. I know that would have answered some questions for you. Only two direct lines of Merovingians remain. Their family names are Plantard and Saint-Clair. Both families live in hiding, probably protected by the Priory.'

Sophie repeated the names silently in her mind and then shook her head. There was no one in her family named Plantard or Saint-Clair. She turned quietly back to *The Last Supper* and gazed at Mary Magdalene's long red hair and quiet eyes. There was something in the woman's expression that echoed the loss of a loved one. Sophie could feel it too.

The clicking of Teabing's crutches approached in the hallway, his pace unusually brisk.

'You'd better explain yourself, Robert,' he said, his expression stern. 'I fear you have not been honest with me. You're on television, for Christ's sake. Did you know you were wanted by the authorities? For murder!'

'Yes.'

'Then you abused my trust.'

'I'm being framed, Leigh,' Langdon said. 'I didn't kill anyone.'

'Jacques Saunière is dead, and the police say you did it.' Teabing looked saddened. 'Such a contributor to the arts . . .'

'Sir?' The manservant had appeared now, standing behind Teabing in the doorway, his arms crossed. 'Shall I show them out?'

'Allow me.' Teabing hobbled across the study, unlocked a set of wide glass doors and swung them open on to a side lawn. 'Please find your car and leave.'

Sophie did not move. 'We have information about the *clef de voûte. The Priory keystone.*'

Teabing stared at her for several seconds and scoffed derisively. 'A desperate ploy. Robert knows how I've sought it.'

'She's telling the truth,' Langdon said. 'That's why we came to you tonight. To talk to you about the keystone.'

The manservant intervened now. 'Leave, or I shall call the authorities.'

'Leigh,' Langdon whispered, 'we know where it is.'

Teabing's balance seemed to falter.

Rémy now marched stiffly across the room. 'Leave at once! Or I will forcibly –'

'Rémy!' Teabing spun, snapping at his servant. 'Excuse us for a moment.'

The servant's jaw dropped. 'Sir? I must protest. These people are –'

'I'll handle this.' Teabing pointed to the hallway.

After a moment of stunned silence, Rémy skulked out like a banished dog.

In the cool night breeze coming through the open doors, Teabing turned back to Sophie and Langdon, his expression still wary. 'This had better be good. What do you know of the keystone?'

In the thick brush outside Teabing's study, Silas clutched his pistol and gazed through the glass doors. *The keystone is somewhere inside the house.* He could feel it.

Staying in the shadows, he inched closer to the glass, eager to hear what was being said. He would give them five minutes. If they did not reveal where they had placed the keystone, he would have to enter and persuade them with force.

*

Inside the study, Langdon could sense their host's bewilderment.

'Grand Master?' Teabing choked, eyeing Sophie. 'Jacques Saunière?'

Sophie nodded, seeing the shock in his eyes.

'But you could not possibly know that!'

'Jacques Saunière was my grandfather.'

Teabing staggered back on his crutches, shooting a glance at Langdon, who nodded. Teabing turned back to Sophie. 'Miss Neveu, I am speechless. If this is true, then I am truly sorry for your loss.' He was silent a moment and then shook his head. 'But it still makes no sense. Even if your grandfather were the Priory Grand Master and created the keystone himself, he would never tell you how to find it. The keystone reveals the pathway to the brotherhood's ultimate treasure. Granddaughter or not, you are not eligible to receive such knowledge.'

'Mr Saunière was dying when he passed on the information,' Langdon said. 'He had limited options.'

'He didn't *need* options,' Teabing argued. 'There exist three *sénéchaux* who also know the secret. That is the beauty of their system. One will rise to Grand Master and they will induct a new *sénéchal* and share the secret of the keystone.'

'I presume you didn't see the entire news broadcast,' Sophie said. 'In addition to my grandfather, *three* other prominent Parisians were murdered today. All in similar ways.'

Teabing's jaw fell. 'And you think they were . . .'

'The *sénéchaux*,' Langdon said.

'But how? A murderer could not possibly learn the identities of *all four* top members of the Priory of Sion! Look at *me* – I have been researching them for decades and I can't even name *one* Priory member for certain. It seems inconceivable that all three *sénéchaux* and the Grand Master could be discovered and killed in one day.'

'I doubt the information was gathered in a single day,' Sophie said. 'It sounds like a well-planned operation – it's possible someone patiently watched the Priory and then attacked, hoping the top people would reveal the location of the keystone.'

Teabing looked unconvinced. 'But the brothers would never talk. They are sworn to secrecy. Even in the face of death.'

'Exactly,' Langdon said. 'Meaning, if they never divulged the secret *and* they were killed . . .'

Teabing gasped. 'Then the location of the keystone would be lost forever!'

'And with it,' Langdon said, 'the location of the Holy Grail.'

Teabing's body seemed to sway with the weight of Langdon's words. Then, as if too tired to stand another moment, he flopped into a chair and stared out of the window.

Sophie walked over, her voice soft. 'It seems possible that in total desperation my grandfather may have tried to pass the secret on to someone outside the brotherhood. Someone he thought he could trust. Someone in his family.'

Teabing was pale. 'Someone capable of such an attack . . . of discovering so much about the brotherhood . . .' He paused, radiating a new fear. 'It could only be one force. This attack could only have come from the Priory's oldest enemy.'

Langdon glanced up. 'The Church?'

'Who else? Rome has been seeking the Grail for centuries.'

Sophie was sceptical. 'You think the *Church* killed my grandfather?'

Teabing replied, 'It would not be the first time in history the Church has killed to protect itself. The documents that accompany the Holy Grail are explosive, and the Church has wanted to destroy them for years.'

'Leigh,' Langdon said, 'it doesn't make sense. Why would members of the Catholic clergy *murder* Priory members in an effort to find and destroy documents they believe are false?'

Teabing chuckled. 'The clergy in Rome are indeed blessed with strong faith, and so their beliefs can weather any storm, including documents that contradict everything they hold dear. But what about the *rest* of the world? What about those who look at the cruelty in the world and say, where is God today? Those who look at Church scandals and ask, who are these men who claim to speak the truth about Christ and yet try to cover up – for instance – the terrible misdeeds of their own priests?' He paused. 'What happens to those people, Robert, if real evidence comes out that the Church's version of the Christ story is inaccurate – and that the greatest story ever told is, in fact, the greatest story ever *sold*?'

Langdon did not respond.

'I'll tell you what happens if the documents get out,' Teabing said. 'The Vatican faces a crisis of faith never seen before in its two-millennium history.'

After a long silence, Sophie said, 'But if it is the Church that is responsible for this attack, why would they act *now*? The Priory keeps the Sangreal documents hidden – surely they pose no immediate threat to the Church.'

Teabing heaved an ominous sigh. 'Miss Neveu,' he said, 'the Church and the Priory have had an understanding for years. That is, the Church does not attack the Priory, and the Priory keeps the Sangreal documents hidden. However, part of the Priory history has always included a plan to unveil the secret. When we reach a specific date in history, the brotherhood plans to shout the true story of Jesus Christ from the mountaintops.'

Sophie stared at Teabing. 'And you think that date is approaching? And the Church knows it?'

'It could be,' he said, 'and that would certainly provide the Church with a reason to go all-out to find the documents before it was too late. Even if they don't have the exact date, their superstitions may be getting the better of them.'

'Superstitions?' Sophie asked.

'In terms of prophecy,' Teabing said, 'we are in a period of enormous change. The millennium has recently passed, and with it has ended the two-thousand-year-long astrological Age of Pisces – the fish, which is also the sign of Jesus. Now we are entering the Age of Aquarius.'

Langdon felt a shiver. 'The Church calls this transitional period the End of Days.'

'Many Grail historians,' Teabing added, 'believe that *if* the Priory is indeed planning to release this truth, *this* point in history would be an appropriate time. Admittedly, the Roman calendar does not mesh perfectly with the astrology, so there is some uncertainty about the dates. Whether the Church now has inside information that an exact date to release the information is looming, or whether they are just getting nervous, I don't know. But believe me' – he frowned – 'if the Church finds the Holy Grail, they will destroy it. The documents – and the relics of the blessed Mary Magdalene.' His eyes grew heavy. 'Then, my dear, all evidence will be lost. The Church will have won their age-old war to rewrite history, and the past will be erased forever.'

Slowly, Sophie pulled the cruciform key from her pocket and held it out to Teabing.

He took the key and studied it. 'My goodness. The Priory seal. Where did you get this?'

'My grandfather gave it to me tonight before he died. It provides access to the keystone.'

Teabing's head snapped up in disbelief. 'Impossible! I've searched every church in France!'

'It's not in a church,' Sophie said. 'It's in the vault of a Swiss depository bank.'

Teabing shook his head violently. 'That's impossible. The keystone is supposed to be hidden beneath the sign of the Rose.'

'It is,' Langdon said. 'It was stored in a rosewood box inlaid with a five-petal Rose.'

Teabing came over to them, his eyes wild with fear. 'You've seen it? Then the keystone is in danger! We have a duty to protect it. What if there are other keys? Perhaps stolen from the murdered *sénéchaux*? If the Church can gain access to the bank as you have –'

'Then they will be too late,' Sophie said. 'We removed the keystone.'

'What! You removed it from its hiding place?'

'Don't worry,' Langdon said. 'It's well hidden.'

'*Extremely* well hidden, I hope!'

'Actually,' Langdon said, unable to hide his grin, 'that depends on how often you dust under your couch.'

The wind outside Château Villette had picked up, and Silas's robe danced in the breeze as he crouched near the window. Although he had been unable to hear much of the conversation, the word *keystone* had sifted through the glass on numerous occasions.

*It is inside.*

# Chapter 51

Lieutenant Collet stood alone at the end of Leigh Teabing's driveway and gazed up at the massive house. *Isolated. Dark. Good ground cover.* He watched his agents spreading silently out along the length of the fence. They could be over it and have the place surrounded in a matter of minutes. Langdon could not have chosen a more ideal spot for Collet's men to make a surprise assault.

He was about to call Fache himself when at last his phone rang.

Fache sounded not nearly as pleased with the developments as Collet would have imagined. 'Why didn't someone tell me we had a lead on Langdon?'

'You were on a phone call and –'

'Where exactly are you, Lieutenant Collet?'

Collet gave him the address. 'The estate belongs to a British national named Teabing. Langdon drove a fair distance to get here, and the vehicle is inside the security gate, with no signs of forced entry, so chances are good that Langdon knows the occupant.'

'I'm coming out,' Fache said. 'Don't make a move. I'll handle this personally.'

Collet's jaw dropped. 'But, Captain, you're twenty minutes away! We should act immediately. I have him staked out. I'm with eight men total – and we are all armed.'

'Wait for me.'

'Captain, what if Langdon has a hostage in there? What if he sees us and decides to leave on foot? We need to move *now!*'

'Lieutenant Collet, you will wait for me to arrive before taking action. That is an order.' Fache hung up.

Stunned, Lieutenant Collet switched off his phone. *Why on earth is Fache asking me to wait?*

'Lieutenant?' One of the field agents came running over. 'We found a car.'

Collet followed the man about fifty yards past the driveway. The agent pointed to a wide shoulder on the opposite side of the road. There, parked in the brush, almost out of sight, was a black Audi. It had rental plates. The lieutenant felt the hood. Still warm. Hot, even.

'That must be how Langdon got here,' he said. 'Call the rental company. Find out if it's stolen.'

'Yes, sir.'

Another agent waved Collet back over in the direction of the fence. 'Lieutenant, have a look at this.' He handed Collet a pair of night-vision binoculars. 'The grove of trees near the top of the driveway.'

Collet aimed the binoculars up the hill and adjusted the dials.

Slowly, the greenish shapes came into focus – and all he could do was stare. There, shrouded in the greenery, was an armoured truck. A truck just like the one Collet had allowed to leave the bank earlier tonight.

'It seems obvious,' the agent said, 'that this truck is how Langdon and Neveu got away from the bank.'

Collet thought back to the armoured truck he had stopped at the roadblock. The Rolex on the driver's wrist . . .

*I never checked the back of the truck.*

Incredulous, he realized that someone at the bank had actually helped Langdon and Agent Neveu to escape. *But who? And why? And if the fugitives had arrived in the armoured truck, then who had driven there in the Audi?*

Hundreds of miles to the south, a small plane raced northwards over the sea. Despite the calm skies, Bishop Aringarosa clutched an airsickness bag – he felt he might be ill at any moment. His conversation with Captain Fache in Paris had not been at all what he had imagined.

Alone in the small cabin, he twisted the gold ring on his finger and tried to ease his overwhelming sense of fear and desperation.

*Everything in Paris has gone terribly wrong.*

Closing his eyes, he said a prayer that Bezu Fache would be able to fix it.

# Chapter 52

Teabing sat on the divan, cradling the wooden box on his lap and admiring the lid's intricate inlaid rose. *Tonight has become the strangest and most magical night of my life.*

'Lift the lid,' Sophie whispered, standing over him, beside Langdon.

Teabing smiled. *Do not rush me.* Having spent over a decade searching for this keystone, he wanted to savour every millisecond of this moment. He ran a palm across the wooden lid, feeling the texture of the inlaid flower.

'The Rose,' he whispered. *The Rose is Magdalene is the Holy Grail. The Rose is the compass that guides the way.* Teabing felt foolish. For years he had travelled to cathedrals and churches all over France, paying for special access, examining hundreds of archways beneath rose windows, searching for an encrypted keystone. *La clef de voûte – a stone key beneath the sign of the Rose.*

He slowly unlatched the lid and raised it, and as his eyes finally gazed upon the contents, he knew in an instant it could only be the keystone. He was staring at a stone cylinder crafted of interconnecting lettered dials. The device seemed surprisingly familiar to him.

'Designed from Da Vinci's diaries,' Sophie said. 'My grandfather made them as a hobby.'

*Of course*, Teabing realized. He had seen the sketches and blueprints. *The key to finding the Holy Grail lies inside this stone.* He lifted the heavy cryptex from the box, holding it gently. Although he had no idea how to open the cylinder, he sensed his own destiny lay inside. In moments of failure, Teabing had questioned whether his life's quest would ever be rewarded. Now those doubts were gone forever. He could hear the ancient words . . . the foundation of the Grail legend:

*Vous ne trouvez pas le Saint-Graal; c'est le Saint-Graal qui vous trouve.*

*You do not find the Grail; the Grail finds you.*

And tonight, incredibly, the key to finding the Holy Grail had walked right through his front door.

While Sophie and Teabing sat with the cryptex and talked about the vinegar, the dials and what the password might be, Langdon carried the rosewood box across the room to a well-lit table to get a better look at it. Something Teabing had just said was now running through his mind.

*The key to the Grail is hidden beneath the sign of the Rose.*

He held the wooden box up to the light and looked again at the rose.

*Beneath the Rose.*

*Sub Rosa.*

*Secret.*

A bump in the hallway behind him made him turn. He saw nothing but shadows – most likely Teabing's manservant had passed through. He turned back to the box and ran his finger over the smooth edge of the inlay, wondering if he could prise the rose out, but the craftsmanship was perfect.

Opening the box, he examined the inside of the lid. It was smooth. As he shifted its position, though, the light caught what appeared to be a small hole on the underside of the lid, positioned in the exact centre. Langdon closed the lid and examined the inlaid symbol from the top. No hole.

*It doesn't go all the way through.*

Setting the box on the table, he looked around the room and spied a stack of papers secured with a paper clip. Borrowing the clip, he returned to the box, opened it and studied the hole again. Carefully, he unbent the paper clip and inserted one end into the hole. He gave a gentle push . . . and something clattered quietly on to the table. The wooden rose – a small piece of wood, like a puzzle piece – had popped out of the lid.

Speechless, Langdon stared at the bare spot on the lid where the rose had been. There, engraved in the wood, written in an immaculate hand, were four lines of text in a language he had never seen.

*I don't recognize the language!* he thought. *And yet . . .*

A sudden movement behind him caught his attention and, out of nowhere, a crushing blow to the head knocked him to his knees. As he fell, he thought for a moment he saw a pale ghost hovering over him.

Then everything went black.

# Chapter 53

Despite working for the police, Sophie Neveu had never found herself at gunpoint until tonight. Almost inconceivably, the gun into which she was now staring was clutched in the pale hand of an enormous albino with long white hair, dressed in a wool robe with a rope tie, like some medieval cleric.

'You know what I have come for,' the monk said, his voice hollow. His eyes fell immediately to the keystone on Teabing's lap.

Teabing's tone was defiant. 'You will not be able to open it.'

'My Teacher is very wise,' the monk replied, inching closer, the gun shifting between Teabing and Sophie.

'Who is your teacher?' Teabing asked. 'Perhaps we can make a financial arrangement.'

'The Grail is priceless.' The albino moved closer. 'Now hand me the keystone.'

'You know of the keystone?' Teabing said, sounding surprised.

'Never mind what I know. Stand up slowly, and give it to me.'

'Standing is difficult for me.'

'Precisely. I would prefer nobody attempt any quick moves.'

Teabing slipped his right hand through one of his crutches and grasped the keystone in his left. Lurching to his feet, he stood erect, palming the heavy cylinder and leaning unsteadily on his crutch. 'You will not succeed,' he said as the monk reached out to take the cylinder from him. 'Only the worthy can unlock this stone.'

*God alone judges the worthy,* Silas thought.

'It's quite heavy,' the man on crutches said, his arm wavering now. 'If you don't take it soon, I'm afraid I shall drop it!' He swayed perilously.

Silas stepped quickly forward to take the stone, and as he did, the man on crutches lost his balance. The crutch slid out from under him, and he began to topple to his right. *No!* Silas lunged to save the stone, lowering his weapon in the process. But as the man fell to his right, his left hand swung backwards and the cylinder tumbled from his palm on to the couch. At the same instant, the metal crutch that had been sliding out from under the man seemed to accelerate, cutting a wide arc through the air towards Silas's leg.

Splinters of pain tore up Silas's body as the crutch made contact with the spiked belt around his thigh. The pistol discharged with a deafening roar, the bullet burying itself harmlessly in the floorboards. Buckling, he crumpled to his knees. And before he could raise the gun and fire again, the woman's foot caught him square on the jaw.

★

At the bottom of the driveway, Collet heard the gunshot. The muffled pop sent panic through his veins. He knew that if he stood idly by for another second, his entire career could be history by morning.

Eyeing the estate's iron gate, he made his decision.

'Pull it down.'


In the distant recesses of his groggy mind, Robert Langdon also heard the gunshot. And a scream of pain. His own? A drill was boring a hole into the back of his skull. Somewhere nearby, people were shouting.

'Where *were* you?' Teabing was yelling.

The manservant hurried in. 'Oh my God! Who is that? I'll call the police!'

'No! Don't call the police. Make yourself useful and get us something with which to restrain this monster.'

'And some ice!' Sophie added.

Langdon drifted out again. More voices. Movement. Now he was seated on the divan and Sophie was holding an ice pack to his head. His skull ached. As his vision finally began to clear, he found himself staring at a body on the floor. *Am I imagining things?* The massive body of an albino monk lay bound and gagged with duct tape.

He turned to Sophie. 'Who is *that*? What . . . happened?'

Teabing hobbled over. 'You were rescued by a knight brandishing an Excalibur made by Acme Orthopaedic.'

*Huh?* Langdon tried to sit up.

'I fear,' Teabing said, 'that I've just demonstrated for your lady friend a feature of my condition – everyone underestimates you.'

Langdon gazed down at the monk and tried to imagine what had happened. The man's chin was split open, and the robe over his right thigh was soaked with blood.

'He was wearing a *cilice*,' Teabing explained.

'A what?'

Teabing pointed to a bloodstained strip of barbed leather that lay on the floor. 'A discipline belt. He wore it on his thigh. I took careful aim.'

Langdon rubbed his head. He knew of discipline belts. 'But how . . . did you know?'

Teabing grinned. 'Christianity is my field of study, Robert, and there are certain sects who wear their hearts on their sleeves.' He pointed his crutch at the blood soaking through the monk's cloak. 'As it were.'

'Opus Dei,' Langdon whispered, recalling recent media coverage of the group, especially details of the practices of the sect's more dedicated members, some of whom took the teachings and twisted them into something that those outside the group would think too extreme . . . members like the monk now lying on the floor before him.

'Robert,' Sophie said, walking to the wooden box. 'What's this?' She was holding the small rose inlay he had removed from the lid.

'It covered an engraving on the box. I think the text might tell us how to open the keystone.'

Before Sophie and Teabing could respond, a sea of blue police lights and sirens erupted at the bottom of the hill and began snaking their way up the half-mile drive.

Teabing frowned. 'My friends, it seems we have a decision to make. And we'd better make it fast.'

# Chapter 54

Collet and his agents burst through the front door of Sir Leigh Teabing's estate. Fanning out, they began searching all the rooms on the ground floor. The entire floor seemed deserted.

Just as Collet was about to divide up his men to search the basement and grounds behind the house, they heard the sound of a car engine.

Collet was outside again in seconds, running towards the back door, grabbing one of his agents on the way. The men crossed the rear lawn and arrived breathless at the front of a weathered grey barn. Collet drew his weapon, rushed in and flicked on the lights.

A long line of horse stalls. But no horses. Apparently the owner preferred a different kind of horsepower: the stalls had been converted into a storage area for an astonishing collection of cars – a black Ferrari, a pristine Rolls-Royce, an antique Aston Martin sports coupé, a vintage Porsche 356.

The last bay was empty. Oil stains on the floor.

Collet ran over. *They can't get out of the grounds.* The driveway and gate were barricaded with two patrol cars to prevent this very situation.

'Sir?' The agent pointed down the length of the barn.

The rear doors were wide open, giving way to a dark, muddy slope of rugged fields. All the police lieutenant could make out was the faint shadow of a forest in the distance. No headlights. This wooded valley was probably crisscrossed by dozens of unmapped small roads and trails, but Collet was confident his quarry would never make it to the forest. 'Get some men spread out down there. They're probably already stuck somewhere nearby. These fancy sports cars can't handle terrain.'

'Um, sir?' The agent pointed to a nearby pegboard on which hung several sets of keys. The labels above the keys bore familiar names.

DAIMLER . . . ROLLS-ROYCE . . . ASTON MARTIN . . . PORSCHE . . .

The last peg was empty.

When Collet read the label above the empty peg, he knew he was in trouble.

The Range Rover was four-wheel drive, standard gears, with high-power lights and a steering wheel on the right. Langdon was pleased he was not driving.

Teabing's manservant Rémy, on orders from his master, was making an impressive job of manoeuvring the vehicle across the moonlit fields behind the château. With no headlights, he had crossed an open knoll and now seemed to be heading towards a jagged silhouette of wooded land in the distance.

Langdon, cradling the keystone in its box, turned in the passenger seat and eyed Teabing and Sophie in the back seat.

'So glad you popped in this evening, Robert,' Teabing said, grinning as if he were having fun for the first time in years.

'Sorry to get you involved in this, Leigh.'

'Oh, please, I've waited my entire life to be involved.' Teabing tapped Rémy on the shoulder from behind. 'Remember, no brake lights. I want to get into the woods a bit. No reason to risk them seeing us from the house.'

Rémy coasted to a crawl and guided the Range Rover through an opening in a long hedge. As the vehicle lurched on to an overgrown pathway, almost immediately the trees overhead blotted out the moonlight. He leaned over and pressed a small button, and a muted yellow glow fanned out across the path in front of them, revealing thick underbrush on either side. *Fog lights*, Langdon realized. They gave off just enough light to keep them on the path, and yet they were deep enough into the woods now that the lights would not give them away.

'Where are we going?' Sophie asked.

'This trail continues a couple of miles into the forest,' Teabing said. 'Cutting across the estate and then arching north. Provided we don't hit any standing water or fallen trees, we shall emerge unscathed on the main road.'

*Unscathed*. Langdon's head begged to differ. He turned his eyes down to his own lap, where the keystone was safely stowed in its wooden box. The inlaid rose on the lid was back in place, and although his head felt muddled, he was eager to remove the inlay again and examine the engraving beneath more closely. He unlatched the lid and began to raise it when Teabing laid a hand on his shoulder from behind.

'Patience, Robert,' he said. 'It's bumpy and dark. God save us if we break anything. Let's focus on getting away in one piece, shall we? There will be time for that very soon.'

Langdon knew Teabing was right. With a nod, he relatched the box.

The monk in the back was moaning now, struggling against his trusses. Suddenly, he began kicking wildly.

'Are you sure we should have brought him?' Langdon asked.

'Absolutely positive!' Teabing exclaimed. 'Don't forget – you're wanted for murder, Robert, and the police apparently want you badly enough to have tailed you to my home.'

'My fault,' Sophie said. 'The armoured car probably had a transmitter.'

'Not the point,' Teabing said. 'I'm not surprised the *police* found you, but I *am* surprised that this Opus Dei character found you. I can't imagine how he could have tailed you to my home unless he had a contact within the police – or at the bank.'

Langdon considered it. Bezu Fache certainly seemed to want to find a scapegoat for tonight's murders. And Vernet had turned on them rather suddenly, although considering Langdon was wanted by the police for four murders, the banker's change of heart seemed understandable.

'This monk is not working alone, Robert,' Teabing said, 'and until you learn who is behind all this, you are both in danger. The good news, my friend, is that you are now in a position of power, because this monster behind me has that information.' He pointed to the car phone on the dash. 'Robert, would you be so kind as to hand me that?' Taking the phone, Teabing dialled a number. 'Richard? Did I wake you? Of course I did. Silly question. I'm sorry. I have a small problem. I'm feeling a bit off, so Rémy and I need to pop up to the Isles for my treatments. Well, right away, actually. Sorry for the short notice. Can you have Elizabeth ready in about twenty minutes? I know, do the best you can. See you shortly.' He hung up.

'Elizabeth?' Langdon said.

'My plane. She cost me a queen's ransom.'

Langdon turned right round and looked at him.

'What?' Teabing demanded. 'You two can't expect to stay in France when the whole of the French police force is after you. London will be much safer.'

Sophie had turned to Teabing as well. 'You really think we should leave the country?'

'My friends, the Grail is now believed to be in Great Britain. If we unlock the keystone, I am certain we will discover a map showing that we are going in the right direction.'

'You're running a big risk by helping us,' Sophie said.

Teabing gave a wave of disgust. 'I am finished with France. I moved here to find the keystone. I shan't care if I never see Château Villette again.'

Sophie sounded uncertain. 'How will we get through airport security?'

Teabing chuckled. 'I fly from Le Bourget – a private airfield near here. Once a fortnight I fly north to see my doctors in England – and I pay for certain special privileges at both ends.'

'Sir?' Rémy said. 'Are you truly thinking of returning to England for good?'

'Rémy, you needn't worry,' Teabing assured. 'Just because I am returning to the Queen's realm does not mean I intend to subject my taste buds to bangers and mash for the rest of my days. I expect you to join me there. I will buy a splendid villa in Devon, and we'll have all your things shipped out immediately. An adventure, Rémy. I say, an adventure!'

Wedged in the back of the Range Rover, Silas could barely breathe. His arms were wrenched back and lashed to his ankles with kitchen twine and duct tape. Every bump in the road sent pain shooting through his twisted shoulders. At least his captors had removed the *cilice*. Unable to inhale through the strip of tape over his mouth, he could only breathe through his nostrils, which were slowly clogging up with dust from the cargo area. He began coughing.

'I think he's choking,' the French driver said, sounding concerned.

The British man who had struck Silas with his crutch now turned and peered over the seat, frowning coldly at Silas. 'Fortunately for you, we British judge man's civility not by his compassion for his friends, but by his compassion for his enemies.' He reached down and grabbed the duct tape on Silas's mouth. In one fast motion, he tore it off.

Silas felt as if his lips had just caught fire, but the air pouring into his lungs was sent from God.

'Whom do you work for?' the British man demanded.

'I do the work of God,' Silas spat back through the pain in his jaw where the woman had kicked him.

'You belong to Opus Dei,' the man said. It was not a question.

'You know nothing of who I am.'

'Why does Opus Dei want the keystone?'

Silas had no intention of answering. The keystone was the link to the Holy Grail, and the Holy Grail was the key to protecting the Faith.

*I do the work of God. The Way is in peril.*

In the stifling darkness, Silas prayed.

*A miracle, Lord. I need a miracle.*

He had no way of knowing that, hours from now, he would get one.

'Robert?' Sophie was still watching him. 'A funny look just crossed your face.'

Langdon glanced back at her. An incredible thought had just occurred to him. *Could it really be that simple?* 'I need to use your cellphone, Sophie.'

'Now?'

'I think I just worked something out.'

Sophie looked wary. 'I doubt Fache is tracing it now, but keep it under a minute just in case.' She gave him her phone.

'How do I dial the States?'

# Chapter 55

New York editor Jonas Faukman had just climbed into bed for the night when the telephone rang. *A little late,* he grumbled, picking up the receiver.

The line clicked. 'Jonas?'

'Robert? Why are you waking me up in the middle of the night?'

'Jonas, forgive me,' Langdon said. 'I'll keep this short. I really need to know. The manuscript I gave you. I need to know if you sent any copies out for advance quotes without telling me.'

Faukman hesitated. Langdon's newest manuscript – a book about the history of goddess worship – included several sections about Mary Magdalene that were going to raise some eyebrows, and he didn't want to print advance proofs without at least a few quotes from well-known art experts. He had chosen ten big names in the art world and sent them all sections of the manuscript, along with a polite letter asking if they would be willing to write a short endorsement for the cover of the book. In his experience, most people jumped at the opportunity to see their name in print.

'Jonas?' Langdon pressed. 'You sent out my manuscript, didn't you?'

Faukman frowned. 'I wanted to surprise you with some terrific quotes.'

A pause. 'Did you send one to the curator of the Louvre?'

'What do you think? His books are listed in your bibliography – Saunière was a no-brainer.'

The silence on the other end lasted a long time. 'When did you send it?'

'About a month ago. I also mentioned you would be in Paris soon and suggested you two chat. Did he arrange to meet you?' Faukman paused, rubbing his eyes. 'Hold on, aren't you supposed to *be* in Paris this week?'

'I *am* in Paris.'

Faukman sat upright. 'Did you see Saunière? Did he like the manuscript?'

But Langdon was gone.

Inside the Range Rover, Leigh Teabing let out a guffaw. 'Robert, you're saying you wrote a manuscript that delves into a secret society, and your editor *sent* a copy to that secret society?'

Langdon slumped. 'Evidently.'

'Here's the million-dollar question,' Teabing said, still chuckling. 'Was your position on the Priory favourable or *un*favourable?'

Langdon could hear his true meaning loud and clear. Many historians questioned why the Priory was still keeping the Sangreal documents hidden; some felt the information should have been shared with the world long ago. 'I simply provided a history of the brotherhood and described them as a modern goddess-worship society, keepers of the Grail and guardians of ancient documents.'

Sophie looked at him. 'Did you mention the keystone?'

Langdon winced. He had. Numerous times. 'I talked about the supposed keystone as an example of the lengths to which the Priory would go to protect the Sangreal documents.'

Sophie looked amazed. 'I guess that explains *P.S. Find Robert Langdon*. So,' she added, 'you lied to Captain Fache.'

'What?' Langdon demanded.

'You told him you had never corresponded with my grandfather.'

'I didn't! My editor sent him a manuscript.'

'Think about it, Robert. If Captain Fache didn't find the envelope in which your editor sent the manuscript or the letter he sent with it, he would think that *you* sent it.' She paused. 'Or worse, that you hand-delivered it and lied about it.'


When the Range Rover arrived at Le Bourget, Rémy drove to a small hangar at the far end of the airstrip. A tousled man in wrinkled khakis hurried out, waved and slid open the enormous corrugated metal door to reveal a sleek white jet within.

Langdon stared at the glistening fuselage. '*That's* Elizabeth?'

Teabing grinned. 'Beats going by Eurostar.'

The man in khakis hurried towards them, squinting into the headlights. 'Almost ready, sir,' he called in a British accent. 'My apologies for the delay, but you took me by surprise and –' He stopped short as the group got out.

Teabing said, 'My associates and I have urgent business in London. We've no time to waste. Please prepare to depart immediately.'

'Sir, my humble apologies, but my flight permit means I can only take you and your manservant. I cannot take any additional passengers.'

'Richard,' Teabing said, smiling warmly, 'two thousand pounds sterling say you *can* take my guests.' He motioned to the Range Rover. 'And the unfortunate fellow in the back.'

Less than five minutes later, the Hawker 731's twin engines were powering the plane skywards with gut-wrenching force. Outside the window, the airfield dropped away with startling speed.

*I'm fleeing the country,* Sophie thought, her body forced back into the leather seat. Until this moment, she had believed her game of cat and mouse with Fache was somehow justifiable. *I was attempting to protect an innocent man. I was trying to fulfil my grandfather's dying wishes.* Now she was leaving the country, without documentation, accompanying a wanted man and transporting a bound hostage. If a 'line of reason' had ever existed, she had just crossed it. *At almost the speed of sound.*

She was seated with Langdon and Teabing near the front of the cabin. In the rear of the plane, in a separate seating area near the toilet, Teabing's manservant Rémy, a pistol in his hand, stood guard over the albino monk, who lay trussed at his feet like a piece of luggage.

'Before we turn our attention to the keystone,' Teabing said, 'I was wondering if you would permit me a few words.' He sounded apprehensive. 'My friends, as someone who has spent his life in search of the Grail, I feel it is my duty to warn you that you are about to step on to a path from which there is no return, regardless of the dangers involved.' He turned to Sophie. 'Miss Neveu, your grandfather gave you this cryptex in hopes you would keep the secret of the Holy Grail alive.'

'Yes.'

'Understandably, you feel obliged to follow the trail wherever it leads.'

Sophie nodded, although she felt a second motivation still burning within her. *The truth about my family.* Despite Langdon's telling her that the keystone had nothing to do with her past, she still sensed something deeply personal entwined within this mystery.

'Your grandfather and three others died tonight,' Teabing continued, 'and they did so to keep this keystone away from the Church. Opus Dei came within inches of possessing it. You understand, I hope, that this puts you in a position of exceptional responsibility. You have been handed a torch – a two-thousand-year-old flame that cannot be allowed to go out. It cannot fall into the wrong hands.' He paused, glancing at the rosewood box. 'I realize you have been given no choice in this matter, Miss Neveu, but you must either fully embrace this responsibility . . . or you must pass it on to someone else.'

'My grandfather gave the cryptex to me. I'm sure he thought I could handle it.'

Teabing looked encouraged but unconvinced. 'Good. A strong will is necessary. And yet, do you understand that successfully unlocking the keystone will bring with it a far greater test?'

'How so?'

'My dear, imagine that you are suddenly holding a map that reveals the location of the Holy Grail. In that moment, you will be in possession of a truth capable of altering history forever – a truth that man has sought for centuries. Will you reveal that truth to the world? The individual who does so will be revered by many and despised by others. Do you have the necessary strength to carry out that task?'

Sophie paused. 'I'm not sure that is my decision to make.'

Teabing's eyebrows arched. 'No? If not the possessor of the keystone, then who?'

'The brotherhood who have successfully protected the secret for so long.'

'The Priory?' Teabing looked sceptical. 'How? The brotherhood was shattered tonight. Someone uncovered the identities of their four top members – and killed them. I would not trust anyone who stepped forward from the brotherhood at this point.'

'So what do you suggest?' Langdon asked.

'Robert, you know that the Priory has not protected the truth all these years just to have it gather dust until eternity. They have been waiting for the right moment in history to share their secret.'

'And you believe that moment has come?'

'Absolutely. Besides, if the Priory did not intend to make their secret known, why has the Church now attacked?'

Sophie argued, 'The monk has not yet told us his purpose.'

'The monk's purpose is the Church's purpose,' Teabing replied. 'To destroy the documents that reveal the great deception. The Church came closer tonight than they have ever come, and the Priory has put its trust in *you*, Miss Neveu. I believe that the task of saving the Holy Grail clearly includes carrying out the Priory's final wishes of sharing the truth with the world, so it is important that you begin to think about what happens should we succeed in opening the keystone.'

'Gentlemen,' Sophie said, her voice firm, 'I have heard the saying, "You do not find the Grail; the Grail finds you." I am going to trust that the Grail has found me for a reason, and when the time comes, I will know what to do.'

Both of them looked startled.

'So then,' she said, motioning to the rosewood box, 'let's move on.'

# Chapter 56

As the Hawker levelled off, its nose aimed for England, Langdon carefully lifted the rosewood box from his lap, where he had been protecting it during takeoff.

Unlatching the lid and opening the box, he turned his attention not to the lettered dials of the cryptex, but rather to the tiny hole on the underside of the box lid. Using the tip of a pen, he carefully removed the inlaid rose and revealed the text beneath it. *Sub Rosa*, he mused, hoping a fresh look at the text would bring clarity. He hunched over the box and studied the strange text.

'Leigh, I just can't seem to place it. My first guess is an ancient language from the Hebrew or Arabic world – but now I'm not so sure.'

Reaching over, Teabing edged the box away from Langdon and pulled it towards himself. But his shoulders soon slumped. 'I'm astonished,' he said. 'This language looks like nothing I've ever seen!'

'Might I see it?' Sophie asked. Teabing pretended not to hear her. 'Leigh?' she repeated, clearly not appreciating being left out of the discussion. 'Might I have a look at the box my grandfather made?'

'Of course, dear,' Teabing said, pushing it over to her, though he felt Sophie Neveu was light-years out of her league. If a British Royal Historian and a Harvard expert on symbols could not even identify the language –

'Ah,' Sophie said, seconds after examining the box. 'I should have guessed.'

Teabing and Langdon turned in unison, staring at her.

'Guessed *what*?' Teabing demanded.

Sophie shrugged. 'Guessed that *this* would be the language my grandfather used.'

'You're saying you can *read* this text?' Teabing exclaimed.

'Quite easily,' Sophie chimed, obviously enjoying herself now. 'My grandfather taught me how to when I was only six years old. I'm fluent.' She leaned across the table and fixed Teabing with an admonishing glare. 'And frankly, sir, I'm a little surprised you didn't recognize it.'

In a flash, Langdon knew. Sophie had cracked it, but he got it too. *No wonder the script looks so familiar!*

Langdon had forgotten that one of Da Vinci's numerous artistic talents was an ability to write in a mirrored script that was virtually illegible to anyone other than himself.

Sophie smiled inwardly to see that Robert understood her meaning. 'I can read the first few words,' she said. 'It's in English.'

Teabing was still spluttering. 'What's going on?'

'Reverse text,' Langdon said. 'We need a mirror.'

'No we don't,' Sophie said. 'I bet the veneer on the box is thin enough.' She lifted the rosewood box up to a light on the wall of the plane and began to examine the underside of the lid. Her grandfather couldn't actually write in reverse, so he always cheated by writing *normally* and then flipping the paper over and tracing the reversed impression. Sophie guessed that he had burned *normal* text on to a block of wood, then sanded down the back of the block until the wood was paper thin and the text could be seen *through* the wood. As she moved the lid closer to the light, she saw she was right. The bright beam sifted through the thin layer of wood, and the script appeared in reverse on the underside.

Instantly legible.

'English,' Teabing croaked, hanging his head in shame. 'My native tongue.'

Sophie quickly found some paper and copied it down longhand. When she was done, the three of them took turns reading the text, a riddle that promised to reveal how to open the cryptex.

*An ancient word of wisdom frees this scroll . . . and helps us keep her scatter'd family whole . . . A headstone praised by templars is the key . . . and atbash will reveal the truth to thee.*

Langdon read the verse slowly:

'*An ancient word of wisdom frees this scroll . . . and helps us keep her scatter'd family whole . . . A headstone praised by templars is the key . . . and atbash will reveal the truth to thee.*'

Before he could even consider what ancient password the verse was trying to reveal, he felt something far more fundamental resonate within him – the metre of the poem. *Iambic pentameter: two syllables with opposite emphasis, arranged in strings of five.*

'It's pentameter!' Teabing blurted, turning to Langdon. 'And the verse is in English! *La lingua pura!*'

Langdon nodded. The Priory had considered English the only European *pure* language for centuries. Unlike French, Spanish and Italian, which were rooted in Latin – *the tongue of the Vatican* – English was separate from Rome.

'This poem,' Teabing gushed, 'refers not only to the Grail, but the Knights Templar and the scattered family of Mary Magdalene! What more could we ask for?'

'The password – to open the cryptex,' Sophie said, looking again at the poem. 'It sounds like we need some kind of ancient word of wisdom?'

'Abracadabra?' Teabing ventured, his eyes twinkling.

*A word of five letters,* Langdon thought, pondering the staggering number of ancient words that might be considered words of wisdom: extracts from mystic chants, incantations, magic spells, pagan mantras . . . The list was endless.

'The password,' Sophie said, 'appears to have something to do with the Templars.' She read the text aloud. ' "A headstone praised by Templars is the key." '

'Leigh,' Langdon said, 'you're the Templar specialist. Any ideas?'

Teabing was silent for several seconds and then sighed. 'Well, a headstone is obviously a grave marker of some sort. It's possible the poem means a gravestone at the tomb of Magdalene, but that doesn't help us much because we have no idea where her tomb is.'

'The last line,' Sophie said, 'says that *Atbash* will reveal the truth. I've heard that word before. Atbash.'

'I'm not surprised,' Langdon replied. 'The Atbash Cipher is one of the oldest codes known to man. I'm sure you know it; it's the famous Hebrew encoding system.'

Sophie had indeed learned about the Atbash Cipher. It had been part of her early training.

Langdon continued, 'It dates back to 500 BC; it was a simple substitution code based on the twenty-two-letter Hebrew alphabet. In Atbash, the first letter was substituted by the last letter, the second letter by the next to last letter, and so on.'

'Atbash is sublimely appropriate,' Teabing said. 'Text encrypted with Atbash is found throughout the Kabbala, the Dead Sea Scrolls, and even the Old Testament. Jewish scholars and mystics are *still* finding hidden meanings using Atbash. The Priory would certainly include the Atbash Cipher as part of their teachings.' He sighed.

Langdon continued, 'Yes, there must be a code word on the headstone. We must find this "headstone praised by Templars".'

But it wasn't long before Teabing heaved a frustrated sigh and shook his head. 'My friends, I'm stymied. Let me ponder this while I get us some nibbles and check on Rémy and our guest.' He stood up and headed for the back of the plane.

Sophie felt tired as she watched him go. *There is more there,* she told herself. *Ingeniously hidden . . . but present nonetheless.* She also feared that what they eventually found inside this cryptex would not be as simple as a map to the Holy Grail. She had solved enough of her grandfather's treasure hunts to know that Jacques Saunière did not give up his secrets easily.

# Chapter 57

'You're quiet,' Langdon said, gazing across the Hawker's cabin at Sophie.

'Just tired,' she replied. 'And the verses. I don't know.'

Langdon was feeling the same way. The hum of the engines and the gentle rocking of the plane were hypnotic, and his head still throbbed where he'd been hit by the monk. Teabing was still in the back of the plane, so Langdon decided to take advantage of the moment alone with Sophie to tell her something that had been on his mind. 'I think I know another reason why your grandfather wanted to bring us together. I think there's something he wanted me to explain to you.'

'The history of the Holy Grail and Mary Magdalene isn't enough?'

Langdon felt unsure how to proceed. 'The rift between you. Why you haven't spoken to him for ten years. I think maybe he was hoping I could somehow make that right . . . by explaining what may have driven you apart.' He eyed her carefully. 'You witnessed a ritual, didn't you?'

Sophie recoiled. 'How do you know that?'

'Sophie, you told me you saw something that convinced you your grandfather was in a secret society. And whatever you saw upset you.'

Sophie stared.

'Was it in the spring?' Langdon asked. 'Sometime around the equinox? Late March?'

Sophie looked out the window. 'It was my spring break from university. I came home a few days early.'

'You want to tell me about it?'

'I'd rather not.' She suddenly turned back, her eyes welling with emotion. 'I don't know what I saw.'

'Were both men and women present?'

After a beat, she nodded.

'Dressed in white and black?'

She wiped her eyes and nodded again, seeming to open up a little. 'The women were in white gossamer gowns with golden shoes. They held golden orbs. The men wore black tunics and black shoes.'

'Masks?' Langdon asked, trying to keep his voice calm. Sophie had unwittingly witnessed a two-thousand-year-old sacred ceremony!

'Yes. Everyone. Identical masks. White on the women. Black on the men.'

Langdon had read descriptions of this ceremony and understood its roots. 'It's called Hieros Gamos,' he said softly. 'It dates back more than two thousand years. Egyptian priests and priestesses performed it regularly to celebrate the reproductive power of the female.' He paused, leaning towards her. 'And if you witnessed the rite without being prepared, unable to understand its meaning, I imagine it would look pretty shocking.'

Sophie said nothing.

'Hieros Gamos is Greek,' he continued. 'It means *sacred marriage*. The ancients believed that the male was spiritually incomplete until he had carnal knowledge of the sacred feminine. A physical union with the female was the only way a man could become complete and ultimately achieve *gnosis* – knowledge of the divine.'

Sophie was silent, but Langdon hoped she was starting to understand her grandfather better.

# Chapter 58

Le Bourget airfield's night-shift air-traffic controller had been dozing before a blank radar screen when the captain of the Judicial Police practically broke down his door.

'Teabing's jet,' Bezu Fache blared, marching into the small tower. 'Where did it go?'

The controller's initial response was a babbling, lame attempt to protect the privacy of one of the airfield's most respected customers.

'I am placing you under arrest for permitting a private plane to take off without registering a flight plan,' Fache said.

'Wait!' the controller heard himself whimper. 'I can tell you this much. Sir Leigh Teabing makes frequent trips to London for medical treatments. He has a hangar at Biggin Hill Executive Airport in Kent. On the outskirts of London.'

'Is Biggin Hill his destination tonight?' Fache demanded to know.

'The plane left on its usual tack, and his last radar contact suggested the United Kingdom,' the controller said honestly.

'Did he have others on board?'

'I swear, sir, there is no way for me to know. Our clients drive directly to their hangars. Who is on board is the responsibility of the customs officials at the receiving airport.'

'If they're going to Biggin Hill, how long until they land?'

'It's a short flight. His plane could be on the ground by . . . around six thirty. Fifteen minutes from now,' the controller replied.

Fache frowned and turned to one of his men. 'I'm going to London. Call the Kent local police. Not British MI5. I want this quiet. Kent *local*. Tell them I want Teabing's plane to be permitted to land. Then I want it surrounded on the tarmac. Nobody to be allowed off until I get there.'

The small chartered plane was just passing over the twinkling lights of Monaco when Aringarosa hung up on Fache for the second time. He reached for the airsickness bag again but felt too drained even to be sick.

*Just let it be over!*

Fache's newest update seemed unfathomable. Everything had spiralled wildly out of control. *What have I got Silas into? What have I got myself into!*

On shaky legs, the bishop walked to the cockpit. 'I have to get to London immediately. I will pay you. London is only one hour further north and requires almost no change of direction, so –'

'It's not a question of money, Father. There are other issues.'

'Ten thousand euros. Right now.'

The pilot turned, his eyes wide with shock. Aringarosa walked back to his black briefcase, opened it and removed one of the bearer bonds. He handed it to the pilot.

'What is this?'

'A ten-thousand-euro bearer bond drawn on the Vatican Bank. It's the same as cash.'

'Only cash is cash,' the pilot said, handing the bond back. He eyed the bishop's gold ring. 'Real diamonds?'

Aringarosa looked at the ring. Everything it represented was about to be lost anyway. He slid the ring from his finger and placed it gently on the instrument panel.

Fifteen seconds later, he could feel the pilot banking a few more degrees to the north.

# Chapter 59

Langdon could see Sophie was still shaken from recounting her experience. He was amazed to have heard it. Not only had Sophie witnessed the full-blown ritual, but her own grandfather was the Grand Master of the Priory of Sion. He was in heady company. *Da Vinci, Botticelli, Isaac Newton, Victor Hugo, Jean Cocteau* ... *Jacques Saunière.*

'He raised me like his own daughter,' Sophie said tearfully. She had shunned her grandfather and was now seeing him in an entirely different light.

'Victuals, my dears?' Teabing rejoined them with a flourish, presenting several cans of Coke and a box of old crackers. He apologized profusely for the limited fare. 'Our friend the monk isn't talking yet, but give him time.' He bit into a cracker and eyed the poem. 'So, what is your grandfather trying to tell us? Where *is* this headstone praised by Templars?'

Sophie shook her head.

Langdon popped a Coke and turned to the window, his thoughts awash with images of secret rituals and unbroken codes. Below them now, he saw a shimmering ocean. *The English Channel*. It wouldn't be long now.

*A headstone praised by Templars.*

The plane was over land again. 'You won't believe this,' he said, turning to the others. 'The Templar "headstone" – I figured it out.'

Teabing's eyes turned to saucers. 'You *know* where the headstone is?'

Langdon smiled. 'Not *where* it is. *What* it is.'

Sophie leaned in to hear.

'I think the headstone is a literal *stone head*,' Langdon explained, enjoying the familiar excitement of an academic breakthrough. 'Not a grave marker.' He turned to Teabing. 'Leigh, during the Inquisition – right through the twelfth to fourteenth centuries – the Church accused the Knights Templar of all kinds of heresies, right?'

'Correct. They made up all kinds of charges.'

'And on that list was the worship of false idols. They accused the Templars of performing rituals in which they prayed to a carved stone head . . . the pagan god –'

'Baphomet!' Teabing blurted. 'My heavens, Robert, you're right! A headstone praised by Templars!'

Baphomet was a pagan fertility god, associated with the creative force of reproduction. His head was represented as that of a ram or goat, and the Templars used to honour Baphomet by encircling a stone replica of his head and chanting prayers.

Teabing tittered. 'The pope convinced everyone that

Baphomet's head was in fact an image of the Devil. It *must* be what the poem is referring to.'

Sophie said, 'But if Baphomet is the right answer, then we have a new dilemma.' She pointed to the dials on the cryptex. 'Baphomet has eight letters. We only have room for five.'

Teabing grinned broadly. 'My dear, this is where the Atbash Cipher comes into play.'

He wrote out the entire twenty-two-letter Hebrew alphabet – *alef-beit* – from memory. He used Roman equivalents rather than Hebrew characters.

$$A \; B \; G \; D \; H \; V \; Z \; Ch \; T \; Y \; K \; L \; M \; N \; S \; O \; P$$
$$Tz \; Q \; R \; Sh \; Th$$

'Alef, Beit, Gimel, Dalet, Hei, Vav, Zayin, Chet, Tet, Yud, Kaf, Lamed, Mem, Nun, Samech, Ayin, Pei, Tzadik, Kuf, Reish, Shin and Tav.' Teabing dramatically mopped his brow and ploughed on. 'In formal Hebrew spelling, however, the five vowel sounds are not written. Therefore, when we write the word *Baphomet* using the Hebrew alphabet, it will lose the three vowels in the word, leaving us –'

'Five letters,' Sophie blurted.

Teabing nodded and began writing again. 'OK, here is the proper spelling of *Baphomet* in Hebrew letters. I'll sketch in the missing vowels for clarity's sake.'

$$\underline{B} \; a \; \underline{P} \; \underline{V} \; o \; \underline{M} \; e \; \underline{Th}$$

'Remember, of course,' he added, 'that Hebrew is normally written in the opposite direction, but we can just as easily use Atbash this way. Next, all we have to do is create our substitution scheme by rewriting the entire alphabet in reverse order opposite the original alphabet.'

'There's an easier way,' Sophie said, taking the pen from Teabing. 'It works for all mirror substitution ciphers, including the Atbash. A little trick I learned at university.' She wrote the first half of the alphabet from left to right, and then, beneath it, wrote the second half, right to left. 'Code-breakers call it the fold-over. Half as complicated. Twice as clean.'

| A | B | G | D | H | V | Z | Ch | T | Y | K |
|----|----|----|----|----|----|----|----|----|----|----|
| Th | Sh | R | Q | Tz | P | O | S | N | M | L |

Teabing eyed her handiwork and chuckled. 'Right you are.'

Langdon felt a rising thrill. 'We're getting close,' he whispered.

'Inches, Robert,' Teabing said. He glanced over at Sophie and smiled. 'You ready?'

She nodded.

'OK, *Baphomet* in Hebrew without the vowels reads: *B-P-V-M-Th*. Now we simply apply your Atbash substitution matrix to translate the letters into our five-letter password.' He was grinning. 'And the Atbash Cipher reveals –' He stopped short. 'Good God!' His face went white.

'What's wrong?' Sophie demanded.

'This is . . . ingenious,' Teabing whispered. 'Utterly ingenious!' He wrote again on the paper. 'Drumroll, please. Here is your password.' He showed them what he had written.

Sh–V–P–Y–A

Sophie scowled. 'What is it?'

Teabing's voice seemed to tremble with awe. 'This, my friend, is actually *an ancient word of wisdom*.'

Langdon read the letters again. *An ancient word of wisdom frees this scroll.* An instant later he got it. 'An ancient word of wisdom!'

Teabing was laughing. 'Quite literally!'

Sophie looked at the word and then at the dial. 'Hold on!' she argued. 'This can't be the password. The cryptex doesn't have a Sh on the dial. It uses a traditional Roman alphabet.'

'*Read* the word,' Langdon urged. 'And keep in mind two things. In Hebrew, the symbol for the sound *Sh* can also be pronounced as *S*, depending on the accent. Just as the letter *P* can be pronounced *F*.'

*SVFYA?* she thought, puzzled.

'Genius!' Teabing added. 'And the letter *Vav* often stands for the vowel sound *O*!'

Sophie again looked at the letters, attempting to sound them out.

'*S . . . o . . . f . . . y . . . a.*'

She heard the sound of her voice and could not believe what she had just said. 'Sophia? This spells *Sophia*?'

Langdon was nodding enthusiastically. 'Yes! *Sophia* literally means *wisdom* in Greek. The root of your name, Sophie, is literally a "word of wisdom".'

Sophie suddenly missed her grandfather immensely. *He encrypted the Priory keystone with my name.* A knot caught in her throat. It all seemed so perfect. Then she realized a problem still existed. 'Wait . . . the word Sophia has *six* letters.'

Teabing's smile never faded. 'Look at the poem again. Your grandfather wrote, "an *ancient* word of wisdom".'

'Yes?'

Teabing winked. 'In ancient Greek, *wisdom* is spelled S-O-F-I-A.'

# Chapter 60

*An ancient word of wisdom frees this scroll.*

Sophie felt a wild excitement as she cradled the cryptex and began dialling in the letters. S . . . O . . . F . . .

'Carefully,' Teabing urged. 'Ever so carefully.'

. . . I . . . A.

Sophie aligned the final dial. 'OK,' she whispered, glancing up at the others. 'I'm going to pull it apart.'

'Remember the vinegar,' Langdon whispered with fearful exhilaration. 'Be careful.'

*Pull gently,* she told herself.

Teabing and Langdon both leaned in as she wrapped her palms around the ends of the cylinder, double-checked that all the letters were properly aligned with the indicator, and then slowly pulled. Nothing happened. Sophie applied a little more force. Suddenly, the stone slid apart like a well-crafted telescope. Langdon and Teabing almost jumped to their feet. Sophie's heart rate climbed as she set the end cap on the table and tipped up the cylinder to peer inside.

*A scroll!* Sophie could see it had been wrapped around a cylindrical object – the vial of vinegar, she assumed. Strangely, though, the paper around the vinegar was not the customary delicate papyrus but vellum. *That's odd,* she thought. *Vinegar can't dissolve a lambskin vellum.* She looked again down the hollow of the scroll and realized the object in the centre was not a vial of vinegar after all. It was something else entirely.

'What's wrong?' Teabing asked. 'Pull out the scroll.'

Frowning, Sophie grabbed the vellum and the object around which it was wrapped, pulling them both out of the container.

'That's not papyrus,' Teabing said. 'It's too heavy.'

'I know. It's padding.' Sophie unrolled the scroll and revealed what was wrapped inside. 'For *this.*' She put it on the table.

Langdon stared in amazement. *I see Saunière has no intention of making this easy.*

In front of them sat a second cryptex. Smaller. Made of black onyx. It had been nested within the first. Saunière's passion for dualism. *Two cryptexes.* Everything in pairs. *Double entendres. Male female. Black nested within white. White gives birth to black.*

*Every man sprang from woman.*

*White – female.*

*Black – male.*

Reaching over, Langdon lifted the smaller cryptex. It looked identical to the first, except that it was half the size and black. He heard the familiar gurgle. Apparently, the vial of vinegar they had heard earlier was inside this smaller cryptex.

'Well, Robert,' Teabing said, sliding the page of vellum over to him, 'you'll be pleased to hear that at least we're flying in the right direction.'

Langdon examined the thick vellum sheet. Written in ornate penmanship was another four-line verse. He needed to read only as far as the first line to realize that Teabing's plan to come to Britain was going to pay off.

*In London lies a knight a Pope interred.*

The remainder of the poem clearly implied that the password for opening the second cryptex could be found by visiting this knight's tomb, somewhere in the city.

Langdon turned excitedly to Teabing. 'Do you have any idea what knight this poem is referring to?'

Teabing grinned. 'No. But I know in precisely which crypt we should look.'

At exactly that moment, fifteen miles ahead of them, six Kent police cars streaked down rain-soaked streets towards Biggin Hill Executive Airport.

# Chapter 61

'Seat belts, please,' Teabing's pilot announced as the Hawker 731 descended into a gloomy morning drizzle. 'We'll be landing in five minutes.'

Teabing felt joyous as he saw the misty hills of Kent spreading wide beneath the descending plane. *My time in France is over. I am returning to England victorious. The keystone has been found.*

'Sir?' the pilot called back suddenly. 'The tower just radioed. They've got some kind of maintenance problem out near your hangar, and they're asking me to bring the plane directly to the terminal instead.'

Teabing had been flying to Biggin Hill for over a decade, and this was a first. 'Did they mention what the problem is?'

'The controller was vague. Something about a petrol leak? They asked me to park in front of the terminal and keep everyone on board until further notice. Safety precaution. We're not supposed to deplane until we get the all-clear from the airport authorities.'

Teabing turned to Sophie and Langdon. 'My friends, I have an unpleasant suspicion that we are about to be met by a welcoming committee.'

Langdon gave a bleak sigh. 'I guess Fache still thinks I'm his man.'

'Either that,' Sophie said, 'or he is too deep into this to admit his error.'

Teabing was not listening. *Don't lose sight of the ultimate goal. The Grail. We're so close . . .* He hobbled towards the cockpit, wondering how much it would cost him to persuade his pilot to perform one highly irregular manoeuvre.

*The Hawker is on final approach.*

Simon Edwards – Executive Services Officer at Biggin Hill Airport – paced the control tower. He never appreciated being awoken early on a Saturday morning, but it was particularly distasteful that he had been called in to oversee the arrest of one of his most lucrative clients – Sir Leigh Teabing. The charges were obviously serious. At the French authorities' request, Kent police had ordered the Biggin Hill air-traffic controller to instruct the Hawker's pilot to go directly to the terminal. And although the British police did not generally carry weapons, the situation had brought out an armed response team inside the terminal building, awaiting the moment when the plane's engines powered down.

The Hawker was low in the sky now, skimming the treetops to their right. Out on the runway, the jet's nose tipped up and the tyres touched down in a puff of smoke. But . . . rather than braking and turning into the terminal, as instructed, the jet coasted calmly past and continued on towards Teabing's hangar in the distance.

All the police spun and stared at Edwards. 'You said the pilot agreed to come to the terminal!'

Edwards was bewildered. 'He *did*!'

Seconds later, he was in a police car and racing across the tarmac. They were still a good five hundred yards away when Teabing's Hawker taxied calmly into the private hangar. As the police skidded to a stop outside the gaping hangar door, the officers poured out.

Edwards jumped out too.

The noise was deafening. The Hawker's engines were still roaring as the jet finished its usual turn inside the hangar, positioning itself nose-out, ready for departure. The pilot brought it to a final stop, powering down the engines. After several seconds, the fuselage door popped open.

Leigh Teabing appeared in the doorway as the plane's electronic stairs smoothly dropped down. He propped himself on his crutches and scratched his head. 'Did I win the policemen's lottery while I was away?' He sounded more bewildered than concerned.

Simon Edwards stepped forward, swallowing the frog in his throat. 'Good morning, sir. I apologize for the confusion. We've had a petrol leak and your pilot said he was coming to the terminal.'

'Yes, yes, well, I told him to come here instead. I'm late for an appointment. I pay for this hangar, and this rubbish about avoiding a petrol leak sounded overcautious.'

'Sir,' the Kent chief inspector said, stepping forward, 'I need to ask you to stay on board for another half-hour or so.'

Teabing looked unamused as he hobbled down the stairs. 'I'm afraid that is impossible. I have a medical appointment, and I cannot afford to miss it.'

The chief inspector blocked his way. 'This is serious, sir. The French police have claimed that you are transporting fugitives from the law on this plane. Also that you may have a hostage on board. I'm afraid we cannot let you leave.'

'Inspector, *I'm* afraid I don't have time to indulge in your games. I'm late, and I'm leaving. If it is that important to you to stop me, you'll just have to shoot me.' With that, Teabing and Rémy walked round the chief inspector and headed across the hangar towards the parked limousine. Without breaking stride or glancing back, Teabing added, 'And do not dare to board my plane without a warrant.'

The chief inspector knew that Teabing was correct – the police needed a warrant to board his jet – but the plane had taken off in France, and the powerful Bezu Fache had requested the action. He gripped his gun and marched up the plane's gangway, peered inside, then stepped into the cabin. *What on earth?*

With the exception of the frightened-looking pilot in the cockpit, the aircraft was completely empty.

The Kent chief inspector swallowed hard. 'Let them go,' he ordered. 'We received a bad tip.'

Teabing's eyes were menacing. 'You can expect a call from my lawyers.' With that, his manservant opened the door at the rear of the stretch limousine and helped him into the back seat. Then the man climbed in behind the wheel, and the Jaguar peeled out of the hangar.

As it accelerated away, Teabing turned his eyes to the dimly lit front recesses of the spacious interior. 'Everyone comfy?'

Langdon gave a weak nod. He and Sophie were still crouched on the floor there beside the bound and gagged albino.

Moments earlier, as the Hawker had taxied into the deserted hangar, Rémy had popped the hatch when the plane jolted to a stop halfway through its turn. With the police closing in fast, Langdon and Sophie dragged the monk down the gangway to ground level and out of sight behind the limousine. Then the jet engines had roared again, rotating the plane and completing its turn as the police cars came skidding into the hangar.

Now, as the limousine raced towards London, Langdon and Sophie clambered into the rear of the limo's long interior, leaving the monk bound on the floor. They settled on to the long seat facing Teabing. The Englishman gave them both a roguish smile and opened the cabinet on the limo's bar. 'Could I offer you a drink? Some nibbles? Crisps? Nuts?'

Sophie and Langdon both shook their heads.

Teabing grinned and closed the bar. 'So then, about this knight's tomb . . .'

# Chapter 62

'Fleet Street?' Langdon asked, eyeing Teabing in the back of the limo. *There's a crypt on Fleet Street?*

'Miss Neveu, give the Harvard boy one more shot at the verse, will you?' Teabing said.

Sophie fished in her pocket and pulled out the black cryptex, still wrapped in the vellum. They had agreed to leave the rosewood box and larger cryptex in the plane's strongbox. Sophie unwrapped the vellum and handed the sheet to Langdon.

Although Langdon had read the poem several times on board the jet, he had been unable to think of any specific location. Now he processed them slowly and carefully, hoping the rhythms would reveal a clearer meaning.

> *In London lies a knight a Pope interred.*
> *His labour's fruit a Holy wrath incurred.*
> *You seek the orb that ought be on his tomb.*
> *It speaks of Rosy flesh and seeded womb.*

The language seemed simple enough. There was a knight buried in London. A knight who laboured at something that angered the Church. A knight whose tomb was missing an orb that *should* be present. The poem's final reference – *Rosy flesh and seeded womb* – was a clear reference to Mary Magdalene, the Rose who bore the seed of Jesus.

However, Langdon still had no idea who this knight was or where he was buried.

'No thoughts?' Teabing clucked. 'Very well, I will walk you through it. It's quite simple, really. The first line is the key. Would you read it, please?'

Langdon read aloud. '"In London lies a knight a Pope interred."'

'Precisely. A knight a *Pope* interred.' He eyed Langdon. 'What does that mean to you?'

Langdon shrugged. 'A knight buried by a pope? A knight whose funeral was presided over by a pope?'

Teabing laughed loudly. 'Oh, that's rich. Always the optimist, Robert. Look at the second line. This knight obviously did something that incurred the holy wrath of the Church.'

'A knight a pope *killed*?' Sophie asked.

Teabing smiled and patted her knee. 'Well done, my dear. A knight a pope *buried*. Or killed.'

Langdon thought of the notorious Templar roundup in 1307 – unlucky Friday the thirteenth – when Pope Clement killed and interred hundreds of Knights Templar. 'But there must be endless graves of "knights killed by popes".'

'Aha, not so!' Teabing said. 'Many of them were burned at the stake and tossed unceremoniously into the Tiber in Rome. But this poem refers to a *tomb*. A tomb in London. And there are few knights buried in London. Robert, for heaven's sake! The church built in London in 1185 by the Priory's military arm – the Knights Templar themselves!'

'The Temple Church?' Langdon drew a startled breath. 'It has a crypt?'

'Ten of the most frightening tombs you will ever see.'

Langdon had come across many references to the Temple Church in his Priory research. Once the epicentre of all Templar and Priory activities in the United Kingdom, named in honour of Solomon's temple, tales abounded of knights performing strange, secretive rituals there. 'The Temple Church is on Fleet Street?'

'Actually, it's just off Fleet Street on Inner Temple Lane.' Teabing looked mischievous. 'It's hidden now behind much larger buildings, so few people even know it's there. Eerie old place. The architecture is pagan to the core.'

Sophie looked surprised. 'Pagan?'

'Totally!' Teabing exclaimed. 'The church is *round*. The Templars ignored the traditional Christian cruciform layout and built a perfectly circular church in honour of the *sun*.' His eyebrows did a devilish dance.

Sophie eyed Teabing. 'What about the rest of the poem?'

'It's puzzling. We will need to examine each of the ten tombs carefully. With luck, one of them will have a conspicuously absent orb.'

Langdon eyed the poem again. *A five-letter word that speaks of the Grail?* He suddenly realized how close they really were. If the missing orb revealed the password, they would be able to open the second cryptex.

'Sir Leigh?' Rémy called over his shoulder. He was watching them in the rearview mirror through the open divider. 'You said Fleet Street is near Blackfriars Bridge?'

'Yes, take Victoria Embankment.'

'I'm sorry. I'm not sure where that is. We usually go only to the hospital.'

Teabing rolled his eyes at Langdon and Sophie and grumbled, 'One moment, please. Help yourself to a drink and savoury snacks.' He left them, clambering awkwardly towards the open divider to talk to Rémy.

Langdon's Mickey Mouse wristwatch read almost seven thirty in the morning when he, Sophie and Teabing emerged from the Jaguar. The threesome wound their way through a maze of buildings to a small courtyard outside the Temple Church.

*The simplicity of the circle,* Langdon thought, admiring the building for the first time.

'It's early on a Saturday,' Teabing said, hobbling towards the entrance. 'They don't open to sightseers for another couple of hours.' He peered at the bulletin board outside, reading the notices there, and then tried the door. It didn't budge.

Inside, an altar boy had almost finished vacuuming the communion kneelers when he heard a knocking on the sanctuary door. He ignored it – the church wasn't open yet for another two hours – but the knocking turned to a forceful banging, as if someone were hitting the door with a metal rod. The young man switched off his vacuum cleaner and marched angrily towards the door. Unlatching it from within, he swung it open. Three people stood in the doorway. *Tourists,* he though. 'We open at nine thirty,' he told them.

A heavy-set man using crutches stepped forward. 'I am Sir Leigh Teabing,' he said, his accent highbrow British. 'As Reverend Knowles will no doubt have told you, I am escorting Mr and Mrs Christopher Wren the Fourth.' He stepped aside, flourishing his arm towards the attractive couple behind him. The altar boy had no idea how to reply.

The man on crutches frowned. He leaned forward, whispering as if to save everyone from embarrassment. 'Young man, apparently you are new here. Every year Sir Christopher Wren's descendants bring a pinch of the old man's ashes to scatter in the Temple sanctuary. It is part of his last will and testament.'

The altar boy had never heard of this custom. 'It would be better if you waited until nine thirty . . .'

The man on crutches glared angrily. 'Mrs Wren,' he said, 'would you be so kind as to show this impertinent young man the reliquary of ashes?'

The woman hesitated a moment and then, as if awaking from a trance, reached into her sweater pocket and pulled out a small cylinder wrapped in protective fabric.

'There, you see?' the man on crutches snapped. 'Now, you can either grant his dying wish and let us sprinkle Wren's ashes in the sanctuary, or I tell Reverend Knowles how we've been treated.'

*What harm could it do?* The boy stepped aside to let the three people pass.

As he moved through the rectangular annexe towards the archway leading into the main church, Langdon was surprised by its barren austerity. The furnishings were stark and cold, bearing none of the traditional ornamentation. 'Bleak,' he whispered.

'It looks like a fortress in there,' Sophie whispered.

'The Knights Templar were warriors,' Teabing reminded them, the sound of his aluminium crutches echoing in this reverberant space. 'Their churches were their strongholds – and their banks.'

'Banks?' Sophie asked, glancing at Leigh.

'Heavens, yes. The Templars *invented* the concept of modern banking. For European nobility, travelling with gold was perilous, so the Templars allowed nobles to deposit gold in their nearest Temple Church and then draw it from any *other* Temple Church across Europe. For a small commission, of course.' He winked. 'They were the original cash machines.' He shot a glance over his shoulder at the altar boy, who was vacuuming in the distance. 'You know,' he whispered to Sophie, 'the Holy Grail is said to have been stored in this church overnight while the Templars moved it from one hiding place to another. Can you imagine the four chests of Sangreal documents sitting right here with Mary Magdalene's sarcophagus? It gives me goosebumps.'

Langdon eyed the curvature of the chamber's pale stone perimeter, taking in the carvings of gargoyles, demons, monsters and pained human faces, all staring inwards. A single stone pew curled around the entire circumference of the room.

'Like a theatre in the round,' he whispered.

Teabing raised a crutch, pointing towards the far left of the room and then to the far right.

But Langdon had already seen them.

*Ten stone knights.*

*Five on the left. Five on the right.*

*In London lies a knight a Pope interred.*

This had to be the place.

# Chapter 63

In a garbage-strewn alley very close to Temple Church, Rémy Legaludec pulled the Jaguar limousine to a stop behind a row of industrial waste bins. Killing the engine, he checked the area. Deserted. He got out of the car, walked towards the rear and climbed into the back where the monk was.

Loosening his bow tie, he went to the limousine's bar, where he poured himself a strong drink. Then he picked up a corkscrew and flicked open the sharp blade on it that was used to slice the foil from corks on bottles of wine.

He turned and faced Silas, holding up the glimmering blade. 'Be still,' Rémy whispered, raising the blade.

Silas could not believe that God had forsaken him. He clenched his eyes shut and cried out, unable to believe he was going to die, here in the back of this limousine, unable to defend himself. *I was doing God's work* . . .

'Take a drink,' the tuxedoed man whispered as Silas felt a biting warmth spread across his back and shoulders. 'The pain you feel is the blood rushing into your muscles.'

Silas's eyes flew open in surprise. A blurry image was leaning over him, offering a glass of liquid. A mound of shredded duct tape lay on the floor beside the bloodless knife.

*God has not forsaken me.*

'I wanted to free you earlier,' the man apologized, 'but it was impossible. This was the first possible moment. You understand, don't you, Silas?'

Silas recoiled, startled. 'You know my name?' He sat up, rubbing his stiff muscles. 'Are you . . . the Teacher?'

Rémy shook his head, laughing at the idea. 'No, I am not the Teacher. Like you, I serve him. But the Teacher speaks highly of you. My name is Rémy.'

Silas was amazed. 'I don't understand. If you work for the Teacher, why did Langdon bring the keystone to *your* home?'

'Not *my* home. The home of the world's foremost Grail historian, Sir Leigh Teabing – the man to whom Robert Langdon would run once he was in possession of the keystone and needed help.' He smiled. 'How do you think the Teacher knows so much about the Grail research?'

Silas was stunned. The Teacher had recruited a servant who had access to all that Sir Leigh Teabing knew. It was brilliant.

'There is much I have to tell you,' Rémy said, handing Silas his loaded pistol. Then he reached through the open partition and took a small revolver from the glove box. 'But first, you and I have a job to do.'

# Chapter 64

*You seek the orb that ought be on his tomb.*

Each of the carved, life-sized figures rested on the floor in peaceful poses, their heads resting on rectangular stone pillows. They were shown wearing full armour, shields and swords.

Sophie felt a chill as she advanced with Langdon and Teabing towards the first group of knights. The poem's reference to an 'orb' conjured images of the night in her grandfather's basement.

*Hieros Gamos. The orbs.*

Scrutinizing the first tombs – the five knights on the left – she noted the similarities and differences between them. Every knight was on his back, but three of the knights had their legs extended straight out while two had their legs crossed. Two wore tunics over their armour, while the other three wore ankle-length robes. Two knights clutched swords, two prayed, and one had his arms at his sides. There was no hint anywhere of a conspicuously absent orb. She glanced back at Langdon and Teabing, then crossed over to the other five knights.

This group was similar to the first. All lay with varied body positions, wearing armour and swords.

That was, all except the tenth and final tomb.

Hurrying over to it, Sophie stared down.

*No pillow. No armour. No tunic. No sword.*

'Robert? Leigh?' she called, her voice echoing around the chamber. 'There's something missing over here.'

Both men looked up and crossed the room towards her.

'An orb?' Teabing called excitedly. His crutches clicked out a rapid staccato. 'Are we missing an orb?'

'Not exactly,' Sophie said, frowning at the tenth tomb. 'We seem to be missing an entire knight.'

Arriving beside her, both men gazed down in confusion. Rather than a knight lying in the open air, this tomb was a sealed stone coffin. It was shaped like a narrow trapezium, tapered at the feet, widening towards the top, with a peaked lid.

'Why isn't this knight shown?' Langdon asked.

'Fascinating,' Teabing said, stroking his chin. 'I had forgotten about this oddity. It's been years since I was here.'

'This coffin,' Sophie said, 'looks like it was carved at the same time and by the same sculptor as the other nine tombs. So why is this knight in a coffin rather than in the open?'

Teabing shook his head. 'One of this church's mysteries. To the best of my knowledge, nobody has ever found any explanation for it.'

'Hello?' the altar boy said, arriving with a perturbed look on his face. 'Forgive me if this seems rude – but you told me you wanted to spread ashes, and yet you seem to be sightseeing.'

Teabing scowled at the boy and turned to Langdon. 'Mr Wren, perhaps we should take out the ashes and get on with it. Now then,' he snapped at the boy, 'if you would give us some privacy?'

'I realize this is an intrusion,' Langdon added politely, 'but I have travelled a great distance to scatter ashes amongst these tombs.' He spoke his lines with Teabing-esque believability.

The altar boy's expression turned sceptical. 'These are not *tombs*.'

'I'm sorry?' Langdon said.

'Of course they are tombs,' Teabing declared. 'What are you talking about?'

The altar boy shook his head. 'Tombs contain bodies. These are effigies. Stone tributes to real men. There are no bodies beneath these figures.'

'This is a crypt!' Teabing said.

'Only in outdated history books. This was believed to be a crypt but was revealed as nothing of the sort during the 1950 renovation.' He turned back to Langdon. 'And I imagine Mr Wren would *know* that. Considering it was his family that uncovered that fact.'

An uneasy silence fell.

It was broken by the sound of a door slamming out in the annexe.

'That must be Reverend Knowles,' Teabing said. 'Perhaps you should go and see?'

The altar boy looked doubtful but stalked back towards the annexe, leaving Langdon, Sophie and Teabing to eye one another gloomily.

'Leigh,' Langdon whispered. 'No bodies? What is he talking about?'

Teabing looked distraught. 'I don't know. I always thought . . . certainly, this *must* be the place. I can't imagine he knows what he is talking about. It makes no sense!' He frowned. 'Could the poem be . . . wrong? Could Jacques Saunière have made the same mistake I just did?'

Langdon shook his head. 'Leigh, you said it yourself. This church was built by Templars, the military arm of the Priory. Something tells me the Grand Master of the Priory would have a pretty good idea if there were knights buried here.'

Teabing looked flabbergasted. 'But this place is perfect.' He wheeled back towards the knights. 'We must be missing something!'

Entering the annexe, the altar boy was surprised to find it deserted. 'Mr Knowles?' *I know I heard the door,* he thought, moving forward.

A thin man in a tuxedo stood near the doorway, scratching his head and looking lost. The altar boy gave an irritated huff, realizing he had forgotten to relock the door when he let the others in. 'I'm sorry,' he called out, passing a large pillar, 'we're closed.'

A flurry of cloth ruffled behind him, and before the altar boy could turn, his head snapped backwards and a powerful hand clamped hard over his mouth, muffling his scream. The hand was snow-white.

The prim man in the tuxedo calmly produced a very small revolver. 'Listen carefully,' he whispered. 'You will leave this church now, silently, and you will run. You will not stop. Is that clear?'

The boy nodded as best he could with the hand over his mouth.

'If you call the police . . .' The tuxedoed man pressed the gun to his skin. 'I will find you.'

The next thing the boy knew, he was sprinting across the outside courtyard with no plans of stopping until his legs gave out.

# Chapter 65

Like a ghost, Silas drifted silently behind his target. Sophie sensed him too late. Before she could turn, Silas had pressed the gun barrel into her spine and wrapped a powerful arm across her chest, pulling her back against his hulking body. She yelled in surprise. Teabing and Langdon both turned now, their expressions astonished and fearful.

'What . . .?' Teabing choked out. 'What did you do to Rémy?'

'Your only concern,' Silas said calmly, 'is that I leave here with the keystone.' This recovery mission, as Rémy had described it, was to be clean and simple: *Enter the church, take the keystone and walk out. No killing, no struggle.*

Holding Sophie firm, he dropped his hand from her chest down to her waist, slipping it inside her deep sweater pockets, searching. 'Where is it?' he whispered. *The keystone was in her pocket earlier. So where is it now?*

'It's over here.' Langdon's deep voice resonated from across the room.

Silas turned to see Langdon holding the black cryptex before him, waving it back and forth.

'Set it down,' Silas demanded.

'Let Sophie and Leigh leave the church first,' Langdon replied.

Silas pushed Sophie away from him and aimed the gun at Langdon, moving towards him.

'Not a step closer,' Langdon said. 'Not until they leave the building.' He raised the cryptex high over his head. 'I will not hesitate to smash this on the floor and break the vial inside.'

Silas felt a flash of fear. This was unexpected. He aimed the gun at Langdon's head and kept his voice as steady as his hand. 'You would never break the keystone. You want to find the Grail as much as I do.'

'You're wrong. You want it much more. You've proven you're willing to kill for it.'

Forty feet away, peering out from the annexe pews near the archway, Rémy Legaludec felt a rising alarm. The manoeuvre had not gone as planned, and he could see that Silas was uncertain what to do next. Following the Teacher's orders, Rémy had forbidden Silas to fire his gun.

*The cryptex cannot fall!* he thought fearfully. If Langdon dropped it, all would be lost. That cryptex was to be Rémy's ticket to freedom and wealth. A little over a year ago, he had been simply a fifty-five-year-old manservant catering to the whims of Sir Leigh Teabing – the most notable Grail historian on earth. Then he had been approached with an extraordinary proposition that would bring him everything he had ever dreamed of. Rémy felt giddy every time he thought of the money he soon would have. *One third of twenty million euros.* He planned to live out his days basking on the sunny beaches of the Côte d'Azur and letting others serve him.

*Am I willing to show my face?* It was something the Teacher had strictly forbidden, for Rémy was the only one who knew the Teacher's true identity.

'Are you certain you want *Silas* to carry out this task?' Rémy had asked the Teacher less than half an hour ago, upon getting orders to steal the keystone. 'I myself could do this.'

The Teacher was resolute. 'Silas served us well with the four Priory members. He will recover the keystone. *You* must remain anonymous. Do not reveal your face.'

'Understood,' Rémy said.

'For your own knowledge, Rémy,' the Teacher had told him, 'the tomb in question is not in the Temple Church. So have no fear. They are looking in the wrong place.'

Rémy was stunned. 'And you know where the tomb is?'

'Of course. Later, I will tell you. For the moment, you must act quickly. If the others work out the true location of the tomb and leave the church before you take the cryptex, we could lose the Grail forever.'

Rémy didn't care about the Grail, except that the Teacher refused to pay him until it was found. Now, with Langdon threatening to break the keystone, his future was at risk. Unable to bear the thought of coming this close only to lose it all, he made the decision to take bold action. Stepping from the shadows,

Rémy marched into the circular chamber and aimed the gun directly at Teabing's head.

'Old man, I've been waiting a long time to do this.'

'Rémy?' Sir Leigh Teabing spluttered in shock. 'What is going on? I don't –'

'I'll make it simple,' Rémy snapped, eyeing Langdon over Teabing's shoulder. 'Set down the keystone, or I pull the trigger and kill Sir Leigh.'

'The keystone is worthless to you,' Langdon said. 'You cannot possibly open it.'

'Arrogant fools,' Rémy sneered. 'I have been listening tonight as you discussed these verses. Everything I heard, I have shared with others. Others who know more than you. You are not even looking in the right place. The tomb you seek is in another location entirely!'

Teabing felt panicked. *What is he saying?*

Rémy called over to the monk. 'Silas, take the keystone from Mr Langdon.'

As the monk advanced, Langdon stepped back, raising the keystone high, looking fully prepared to hurl it at the floor.

'I would rather break it,' he said, 'than see it in the wrong hands.'

Teabing now felt a wave of horror. He could see his life's work evaporating before his eyes. All his dreams about to be shattered. 'Robert, no!' he exclaimed. 'Don't! That's the Grail you're holding! Rémy would *never* shoot me. We've known each other for ten –'

Rémy aimed at the ceiling and fired the revolver. The blast was enormous for such a small weapon, the gunshot echoing like thunder inside the stone chamber.

Everyone froze.

'The next one is in his back,' Rémy said. 'Hand the keystone to Silas.'

Langdon reluctantly held out the cryptex, and Silas stepped forward and took it, his red eyes gleaming with satisfaction. Slipping the keystone into the pocket of his robe, the albino backed off slowly, the gun still in his hand.

Teabing felt an arm clamp hard around his neck; Rémy was backing out of the building, dragging Teabing with him, the gun still pressed into his back.

'Let him go,' Langdon demanded.

'We're taking Mr Teabing for a drive,' Rémy said, still backing up. 'If you call the police, he will die. If you do anything to interfere, he will die. Is that clear?'

'Take me,' Langdon demanded, his voice cracking with emotion. 'Let Leigh go.'

Rémy laughed. 'I don't think so. He and I have such a nice history. Besides, he still might prove useful.'

Sophie's voice was unwavering. 'Who are you working for?'

The question brought a smirk to the departing Rémy's face. 'You would be surprised, Mademoiselle Neveu.'

# Chapter 66

Utterly frustrated, Lieutenant Collet helped himself to a bottle of water from Teabing's fridge and strode back out through the drawing room. Rather than accompanying Fache to London where the action was, he was now babysitting the police team that had spread out through the château.

So far, the evidence they had uncovered was unhelpful: a single bullet buried in the floor, a paper with several symbols scrawled on it, along with the words *blade* and *chalice,* and a spiked leather belt that the crime-scene officers had told Collet was of the sort worn by members of the conservative Catholic group Opus Dei.

In the vast ballroom study, the chief crime-scene examiner was busy dusting for fingerprints.

'Anything?' Collet asked, entering.

The man shook his head. 'Nothing new. Multiple sets matching those in the rest of the house.'

Collet picked up an evidence bag. Through the plastic, he could see a large glossy photograph of what appeared to be an old document. The heading at the top read:

*Les Dossiers Secrets – Number 4 ° lm1 249*

'What's this?' he asked.

'No idea, but he's got copies of it all over the place, so I bagged it.'

Collet studied the document.

## PRIEURE DE SION – LES NAUTONIERS/ GRAND MASTERS

JEAN DE GISORS: *1188–1220*

MARIE DE SAINT-CLAIR: *1220–1266*

GUILLAUME DE GISORS: *1266–1307*

EDOUARD DE BAR: *1307–1336*

JEANNE DE BAR: *1336–1351*

JEAN DE SAINT-CLAIR: *1351–1366*

BLANCHE D'EVREUX: *1366–1398*

NICOLAS FLAMEL: *1398–1418*

RENE D'ANJOU: *1418–1480*

IOLANDE DE BAR: *1480–1483*

SANDRO BOTTICELLI: *1483–1510*

LEONARDO DA VINCI: *1510–1519*

CONNETABLE DE BOURBON: *1519–1527*

FERDINAND DE GONZAQUE: *1527–1575*

LOUIS DE NEVERS: *1575–1595*

ROBERT FLUDD: *1595–1637*

J. VALENTIN ANDREA: *1637–1654*

ROBERT BOYLE: *1654–1691*

ISAAC NEWTON: *1691–1727*

CHARLES RADCLYFFE: *1727–1746*

CHARLES DE LORRAINE: *1746–1780*

MAXIMILIAN DE LORRAINE: *1780–1801*

CHARLES NODIER: *1801–1844*

VICTOR HUGO: *1844–1885*

CLAUDE DEBUSSY: *1885–1918*

JEAN COCTEAU: *1918–1963*

*Prieuré de Sion?* Collet wondered.

'Lieutenant?' Another agent stuck his head in. 'The switchboard has an urgent call for Captain Fache, but they can't reach him. Will you take it?'

It was André Vernet. The banker's refined accent did little to mask the tension in his voice. 'Captain Fache said he would call me, but I have not yet heard from him.'

'The captain is quite busy,' Collet replied. 'May I help you? My name is Lieutenant Collet.'

There was a long pause on the line. 'Lieutenant, I have another call coming in. Please excuse me. I will call you later.'

For several seconds, Collet held the receiver. *I've heard that voice before!* Then it dawned on him and the revelation made him gasp.

*The armoured truck driver. With the fake Rolex.*

*Vernet is involved,* he realized. This lucky break could be his moment to shine. He immediately called Interpol and requested – without delay – every shred of information they could find on the Depository Bank of Zurich and its president, André Vernet.

On the other side of the Channel, Captain Fache had just descended from his transport plane at Biggin Hill and was listening in disbelief to the Kent chief inspector's account of what had happened in Teabing's hangar.

'I searched the plane myself,' the inspector insisted, 'and there was no one inside.'

'Did you interrogate the pilot?'

'Of course not. He is a Frenchman, so –'

'Take me to the plane.'

Arriving at the hangar, Fache walked up to the plane and rapped loudly on the fuselage.

'This is the captain of the French Judicial Police. Open the door!'

The terrified pilot opened the hatch and lowered the stairs.

Three minutes later, with the help of his sidearm, Fache had a full confession, including a description of the bound albino monk. He also learned that Langdon and Sophie had left something behind in Teabing's safe, a wooden box of some sort.

'Open the safe,' Fache demanded.

'I don't have the combination,' the pilot said.

'Then drill it. You have half an hour.'

The pilot leaped into action.

Fache strode to the back of the plane and poured himself a drink. He closed his eyes, trying to sort out what was going on.

*The Kent police's blunder could cost me dearly,* he thought. Suddenly, his phone rang. *'Allo?'*

'I'm en route to London.' It was Bishop Aringarosa. 'I'll be arriving in an hour.'

Fache sat up. 'I thought you were going to Paris.'

'I am deeply concerned. I have changed my plans. Do you have Silas?'

'No. They got away from the local police before I landed, taking Silas with them.'

Aringarosa's anger rang sharply. 'You assured me you would stop that plane!'

Fache lowered his voice. 'Bishop, I will find Silas and the others as soon as possible. Tell your pilot to land here at Biggin Hill Executive Airport in Kent. I'll have a car waiting for you.'

'Thank you.'

'You would do well to remember, Bishop, that you are not the only man on the verge of losing everything.'

The fireplace in Château Villette's drawing room was cold, but Collet paced before it as he read the information that had rapidly come back from Interpol.

André Vernet, according to official records, was a model citizen. No police record – not even a parking ticket.

*Zero.* Collet sighed.

The only red flag had been a set of fingerprints that apparently belonged to Teabing's servant. 'Prints belong to Rémy Legaludec,' his chief forensic examiner reported. 'Wanted for petty theft. Breaking and entering. Skipped out on a hospital bill for an emergency tracheotomy once.' He glanced up, chuckling. 'Peanut allergy.'

Collet sighed. 'All right, you better forward this info to Captain Fache.'

The examiner headed off just as another agent burst into the living room. 'Lieutenant! We just found something in the barn.'

From the anxious look on the agent's face, Collet could only guess. 'A body?'

'No, sir. Something more . . .' He hesitated. 'Unexpected.'

Rubbing his eyes, Collet followed the agent out to the barn. As they entered the musty, cavernous space, the agent motioned towards the centre of the room, where a wooden ladder ascended high into the rafters.

Collet's eyes followed it up to the soaring hayloft. *Someone goes up there regularly?*

A senior agent appeared at the top of the ladder, looking down. 'You'll definitely want to see this, Lieutenant,' he said, waving Collet up with a latex-gloved hand.

Nodding tiredly, the lieutenant walked over to the base of the old ladder and grasped the bottom rungs. The ladder was an antique tapered design and narrowed as Collet ascended. As he neared the top, he almost lost his footing on a narrow rung. The barn below him spun. The agent above him reached out, offering his wrist. Collet grabbed it and made the awkward transition on to the platform.

'It's over there,' the agent said, pointing into the immaculately clean loft. 'Only one set of prints up here. We'll have an ID shortly.'

Collet squinted through the dim light towards the far wall. *What* –? Nestled against the far wall sat an elaborate computer workstation with a flat-screen monitor and what looked like speakers and a multichannel console. He moved towards the gear. 'Have you examined the system?'

'It's a listening post.'

Collet spun. 'Surveillance?'

The agent nodded. 'Very advanced surveillance.'

'Do you have any idea what target is being bugged?'

'Well, Lieutenant,' the agent said, 'it's the strangest thing . . .'

# Chapter 67

Langdon felt utterly exhausted as he and Sophie hurdled a turnstile at Temple tube station and dashed deep into the grimy labyrinth of tunnels and platforms. The guilt ripped through him.

*I involved Leigh, and now he's in enormous danger.*

Rémy's involvement had been a shock, and yet it made sense. Whoever was pursuing the Grail had recruited someone on the inside. He followed Sophie to the westbound District and Circle Line platform, where she hurried to a pay phone to call the police, despite Rémy's warning to the contrary.

'The best way to help Leigh,' Sophie reiterated as she dialled, 'is to involve the London authorities immediately. Trust me.'

Langdon had not initially agreed with her, but as they had hatched their plans, Sophie's logic began to make sense. Teabing was safe at the moment. Even if Rémy and the others believed they knew where the knight's tomb was located, they might still need Teabing's help to decipher the orb reference. What worried Langdon was what might happen *after* the Grail map had been found. *Leigh will no longer be of use to them.*

If Langdon were to have any chance of helping Leigh, or of ever seeing the keystone again, it was essential that he find the tomb first.

Slowing Rémy down had become Sophie's task.

Finding the right tomb had become Langdon's.

Sophie had finally got through to the London police.

'I'm reporting a kidnapping.' She knew to be concise.

'Name, please?'

Sophie paused. 'Agent Sophie Neveu with the French Judicial Police.'

The title had the desired effect. 'Right away, ma'am. Let me get a detective on the line for you.'

Fifteen seconds passed.

Finally, a man came on the line. 'Agent Neveu?'

Stunned, Sophie registered the gruff tone immediately.

'Agent Neveu,' Bezu Fache demanded. 'Where *are* you?'

Sophie was speechless.

'Listen,' Fache said, speaking to her in terse French. 'I made a terrible mistake tonight. Robert Langdon is innocent. All charges against him have been dropped.'

Sophie's jaw fell slack. She had no idea how to respond. Fache *never* apologized for anything.

'You did not tell me,' Fache continued, 'that Jacques Saunière was your grandfather. But both you and Langdon are in danger – you need to go to the nearest London police headquarters for refuge.'

*He knows I'm in London? What else does Fache know?* Sophie heard what sounded like machinery in the background. She also heard an odd clicking on the line. 'Are you tracing this call, Captain?'

Fache's voice was firm now. 'You and I need to cooperate, Agent Neveu. We both have a lot to lose here . . .'

'The man you want is Rémy Legaludec,' she told Fache. 'He is Teabing's servant. He just kidnapped Sir Leigh Teabing inside the Temple Church and –'

'Agent Neveu!' Fache bellowed as the train thundered into the station. 'This is not something to discuss on an open line. You and Langdon will come in now. That is a direct order!'

Sophie hung up and dashed with Langdon on to the train.

# Chapter 68

The immaculate cabin of Teabing's Hawker was now covered with steel shavings. Bezu Fache had sent everyone away and sat alone with his drink and the heavy wooden box found in Teabing's safe.

Running his finger across the inlaid rose, he lifted the ornate lid. Inside he found a stone cylinder with lettered dials. The five dials were arranged to spell SOFIA. Fache stared at the word and then lifted the cylinder from its padded resting place and examined every inch. Then, pulling slowly on the ends, he slid off one of the end caps. The cylinder was empty.

He set it back in the box and gazed absently out of the window at the hangar. The sound of his phone shook him from his daydream. A call via the police switchboard from the president of the Depository Bank of Zurich.

'Monsieur Vernet,' Fache said before the man could even speak, 'I am sorry I did not call you earlier. I have been busy. As promised, the name of your bank has not appeared in the media. So what precisely is your concern?'

Vernet's voice was anxious as he told Fache how Langdon and Sophie had extracted a small wooden box from the bank and then persuaded him to help them escape. 'When I heard on the radio that they were criminals,' he said, 'I pulled over and demanded the box back, but they attacked me and stole the truck.'

'You are concerned for a wooden box,' Fache said, eyeing the rose inlay on the cover and again gently opening the lid to reveal the white cylinder. 'Can you tell me what was in it?'

'The contents don't matter,' Vernet fired back. 'I am concerned with the reputation of my bank. We have never had a robbery. *Ever.* It will ruin us if I cannot recover this property on behalf of my client.'

'But if they had a key – and the right password – what makes you say they *stole* the box?'

'They *murdered* people tonight. Including Sophie Neveu's grandfather.' The banker sounded distraught. 'The key and password were obviously ill-gotten.'

'Mr Vernet,' Fache said slowly, 'I appreciate that you are a man of honour. As am I. That said, I give you my word that your box – and your bank's reputation – is in the safest of hands.'

High in the hayloft at Château Villette, Collet stared at the computer monitor in amazement. 'This system is eavesdropping on *all* these locations?'

'Yes,' the agent said. 'For over a year, I believe.'

Collet read the list again, speechless.

Colbert Sostaque – Chairman of the Conseil
   Constitutionnel
Jean Chaffée – Curator, Musée du Jeu de Paume
Edouard Desrochers – Senior Archivist,
   Mitterrand Library
Jacques Saunière – Curator, Musée du Louvre
Michel Breton – Head of DAS (French
   Intelligence)

The agent pointed to the screen. 'Number four is of obvious interest.'

Collet nodded. He had noticed it immediately. *Jacques Saunière was being bugged.* He looked at the rest of the list again. *How could anyone possibly manage to bug these prominent people?* 'Have you heard any of the files?'

'Here's one of the most recent.' The agent clicked a few computer keys. The speakers crackled to life. *'Capitaine, un agent du Département de Cryptographie est arrivé.'*

Collet could not believe his ears. 'That's me! That's my voice!' He remembered sitting at Saunière's desk and radioing Fache in the Grand Gallery to alert him of Sophie Neveu's arrival.

The agent nodded. 'A lot of our investigation at the gallery tonight would have been audible if someone had been interested.'

'Have you sent anyone in to sweep for the bug?'

'No need. I know exactly where it is.' The agent went to a pile of old notes and blueprints on the worktable. He selected a page and handed it to Collet. 'Look familiar?'

Collet was amazed. He was holding a photocopy of an ancient diagram, which depicted a rudimentary machine. He was unable to read the handwritten Italian labels, and yet he knew what he was looking at. A fully articulated model of a medieval French knight.

*The knight sitting on Saunière's desk!*

Collet's eyes moved to the margins, where someone had scribbled notes on the photocopy in red felt-tip. The notes were in French and appeared to be ideas on how best to insert a listening device into the knight.

# Chapter 69

Silas sat in the passenger seat of the parked Jaguar near the Temple Church. His hands felt damp on the keystone as he waited for Rémy to finish tying up and gagging Teabing with the rope they had found in the trunk.

Finally, Rémy slid into the driver's seat beside Silas. He chuckled, shaking off the rain and glancing over his shoulder through the open partition at the crumpled form of Leigh Teabing, who was barely visible in the shadows in the rear. 'He's not going anywhere.'

Silas could hear Teabing's muffled cries and realized Rémy must have used some of the old duct tape to gag him.

'*Ferme ta gueule!*' Rémy shouted over his shoulder at Teabing. *Shut up!* Reaching for the control panel, he pressed a button. An opaque partition raised behind them, sealing off the back. Teabing disappeared, and his voice was silenced.

Minutes later, as the stretch limo powered through the streets, Silas's phone rang. *The Teacher.* He answered excitedly. 'Hello?'

'Silas,' the Teacher's familiar French accent said, 'I am relieved to hear your voice. This means you are safe.'

Silas was equally comforted to hear the Teacher. It had been hours, and the operation had veered wildly off course. Now, at last, it seemed to be back on track. 'I have the keystone.'

'This is superb news,' the Teacher told him. 'Is Rémy with you?'

Silas was surprised to hear the Teacher use Rémy's name. 'Yes. Rémy freed me.'

'As I ordered him to do. I am only sorry you had to endure captivity for so long.'

'Physical discomfort has no meaning. The important thing is that the keystone is ours.'

'Yes. I need it delivered to me at once. Time is of the essence.'

Silas was eager to meet the Teacher face to face at last. 'Yes, sir, I would be honoured.'

'Silas, I would like *Rémy* to bring it to me.'

After everything Silas had done for the Teacher, he thought he would be the one to hand over the prize.

'I sense your disappointment,' the Teacher said, 'which tells me you do not understand my meaning.' He lowered his voice to a whisper. 'You must believe that I would much prefer to receive the keystone from *you* – a man of God rather than a criminal – but Rémy must be dealt with. He disobeyed my orders and made a grave mistake that has put our entire mission at risk.'

Silas felt a chill and glanced over at Rémy. Kidnapping Teabing had not been part of the plan, he knew.

'You and I are men of God,' the Teacher whispered. 'We cannot be deterred from our goal.' There was an ominous pause on the line. 'For this reason alone, I will ask Rémy to bring me the keystone. Do you understand?'

Silas sensed anger in the Teacher's voice and was surprised the man was not more understanding. *Rémy did what he had to do. Showing his face could not be avoided,* he thought. *He saved the keystone.* 'I understand,' he managed to say.

'Good. Now, you need to get off the street immediately. The police will be looking for the limousine, and I do not want you caught. Opus Dei has a residence in London, no?'

'Of course.'

'And you are welcome there?'

'As a brother.'

'Then go there and stay out of sight – I will tell Rémy to drive you there. I will call you the moment I am in possession of the keystone.' The Teacher heaved a sigh. 'It's time I speak to Rémy.'

Silas handed Rémy the phone, sensing it might be the last call Rémy Legaludec ever took.

As Rémy took the phone, he knew this poor, twisted monk had no idea what fate awaited him now that he had served his purpose.

*The Teacher used you, Silas.*

Rémy did not particularly like the Teacher, but he felt proud that he had gained the man's trust and helped him so much. *I have earned my payday.*

'Listen carefully,' the Teacher said. 'Take Silas to the Opus Dei residence hall and drop him off a few streets away. Then drive to St James's Park, adjacent to The Mall, and park the limousine on Horse Guards Parade. We'll talk there.'

With that, the connection went dead.

# Chapter 70

Langdon still felt shaky as he and Sophie came in from the rain and entered the library at King's College. The Theology and Religious Studies department possesses one of the most complete religious research databases in the world.

On the far side of the room, a reference librarian was just pouring a pot of tea and settling in for her day of work.

'Lovely morning,' she said cheerfully, leaving the tea and walking over. 'Pamela Gettum.' She offered her hand. She had a pleasingly fluid voice. The horn-rimmed glasses hanging around her neck were thick. 'May I help you?'

'Thank you, yes,' Langdon replied. 'My name is –'

'Robert Langdon.' She gave a pleasant smile. 'I recognize you – we have some of your books and research papers here.'

Langdon smiled back. 'This is my friend Sophie Neveu. If it's not too much trouble, we could really use your help finding some information.' He paused. 'I'm afraid we've come unannounced. A friend of mine speaks very highly of you. Sir Leigh Teabing?'

He felt a pang of gloom as he said the name. 'The British Royal Historian.'

Gettum brightened, laughing. 'Heavens, yes. What a character. Fanatical! Always the same search strings. Grail. Grail. Grail. I swear that man will die before he gives up on that quest.'

'Is there any chance you can help us?' Sophie asked. 'It's quite important.'

Gettum glanced around the deserted library and then winked at them. 'Well, I can't very well claim I'm too busy, now can I? What did you have in mind?'

'We're trying to find a tomb in London.'

Gettum looked dubious. 'We've got about twenty thousand of them. Can you be a little more specific?'

'It's the tomb of a knight. We don't have a name.'

'A knight. That tightens the net quite a lot. Much less common.'

'We don't have much information about the knight we're looking for,' Sophie said, 'but this is what we know.' She produced a slip of paper.

> *In London lies a knight a Pope interred.*
> *His labour's fruit a Holy wrath incurred.*

She glanced at her guests, feeling intrigued. 'According to this rhyme, a knight did something that incurred displeasure with God, and yet a pope was kind enough to bury him in London?'

Langdon nodded. 'Does it ring any bells?'

Gettum moved towards one of the workstations. 'Not off hand, but let's see what we can pull up from the database.' She eyed the slip of paper and began typing. 'To begin, we'll run a straight Boolean search with a few obvious keywords and see what happens.'

'Thank you.'

Gettum typed in a few words:

London, Knight, Pope

As she clicked the SEARCH button, she said, 'I'm asking the system to show us any documents whose complete text contains all three of these keywords. We'll get more hits than we want, but it's a good place to start.'

The screen was already showing the first of the hits now, and Gettum shot a quick glance to a numeric field at the bottom of the screen – a rough guess of how much information would be found. This particular search looked like it was going to return far too many possibilities.

Estimated number of total hits: 2,692

She frowned, stopping the search. 'There's nothing else to go on?' She knew the most common reason people came to London to look for knights. *The Grail.* 'You are friends with Leigh Teabing, you are in England, and you are looking for a knight.' She folded her hands. 'I can only assume you are on a Grail quest.'

Langdon and Sophie exchanged startled looks.

Gettum laughed. 'My friends, I wish I had a shilling for every time I'd run searches for the Rose, Mary Magdalene, Sangreal, Merovingian, Priory of Sion, et cetera, et cetera. Everyone loves a conspiracy.' She took off her glasses and eyed her guests. 'I need more information.'

In the silence, the librarian sensed their desire for secrecy was quickly being outweighed by their eagerness for a fast result.

'Here,' Sophie Neveu blurted. 'This is everything we know.' Borrowing a pen from Langdon, she wrote two more lines on the slip of paper and handed it to Gettum.

> *You seek the orb that ought be on his tomb.*
> *It speaks of Rosy flesh and seeded womb.*

Gettum gave a small smile. *The Grail indeed,* she thought. She looked up from the slip of paper. 'Might I ask where this verse came from? And why you are seeking an orb?'

'You might ask,' Langdon said with a friendly smile, 'but it's a long story and we have very little time.'

'Sounds like a polite way of saying "mind your own business".'

'We would be forever in your debt, Pamela,' Langdon said, 'if you could find out who this knight is and where he is buried.'

'Very well,' Gettum said, typing again.

*Search for:*
Knight, London, Pope, Tomb

*Within 100 word proximity of:*
Grail, Rose, Sangreal, Chalice

'How long will this take?' Sophie asked.

The librarian's eyes glimmered as she clicked the SEARCH key. 'A mere fifteen minutes.'

# Chapter 71

The London Opus Dei Centre is a modest brick building at 5 Orme Court in Kensington. Silas had never been there before, but he felt a rising sense of refuge and asylum as he approached the building on foot – Rémy had dropped him off a short distance away so he could keep the limousine off the main streets.

The rain began to fall harder now, soaking Silas's heavy robe. It felt cleansing. Silas felt lighter now – he had wiped down his gun and thrown it down a drain. He was glad to get rid of it. His legs still ached from being bound all that time, but he had endured far greater pain. He wondered, though, about Teabing, whom Rémy had left bound in the back of the limousine.

'What will you do with him?' Silas had asked Rémy as they drove over here.

Rémy had shrugged. 'That is a decision for the Teacher.' There was an odd finality in his tone.

Now Silas was ready to leave behind the sins of the last twenty-four hours and purge his soul. His work was done.

Moving across a small courtyard, he was not surprised to find the front door unlocked. He opened it and stepped into a simple foyer. As he stepped on to the carpet, a muted chime sounded upstairs.

A man in a cloak came down the stairs. 'May I help you?' He had kind eyes and seemed not even to notice Silas's unusual appearance.

'Thank you. My name is Silas. I am an Opus Dei numerary, in town only for the day. Might I rest here?'

'You need not even ask. There are two empty rooms on the third floor. Shall I bring you some tea and bread?'

'Thank you.' Silas was famished.

He went upstairs to a modest room with a window, where he took off his wet robe and knelt down to pray. He heard his host come up and lay a tray outside his door. Then Silas finished his prayers, ate his food and lay down to sleep.

Three floors below, a phone began ringing. The Opus Dei resident who had welcomed Silas answered.

'This is the London police,' the caller said. 'We are trying to find an albino monk. We've had a tip-off that he might be there. Have you seen him?'

The numerary was startled. 'Yes, he is here. Is something wrong?'

'He is there *now*?'

'Yes, upstairs praying. What is going on?'

'Don't say a word to anyone,' the policeman commanded. 'I'm sending officers over right away.'

# Chapter 72

St James's Park is a sea of green in the middle of London, a public park bordering the palaces of Westminster, Buckingham and St James. On sunny afternoons, Londoners picnic beneath the willow trees and feed the pond's resident pelicans.

The Teacher saw no pelicans today. The stormy weather had brought seagulls instead. The lawns were covered with them – hundreds of white bodies all facing the same direction, patiently riding out the damp wind. Despite the morning fog, there were splendid views from the park of the Houses of Parliament and Big Ben. Gazing across the sloping lawns, the Teacher could see the spires of the building that housed the knight's tomb – the real reason he had told Rémy to come to this spot.

As he approached the front passenger door of the parked limousine, Rémy leaned across and opened the door. The Teacher paused outside, taking a pull from a flask of cognac he was carrying. Then, dabbing his mouth, he slid in beside Rémy and closed the door.

Rémy held up the keystone like a trophy. 'It was almost lost.'

'You have done well,' the Teacher said.

'*We* have done well,' Rémy replied, laying the keystone in the Teacher's eager hands.

The Teacher admired it, smiling. 'And the gun? You wiped it down?'

'Back in the glove box where I found it.'

'Excellent.' The Teacher took another drink of cognac and handed the flask to Rémy. 'Let's toast our success. The end is near.'

Rémy accepted the bottle gratefully. The cognac tasted salty, but he didn't care – he could feel it warming his blood. The warmth in Rémy's throat, however, mutated quickly to an uncomfortable heat. Loosening his bow tie, he handed the flask back to the Teacher.

Pocketing the flask and the keystone, the Teacher reached for the glove box and pulled out the tiny revolver, slipping it in his trousers pocket. 'Rémy,' he said, his voice now sounding regretful, 'as you are aware, you are the only one who knows my face. I placed enormous trust in you.'

'Yes,' Rémy said, feeling feverish as he loosened his tie further. 'And your identity shall go with me to the grave.'

The Teacher was silent. 'I believe you.'

The swelling in Rémy's throat came on like an earthquake, and he lurched against the steering column, grabbing his throat. The saltiness in the cognac now registered.

Rémy turned to see the Teacher sitting calmly beside him, staring straight ahead through the windshield. He tried to lunge for him, but his stiffening body could barely move. He tried to lift his clenched fists to blow the horn, but instead he slipped sideways, rolling on to the seat, lying on his side beside the Teacher, clutching at his throat as his world slowly went black.

The Teacher stepped out of the limousine, pleased to see that nobody was looking in his direction. *I had no choice,* he told himself. *Rémy sealed his own fate.*

Robert Langdon's unexpected visit to Château Villette had brought the Teacher both a stroke of luck and a problem. Langdon had brought the keystone with him, which had been a pleasant surprise, but he had also brought the police on his tail. Rémy's prints were all over the château, as well as in the barn's listening post – where Rémy had been in charge of all the surveillance – but there were no ties between Rémy's activities and his own. Nobody could implicate the Teacher unless Rémy talked, and that was no longer a concern.

Minutes later, the Teacher was gazing triumphantly across St James's Park at his destination. *In London lies a knight a Pope interred.* As soon as the Teacher heard the poem, he had known the answer – having listened to Saunière's conversations for months now, he had heard the Grand Master mention this famous knight several times, and the poem's reference was brutally simple once one saw it. Yet how this tomb would reveal the final password was still a mystery.

*You seek the orb that ought be on his tomb.*

He tucked the cryptex deep in his right-hand pocket, keeping the tiny revolver in his left, out of sight, as he stepped into the quiet sanctuary of the nine-hundred-year-old building.

Just as the Teacher was stepping out of the rain, Bishop Aringarosa was stepping into it. On the rainy tarmac at Biggin Hill in Kent, Aringarosa emerged from his cramped plane, bundling his cassock against the cold damp. He had hoped to be greeted by Captain Fache. Instead, a young British police officer approached with an umbrella.

'Bishop Aringarosa? Captain Fache asked me to look after you. He suggested I take you to Scotland Yard. He thought it would be safest.'

*Safest?* Aringarosa looked down at the heavy briefcase of Vatican bonds clutched in his hand. He had almost forgotten them. 'Yes, thank you.'

He climbed into the police car, wondering where Silas could be. Minutes later, he got his answer as the police scanner crackled.

*'Five Orme Court.'*

Aringarosa recognized the address instantly.

*The Opus Dei Centre in London.*

He turned to the driver. 'Forget about Scotland Yard. Take me to Orme Court at once!'

# Chapter 73

Langdon's eyes had not left the computer screen since the search began.

*Five minutes. Only two hits. Both irrelevant.*

He was starting to get worried.

Finally, the computer pinged again.

'Sounds like you got another,' Gettum called from the next room. 'What's the title?'

Langdon eyed the screen.

Grail Allegory in Medieval Literature:
A Treatise on Sir Gawain and the Green Knight

'A paper about the Green Knight,' he called back.

'No good.' Gettum peeked back through the doorway, holding a jar of instant coffee. 'Not many mythological green giants buried in London. But just be patient. It's a numbers game. Let the machine run.'

Over the next few minutes, the computer returned several more Grail references.

Four minutes later, as Langdon began feeling fearful they would not find what they had come for, the computer produced another hit.

The Gravity of Genius:
Biography of a Modern Knight

*'Gravity of Genius?'* Langdon called out to Gettum. 'Life story of a modern knight? Let's have a look.' He clicked on the link.

. . . honourable **knight**, Sir Isaac Newton . . .
. . . in **London** in 1727 and . . .
. . . his **tomb** in Westminster Abbey . . .
. . . Alexander **Pope**, friend and colleague . . .

'I suppose he is "modern" if you compare him to medieval knights,' Sophie called to the librarian. 'It's an old book. About Sir Isaac Newton.'

Gettum shook her head in the doorway. 'No good. Newton was buried in Westminster Abbey – that's for English Protestants. There's no way a Catholic pope would have been present. Milk and sugar?'

Sophie nodded.

Gettum waited. 'Robert?'

Langdon pulled his eyes from the screen and stood up. 'Sir Isaac Newton is our knight.'

Sophie remained seated. 'What are you talking about?'

'Newton is buried in London,' Langdon said to her in a whisper. 'His labours produced new science that incurred the wrath of the Church. And he was a Grand Master of the Priory of Sion. What more could we want?'

'What more?' Sophie pointed to the poem. 'How about a knight a pope interred? You heard Ms Gettum. Newton was not buried by a Catholic pope.'

Langdon reached for the mouse. 'Who said anything about a *Catholic* Pope?' He clicked on the 'Pope' hyperlink, and the complete sentence appeared.

> Sir Isaac Newton's burial, attended by kings and nobles, was presided over by Alexander Pope, friend and colleague, who gave a stirring eulogy before sprinkling dirt on the tomb.

Langdon looked at Sophie. 'Alexander Pope.' He paused. 'A. Pope.'

*In London lies a knight A. Pope interred.*

Sophie stood up, looking stunned.

Jacques Saunière, the master of double entendres, had proved once again that he was a very clever man.

# Chapter 74

Silas awoke with a start.

He had no idea how long he had been asleep. *Was I dreaming?* Sitting up on his straw mat, he listened to the quiet breathing of the Opus Dei residence hall, heard the soft murmurs of someone praying aloud in a room below him. These were familiar sounds and should have comforted him.

And yet he felt a sudden and unexpected wariness.

Standing, wearing only his undergarments, Silas walked to the window. *Was I followed?* The courtyard below was deserted, exactly as he had seen it when he entered. He listened. Silence. Long ago Silas had learned to trust his intuition. Intuition had kept him alive as a child on the streets . . . long before he was born again at the hands of Bishop Aringarosa. Peering out of the window, he now saw the faint outline of a car through the hedge. On the car's roof was a police siren. A floorboard creaked in the hallway. A door latch moved.

Silas reacted on instinct, surging across the room and sliding to a stop just behind the door as it crashed open. The first police officer stormed through, swinging his gun left, then right at what appeared an empty room. Before he realized where Silas was, Silas had thrown his shoulder into the door, crushing a second officer as he came through. As the first officer wheeled to shoot, Silas dived for his legs. The gun went off, the bullet sailing above Silas's head just as he connected with the officer's shins; the man fell down, his head hitting the floor.

Silas hurled his pale body down the staircase. He knew he had been betrayed, but by whom? When he reached the foyer, more officers were surging through the front door. Silas turned the other way and dashed deeper into the residence hall. *The women's entrance. Every Opus Dei building has one.* Winding down narrow hallways, Silas snaked through a kitchen, past terrified workers, bursting into a dark hallway near the boiler room. He now saw the door he sought, an exit light gleaming at the end.

Running full speed through the door out into the rain, Silas leaped off the low landing, not seeing the officer coming the other way until it was too late. The two men collided, Silas's broad shoulder grinding into the man's chest with crushing force. He drove the officer backwards on to the pavement, landing hard on top of him. The man's gun clattered away. Rolling, Silas grabbed the loose gun just as the other officers emerged. A shot rang out from the stairs, and Silas felt a searing pain below his ribs. Filled with rage, he opened fire at all three officers.

A dark shadow loomed behind, coming out of nowhere, and

angry hands grabbed at his bare shoulders. The man roared in his ear, *'Silas, no!'*

Silas spun and fired. Their eyes met. Silas was already screaming in horror as Bishop Aringarosa fell.

# Chapter 75

More than three thousand people are entombed or enshrined within the colossal stone interior of Westminster Abbey – tombs of kings, statesmen, scientists, poets and musicians, packed into every last niche and alcove. They range in grandeur from the most regal of mausoleums – that of Queen Elizabeth I, whose canopied sarcophagus sits in its own private chapel – down to a simple modest etched floor tile.

*In London lies a knight a Pope interred.*

Stepping across the threshold into the abbey – after passing through the abbey's newest addition of a walk-through metal detector – Langdon felt the outside world evaporate with a sudden hush. No rumble of traffic. No hiss of rain. Just a deafening silence, which seemed to reverberate back and forth as if the building were whispering to itself.

His and Sophie's eyes, like those of almost every visitor, shifted immediately skyward. Grey stone columns ascended like redwood trees into the shadows, arching gracefully over dizzying space and then shooting back down to the stone floor. Before them, the wide alley of the north transept stretched out like a deep canyon, flanked by sheer cliffs of stained glass. 'It's practically empty,' Sophie whispered.

Today was a rainy April morning. Rather than crowds and shimmering stained glass, all Langdon saw were acres of desolate floor and shadowy, empty alcoves.

'We passed through a metal detector,' Sophie reminded him, sensing his apprehension. 'If anyone is in here, they can't be armed.'

Langdon nodded but still felt worried. He had wanted to bring the London police with them, but Sophie's fears of who might be involved made her wary of contacting the authorities again. *We need to recover the cryptex,* Sophie had insisted. *It is the key to everything.*

She was right, of course.

*The key to getting Leigh back alive.*

*The key to finding the Holy Grail.*

*The key to learning who is behind this.*

Unfortunately, their only chance to recover the keystone seemed to be here and now . . . at the tomb of Isaac Newton. Whoever held the cryptex would have to pay a visit to the tomb to decipher the final clue, and if they had not already come and gone, Sophie and Langdon planned to intercept them.

'Which way is it?' Sophie asked, looking around.

*Newton's tomb.* 'We should find a guide and ask.'

Westminster Abbey was a tangled warren of mausoleums, chambers and walk-in burial niches. Keeping to tradition, the abbey was laid out in the shape of a giant crucifix. Unlike most churches, however, it had its entrance at the *side,* rather than the standard rear of the church. Moreover, the abbey had a series of sprawling cloisters attached. One step through the wrong archway, and a visitor could be lost in a labyrinth of outdoor passageways surrounded by high walls. Easy to find your way in – like the Louvre gallery, it had a lone point of entry – but impossible to find your way out.

'Guides wear crimson robes,' Langdon said, approaching the centre of the church.

'I don't see any about,' Sophie said. 'Maybe we can find the tomb on our own?'

Without a word, Langdon led her to the centre of the abbey and pointed to the right.

Sophie drew a startled breath. 'Let's find that guide,' she said.

At that moment, a hundred yards down the nave, out of sight behind the choir screen, the stately tomb of Sir Isaac Newton had a lone visitor. The Teacher had been scrutinizing the monument for ten minutes now.

Newton's tomb consisted of a massive black marble sarcophagus on which reclined his sculpted form, wearing classical costume and leaning proudly against a stack of his own books – *Divinity, Chronology, Opticks* and *Philosophiae Naturalis Principia Mathematica.* At Newton's feet stood two winged boys holding a scroll. Behind him rose an austere pyramid. Although the pyramid itself seemed odd, it was the giant shape mounted halfway *up* the pyramid that most intrigued the Teacher.

*An orb.*

The Teacher thought of Saunière's beguiling riddle. *You seek the orb that ought be on his tomb.* The massive orb protruding from the face of the pyramid showed all kinds of heavenly bodies – constellations, signs of the zodiac, comets, stars and planets.

*Countless orbs.*

The Teacher had been convinced that once he found the tomb, it would be easy to unravel the riddle. Now he was not so sure. He was gazing at a complicated map of the heavens. Was there a missing planet? He had no idea. Even so, the Teacher could not help but suspect that the solution would be ingeniously simple – it would be unlikely that someone searching for the Holy Grail would need advanced knowledge of astronomy.

*It speaks of Rosy flesh and seeded womb.*

He stepped closer to the tomb, scanning it from bottom to top. *What orb ought to be here . . . and yet is missing?* He touched the cryptex in his pocket as if he could somehow divine the answer from Saunière's crafted marble. *Only five letters separate me from the Grail.*

Pacing now near the corner of the choir screen, he took a deep breath and glanced up the long nave towards the main altar in the distance. His gaze dropped from the gilded altar down to the bright crimson robe of an abbey guide – and two very familiar individuals.

Langdon and Neveu.

Calmly, the Teacher moved two steps back behind the choir screen. *That was quick.* Sooner than he had imagined. Taking a deep breath, he considered his options.

*I am holding the cryptex.*

Reaching into his pocket, he touched the second object that gave him his confidence: the small revolver. As expected, the abbey's metal detectors had blared as the Teacher passed through with the concealed gun. Also as expected, the guards had backed off at once when the Teacher glared indignantly and flashed his identification card. An official rank like his always commanded the proper respect.

Although the Teacher had hoped to solve the riddle alone and avoid any further complications, the arrival of Langdon and Neveu was actually a welcome development. He might be able to use their expertise. After all, if Langdon had deciphered the poem to find the tomb, there was a reasonable chance he also knew something about the orb. It would just be a matter of applying the right pressure.

*Not here, of course.*

*Somewhere private.*

The Teacher recalled a small announcement sign he had seen on his way into the abbey. Immediately, he knew the perfect place to lure them.

The only question now . . . what to use as bait.

# Chapter 76

Langdon and Sophie moved slowly down the north aisle. They still had no clear view of Newton's tomb. The sarcophagus was recessed in a niche, obscured from this angle.

'At least there's nobody over there,' Sophie whispered.

Langdon nodded, relieved. The entire section of the nave near Newton's tomb was deserted. 'I'll go over,' he whispered. 'You should stay hidden just in case someone –'

Sophie had already stepped from the shadows and was headed across the open floor.

'– is watching,' Langdon sighed, hurrying to join her.

Crossing the massive nave on a diagonal, Langdon and Sophie remained silent as the elaborate tomb revealed itself . . . a black marble sarcophagus . . . a reclining statue of Newton . . . two winged boys . . . a huge pyramid . . . and . . . *an enormous orb.*

'Did you know about that?' Sophie said, sounding startled.

Langdon shook his head, also surprised.

'Those look like constellations carved on it,' Sophie added.

As they approached the niche, Langdon felt a slow sinking

sensation. Newton's tomb was covered with orbs – stars, comets, planets. *You seek the orb that ought be on his tomb?* It could turn out to be like trying to find a missing blade of grass on a golf course. He frowned. The only link between the planets and the Grail that Langdon could imagine was the pentacle of Venus, and he had already tried the password 'Venus' en route to the Temple Church.

Sophie moved directly to the sarcophagus. *'Divinity,'* she said, tilting her head and reading the titles of the books on which Newton was leaning. *'Chronology. Opticks. Philosophiae Naturalis Principia Mathematica?'* She turned to him. 'Ring any bells?'

Langdon stepped closer, considering it. *'Principia Mathematica* has something to do with the gravitational pull of planets . . . which admittedly are orbs, but it seems a little far-fetched.'

'How about the signs of the zodiac?' Sophie asked, pointing to the constellations on the orb. 'You and Teabing were talking about Pisces and Aquarius earlier, weren't you?'

*The End of Days,* Langdon thought. 'The end of the Age of Pisces and the beginning of the Age of Aquarius could be the time when the Priory planned to release the Sangreal documents to the world . . .'

'Maybe,' Sophie said, 'the Priory's plans to reveal the truth are related to the last line of the poem?'

*It speaks of Rosy flesh and seeded womb.*

'Look!' She grabbed Langdon's arm and stared aghast at the top of the black marble sarcophagus. 'Someone was here,' she whispered, pointing to a spot on the sarcophagus near Newton's outstretched right foot.

Langdon did not understand her concern. A careless tourist had left a charcoal grave-rubbing pencil on the sarcophagus lid. *It's nothing.* Langdon reached out to pick it up, but as he leaned towards the sarcophagus, the light shifted on the polished marble slab, and he froze. Suddenly, he saw why Sophie was afraid.

Scrawled on the sarcophagus lid, at Newton's feet, shimmered a barely visible charcoal-pencil message:

> I have Teabing.
> Go through Chapter House,
> out south exit, to public garden.

Langdon read the words twice, his heart pounding wildly as he told himself this was actually good news. *Leigh is still alive.* There was another implication here too. 'They don't know the password either,' he whispered.

Sophie nodded. Otherwise why make their presence known?

'They may want to trade Leigh for the password.'

'Or it's a trap.'

Langdon shook his head. 'I don't think so. The garden is *outside* the abbey walls. A very public place.' He had once visited the abbey's famous College Garden – a small fruit orchard and herb garden, left over from the days when monks grew natural remedies there. Boasting the oldest living fruit trees in Great Britain, College Garden was a popular spot for tourists to visit without having to enter the abbey. 'I think sending us outside is a show of faith. So we feel safe.'

Sophie looked dubious. 'Outside . . . where there are no metal detectors?'

She had a point. Gazing back at the orb-filled tomb, Langdon wished he had some idea about the cryptex password . . . something with which to negotiate. *I got Leigh involved in this, and I'll do whatever it takes if there is a chance to help him.*

'The note says to go through the Chapter House to the south exit,' Sophie said. 'Maybe from the exit we would have a view of the garden? That way we could check out the situation before we walked out there and put ourselves in any danger?'

The idea was a good one. Langdon vaguely recalled the Chapter House as a huge octagonal hall where the original British Parliament convened in the days before the modern Parliament building existed. It had been years since he had been there, but he remembered it being out through the cloisters somewhere. Taking several steps back from the tomb, he peered round the choir screen to his right.

A gaping vaulted passageway stood nearby, with a large sign.

**THIS WAY TO:**
**Cloisters**
**Deanery**
**College Hall**
**Museum**
**Pyx Chamber**
**St Faith's Chapel**
**Chapter House**

They were jogging as they headed into the passageway, moving too quickly to notice the small announcement under the sign apologizing that certain areas were closed for renovation.

They hurriedly followed the signs for the Chapter House.

Forty yards down, an archway materialized on their left, giving way to another hallway. Although this was the entrance they were looking for, the opening was cordoned off by a rope and an official-looking sign.

## CLOSED FOR RENOVATION
### Pyx Chamber
### St Faith's Chapel
### Chapter House

The long, deserted corridor beyond the rope was littered with scaffolding and dust sheets. The entrance to the Chapter House was at the far end. Even from here, Langdon could see that its heavy wooden door was wide open, and the spacious octagonal interior was bathed in a greyish natural light from the room's enormous windows that looked out on College Garden.

*Go through Chapter House, out south exit, to public garden.*

Sophie was already stepping over the rope and moving forward.

As they hurried down the dark corridor, the sounds of the wind and rain from the open cloister faded behind them.

'It looks huge,' Sophie whispered as they approached the Chapter House.

Even from outside the entrance, Langdon could gaze across

the vast expanse of floor to the breathtaking windows on the far side of the octagon, which rose five storeys to a vaulted ceiling. They would certainly have a clear view of the garden from in here.

They were a good ten feet into the room, searching the south wall, when they realized the exit they had been promised was not there. They were standing in an enormous dead end.

The creaking of the heavy door behind them made them turn. It closed with a resounding thud and the latch fell into place. The lone man who had been standing behind it looked calm as he aimed a small revolver at them.

He was portly and was propped on a pair of aluminium crutches.

For a moment Langdon thought he must be dreaming.

It was Leigh Teabing.

# Chapter 77

Sir Leigh Teabing could see the expressions of shock and betrayal as he gazed out over the barrel of his revolver at Robert Langdon and Sophie Neveu.

'My friends,' he said, 'since the moment you walked into my home last night, I have done everything in my power to keep you out of harm's way. I never had any intention of your being involved. But *you* came to my home. *You* came searching for *me.*'

'Leigh?' Langdon finally managed. 'What are you doing? We thought you were in trouble. We came here to *help* you!'

'As I trusted you would,' he said. 'We have much to discuss.' *There is so much I have to tell you both . . . so much you do not yet understand.*

Langdon and Sophie seemed unable to tear their stunned gazes from the revolver aimed at them.

'It is simply to ensure your full attention,' Teabing said. 'If I had wanted to harm you, you would be dead by now. I am a man of honour, and I vowed in my deepest conscience only to sacrifice those who had betrayed the Sangreal.'

'What are you talking about?' Langdon said. 'Betrayed the Sangreal?'

'I discovered a terrible truth,' Teabing said, sighing. 'I learned *why* the Sangreal documents were never revealed to the world. I learned that the Priory had decided not to release the truth after all . . . why nothing happened as we entered the End of Days.'

Langdon drew a breath, about to protest.

'The Priory,' Teabing continued, 'was given a sacred charge to share the truth. *To release the Sangreal documents when the End of Days arrived.* For centuries, men like Da Vinci, Botticelli and Newton risked *everything* to protect the documents and carry out that charge. And now, at the ultimate moment of truth, Jacques Saunière *changed his mind*. The man honoured with the greatest responsibility in Christian history turned from his duty. He decided the time was not right.' Teabing turned to Sophie. 'He failed the Grail. He failed the Priory. And he failed the memory of all the generations that had worked to make that moment possible.'

'You?' Sophie declared, glancing up now, her green eyes boring into him with rage and realization. '*You* are the one responsible for my grandfather's murder?'

Teabing scoffed. 'Your grandfather and his *sénéchaux* were traitors to the Grail.' His voice was relentless. 'Your grandfather sold out to the Church. It is obvious they pressured him to keep the truth quiet.'

Sophie shook her head. 'The Church had no influence on my grandfather!'

Teabing laughed coldly. 'My dear, the Church has two thousand years of experience pressuring those who threaten to unveil its lies. Since the days of the Emperor Constantine – at the very birth of Christianity – the Church has successfully hidden the truth about Mary Magdalene and Jesus. We should not be surprised that, once again, they have found a way to keep the world in the dark.' He paused, as if to punctuate his next point. 'Miss Neveu, for some time your grandfather has wanted to tell you the truth about your family.'

'How could you know that?'

'My methods are immaterial. The important thing for you to grasp right now is this.' He took a deep breath. 'The deaths of your mother, father, grandmother and brother were *not* accidental.'

The words sent Sophie's emotions reeling. She opened her mouth to speak but was unable.

'What are you saying?' Langdon asked.

'Robert, it explains everything. All the pieces fit. History repeats itself. The Church turns to murder when it comes to silencing the Sangreal. With the End of Days imminent, killing the Grand Master's loved ones sent a very clear message. Be quiet – or you and Sophie will be next.'

'It was a car accident,' Sophie stammered, feeling the childhood pain welling inside her. 'An *accident*!'

'Just a story to protect you,' Teabing said. 'Consider that only two family members went untouched: the Priory's Grand Master and his lone granddaughter – a perfect pair to provide the

Church with control over the brotherhood. I can only imagine the terror the Church wielded over your grandfather these past years, threatening to kill you if he dared release the Sangreal secret, threatening to finish the job they started unless Saunière influenced the Priory to reconsider its ancient vow.'

'Leigh,' Langdon argued, 'you can have no proof that the Church had anything to do with those deaths, or that it influenced any decision by the Priory to remain silent.'

'Proof?' Teabing fired back. 'You want proof? The new millennium is here – and yet the world remains ignorant! Is that not proof enough?'

In the echoes of Teabing's words, Sophie heard another voice speaking. *Sophie, I must tell you the truth about your family.* She realized she was trembling. Could *this* possibly be what her grandfather had wanted to tell her? That her family had been *murdered*? What did she truly know about the crash? Only sketchy details. Even the stories in the newspaper had been vague. Her mind flashed suddenly on her grandfather's overprotectiveness, how he never liked to leave her alone when she was young. Even when Sophie was older, away at university, she had felt her grandfather was watching over her.

'You suspected that Saunière was being put under pressure,' Langdon said, glaring with disbelief at Teabing. 'So you *murdered* him?'

'I did not pull the trigger,' Teabing said. 'Saunière is free now, released from the shame caused by his failure to carry out his sacred duty. And now we are poised to carry out his legacy and right a terrible wrong.' He paused. 'The three of us. Together.'

'How could you *possibly* believe that we would help you?' Sophie said.

'Because, my dear, *you* are the reason the Priory failed to release the documents. Your grandfather's love for you prevented him from challenging the Church. It crippled him. He never had a chance to explain the truth because you turned away from him, tying his hands, making him wait. Now you owe the world the truth. You *owe* it to the memory of your grandfather.'

Despite the torrent of questions running through Langdon's mind, he knew only one thing mattered: getting Sophie out alive. She looked shaken. *The Church murdered her family to silence the Priory?* Langdon felt certain the modern Church did not go about murdering people. There had to be some other explanation.

'Let Sophie leave,' he declared, staring at Leigh. 'You and I should deal with this alone.'

Teabing gave an unnatural laugh. 'I'm afraid that is one show of faith I cannot afford. I can, however, offer you *this*.' He propped himself fully on his crutches, keeping the gun aimed at Sophie, and removed the keystone from his pocket. He swayed a bit as he held it out for Langdon. 'A token of trust, Robert.'

Langdon didn't move. *Leigh is giving the keystone back to us?*

'Take it,' Teabing said, thrusting it awkwardly towards him.

Langdon could imagine only one reason why Teabing would give it back. 'You opened it already. You removed the map.'

Teabing was shaking his head. 'Robert, if I had solved the

keystone, I would have disappeared to find the Grail myself and kept you uninvolved. No, I do not know the answer. I can admit that freely. A true knight learns humility in the face of the Grail. He learns to obey the signs placed before him. When I saw you enter the abbey, I understood. You were here for a reason. To help. I am not looking for personal glory. I serve a far greater master than my own pride. The Truth. Mankind deserves to know that truth. The Grail found us all, and now she is begging to be revealed. We must work together.'

Despite Teabing's pleas for cooperation and trust, his gun remained trained on Sophie as Langdon stepped forward and accepted the cold marble cylinder. The vinegar inside gurgled as he grasped it and stepped backwards. The dials were still in random order, and the cryptex remained locked.

Langdon eyed Teabing. 'How do you know I won't smash it right now?'

Teabing's laugh was an eerie chortle. 'I should have realized your threat to break it in the Temple Church was an empty one. Robert Langdon would never break the keystone. You are a historian, Robert. You are holding the key to two thousand years of history – the lost key to the Sangreal. You can feel the souls of all the knights burned at the stake to protect her secret. Would you have them die in vain? No – you will prove their sacrifice was worthwhile. You will join the ranks of the great men you admire – Da Vinci, Botticelli, Newton – each of whom would have been honoured to be in your shoes right now. The contents of the keystone are crying out to us. Longing to be set free. The time has come. Destiny has led us to this moment.'

'I cannot help you, Leigh. I have no idea how to open this. I only saw Newton's tomb for a moment. And even if I knew the password . . .' Langdon paused, realizing he had said too much.

'You would not tell me?' Teabing sighed. 'I am disappointed and surprised, Robert, that you do not appreciate the extent to which you are in my debt. My task would have been far simpler had Rémy and I simply eliminated you both when you walked into Château Villette. Instead, I risked everything to take a nobler course.'

'This is *noble*?' Langdon demanded, eyeing the gun.

'Saunière's fault,' Teabing said. 'He and his *sénéchaux* lied to Silas – yes, the albino monk is the one who pulled the trigger on them. But how was I to know the Grand Master would deceive me and bequeath the keystone to a granddaughter he never saw?' He looked at Sophie with disdain, then glanced back at Langdon. 'Fortunately, Robert, your involvement turned out to be my saving grace. Rather than the keystone remaining locked in the bank forever, you went and collected it and then walked into my home.'

Teabing now looked smug. 'When I learned Saunière left you a dying message, I had a suspicion you might arrive on my doorstep. The fact that you did arrive and delivered the keystone into my waiting hands only serves as proof that my cause is just.'

'What?' Langdon was appalled.

'Silas was supposed to break in and steal the keystone from you in Château Villette – without hurting you, or giving away my involvement. However, when I saw the intricate nature of Saunière's codes, I decided to include you both in my quest for a bit longer. I could have Silas steal the keystone later, once I knew enough to carry on alone.'

'The Temple Church . . .' Sophie said, her tone awash with betrayal.

*Light begins to dawn,* Teabing thought. The Temple Church had been a perfect location and Rémy's orders had been clear – stay out of sight while Silas recovers the keystone. Unfortunately, Langdon's threat to smash the keystone on the chapel floor had caused Rémy to panic. *If only Rémy had not revealed himself,* Teabing thought ruefully. *Rémy was the sole link to me, and he showed his face!*

Fortunately, the monk Silas had no idea of Teabing's true identity and had been easily fooled into helping Rémy 'kidnap' him from the church, sitting naively in the front of the Jaguar while Rémy pretended to tie Teabing up in the back of the limo. With the soundproof divider raised, Teabing had been able to phone Silas in the front seat – using the fake French accent of the Teacher – and direct him to go straight to Opus Dei. A simple anonymous tip to the police was all it would then take to remove the albino from the picture.

*One loose end tied up.*

The other loose end had been harder. *Rémy.*

Rémy had proven himself a liability. *Every Grail quest requires sacrifice.* In the end a flask, some cognac and a can of peanuts to trigger Rémy's deadly allergy had made it simple.

Westminster Abbey had only been a short walk away, and

although Teabing's leg braces, crutches and gun had set off the metal detector, the guards on duty never knew what to do. *Do we ask a disabled man to remove his leg braces and crawl through?* Teabing had presented them with a far easier solution – an embossed card identifying him as a Knight of the Realm. The poor fellows practically tripped over one another ushering him in.

Now he eyed the bewildered Langdon and Neveu. '*Mes amis,*' Teabing declared in flawless French, '*vous ne trouvez pas le Saint-Graal; c'est le Saint-Graal qui vous trouve.*' He smiled. '*You do not find the Holy Grail; it is the Holy Grail that finds you.* Our paths together could not be more clear. The Grail has found us.'

Silence.

He was whispering to them now. 'Listen. Can you hear it? The Grail is speaking to us across the centuries. She is begging to be saved from the Priory's folly. I beg you both to recognize this opportunity. There could not possibly be three more capable people assembled at this moment to break the final code and open the cryptex.' Teabing paused, his eyes alight. 'We need to swear an oath together. A pledge of faith to one another. A knight's allegiance to uncover the truth and make it known.'

'I will *never* swear an oath with my grandfather's murderer. Except an oath that I will see you go to prison,' Sophie said in a steely tone.

'I am sorry you feel that way, mademoiselle.' Teabing turned and aimed the gun at Langdon. 'And you, Robert? Are you with me . . . or against me?'

# Chapter 78

Bishop Manuel Aringarosa's body had endured many kinds of pain, and yet the searing heat of the bullet wound in his chest felt deep and grave. Not a wound of the flesh . . . but closer to the soul.

He opened his eyes, trying to see, but the rain on his face blurred his vision. *Where am I?* He could feel powerful arms holding him, carrying his limp body like a rag doll, his black cassock flapping.

Lifting a weary arm, he mopped his eyes and saw the man holding him was Silas. The great albino was struggling down a misty sidewalk, shouting for a hospital, his voice a wail of agony. Tears were streaming down his pale, blood-spattered face.

'My son,' Aringarosa whispered, 'you're hurt.'

Silas glanced down, his visage contorted in anguish. 'I am so very sorry, Father.' He seemed almost too pained to speak.

'No, Silas,' Aringarosa replied. 'It is I who am sorry. This is my fault. You and I were deceived . . .'

His mind flashed back. To Spain. To his modest beginnings, building a small Catholic church in Oviedo with Silas. And later, to New York City, where he had proclaimed the glory of God with the towering Opus Dei building.

Five months ago, Aringarosa had received devastating news. He recalled, in vivid detail, the meeting inside Castel Gandolfo that had changed his life.

He had entered the Astronomy Library with his head held high, fully expecting to be praised for his work upholding and promoting Catholicism in America.

But only three people were present.

The Vatican secretarius – the man in charge of the pope's legal affairs. Obese. Dour.

Two high-ranking Italian cardinals. Sanctimonious. Smug.

'Secretarius?' Aringarosa said, puzzled.

The secretarius shook his hand and motioned to the chair opposite him. 'Please, make yourself comfortable.'

Aringarosa sat, sensing something was wrong.

'I am not skilled in small talk, Bishop,' the secretarius said, 'so let me be direct about the reason for your visit.'

'Please. Speak openly.'

'As you are well aware, His Holiness and others in Rome have been concerned lately with the impact on the Church of some of the recent media coverage of Opus Dei's more *controversial* practices.'

Aringarosa felt himself bristle instantly.

'I want to assure you,' the secretarius added quickly, 'that His Holiness does not seek to change anything about the way you run your ministry.'

*I should hope not!* 'Then why am I here?'

The enormous man sighed. 'Bishop, I am not sure how to say this delicately, so I will state it directly. Two days ago, the Secretariat Council voted unanimously to revoke the Vatican's sanction of Opus Dei.'

Aringarosa was certain he had heard incorrectly. 'I beg your pardon?' *The Secretariat Council – the group at the Vatican responsible for so much of the Holy See's affairs – had voted to cut off support for Opus Dei?*

'Plainly stated, six months from today, Opus Dei will no longer be considered part of the established Catholic Church. You will be a church unto yourself. The Holy See will be disassociating itself from you. His Holiness agrees, and we are already drawing up the legal papers.'

'But . . . that is impossible!'

'On the contrary, it is quite possible. And necessary. His Holiness has become uneasy with some of Opus Dei's practices.' He paused. 'Also your policies regarding women. Opus Dei has, quite frankly, become an embarrassment.'

Bishop Aringarosa was stupefied. 'An embarrassment? Opus Dei is the only Catholic organization whose numbers are growing! We now have over eleven hundred priests!'

'True. Which in itself is troubling.'

Aringarosa shot to his feet. 'Ask His Holiness if Opus Dei

388

was an embarrassment in 1982 when we helped the Vatican Bank!'

'The Vatican will always be grateful for that,' the secretarius said, his tone appeasing, 'and yet there are those who still believe this . . . generosity . . . was the only reason you were granted official support.'

'That is not true!' Aringarosa was deeply offended.

'Whatever the case, we plan to act in good faith. The terms that separate us will include a reimbursement of that money. It will be paid back in five instalments.'

'You are buying me off?' Aringarosa demanded. 'Paying me to go quietly?' He leaned across the table to glare at one of the cardinals, sharpening his tone. 'Do you really wonder why Catholics are leaving the Church? Look around you. People have lost respect. The rigours of faith are gone. It's become more like a buffet! Abstinence, confession, communion, baptism, mass – take your pick. What kind of spiritual guidance is the Church offering?'

'Third-century laws,' the cardinal said, 'cannot be applied to the modern followers of Christ. The rules are not workable in today's society.'

'Well, they seem to be working for Opus Dei!'

'Bishop Aringarosa,' the secretarius said, his voice decisive. 'Out of respect for your relationship with the previous pope, His Holiness will be giving Opus Dei six months to *voluntarily* break away from the Vatican. I suggest you publicly state that you wish to establish yourself as your own Christian organization.'

'I refuse!' Aringarosa declared. 'And I'll tell the pope that in person!'

'I'm afraid His Holiness will no longer meet you.' The secretarius's eyes did not flinch. 'The Lord giveth and the Lord taketh away.'

Aringarosa had staggered from that meeting in bewilderment and panic, fearful for the future of Christianity. But that all changed when, several weeks later, he received a phone call.

The caller sounded French and identified himself as the Teacher. He said he knew of the Vatican's plans to pull support from Opus Dei. 'I have ears everywhere, Bishop,' the Teacher whispered, 'and with these ears I have gained certain knowledge. With your help, I can uncover the hiding place of a sacred relic that will bring you enormous power . . . enough power to make the Vatican bow before you. Enough power to save the Faith.' He paused. 'Not just for Opus Dei. But for all of us.'

*The Lord taketh away . . . and the Lord giveth.* Bishop Aringarosa had felt a glorious ray of hope. 'Tell me your plan.'

The bishop was unconscious when the doors of St Mary's Hospital opened. The doctor who helped the albino heave the delirious bishop on to a gurney looked gloomy as he felt Aringarosa's pulse. 'He's lost a lot of blood. I am not hopeful.'

The bishop's eyes flickered, and he gathered strength for a moment, his gaze locating Silas. 'My child . . .'

Silas's soul thundered with rage. 'Father, I will find the one who deceived us – and I will kill him.'

Aringarosa shook his head, looking sad. 'Silas . . . if you have learned nothing from me, please . . . learn this.' He took the albino's hand and gave it a firm squeeze. 'Forgiveness is God's greatest gift.'

'But, Father . . .'

Aringarosa closed his eyes. 'Silas, you must pray.'

# Chapter 79

*Robert, are you with me . . . or against me?* The Royal Historian's words echoed in the silence of Langdon's mind.

There was no good answer, Langdon knew. Answer yes, and he would be selling out Sophie. Answer no, and Teabing would have no choice but to kill them both.

Langdon decided on the grey area between yes and no.

*Silence.*

Staring at the cryptex in his hands, Langdon chose simply to walk away. Without ever lifting his eyes, he stepped backwards, out into the room's vast empty spaces. *Neutral ground.* He hoped his focus on the cryptex signalled to Teabing that collaboration might be an option, and that his silence signalled to Sophie he had not abandoned her.

The act of thinking, Langdon suspected, was exactly what Teabing wanted him to do. *That's why he handed me the cryptex. So I could feel the weight of my decision. If I can free the map, Teabing will negotiate,* he told himself as he moved slowly across the room . . .

allowing his mind to fill with the numerous astronomical images on Newton's tomb.

> *You seek the orb that ought be on his tomb.*
> *It speaks of Rosy flesh and seeded womb.*

He walked towards the towering windows, searching for any inspiration in their stained-glass mosaics. There was none.

*Place yourself in Saunière's mind.* He thought long and hard, gazing out into College Garden. *What would* Saunière *believe is the orb that ought be on Newton's tomb?* Saunière was not a man of science. He was a man of humanity, of art, of history. *The sacred feminine . . . the chalice . . . the Rose . . . the banished Mary Magdalene . . . the decline of the goddess . . . the Holy Grail.*

Legend had always portrayed the Grail as a cruel mistress, dancing in the shadows just out of sight, whispering in your ear, luring you one more step and then evaporating into the mist.

Gazing out at the rustling trees of College Garden, Langdon sensed the Grail's playful presence. The signs were everywhere. Like a taunting silhouette just visible in the fog, the branches of Britain's oldest apple tree burgeoned with five-petalled blossoms, glistening like the planet Venus. The goddess was in the garden now. She was dancing in the rain, singing songs of the ages, peeking out from behind the bud-filled branches as if to remind

Langdon that the fruit of knowledge was growing just beyond his reach.

Across the room, Sir Leigh Teabing watched confidently as Langdon gazed out of the window.

*Exactly as I hoped,* Teabing thought. *He will come round.* For some time now, he had suspected Langdon might hold the key to the Grail – and it was no coincidence that he had put his plan into action on the same night Langdon was in Paris, scheduled to meet Jacques Saunière. Teabing, listening in on the curator, had been certain the man's eagerness to meet Langdon privately could mean only one thing: *Langdon has stumbled on to a truth, and Saunière fears its release.*

Teabing thought back on how it seemed almost too easy. *I had inside information about Saunière's deepest fears.* Yesterday afternoon, Silas had phoned the curator, pretending to be a distraught priest who had just heard a harrowing admission from a member of his congregation. Anything heard by a priest in a Catholic confessional, of course, should be kept absolutely confidential – a sacred duty of the priest. But in this case . . .

'Monsieur Saunière, forgive me, I must speak to you at once. I just took confession from a man who claimed to have murdered members of your family.'

Saunière's response was startled but wary. 'My family died in an accident. The police report was clear.'

'Yes, a *car* accident,' Silas said, baiting the hook. 'The man I spoke to said he forced their car off the road into a river.'

Saunière fell silent.

'Monsieur Saunière, I would never have phoned you directly – breached the sanctity of the confessional – except this man made a comment that made me now fear for *your* safety.' He paused. 'The man also mentioned a granddaughter. Sophie?'

The mention of Sophie's name had done it. The curator leaped into action. He ordered Silas to come and see him immediately in the safest location Saunière knew – his Louvre office. Then he had phoned Sophie to warn her she might be in danger. His meeting with Robert Langdon had been instantly forgotten.

'He won't open it for you,' Sophie said now, coldly, to Sir Leigh. 'Even if he could.'

At that moment, Langdon turned from the window. 'The tomb . . .' he said suddenly, facing them. 'I know where to look on Newton's tomb. Yes, I think I can find the password!'

Teabing's heart soared. 'Where, Robert? Tell me!'

Sophie sounded horrified. 'Robert, *no*! You're not going to help him, are you?'

Langdon approached with a resolute stride, holding the cryptex before him. 'No,' he said, his eyes hardening as he turned to Leigh. 'Not until he lets you go.'

Teabing's mood darkened. 'We are so close, Robert. Don't start playing games with me!'

'No games,' Langdon said. 'Let her go. Then I'll take you to Newton's tomb and we'll open the cryptex together.'

'I'm not going anywhere,' Sophie declared, her eyes narrowing with rage. 'That cryptex was given to me by my grandfather. It is not *yours* to open.'

Langdon wheeled round, looking fearful. 'Sophie, please! You're in danger. I'm trying to help you!'

'How? By revealing the secret my grandfather died trying to protect? He trusted you, Robert. *I* trusted you!'

'Sophie,' he pleaded. 'Please . . . you must leave.'

She shook her head. 'Not unless you either hand me the cryptex or smash it on the floor.'

'What?' Langdon gasped.

'Robert, my grandfather would prefer his secret lost forever than see it in the hands of his murderer.' Sophie stared directly back at Teabing. 'Shoot me if you have to. I am not leaving my grandfather's legacy in your hands.'

*Very well.* Teabing aimed the weapon.

'No!' Langdon shouted, raising his arm and holding the cryptex precariously over the hard stone floor. 'Leigh, if you even think about it, I will drop this.'

Teabing laughed. 'That bluff worked on Rémy. Not on me. I know you better than that.'

'Do you?'

'Truly, Robert?' Teabing pushed. 'You know where on the tomb to look?'

'I do.'

The falter in Langdon's eyes was fleeting, but Leigh caught it. *I can see that you are lying. You have no idea where on Newton's tomb*

*the answer lies. I am a lone knight, surrounded by unworthy souls. I will
have to decipher the keystone on my own.*

'A show of faith,' he said, lowering the gun from Sophie. 'Set
down the keystone, and we'll talk.'

Langdon knew his lie had failed, knew the moment was upon
them. *When I put this down, he will kill us both.* Even without
looking at Sophie, he felt sure he knew what she was thinking.

*Robert, this man is not worthy of the Grail. Please do not place it in
his hands. No matter what the cost.*

Langdon had already made his decision several minutes ago,
while standing alone at the window.

*Protect Sophie.*

*Protect the Grail.*

He had almost shouted out in desperation. Then the stark
moments had brought with them clarity. *The Truth is right before
your eyes, Robert. The Grail is not mocking you. She is calling out to a
worthy soul.*

He lowered the cryptex to within inches of the stone floor.

'Yes, Robert,' Teabing whispered, aiming the gun at him. 'Set
it down.'

Langdon's eyes moved heavenwards, up into the gaping void
of the Chapter House cupola. Crouching down, he lowered his
gaze to stare at Teabing's gun, aimed directly at him.

'I'm sorry, Leigh.'

In one fluid motion, he leaped up, swinging his arm skyward,
launching the cryptex straight up towards the dome above.

\*

Leigh Teabing did not feel his finger pull the trigger, but the gun went off with a thundering crash. Langdon's crouched form was now vertical, almost airborne, and the bullet exploded in the floor near his feet. Half of Teabing's brain wanted to adjust his aim and fire again in rage, but the more powerful half dragged his eyes upward.

*The keystone!*

Time seemed to freeze as Teabing's entire world became the airborne keystone. He watched it rise to the apex of its climb . . . hover for a moment in the void . . . and then tumble down, end over end, back towards the stone floor.

All of Teabing's hopes and dreams were plummeting to earth. *It cannot strike the floor! I can reach it!* Teabing's body reacted on instinct. He dropped the gun and threw himself forward, dropping his crutches as he reached out with his soft, manicured hands – and snatched the keystone out of mid-air.

Falling forward with the keystone victoriously clutched in his hand, Teabing knew he was falling too fast. With nothing to break his fall, his outstretched arms hit first, and the cryptex collided hard with the floor.

There was a sickening crunch of glass within.

For a full second, Teabing did not breathe. Lying there on the cold floor, staring the length of his outstretched arms at the marble cylinder, he implored the glass vial inside to hold. Then the acrid tang of vinegar cut the air, and he felt the cool liquid flowing out through the dials on to his palm.

Wild panic gripped him. *No!* He pictured the papyrus dissolving within. *Robert, you fool! The secret is lost! The Grail is gone. Everything destroyed.* Shuddering in disbelief, Teabing tried to force the cylinder apart, longing to catch a fleeting glimpse of history before it dissolved forever. To his shock, as he pulled the ends of the keystone, the cylinder separated.

He gasped and peered inside. It was empty except for shards of wet glass. No dissolving papyrus. Teabing rolled over and looked up at Langdon, then back at the keystone. The dials now spelled a five-letter word: APPLE.

'The orb from which Eve partook,' Langdon said coolly, 'incurring the Holy wrath of God. Original Sin. The symbol of the fall of the sacred feminine.'

Teabing felt the truth come crashing down on him in excruciating austerity. The *'orb that ought be on Newton's tomb'* could be none other than the Rosy apple that fell from heaven, struck Newton on the head and inspired his life's work – his work on gravity. *His labour's fruit! The Rosy flesh with a seeded womb!*

'Robert,' Teabing stammered, overwhelmed. 'You opened it. Where . . . is the map?'

Without blinking, Langdon reached into the breast pocket of his coat and carefully extracted a delicate scroll. Only a few yards from where Teabing lay, he unrolled the papyrus and looked at it. A knowing smile crossed his face.

*He knows!* Teabing's heart craved that knowledge. His life's dream was right in front of him. 'Tell me!' he demanded. 'Please! Oh God, please! It's not too late!'

As the sound of heavy footsteps thundered down the hall

towards the Chapter House, Langdon quietly rolled the papyrus and slipped it back in his pocket.

'No!' Teabing cried out, trying in vain to stand.

Then the doors burst open and Bezu Fache entered like a bull into a ring, his fierce eyes finding his target – Leigh Teabing – helpless on the floor. He holstered his gun and turned to Sophie. 'Agent Neveu, I am relieved you and Mr Langdon are safe.'

The British police entered on Fache's heels, seizing the anguished prisoner and placing him in handcuffs.

Sophie was stunned. 'How did you find us?'

Fache pointed to Teabing. 'He showed his ID when he entered the abbey. When the guards heard a police broadcast about our search for him, they notified us.'

'It's in Langdon's pocket!' Teabing was screaming like a madman. 'The map to the Holy Grail!' As they hoisted him up, he threw back his head and howled, 'Robert! Tell me where it's hidden!'

Langdon looked him in the eye as he passed by. 'Only the worthy find the Grail, Leigh. You taught me that.'

# Chapter 80

The mist had settled low on Kensington Gardens as Silas limped into a quiet hollow, out of sight. Kneeling on the wet grass, he could feel a warm stream of blood flowing from the bullet wound below his ribs.

The fog made it look like heaven here. Raising his bloody hands to pray, he watched the raindrops caress his fingers, turning them white again. As the droplets fell harder across his back and shoulders, he could feel his body disappearing bit by bit into the mist.

*I am a ghost.*

A breeze rustled past him, carrying the damp, earthy scent of new life. With every living cell in his broken body, Silas prayed. He prayed for forgiveness. He prayed for mercy. And, above all, he prayed for his mentor, Bishop Aringarosa – that the Lord would not take him before his time. *He has so much work left to do.*

The fog was swirling around him now, and Silas felt so light that he was sure the wisps would carry him away. Closing his eyes, he said a final prayer.

From somewhere in the mist, the voice of Manuel Aringarosa whispered to him.

*Our Lord is a good and merciful God.*

Silas's pain at last began to fade, and he knew the bishop was right.

# Chapter 81

It was late afternoon when the London sun broke through and the city began to dry. Bezu Fache felt weary as he emerged from the interrogation room and hailed a cab. Sir Leigh Teabing had loudly proclaimed his innocence, but from his rantings about the Holy Grail, secret documents and mysterious brotherhoods, Fache suspected the wily historian was just setting the stage for his lawyers to plead mental disorder as a defence.

*Sure*, Fache thought. *Mentally incompetent.* Teabing had shown ingenious precision in coming up with a plan that protected his innocence at every turn.

He had exploited both the Vatican and Opus Dei, two groups that turned out to be completely innocent.

Teabing's dirty work had been carried out unknowingly by a fanatical monk and a desperate bishop.

More cleverness. Teabing had set up his electronic listening post in the *one* place a man with polio could not possibly reach – high in a hayloft, accessible only up a steep ladder. The actual surveillance had been carried out by his manservant,

Rémy – the lone person aware of Teabing's true identity, now conveniently dead after an allergic reaction.

The information coming from Collet out of Château Villette suggested that Teabing's cunning ran so deep that Fache himself might even learn from it. To successfully hide bugs in some of Paris's most powerful offices, the British historian had turned to a lesson from the Ancient Greeks. *Trojan horses.*

Teabing had sent lavish gifts of artwork to some of his targets, with others unwittingly bidding at auctions for items sold by him.

In Saunière's case, the curator had received a dinner invitation to Château Villette to discuss the possibility of Teabing funding a new Da Vinci Wing at the Louvre. Teabing had added a brief P.S. to the invitation, expressing fascination with a robotic knight that Saunière was rumoured to have built from Da Vinci's drawings. *Bring him to dinner,* Teabing had suggested. Saunière clearly had done just that, leaving the knight unattended long enough for Rémy Legaludec to make one small addition – a bug.

Now, sitting in the back of the cab, Fache closed his eyes. *One more thing to deal with before I return to Paris.*

The St Mary's Hospital recovery room was sunny.

'You've impressed us all,' the nurse said, smiling. 'Nothing short of miraculous.'

Bishop Aringarosa gave a weak smile. 'I have always been blessed.'

As she left him alone, he thought despondently of Silas, whose body had been found in the park.

*Please forgive me, my son.*

Aringarosa had longed for Silas to be part of his glorious plan. Last night, however, the bishop had taken a call from a police captain, Bezu Fache – a call that told him that a nun, Sister Sandrine, had been murdered. Knowing he himself had arranged Silas's visit to Saint-Sulpice, Aringarosa realized the evening had taken a horrifying turn, and when he was told about the four additional murders, his horror turned to anguish. *Silas, what have you done?* Unable to reach the Teacher, the bishop knew he had been cut loose. *Used.* The only way to stop the horrific chain of events he had helped put in motion was to confess everything to Fache, a man he had discovered was a committed Catholic who promised to do all in his power to protect his beloved Church. From that moment on, the bishop and the police captain had been racing to catch up with Silas before the Teacher could persuade the flawed albino to kill again.

Feeling bone weary, Aringarosa closed his eyes and listened to the television coverage of the arrest of a prominent British knight, Sir Leigh Teabing. Teabing, having caught wind of the Vatican's plans to separate itself from Opus Dei, had chosen Aringarosa as a perfect pawn in his plan. *Who would be more likely to leap blindly after the Holy Grail than a man like myself with everything to lose? The Grail would have brought enormous power to anyone who possessed it.*

Aringarosa had been far too eager to be suspicious, and the Teacher's price tag of twenty million euros was paltry when compared with the prize of obtaining the Grail. Finding the funds had been no problem – he had simply collected the money the Vatican was repaying to Opus Dei from Castel Gandolfo yesterday. Teabing's ultimate insult, of course, had been to demand payment in Vatican bonds, so that if anything went wrong, the investigation would lead to Rome.

'I am glad to see you're well, My Lord.'

Aringarosa recognized the gruff voice in the doorway, but the face was unexpected – stern, powerful features, slicked-back hair and a broad neck that strained against his dark suit. 'Captain Fache?' he asked. He had imagined a much gentler-looking man.

The captain approached the bed and hoisted a familiar heavy black briefcase on to a chair. 'I believe this belongs to you.'

Aringarosa looked at the briefcase filled with bonds and immediately looked away, feeling only shame. 'Yes . . . thank you.' He paused while working his fingers across the seam of his bedsheet, then continued. 'Captain, I have been giving this deep thought, and I need to ask a favour of you. The families of those in Paris who Silas . . .' He paused, swallowing the emotion. 'I realize no sum could possibly make up for their loss, and yet, if you could be kind enough to divide the contents of this briefcase among them . . . the families of the deceased.'

Fache's dark eyes studied him. 'I will see to it that your wishes are carried out, My Lord.'

A heavy silence fell between them.

On the television, a lean French police officer was giving a press conference in front of a sprawling mansion. Fache saw who it was and turned his attention to the screen.

'Lieutenant Collet,' a BBC reporter said, her voice accusing. 'Last night, your captain publicly charged two innocent people with murder. Will Robert Langdon and Sophie Neveu be seeking compensation from the police? Will this cost Captain Fache his job?'

Lieutenant Collet's smile was tired but calm. 'Captain Bezu Fache seldom makes mistakes. I have not yet spoken to him on this matter, but knowing how he operates, I suspect his public manhunt for Agent Neveu and Mr Langdon was part of a ruse to lure out the real killer.'

The reporters exchanged surprised looks.

Collet continued. 'I can also confirm at this point that the captain has successfully arrested the man responsible for these horrific murders, and that Mr Langdon and Agent Neveu are both innocent and safe.'

Fache had a faint smile on his lips as he turned back to Aringarosa. 'A good man, that Collet.' He ran his hand over his forehead, slicking back his hair as he gazed down at the bishop. 'My Lord, before I return to Paris, there is one final matter I'd like to discuss – your impromptu flight to London. You bribed a pilot to change course.'

Aringarosa slumped. 'I was desperate.'

'Yes. As was the pilot when my men interrogated him.' Fache reached into his pocket and produced a purple amethyst ring with a familiar hand-tooled mitre-crozier appliqué.

Aringarosa felt tears welling as he accepted the ring and slipped it back on his finger. 'You've been so kind.' He held out his hand and clasped Fache's. '*Merci.*'

# Chapter 82

Rosslyn Chapel stands seven miles south of Edinburgh, on the site of an ancient temple built in honour of the god Mithras. Built by the Knights Templar in 1446, the chapel is engraved with a mind-boggling array of symbols – Jewish, Christian, Egyptian, Masonic and pagan.

Its location falls precisely on the north–south meridian that runs through Glastonbury. This Rose Line is the traditional marker of King Arthur's Isle of Avalon and is considered the central pillar of Britain's sacred geometry. It is from this hallowed Rose Line that Rosslyn – originally spelled Roslin – takes its name.

The chapel's rugged spires were casting long evening shadows as Robert Langdon and Sophie Neveu pulled their rental car into the grassy parking area at the foot of the bluff on which it stood. Gazing up at the stark edifice framed against a cloud-swept sky, Langdon felt like Alice falling headlong into the rabbit hole in Lewis Carroll's classic book *Alice's Adventures in Wonderland*. *This must be a dream.* And yet he knew the text of Saunière's final message could not have been more specific.

*The Holy Grail 'neath ancient Roslin waits.*

The Priory's final secret had been revealed in the same way Saunière had spoken to them from the beginning. *Simple verse.* Four explicit lines that pointed without a doubt to this very spot. Not only did the verse identify Rosslyn by name, but it also made reference to several of the chapel's renowned features.

Rosslyn Chapel seemed far too obvious a location to Langdon. For centuries, this stone chapel had echoed with whispers of the Holy Grail's presence. The whispers had turned to shouts in recent decades when ground-penetrating radar had revealed the presence of an astonishing structure *beneath* the chapel – a massive underground chamber. Not only did this deep vault dwarf the chapel atop it, but it also appeared to have no entrance or exit. Archaeologists requested permission to begin blasting through the bedrock to reach the mysterious chamber, but the Rosslyn Trust expressly forbade any excavation of the sacred site.

Rosslyn had now become a pilgrimage site for mystery-seekers. What was the Rosslyn Trust trying to hide? True Grail academics, however, agreed that Rosslyn was a decoy – one of the devious dead ends the Priory liked to present.

Tonight, however, with the Priory's keystone offering a verse that pointed directly to this spot, Langdon no longer felt so smug. A perplexing question had been running through his mind all day:

*Why would Saunière go to such efforts to guide us to so obvious a location?*

There seemed only one logical answer.

*There is something about Rosslyn we have yet to understand.*

'Robert?' Sophie was standing outside the car, looking back at him. 'Are you coming?' She was holding the rosewood box, which Captain Fache had returned to them. Inside, both cryptexes had been reassembled and nested as they had been found. The papyrus verse was locked safely at its core.

The entrance to the chapel was more modest than Langdon expected. The small wooden door had two iron hinges and a simple oak sign.

# ROSLIN

The chapel would be closing soon, and as Langdon pulled open the door, a warm puff of air escaped, as if the ancient building were heaving a weary sigh at the end of a long day. Her entry arches burgeoned with carved cinquefoils.

*Roses. The womb of the goddess.*

Entering with Sophie, Langdon felt his eyes reaching across the famous sanctuary and taking it all in. Although he had read accounts of Rosslyn's intricate stonework, seeing it in person was an overwhelming encounter.

*Symbology heaven*, one of Langdon's colleagues had called it. Every surface in the chapel had been carved with symbols – Christian cruciforms, Jewish stars, Masonic seals, Templar crosses, cornucopias, pyramids, astrological signs, plants, vegetables, pentacles and roses. The Knights Templar had been master stonemasons, erecting Templar churches all over Europe, but Rosslyn was considered their most sublime labour of love and worship. The master masons had left no stone uncarved. Rosslyn Chapel was a shrine to all faiths . . . to all traditions . . . and, above all, to nature and the goddess.

The sanctuary was empty except for a handful of visitors listening to a young man giving the day's last tour. He was leading them in single file along a well-known route on the floor – an invisible pathway that linked six key architectural points within the sanctuary. Generations of visitors had walked these straight lines, connecting the points, and their countless footsteps had engraved an enormous symbol on the floor.

*The Star of David,* Langdon thought. *No coincidence there.* Also known as Solomon's Seal, this hexagram had once been the secret symbol of the stargazing priests.

The guide saw them enter and offered a pleasant smile, motioning for them to feel free to look around.

As Langdon nodded his thanks and began to move deeper into the sanctuary, Sophie stood riveted in the entryway, a puzzled look on her face.

'I think . . . I've been here,' she said slowly.

Langdon was surprised. 'But you said you hadn't even *heard* of Rosslyn.'

'I hadn't . . .' She scanned the sanctuary, looking uncertain. 'My grandfather must have brought me here when I was very young. I don't know. It feels familiar.' She began nodding with more certainty. 'Yes.' She pointed to the front of the sanctuary. 'Those two pillars . . . I've seen them before.'

Langdon looked at the pair of intricately sculpted columns at the far end. Their white lacework carvings seemed to smoulder with a ruddy glow as the last of the day's sunlight streamed in through the west window. The pillars – positioned where the altar would normally stand – were an oddly matched pair. The pillar on the left was carved with simple, vertical lines, while the one on the right was embellished with an ornate, flowering spiral.

Sophie was already moving towards them, nodding. 'Yes, I'm positive I have seen these!'

'I don't doubt you've seen them,' Langdon said, 'but it wasn't necessarily *here*.'

She turned. 'What do you mean?'

'Copies of these two pillars turn up in buildings all over the world.'

'Replicas of Rosslyn?' She looked sceptical.

'No. Of the pillars. Do you remember earlier that I mentioned Rosslyn *itself* is a copy of the Temple of Solomon? Those two pillars are exact replicas of two pillars that stood at its head.' Langdon pointed to the pillar on the left. 'That's called Boaz – or the Mason's Pillar. The other is called Jachin – or the Apprentice Pillar.' He paused. 'In fact, virtually every Masonic temple in the world has two pillars like these.'

Langdon had already told Sophie about the powerful historic ties between the Templars and modern Masonic secret societies – and Sophie's grandfather's final verse made direct reference to the Master Masons whose carvings adorned Rosslyn.

'I've never been in a Masonic temple,' Sophie said, still eyeing the pillars. 'I am almost positive I saw these *here*.' She turned back, as if looking for something else to jog her memory.

The rest of the visitors were now leaving, and the young verger made his way across the chapel to them with a pleasant smile. He was a handsome young man in his late twenties, with a Scottish accent and strawberry-blond hair. 'I'm about to close up for the day. May I help you find anything?'

*How about the Holy Grail?* Langdon wanted to say.

'The code,' Sophie blurted, in sudden revelation. 'There's a code here!'

The verger looked pleased by her enthusiasm. 'Yes, there is, ma'am.'

'It's on the ceiling,' she said, turning to the right-hand wall. 'Somewhere over . . . there.'

He smiled. 'Not your first visit to Rosslyn, I see.'

*The code,* Langdon thought. He had forgotten that little bit of lore. Among Rosslyn's numerous mysteries was a vaulted archway from which hundreds of stone blocks protruded, each block being carved with a symbol, seemingly at random. It created an amazing, massive cipher. Some believed it revealed the entrance to the vault beneath the chapel; others that it told the true Grail legend. Not that it mattered – people had been trying for centuries to work out its meaning. To this day the Rosslyn Trust offered a generous reward to anyone who could solve it, but the code remained a mystery.

'I'd be happy to show . . .'

The verger's voice trailed off as Sophie handed the rosewood box to Langdon to hold, then moved alone, in a trance, towards the encoded archway. *My first code.* She could feel herself momentarily forgetting about the Holy Grail, the Priory of Sion and all the mysteries of the past day. The memories were flooding back. She was recalling her first visit here, and strangely, an unexpected sadness.

She was a little girl . . . a year or so after her family's death. Her grandfather had brought her to Scotland on a short vacation. They had come to see Rosslyn Chapel before going back to Paris. It was late evening, and the chapel was closed. But they were still inside.

'Can we go home, *Grand-père*?' Sophie begged, feeling tired.

'Soon, dear, very soon.' His voice was melancholy. 'I have one last thing I need to do here. How about if you wait in the car?'

'You're doing another big-person thing?'

He nodded. 'I'll be fast. I promise.'

'Can I do the archway code again? That was fun.'

'You won't be frightened in here alone?'

'Of course not!' she said in a huff. 'It's not even dark yet!'

He smiled. 'Very well, then.' He led her over to the elaborate archway he had shown her earlier.

Sophie immediately plopped down on the stone floor, lying on her back and staring up at the collage of puzzle pieces overhead. 'I'm going to break this code before you get back!'

'It's a race then.' Her grandfather bent over, kissed her forehead and walked to the nearby side door. 'I'll be right outside. I'll leave the door open. If you need me, just call.' He went out into the soft evening light.

Sophie lay there on the floor, gazing up at the code. She felt sleepy. After a few minutes, the symbols got fuzzy. And then they disappeared.

When she awoke, the floor felt cold. '*Grand-père?*'

There was no answer. Standing up, she brushed herself off. The side door was still open, so she walked outside. She could see her grandfather standing on the porch of a nearby stone house directly behind the church. He was talking quietly to someone barely visible inside the screened door.

'*Grand-père?*' she called again.

Her grandfather turned and waved, motioning for her to wait just a moment. Then, slowly, he said some final words to the person inside and blew a kiss towards the door. He came to her with tearful eyes.

'Why are you crying, *Grand-père?*'

He picked her up and held her close. 'Oh, Sophie, you and I have said goodbye to a lot of people this year. It's hard.'

Sophie thought of the accident, of saying goodbye to her mother and father, her grandmother and baby brother. 'Were you saying goodbye to *another* person?'

'To a dear friend whom I love very much,' he replied, his voice heavy with emotion. 'And I fear I will not see her again for a very long time.'

Langdon was scanning the chapel walls, worried that a dead end might once again be looming. Although Saunière's poem clearly indicated Rosslyn, he was not sure what to do now that they had arrived. The poem made reference to a 'blade and chalice', which Langdon saw nowhere.

> The Holy Grail 'neath ancient Roslin waits.
> The blade and chalice guarding o'er Her gates.

'I hate to pry,' the verger said, eyeing the rosewood box in Langdon's hands. 'But this box . . . might I ask where you got it?'

Langdon gave a weary laugh. 'That's a very long story.'

The young man hesitated, his eyes on the box again. 'It's just so strange, but my grandmother has a box *exactly* like that – a jewellery box. Identical polished rosewood, same inlaid rose, even the hinges look the same.'

Langdon knew the young man must be mistaken. 'The two boxes may be similar, but –'

The side door closed loudly, drawing both of their gazes. Sophie had gone out without a word and was now wandering down the bluff towards a stone house nearby. Langdon stared after her. *Where is she going?* She had been acting strangely ever since they entered the building. He turned to the guide. 'Do you know what that house is?'

He nodded. 'That's the chapel rectory. The chapel curator lives there. She also happens to be the head of the Rosslyn Trust.' He paused. 'She's my grandmother.'

'Your grandmother heads the Rosslyn Trust?'

The young man nodded. 'I live with her in the rectory and help keep up the chapel and give tours.' He shrugged. 'I've lived here my whole life. My grandmother brought me up in that house.'

*My grandmother brought me up.*

Langdon looked out at Sophie on the bluff, then down at the rosewood box in his hand. *Impossible.* Slowly, Langdon turned back to the young man. 'You said your grandmother has a box like this one?'

'Almost identical.'

'Where did she get it?'

'My grandfather made it for her. He died when I was a baby, but my grandmother still talks about him. She says he was a genius with his hands. He made all kinds of things.'

Langdon glimpsed a web of connections emerging. 'Do you mind my asking what happened to your parents?'

The young man looked surprised. 'They died when I was young.' He paused. 'The same day as my grandfather.'

Langdon's heart pounded. 'In a car accident?'

The guide recoiled, a look of bewilderment in his olive-green eyes. 'Yes. My entire family died that day. I lost my grandfather, my parents and . . .' He hesitated, glancing down at the floor.

'Your sister,' Langdon said.

Out on the bluff, the stone house was exactly as Sophie remembered it. Night was falling now, and the house exuded a warm and inviting aura. The smell of bread wafted through the open screened door, and a golden light shone in the windows. As Sophie approached, she could hear quiet sounds of sobbing from within.

Through the screened door, Sophie saw an elderly woman in the hallway. Her back was to the door, but Sophie could see she was crying. The woman had long, luxuriant silver hair that conjured an unexpected wisp of memory. Feeling herself drawn closer, Sophie stepped on to the porch stairs. The woman was clutching a framed photograph of a man and touching her fingertips to his face with loving sadness.

It was a face Sophie knew well.

*Grand-père.*

The woman had obviously heard the sad news of Jacques Saunière's death.

A board squeaked beneath Sophie's feet, and the woman turned slowly, her sad eyes finding Sophie's. Sophie wanted to run, but she stood transfixed. The woman's fervent gaze never wavered as she set down the photo and approached the door. An eternity seemed to pass as the two women stared at each other through the thin mesh. Then, like the slowly gathering swell of an ocean wave, the woman's expression transformed from one of uncertainty . . . to disbelief . . . to hope . . . and finally, to joy.

Throwing open the door, she came out, reaching with soft hands, cradling Sophie's thunderstruck face. 'Oh, dear child . . . look at you!'

Although Sophie did not recognize her, she knew who this woman was. She tried to speak but found she could not even breathe.

'Sophie,' the woman sobbed, kissing her forehead.

Sophie's words were a choked whisper. 'But . . . *Grand-père* said you were –'

'I know.' The woman placed her tender hands on Sophie's shoulders and gazed at her with familiar eyes. 'Your grandfather and I were forced to say so many things. We did what we thought was right. I'm so sorry. It was for your own safety, princess.'

Sophie heard that final word and immediately thought of her grandfather, who had called her his princess for so many years. The sound of his voice seemed to echo now in the ancient stones of Rosslyn, reverberating in the unknown hollows below.

The woman threw her arms around Sophie, the tears flowing faster. 'Your grandfather wanted so badly to tell you everything. But things were difficult between you two. He tried so hard. There's so much to explain – so very much.' She kissed Sophie's forehead once again, then whispered in her ear, 'No more secrets, princess. It's time you learned the truth about our family.'

*

Sophie and her grandmother were seated on the porch stairs in a tearful hug when the young guide dashed across the lawn, his eyes shining with hope and disbelief.

'Sophie?'

Through her tears, Sophie nodded, standing. She did not know the young man's face, but as they embraced, she could feel the power of the blood coursing through his veins . . . the blood she now understood they shared.

When Langdon walked across the lawn to join them, Sophie could not imagine that only yesterday she had felt so alone in the world. And now, somehow, in this foreign place, in the company of three people she barely knew, she felt at last that she was home.

# Chapter 83

Night had fallen over Rosslyn.

Robert Langdon stood alone, feeling exhausted, on the porch of the stone house, enjoying the sounds of laughter and reunion drifting through the screened door behind him. The fatigue in his body went to the core.

'You slipped out quietly,' a voice behind him said.

He turned. Sophie's grandmother emerged, her silver hair shimmering in the night. Her name, for the last twenty-eight years at least, was Marie Chauvel.

Langdon gave a tired smile. 'I thought I'd give your family some time together.' Through the window, he could see Sophie talking with her brother.

Marie came over and stood beside him. 'Mr Langdon, when I first heard of Jacques's murder, I was terrified for Sophie's safety. Seeing her standing in my doorway tonight was the greatest relief of my life. I cannot thank you enough.'

Langdon had no idea how to respond. Although he had offered to give Sophie and her grandmother time to talk in private, Marie had asked him to stay and listen. *My husband obviously trusted you, Mr Langdon, so I do as well.* And so he had remained, listening in mute astonishment while Marie told the story of Sophie's late parents. Incredibly, both had been from Merovingian families – direct descendants of Mary Magdalene and Jesus Christ. Sophie's parents and ancestors, for protection, had changed their family names of Plantard and Saint-Clair, and their children – the most direct surviving royal bloodline – had been carefully guarded by the Priory. Then Sophie's parents were killed in a mysterious car accident – and the Priory feared the identity of the royal line had been discovered.

'Your grandfather and I,' Marie had explained in a voice choked with pain, 'had to make a serious decision the instant we received the phone call. Your parents' car had just been found in the river.' She dabbed at the tears in her eyes and looked at Sophie and her brother. '*All six of us* – including you two grandchildren – were supposed to be travelling together in that car that very night. Fortunately, we changed our plans at the last moment, so your parents were alone. Jacques and I had no way of knowing what had really happened . . . if this was truly an *accident.*'

Marie looked at Sophie. 'We knew we had to protect our grandchildren, so we did what we thought best. Jacques reported to the police that your brother and I had also been in the car . . . our two bodies apparently washed off in the current. Then your brother and I went underground with the Priory. Jacques, being a prominent man, could not disappear, and it only made sense that Sophie, as the eldest, would stay in Paris to be raised by Jacques, close to the heart and protection of the Priory.'

Her voice fell to a whisper. 'Separating our family was the hardest thing we ever had to do. Jacques and I saw each other only very infrequently, and always in the most secret of settings.' She paused. 'There are certain ceremonies to which the brotherhood always stays faithful.'

Langdon had stepped outside at that point. Now, gazing up at the spires of Rosslyn, he could not help thinking of Rosslyn's unsolved mystery. *Is the Grail really here at Rosslyn? And if so, where are the blade and chalice that Saunière mentioned in his poem?*

Saunière's papyrus. He had taken it from the cryptex once again, hoping to see something he had missed earlier. 'I'll take that,' Marie said, motioning to Langdon's hand.

She looked amused as she took the paper. 'I know of a man at a bank in Paris who is probably very eager to see the return of this rosewood box. André Vernet was a dear friend of Jacques, and Jacques trusted him totally. André would have done anything to honour Jacques's request to look after this box.'

*Including shooting me,* Langdon recalled, deciding not to mention that he had probably broken the poor man's nose. Thinking of Paris, he flashed on the three *sénéchaux* who had also been killed the night before. 'And the Priory? What happens now?'

'The wheels are already in motion, Mr Langdon. The brotherhood has endured for centuries, and it will endure this. There are always those waiting to rebuild.'

All evening Langdon had suspected that Sophie's grandmother was closely tied to the operations of the Priory. After all, the Priory had always had women members. Four Grand Masters had even been women, though the *sénéchaux* – the guardians – were traditionally men.

Langdon thought of Leigh Teabing and what he had said to them at Westminster Abbey. It seemed a lifetime ago. 'Was the Church putting pressure on your husband not to release the Sangreal documents at the End of Days?' he asked.

'Heavens, no. The End of Days is just a legend – there is nothing in the Priory doctrine that gives a date when the Grail should be unveiled. In fact, the Priory has always believed that the Grail should *never* be unveiled.'

'Never?' Langdon was stunned.

'It is the mystery and wonderment that serve our souls, not the Grail itself. The beauty of the Grail lies in her ethereal nature.' Marie Chauvel gazed up at Rosslyn now. 'For some, the Grail is a chalice that will bring them everlasting life. For others, it is the quest for lost documents and secret history. And for most, I suspect the Holy Grail is simply a glorious unattainable treasure that somehow, even in today's world of chaos, inspires us.'

'But if the Sangreal documents remain hidden, the story of Mary Magdalene will be lost forever,' Langdon said.

'Will it? Look around you. Her story is being told in art, music and books. More so every day. The pendulum is swinging. We are starting to sense the dangers from history . . . we are beginning to sense the need to restore the sacred feminine.' Marie paused. 'You mentioned you are writing a manuscript about the symbols of the sacred feminine, are you not?'

'I am.'

She smiled. 'Finish it, Mr Langdon. Sing her song. The world needs modern troubadours.'

Langdon fell silent. *Don't ask,* he told himself. *This is not the moment.* He glanced at the papyrus in Marie's hand, and then back at Rosslyn.

'Ask the question, Mr Langdon,' Marie said, looking amused. 'You have earned the right.'

Langdon felt himself flush.

'You want to know if the Grail is here at Rosslyn.'

'Can you tell me?'

She sighed in mock exasperation. 'Why is it that men simply *cannot* let the Grail rest?' She laughed, obviously enjoying herself. 'Why do you think it's here?'

Langdon motioned to the papyrus in her hand. 'Your husband's poem speaks specifically of Rosslyn, except it also mentions a blade and chalice watching over the Grail. I didn't see any symbols of the blade and chalice up there.'

'The blade and chalice?' Marie asked. 'What exactly do they look like?'

Langdon sensed she was toying with him, but he played along, quickly describing the symbols.

A look of vague recollection crossed her face. 'Ah, yes, of course. The blade represents all that is masculine. I believe it is drawn like this, no?' Using her index finger, she traced a shape on her palm.

'Yes,' Langdon said. Marie had drawn the less common 'closed' form of the blade, although Langdon had seen the symbol portrayed both ways.

'And the inverse,' she said, drawing again on her palm, 'is the chalice, which represents the feminine.'

'Correct,' Langdon said.

'And you are saying that in all the hundreds of symbols we have here in Rosslyn Chapel, these two shapes appear nowhere?'

'I didn't see them.'

'And if I show them to you, will you get some sleep?'

Before Langdon could answer, Marie Chauvel stepped off the porch and was heading towards the chapel. Langdon hurried after her. Entering the ancient building, Marie turned on the lights and pointed to the centre of the sanctuary floor. 'There you are, Mr Langdon. The blade and chalice.'

Langdon stared at the scuffed stone floor. It was blank. 'There's nothing here . . .'

Marie sighed and began to walk along the famous path worn into the chapel floor, the same path Langdon had seen the visitors walking earlier this evening. As his eyes adjusted to see the giant symbol, he still felt lost. 'But that's the Star of Dav—'

Langdon stopped short, mute with amazement as it dawned on him.

*The blade and chalice.*

*Fused as one.*

*The Star of David . . . the perfect union of male and female . . . Solomon's Seal . . . marking the Holy of Holies, where the male and female deities were thought to dwell.*

He needed a minute to find his words. 'The verse does point here to Rosslyn. Completely. Perfectly.'

Marie smiled. 'Apparently.'

The implications chilled him. 'So the Holy Grail is in the vault beneath us?'

She laughed. 'Only in spirit. One of the Priory's most ancient charges was one day to return the Grail to her homeland of France, where she could rest for eternity. For centuries, she was dragged across the countryside to keep her safe. Most undignified. Jacques's charge when he became Grand Master was to restore her honour by returning her to France and building her a resting place fit for a queen.'

'And he succeeded?'

Now her face grew serious. 'Mr Langdon, as curator of the Trust, I can tell you for certain that the Grail is no longer here at Rosslyn.'

Langdon decided to press. 'But the keystone is supposed to point to the place where the Holy Grail is hidden *now*. Why does it point to Rosslyn?'

'Maybe you're misreading its meaning.'

'But how much clearer could it be?' he asked. 'We are standing over an underground vault marked by the blade and chalice, underneath a ceiling of stars, surrounded by the art of Master Masons. Everything speaks of Rosslyn.'

'Very well, let me see this mysterious verse.' She unrolled the papyrus and read the poem aloud in a deliberate tone.

> *'The Holy Grail 'neath ancient Roslin waits.*
> *The blade and chalice guarding o'er Her gates.*
> *Adorned in masters' loving art, She lies.*
> *She rests at last beneath the starry skies.'*

When she finished, she was still for several seconds, until a knowing smile crossed her lips. 'Ah, Jacques.'

Langdon watched her expectantly. 'You *understand* this?'

Marie gave a tired yawn. 'Mr Langdon, I will make a confession to you. I have never officially been privy to the present location of the Grail. But, of course, I was married to a person of enormous influence . . . and my woman's intuition is strong. Something tells me you will eventually find what you seek. One day it will dawn on you.' She smiled.

There was a sound of someone arriving in the doorway. 'Both of you disappeared,' Sophie said, entering.

'I was just leaving,' her grandmother replied, walking over to her. 'Goodnight, princess.' She kissed Sophie's forehead. 'Don't keep Mr Langdon out too late.'

Langdon and Sophie watched her grandmother walk back towards the fieldstone house. When Sophie turned to him, her eyes were awash in deep emotion. 'Not exactly the ending I expected.'

*That makes two of us,* he thought. Langdon could see that Sophie was overwhelmed – everything in her life had changed this night. 'Are you OK? It's a lot to take in.'

She smiled. 'I have a family. That's where I'm going to start. Who we are and where we came from will take some time.'

Langdon remained silent.

'Beyond tonight, will you stay with us?' Sophie asked. 'At least for a few days?'

Langdon sighed, wanting nothing more. 'You need some time here with your family, Sophie. I'm going back to Paris in the morning.'

Neither of them spoke. Then Sophie reached over and, taking his hand, led him out of the chapel. They walked to a small rise on the bluff. From here, the Scottish countryside spread out before them, suffused in a pale moonlight that sifted through the departing clouds.

The stars were just now appearing, but to the west, a single point of light glowed brighter than any other.

Venus. The ancient Goddess shining down with her steady and patient light.

# Epilogue

Robert Langdon awoke with a start. He had been dreaming. The bathrobe beside his bed bore the monogram *Hôtel Ritz Paris*. He saw a dim light filtering through the blinds. *Is it dusk or dawn?* he wondered.

His body felt warm and deeply contented. He had slept solidly for almost two days. Sitting up slowly in bed, he now realized what had awoken him . . . the strangest thought.

*Could it be?*

He remained motionless.

*Impossible.*

Twenty minutes later, after a quick refreshing shower, he stepped out of the hotel, feeling a growing excitement. He walked east, then turned south and continued until he saw what he was looking for . . . the famous royal arcade – a shiny stretch of polished black marble. Moving on to it, Langdon scanned the surface beneath his feet. Within seconds, he found what he knew was there – several bronze medallions embedded in the ground in a perfectly straight line. Each disc was five inches in diameter and embossed with the letters N and S.

*Nord. Sud.*

He turned due south, letting his eye trace the extended line formed by the medallions, and began moving again, following the trail.

The streets of Paris, he had learned years ago, were adorned with 135 of these bronze markers, embedded in sidewalks, courtyards and streets, on a north–south axis across the city. He had once followed the line from Sacré-Coeur, north across the Seine, and finally to the ancient Paris Observatory. There he discovered the significance of the sacred path it traced.

*The earth's original prime meridian.*

*The first zero longitude of the world.*

*Paris's ancient Rose Line.*

Now, as Langdon hurried across a busy road, he could feel his destination within reach. Less than a block away.

> *The Holy Grail 'neath ancient Roslin waits.*

The revelations were coming now in waves. Saunière's ancient spelling of Roslin . . . the blade and chalice . . . the tomb adorned with masters' art.

*Is that why Saunière needed to talk with me? Had I unknowingly guessed the truth?*

He broke into a jog, feeling the Rose Line beneath his feet, guiding him, pulling him towards his destination. As he entered the long tunnel of Passage Richelieu, the hairs on his neck began to bristle with anticipation. He knew that at the end of this tunnel stood the most mysterious of Parisian monuments.

*The Louvre Pyramid.*

Gleaming in the darkness.

He admired it only a moment. Turning, he felt his feet again tracing the invisible path of the ancient Rose Line, carrying him across the courtyard to the Carrousel du Louvre – the enormous roundabout within which lay a great circle of grass surrounded by neatly trimmed hedges – once the site of Paris's primeval nature-worshipping festivals, joyous rites to celebrate fertility and the Goddess.

Langdon felt as if he were crossing into another world as he stepped over the bushes into the grassy area within. This hallowed ground was now marked by one of the city's most unusual monuments. There in the centre, plunging into the earth like a crystal chasm, gaped the giant inverted pyramid of glass that he had seen a few nights ago when he had entered the Louvre.

*La Pyramide Inversée.*

Tremulous, Langdon walked to the edge and peered down into the Louvre's sprawling underground complex, aglow with amber light. His eye was trained not just on the massive inverted pyramid but on what lay directly beneath it. There, on the floor of the chamber below, stood the tiniest of structures . . . a structure Langdon had mentioned in his manuscript.

Langdon felt himself awaken fully now to the thrill of discovery. Raising his eyes again to the Louvre, he sensed the huge wings of the museum enveloping him . . . hallways that burgeoned with the world's finest art.

Da Vinci . . . Botticelli . . .

*Adorned in masters' loving art, She lies.*

Alive with wonder, he stared once again down through the glass at the tiny structure below.

*I must go down there!*

He headed back across the courtyard towards the towering pyramid entrance of the Louvre. The day's last visitors were trickling out of the museum. Pushing through the revolving door, he hurried down the curved staircase. When he reached the bottom, he entered the long tunnel that stretched beneath the Louvre's courtyard, back towards *La Pyramide Inversée*.

At the end of the tunnel, he emerged into a large chamber. Directly before him, hanging down from above, gleamed the inverted pyramid – a breathtaking V-shaped contour of glass.

*The Chalice.*

Langdon's eyes traced its narrowing form down to its tip, suspended only six feet above the floor. There, directly beneath it, stood a tiny structure.

A miniature pyramid. Only three feet tall. The only structure in this colossal complex that had been built on a small scale.

Langdon's manuscript, while discussing the Louvre's elaborate collection of goddess art, had made passing note of this modest pyramid.

*The miniature structure itself protrudes up through the floor as though it were the tip of an iceberg – the apex of an enormous, pyramidical vault, submerged below like a hidden chamber.*

The two pyramids pointed at one another, their bodies perfectly aligned, their tips almost touching.

The Chalice above. The Blade below.

*The blade and chalice guarding o'er Her gates.*

Langdon heard Marie Chauvel's words. *One day it will dawn on you.*

He was standing beneath the ancient Rose Line, surrounded by the work of masters. *What better place for Saunière to keep watch?* Now, at last, he sensed he understood the true meaning of the Grand Master's final verse. Raising his eyes to heaven, he gazed up through the glass to a glorious, star-filled night.

*She rests at last beneath the starry skies.*

Like the murmurs of spirits in the darkness, forgotten words echoed. *The quest for the Holy Grail is the quest to kneel before the bones of Mary Magdalene. A journey to pray at the feet of the outcast one.*

With a sudden upwelling of reverence, Robert Langdon fell to his knees.

For a moment, he thought he heard a woman's voice . . . the wisdom of the ages . . . whispering up from the chasms of the earth.

# Image Credits

**PAGE 1:** Photographs copyright © David Henry, 2004

**PAGE 2:** *Top:* Louvre, Paris, France, Giraudon/Bridgeman Art Library; *bottom left:* Erich Lessing/Art Resource, New York; *bottom right:* Art Resource, New York

**PAGE 3:** *Top:* left and middle panel: Erich Lessing/Art Resource, New York; and right panel: Scala/Art Resource, New York; *middle and bottom right:* Courtesy of Broadway Books, an imprint of the Crown Publishing Group, a division of Penguin Random House LLC

**PAGE 4:** *Top:* Courtesy of owner Olivia Hsu Decker, photographed by Pat Denton. For rental availability and information about Château de Villette, please visit website Frenchvacation.com or email Villette@Frenchvacation.com.

**PAGES 4–5:** *Bottom (spread):* Scala/Art Resource, New York

**PAGE 5:** *Top left:* Photograph by Simon Brighton; *top/bottom right:* Courtesy of Broadway Books, an imprint of the Crown Publishing Group, a division of Penguin Random House LLC

**PAGE 6:** Photographs copyright © David Henry, 2004

**PAGE 7:** *Top left:* Angelo Hornak/CORBIS; *top right:* Werner Forman/CORBIS; *bottom:* Antonia Reeve/Rosslyn Chapel Trust

**PAGE 8:** *Top:* Sandro Vannini/CORBIS; *bottom:* © Brad Braun